THE
PORTAL
GUARDIANS

AMALGAM CHRONICLES

1

ELLIE HOLLAND

to my booktok friend

♡

Ellie Holland

Acknowledgements

Cover design: Jeff Brown www.jeffbrowngraphics.com

Editing: Norma Gambini

Proofreading/Developmental Editing: Camille Caparas

Blurb: Brian Meeks

Formatting: Kari Holloway at KHFormatting.com

Publishing: Ellie Holland Books

Map design: Ellie Holland with www.inkarnate.com

Special thanks to all my beta readers and ARC readers for supporting me and helping me make The Portal Guardians the best it can be.

DEDICATIONS

This book is for anyone who jumped off their bed and believed they could fly.

To my husband, I couldn't have done this without your nerdy love and support.

To my daughters, who remind me every day to continue to believe in dragons and magic.

To my Mom and GrandDot, for passing on the writing genes and believing in me.

To my cat, Bluestar, who has been my spirit animal for over a decade. She is now immortalized in this book.

AUTHOR'S WARNING

The Portal Guardians is a New Adult fantasy book. It contains foul language (in English and in Japanese), bloody violence, sexual tension, mental illness, and alcoholism. I advise anyone who wishes to buy this book for their teenager or grandma to read it first. This will be the most tame book of the entire series. If any of this triggers you, please proceed with caution when reading this book.

INFORMATION

Stay up to date on new releases, see the high resolution map, *Amalgam Chronicles* origins (coming in 2022), *WTF Did I Write* episodes, character art, and more on my social media and website!

Website: www.elliehollandbooks.com

Facebook, TikTok, Instagram

@elliehollandbooks

Twitter
@ehollandbooks

Subscribe to my newsletter on my website to receive a free ebook of *Amalgam Origins: Schism (coming in 2022)*

"She will remember your heart when men are fairy tales in books written by rabbits."
-Schmendrick the Magician
in *The Last Unicorn*

YUMERION

DEVDAN

REVENGE AND MEMORIES

For sixteen years, Devdan Elberos thought of nothing but revenge and French fries. All that time, he lived in solitude in the castle he had demolished with his own hands. Years ago, the damage occurred during his little skirmish with the *verndari* council of the portal guardians. A man of many words, he often had no one to talk to but himself. The silence drove him mad, among other things.

Recounting the last conversation he had with the elder, he paced, waving his arms. A pain in his chest rose as he spoke to himself. "I tried to reason with them. Tried to convince them to train me as a *verndari*, to become a full-fledged portal guardian. I dressed the part, even though I missed my T-shirt and jeans. But no, they couldn't see past those itty-bitty mistakes I made back then. What a crock of shit. I mean, the forest *eventually* grew back. They had chosen who lived and died for centuries, so why couldn't I? How could they not see the great power that I possessed after all that time?"

He placed his trembling hands on his head and pulled at his skin with his fingers, exposing the bottoms of his inner eyelids. As he stared at his reflection in the shattered mirror, a face appeared over his shoulder.

His old mentor.

He whipped around and no one was there. Devdan turned back around and leaned in closer. Squinting, he saw his facial features multiply in the glass shards. "Heh, twelve eyes," he said with a chortle. The twisted, wooden frame leaned against a broken bookshelf with several cracks at the edges. Looking at his shaking hands, he sniffed, then wiped the itchy blood from his nose with the sleeve of his black, white, and green *kamishimo*. It happened often, but he presumed his strange symptom resulted from his lingering exhaustion, due to insufficient sleep.

His brown hair tousled as a small breeze blew past. He stopped, closing his eyes. The coolness comforted him as the sounds of water dripped from the open stone walls.

"What's on the agenda today?"

"Oh, how kind of you to ask. Why, I don't know. How about a stroll through this broken heap of a castle? It's such a lovely day!" He threw his arms above him and placed them on his head.

The man pivoted his body and peered over the half-destroyed wall at the purple, green, and blue swirling sky. Gapureia. The floating islands with green grass and craggy rocks came to points at their bottoms. Faint sounds of swooshing magic faded to near silence. Long ago, the portal entryways teemed with moving colors, allowing guardians from Earth and Yumerion to meet there to discuss important issues in peace. Now, they had grown dark and gray.

The air still smelled musty after all those years. Devdan narrowed his eyes and scoffed. "Only thing I miss are the echoes here."

"Ah!" He placed his hand behind his ear, leaning forward.

Nothing.

"See what I mean?"

"I know, it's terrible, right? So boring."

He contemplated using magic to restore the castle, to pretend someone was replying to his calls from the sound waves bouncing off the enclosed stone, but he appreciated the chaos around him like a work of art. *A work of art. That's exactly what it was.* He relished it all: the screams, the splintering of wood onto stone, cracking of broken bones, and the churns of magic thrown about in all directions. Thinking of his massacre caused Devdan's mouth to fill with saliva. He even remembered the drop of blood that fell into his mouth as he gazed at his victim below, leaning onto his *katana* as it cracked the creature's ribs and pierced its heart. He had licked the metallic liquid from his teeth and swallowed it. *Delicious.*

"Well, now I'm hungry." Facing his palm up, he adjusted his back, grimacing from the hard wood throne he sat on. He conjured a red bowl of French fries and munched; the crunchy, salty, starchy goodness warmed his tongue. He missed greasy, American food after years of eating rice and fish with every meal while he trained in Yumerion. "Now, that's heaven. Best food from both worlds. We humans sure know how to fry a potato."

He snacked on his favorite food, then stopped mid-bite, watching his breath appear as he exhaled. Goosebumps caused the hair on his arms to raise.

Across the open room, a wispy, purple and white figure of a bearded chimera appeared. It had the tail of a serpent and three heads: a lion, a dragon, and a goat. The elder. He floated along, never making eye contact with Devdan. With drooping arms and legs, he looked like a puppet with his limbs tied and controlled by a fiendish puppeteer above. The ghosts of his victims often visited him, their souls tied to the castle for eternity. He knew when they were coming when the temperature of the air declined.

As the elder's ghost vanished, Devdan's memory returned to the last time he saw him alive. He remembered every word and emotion of that day.

"We gave you the chance to prove yourself worthy of a council seat and you burned an entire forest to the ground. Hundreds of lives were lost. Homes destroyed. Do you have no remorse for what you have done? Speak!" the elder demanded.

"So which seat is mine? I bet it's the one next to you, huh, goat-man?" Devdan said with a smirk, his heart unchanged.

"I should have trained him better, should've seen the evil in his heart. I take full responsibility for his actions," his mentor said with a solemn bow, leaning on his staff.

"Orastos, you will escort Devdan home to the human world." The elder turned to him. "You are forthwith banished from Gapureia! You will never be one of us!" the elder screamed, spit dripping from his lion mouth as he extended over his podium. He pointed a claw toward the great doors.

Orastos placed a hand on his shoulder and led him to the entrance.

"You must show them that you are better than this. I trained you to have a good heart and to listen to your instincts," his mentor said. "I believe in you, boy."

A burning light formed around Devdan's body as he shoved Orastos away. The old dragon fell to the floor, staring at the monster he had trained with wide eyes. Devdan sneered at him with clenched fists and a locked jaw. The ounce of humanity he had left allowed his mentor to live for a mere moment longer. The man whipped around and faced his accusers. His body broiled from rage like lava flowing through his veins. Skin crawled, and a power grew inside him that he had never felt before. He swallowed his overwhelming frustration.

With tense muscles, he floated in the air by the door, outstretching his arms. With a wave of his hand, he smiled and locked every exit.

"You're wrong. I feel nothing. If they won't allow me to be a verndari, then the verndari will be no more."

The memory vanished from his mind. It often came to him many times a day. He shook his head and turned away from where the ghost of the elder disappeared. From the corner of his eye, he spotted a faint light. Placing his snack on his seat, he rose and faced the near empty, round hole where the portal orb's power source used to be. Something glowed from a tiny fragment. His heart skipped a beat. He walked closer, frowning. "What the...?"

Stopping, he narrowed his eyes as the flicker of light grew into a picture in black and white. It looked like an old television from the '50s had a baby with a crystal ball. *Wait, are those pointed ears?*

"An elf? He looks familiar. Why has the orb awakened after all this time? There's barely anything left. I slaughtered the last of the council years ago when they wouldn't let me join their stupid club. I was worthy. They just didn't *see* that. They..." He paused and held his breath.

The young elf sat, reading books with a smile, shelves of scrolls and potions surrounding him. Static, neutral colors flashed over his image.

Devdan's frown faded. *Could it be? Is the magic back? Has it chosen a new generation of verndari?* His eyes widened.

"Ha-ha! It's about time! We're going to have some fun with this guy! And if there's one, I know there will be more. Can't have a single council member talking to himself about the fate of the worlds. When I'm finished with whoever these new recruits are, they'll forget all about the portals and cry for their mundane lives back."

He clapped his hands, feeling a rush of serotonin surge through his mind. A huge smile appeared on his face. Chuckling under his breath, with his tongue between his teeth, his body shook. Licking his molars, the laughing continued. "And here I thought I would die of boredom. I've waited years to finish the job!"

He stretched his hands, imagining his destination in his mind. The energy raced through his body as a green aura enveloped him. From his palms, two portals emerged, growing larger until they were the size of doorways. The static screeches of the portals close together reminded him of hanging out with his friends as a teen when they would turn on their cellphones and put them on speakerphone right next to each other. They'd laughed at that creepy, alien-like sound for weeks.

"I still got it." He smiled.

Inside both portals were libraries, with various young creatures and humans studying. He panned side to side and chose the portal on his left. He reached in, and the young human inside gasped, falling out of her chair.

She gazed at him, speechless, half his body floating in front of her as magic swirled around his waist.

"Hey gorgeous. Any elves in here?"

She screamed and threw the book in her hand at the man's head inside the spinning, colored circle in front of her. It hit Devdan in the forehead. With closed fists, the portals disappeared. He placed his palm on his head as a sharp pain resonated down his neck. "Ow! That hurt, you crazy girl!"

He saw the book she'd thrown lying on the floor—*The Oxford English Dictionary*. The letter and page it had opened to intrigued him: *the letter S.*

Devdan bent his knees and retrieved the book. He ran his fingers over the smooth, white pages with small, black type and read aloud. "'*Schism, noun - a split division between strongly opposed sections or parties, caused by differences in opinion or belief.*'"

He lurched forward, licking his lips once more. "Now, now, don't rush in there without thinking. You don't wanna be like those Disney movie villains who don't know their enemy before blundering to their defeat. I'm looking at you, Hades. Oh, that movie kills me. You've waited sixteen years. A few more days won't hurt." He nodded, taking a deep breath. "Observe... from a distance. Learn his weaknesses. Let the others find him. Then, when he least expects it, strike. Good, good. You got it."

For a moment, his mouth salivated. His insatiable hunger would soon be fed. "How perfect."

KERYTH

THE PROPHECY

Souls who had once thrived on their world now roamed in a realm of their own making—The After. It was a peaceful place without external violence or sadness, and much more tranquil than one could hope when spending an eternity there. Souls could feel any manner of internal emotions, but could not hurt another. Keryth developed his own little corner of the realm with the things he loved most from when he was alive. Though not exact replicas, he did his best to conjure a welcoming home for himself. In The After, anything was possible.

Every so often, contact could be made between a living creature and a spirit in The After, if that soul had a deep or personal connection with the creature on the other end from the time that they shared when they were alive. Now, it was between three who had all experienced the same destruction of the famous *verndari* council. Devdan Elberos, Orastos of Lavendale, and Keryth were all there that day, some more present than others.

As a former member of the *verndari* council, Keryth now spent his time as a spirit. Though time was not a concept that he was familiar with anymore, he spent a significant length of his new experience as a soul loathing Devdan Elberos for ending his life. For years, he felt robbed of such a promising path of harnessing the power of the portals and helping to keep everyone from all worlds safe and secure. Anyone in their right mind wanted to be a *verndari,* since tales of the famous council spread through the worlds.

Despite his abrupt and sudden demise, after a while he appreciated the serenity of the afterlife.

Keryth loved the water. When he was alive, he often sat by the shore and watched the vastness of the big blue kiss the golden sun on the horizon. The sounds of the waves lapping on the sand comforted him. He built a boat with his own two hands and sailed in solitude to as many countries of Yumerion as he could, traveling from port to port.

In The After, he recreated a little island for himself to settle as a spirit, complete with a boat that sat upon the turquoise waters of his new home. He conjured scents he loved in life to surround him, from sandalwood, to herbaceous rosemary, and chamomile.

He recreated his time as a living being in his mind. He remembered when he was called to Gapureia to train to become a portal guardian. Reluctantly, he left his sails behind and obeyed, for it was a great honor and privilege to be named a member of the *verndari.* He met with the old dragon, Orastos, who trained him and Devdan for years. When his training ended, Keryth stood before the council, who made their final decision to allow him to gain great power to become a full-fledged member of the *verndari.* They saw promise in his courage and valiance. He passed their test.

The same could not be said for Devdan. The banished former member of portal guardians kept his promise to lay waste to everything his accusers held dear. He slaughtered every last *verndari* council member, all except one.

Keryth never understood how Orastos had escaped, but he was grateful that he had. For years, he tried to make contact with the old dragon but was always met with a dark wall that he could not penetrate, no matter how hard he tried. It pained him not to speak to his mentor.

As much as he hated it, he continued to spy on Devdan from the safety of The After. He alone felt responsible for Devdan. They were training partners when he was alive. For over a decade, he watched the middle-aged man go insane, talking to himself.

One particular day, while Keryth floated in meditation under his favorite glowing orange tree, he was jolted awake. The triangle of connection between Keryth, Devdan, and Orastos sparked like a long connection of magic that pierced the veil of time and space. A surge of pressure consumed his floating body. His *kamishimo* flowed in the citrus and ocean colored breeze. Flowing, dark hair caressed his pointed ears. His heart sank.

"Devdan is back. I must try again to break through the barrier to speak to Orastos. The prophecy will come to pass."

He wanted to speak to his friend in Yumerion to warn him of what was to come. He knew Devdan would not rest until he murdered the last of the *verndari* portal guardians. Keryth didn't understand how the old dragon had managed to evade Devdan's grasp all those years, but he was grateful that he had. He knew if Devdan had his way, Orastos would be next to him in The After. And the *verndari* would be erased forever and diminished to nothing but a myth. Then who would protect the worlds?

Keryth created the prophecy himself, for he saw the ruinous destruction that would rain down upon Yumerion and Earth when the remaining speck of the portal orb awakened. The tiny fragment inadvertently showed Devdan where the first creature of the new generation of *verndari* was located. Orastos was the last remaining council member until the fragment called to a simple elf at a library. The ancient laws of magic carved into the universe that there must always be *verndari* or the universe would become unbalanced as war ravaged the land.

The future would succumb to chaos. Violence would engulf every civilization, from humans to all manner of magical creatures. Dragons would set ablaze twenty-first century, Frozen-themed birthday parties in the human world. And humans would experiment on centaurs and unicorns in Yumerion in medical labs, as the poor creatures shivered in cages, writhing from chemicals infiltrating their veins.

If no one guarded the portals and prevented dangerous travelers from sneaking into their opposing worlds, then everything the *verndari* fought to protect for centuries would perish. *Peace* would no longer be a word spoken on any creatures' tongues. Minds would swell with fear. Not a life would survive.

Keryth feared that the chaos he foresaw in his mind was exactly what Devdan wanted. The tormented man ached to stand upon the ashes of every living creature from both worlds. He wanted to watch the worlds burn.

Time was of the essence, for communicating between the land of the living and The After was unsteady and unpredictable. A black wall always stood between the two. After many years of attempting to speak to the old dragon, one day, he finally broke through the barrier. The connection between the three of them opened the door to allow him to speak to Devdan and Orastos. Keryth chose Orastos. He knew he had to explain as quickly and succinctly as possible. He spoke of his prophecy.

"The owl and the raven,
Send away; do not interfere.
The verndari must rise anew.
Together, while the evil gather,
The dragon may appear.
Fulfill their destiny,
And the owl will kneel,
Before the dragon as he falls.
If he fails, all lives are lost."

Keryth sighed. He closed his eyes, hopeful his message traveled safely from The After to Yumerion. The fate of the worlds was at stake.

"Yutakana tabi, my friend. We shall meet again."

Orastos

The Vision

Through the darkness, the other end of the message was received. The deep, familiar voice echoed the prophecy in the dragon's mind. He froze.

"If he fails, all lives are lost," the voice echoed once more. The same black wall appeared again in his mind and the voice faded to silence.

I have heard that voice before. But where? What do they want from me? Why tell me of this prophecy? I don't know what it all means. They must have the wrong creature. I am but a simple mage who has lived in peace for years. I know not of prophecies and destinies. The dragon swallowed a lump in his throat as he rummaged through his memories for the answer. But they didn't come. No matter how far he reached into his mind, he couldn't remember anything from before his son came to live with him.

His son.

It was the greatest joy of his life, raising the elfling as his own. With gratitude, he safely stored the recollection of the day they met at the front of his thoughts. He ensured the memory would not vanish in the darkness.

Often, he would revisit the time when Braern came into his life.

He remembered the floating cliff where they stood, peering down at the darkened world below. Flames consumed the castle a mile away as smoke rose into the gray sky. His wings ached. He fanned them and winced, squinting his eyes. The two of them fought to catch their breath.

"How did we get here, mentor?" the elfling asked, staring up at him with soot all over his body and crusted tears in his eyes. Blisters formed on his small, burned hands.

"I cannot recall. Perhaps I flew us here. My wings pain me."

"Something happened down there, didn't it?" Braern asked. "And why do my hands hurt?"

Orastos gently wiped the light-colored hair from his son's eyes and placed his claws under his tiny chin.

"It appears so. Braern, would you like to come live with me at the library in Lavendale? I believe fate has brought us together."

The young elf looked up at him with bags under his eyes.

"I would like that very much."

Orastos embraced the boy and wrapped his arms around him. He felt Braern's tears soak through his robe.

"I do not know what happened down there. But I do know that you and I are family now. It is best that we make our way back to Lavendale before whoever did this decides we are their next victims."

Braern nodded.

Orastos gazed above his son's head, off into the far distance. Several fading lights disappeared before his eyes. Without another thought, the old dragon clenched his staff with one hand and his son's in the other. He rotated his wrist in front of them as an oval-shaped wave of magic began and a tiny speck of light then grew to a size larger than them both. Together, they walked through the portal and arrived back home to the library, where they began their life together as father and son.

Orastos shook his head and closed his eyes. His mind jumped. It all began with him hearing a prophecy from a familiar, but strange, voice. Saddened and confused by those words, he fought for a semblance of peace. He thought of the first moment he remembered of his son and when they started their life together. Blinding pains zipped through his mind as he traveled from place to place. He squinted with his claws on his head, trying to make sense of it all.

*****

Finally, a strange world appeared before him, but not one he recognized. With his claws trembling, the ground shook beneath his knees. He peered at his beaten body. A great heaviness pulled him downward, with far too many injuries to know which one to try to treat first. The bitter taste of iron filled his mouth as the warm liquid dripped from his snout. Blood pooled from the deep slash through his belly, sending waves of pain toward his spine and out through his shredded wings. He gasped as the thick smog scorched his eyes; he could hardly see in the distance. Flakes of ash scattered across the crimson-orange sky. All around, the faint groans of the dying filled his ears as he collapsed. A war had ravaged the land. So many were dead that he could hardly see the ground beneath the thousands of bodies.

Was this a memory or premonition? Can I stop this from happening, or is this fate set in stone?

Confused, he flared his nostrils as the sweet scent of lavender overtook the putrescence. He knew he was close. Willing his muscles to move, he fumbled for his staff as his bones cracked while he firmly pressed his claws to his belly. Wincing in searing pain, he clenched his teeth and crawled, quivering with the weight of a boulder crushing his body.

There he was, facedown, more than a few meters away. Hot metal armor burned his hands as he tumbled over armored corpses. With his strength waning, he grasped the hand of the only one he had ever loved. His soft skin soothed the dragon's soul for a mere moment.

"My boy... oh, my Braern. What happened to you?" he rasped, then coughed blood on his son's face as he reached with a trembling arm to be by his side. He gently wiped away the splatters with his claws, caressing his forehead down to his pointed ears and chin. Gasping and gurgling, his head shaking, he lowered himself to the ground. Struggling to breathe, he closed his eyes. The throbbing in his neck ceased as he took his last agonizing breath.

Moments later, the worlds followed.

*****

Back at the workshop in the library, the nightmare vanished. He stared at the wall of potions in front of him. Frozen and lost in deep thought, Orastos involuntarily released his grip on the bottle he was holding. It fell to the floor, shattering in slow motion, causing a deafening explosion that sounded from the workshop. The vibration from the floor shook his bare, reptilian feet as he stood on his hind legs. Coughing from the bitter taste of some vile concoction filling his lungs, he blinked from the burning air. The workshop seeped with red smoke. His eyes watered as he squinted.

Seconds later, the rumbling subsided. Outside the workshop door, he heard his elven son mutter to himself. "How did that old dragon blow himself up this time?"

That is true. I do have frequent accidents in here. I am getting clumsy in my old age, Orastos thought. He shook his head and closed his eyes. *This vision... How do I tell him that I must send him away? What does it all mean? If I do not heed the warning of this prophecy, will I be responsible for the destruction of our world? Will the vision I saw in my mind of so much death come to pass?*

His son bumped into the door and opened it. "Are you hurt, Father? What happened?" he asked, his voice muffled. The smoke cleared.

Orastos faced away from the door. He took deep breaths, his back rising and falling, while he stood hovered over his desk, motionless. "Braern, my boy." He coughed. "I... I had a vision."

"What did you see?" His son arrived at his side, adjusting his strap over his shoulder.

The old dragon felt a heaviness in his chest as he fought the words he desperately wanted to say. He looked to the side; his son's satchel caught his eye—the bird of the night carved into the front leather flap.

The owl and the raven, send away; do not interfere. Orastos remembered the voice from his vision. He paused with his arms outstretched, bracing himself. "I am uncertain. However, when I discover what it all means, I will tell you."

A cool substance grazed his foot. He shook off the last drops. "I was right in the middle of mixing my potion when I must have knocked over the last of the fire wyrm scales." Relaxing his shoulders, he decided it would be best not to alarm the boy. "Those things are deadly in large quantities, you know."

Orastos cleared his throat and shook the last bit of shock from his body. He turned his long neck toward his son, stretched his wrinkled, creaky wings to fan the last of the smoke away, and winced as a sharp pain in his shoulder jolted him. "These old wings aren't what they used to be."

"Let me help." Braern placed a gentle hand on his father's shoulder above his wing. The two shared a glance. The space wasn't big enough for a dragon. Braern pondered why a well-known, powerful mage such as Orastos wouldn't work in an appropriately sized shop, especially when he knew a variety of spells to change such things.

Orastos could hear the thoughts of his son, and Braern could hear his. Over the years, the dragon developed a pocket in his mind where he kept his secrets so his son could not telepathically access them. The pair were close. Everyone around them knew it. He hoped that this would be the last of his deceptions.

The elf scanned the room, placing his light-colored, shoulder-length hair behind his ear. He absorbed the comforting sights of his life with his father. Pots of brown and gray sat on dirty, wooden shelves. Tiny spiders made permanent homes in dark crevices. He was used to the musty stench after all those years. When it became too strong, they would open the windows to let the lavender scent sweep over the room. The remains of creatures not heard nor spoken of in any tongue for thousands of years lay in green jars that looked as fragile as a bird's egg. They had not cleaned the shop in a long time, and yet the sun peeked through faded windows and onto the desks of clutter and chaos. Books opened to random pages and quill pens were thrown about.

They saved kings and queens from the potions created here. Villages and clans stood strong for generations from the magic his father would cast from his old claws. In all its ugliness, beauty and history resided here.

Tapping and clanging of glass sounded as Orastos fumbled to clean his mess. The hunched dragon fiddled with various potions and containers of diluted fluids. He mumbled to himself as he searched for the right combination of ingredients to explore a new formula he'd had on his mind for weeks. His brown, tattered cloak draped over his scaly body; his large wings folded on his back. As he hobbled with the support of his tapered, twisted oak staff, his long, white-tufted tail dragged on the ground, leaving a distinct swiped shape in the dust. The sound of scales scraping stone filled Braern's ears.

Orastos, stroking his long, white beard, paused. "It was here yesterday. Where could it have gone?" he asked himself in an exasperated voice, pausing at an adjacent table.

Braern stepped backward.

"I do not have a suitable substitute for this potion."

"The one you spilled?"

Send away; do not interfere.

Orastos cleared his throat. "Eh, yes. I'm sending you to retrieve more. The mountain griffins are in desperate need to cure their youngest son. He has a case of the ruby fever and needs our help," Orastos said with his confident claw in the air.

"Are you certain we have nothing that would replace it? I believe I read that ruby fever is cured with a mixture of herbs from the dandelion family. Maybe one of these?"

Braern reached high on the shelf in front of him and grasped a tall, thin bottle containing yellow flowers.

"If you want me to turn the hatchling into a newt, then yes!" Orastos chortled, scratching his chest.

Braern placed the jar back. His elbow knocked into a nearby flask of maroon, sending it crashing to the floor. Globs of liquid oozed and spattered on the floor.

"We have made quite a mess today, haven't we?" Orastos joked, placing a loving hand on Braern's arm.

"Oh, I-I apologize. I was not looking where I was going and... I'll help you clean that up." Braern gulped as he frantically gathered the pieces together, careful not to slice his fingers.

The old dragon sniffed the air and closed his eyes as the sweet scent filled his nostrils. "Rosemary tart, lavender, bamboo... and..." He sniffed once more. "Cinnamon! Ah yes, the headache remedy. My boy, this was nearly empty. No harm done." He laughed as his face wrinkled in a smile, showing his worn, off-white, pointed teeth. "And you must stop apologizing for everything. Be confident. There are no accidents, only lessons to be learned!"

Orastos always knew how to put his mind at ease. The young elf sighed and relaxed his shoulders. The dragon was stern and yet kind to him, even when he had been a young elfling. It had been the greatest gift of his life, to raise such a boy.

Braern gathered the glass shards and placed them in a basket near the arched doorway. Orastos nodded in gratitude and waddled toward him with his oak staff.

"Surely, there is a spell that would clean the workshop?" Braern asked, curious, as he surveyed all the dust and dirt everywhere.

"Magic always comes at a price. One must decide if that price is worth it. I might grow a second head if I cast a cleaning spell!" Orastos laughed as his toothy grin reached his ears. "Not to mention, I have more important tasks at hand than cleaning. Lives are at stake, my boy!"

Braern chuckled. "I would never hear silence again with all those heads."

The unlikely pair walked through the arch. Orastos had to duck to avoid scraping his head. The door closed behind them without a touch. Carved designs on the wood came to life to form a face that smiled.

"I'm happy to see you're unharmed from that explosion. And good day to you both," the doorknocker greeted them.

"You as well, Chimon," Orastos said as he waved.

Braern dusted off his pale *kimono* shirt and adjusted his navy-blue, lace-up vest, composing himself once more. Orastos saw his son staring at him, knowing he was eager to begin their day. The elf had arrived early, likely to put in some extra work around the library and workshop, but had broken a potion—not a good start. Alas, the sun had woken from its slumber, and the day was young. There was much to be done.

"Where do I go to collect the scales?" he asked, walking alongside his father.

"I will show you." The old dragon walked much slower these days, but that didn't stop his sharp mind from staying on task.

Orastos and Braern paused to bow as a new family of pale-blue *kappa* strolled through the main entrance and slid open the large wooden-framed *shoji* paper doors. Seven doors of varying sizes and shapes accommodated the needs of any visitors. All creatures from any realm were welcomed to the vast knowledge of the library of Lavendale. There was hardly a time when the great hall was empty, even at night when the dark ones emerged.

The ceiling was much higher and the lighting infinitely brighter. Several mountain giants could fit inside. Reds, oranges, and yellows shone through from the stained-glass windows to the floor in a florid display that swirled and turned every which way. Dozens of diagonal shelves lined each side. Floating magic ovals of glowing white light appeared every so often above the shelves, illuminating the interior. Papers rustled, and feet shuffled, but no one spoke louder than a whisper out of respect for one another.

In the rafters, several forest owls huddled together, reading a tiny parchment about teaching youngsters to fly with confidence. In the corner, a tan centaur with an olive-green vest swished his tail, turning the pages of a large hardback book of remedies, searching for sore hooves. A delicate faun wearing a purple, frilly dress with a rose in her wispy, brown hair sat at a large table, reading a leather-bound book filled with stories of heroes and romance. She played with her locks as she giggled to herself, pursing her lips with twinkling eyes. Trickling sounds came from the back where a pod of hippocampi splashed, reading through the waterproof books on the history of their culture.

The library was known far and wide as a peaceful sanctuary of education due to Orastos's hard work and dedication. He had gathered and protected every parchment and artifact from the vast realms he had traveled to throughout the years. Of course, he didn't use his rugged wings much anymore, but they remained glorious symbols of a life well lived. He chose not to cover them with his cloak. Everyone often saw him stretching them out to remember they were there.

Orastos stopped at a large shelf full of old weapons encased in glass.

Braern stared at him with wide eyes, tapping his foot and pushing back his cuticles.

"Now then, the scales can be found past our Lavendale Forest, over the Ao River, and deep in the Fire Wyrm Swamp."

"The Fire Wyrm Swamp!" Braern exclaimed. He levitated a few feet off the ground, twirling his body in a circle. They had heard stories of such a place, but the boy never ventured there himself—or anywhere, rather. Never had he traveled farther than the ent village—such a great world he had yet to discover. Orastos heard his son swallow and squeal with joy through a closed mouth. A stern gaze from him reminded Braern it was polite to remain quiet.

Everyone in the library stopped their various tasks and narrowed their eyes at him. The elf lowered himself. His face, hot with a reddened neck, turned toward his father.

"A little louder next time. I couldn't hear you," Orastos joked. He cleared his throat and watched his son regain his composure with a sigh and a blink. "This quest will be dangerous and difficult, but I believe you are ready. Braern, my boy, I am tasking you to retrieve seven scales from the wyrm. They carry the properties to heal very rare and deadly illnesses. The griffin leader, as you know, has fought many wars alongside our clans to allow this library to be built here in Lavendale Forest. I intend to conjure a spell that will cure his son." Orastos relished the chance to educate during talk of quests.

"Of course. I'll leave right away." Braern pattered toward the door.

"One moment!" Orastos pointed upward with his claw. He beckoned Braern with a nod to the shelf.

Braern hunched his head into his shoulders and joined his father once again. The young elf tripped over the dragon's tail. He stumbled, flailed his arms to regain his balance, then stood still as Orastos raised an eyebrow and tilted his head.

"I would think you would be used to my tail being in the way after all this time," he told his son, repelling the vision that continued to cloud his mind. His claws trembled.

"Yes, Father, I apologize. Again."

Orastos reached up to a dusty shelf with a large, carved, dark-umber wooden chest. He placed it on the table as Braern's eyes widened. His son slouched closer, his light blond hair covering his eyes. They beheld the carved designs of birds flying and intricate trees as Orastos wiped the dust off with the side of his hand.

"What is it?" Braern asked as the old dragon opened the chest.

Dust particles flew around and disappeared. Inside was a cerulean, velvety-lined interior that shimmered in the light. A weathered tan fabric draped around a long object with a string tied in a bow around the center. Braern flicked his hair over his pointed ear so he could see as the dragon untied it. He liked to watch his father putter about, intrigued by his weathered claws.

Orastos unwrapped the cloth. He unsheathed the sword to reveal an ebony blade with a carved bird below the silver hilt. It was the most stunning object they had ever laid eyes on.

... and the raven...

"This is Raven. Forged from obsidian metal, it is the only sword of its kind. Its blade has seen more wars than any creature I know and works best when coupled with a wielder of magic, like yourself. I have been waiting many years to give this to you."

"Thank you! Where did this come from? I can feel the magic flowing from the blade," Braern said, remembering to keep his voice down.

Orastos paused. He searched his mind for the answer, but was met by an uncomfortable darkness. "I... cannot remember." Orastos frowned, shook his head, and looked to the side. "I thought I knew, but..." He placed his paw on his forehead above his eye. "I will find the answer while you are away, my boy."

"I will hold you to that." Braern fidgeted and reached for the sword.

"One more thing—" Orastos placed an arm between his son and the weapon, whispered a spell, and wiggled his claws over the top as Braern held it between his hands. "Raven only answers to you now. If anyone who means you harm touches it, it becomes heavier than a mountain and will fall to the ground until you retrieve it." He pointed to the sheath and gestured for Braern to strap the sword to his belt. "You must treat Raven with respect at all times. It is not to be played with. There is significant power that you must discover on your own, but remember to always handle this with care. You are the only one who can wield it now." Orastos took a deep breath and forced a grin through the pang of guilt and sadness. He wiped away a tear that pooled in the corner of his wrinkled eye; his son was ready to venture out on his own for the first time.

Braern picked it up—one hand on the hilt and the other under the blade. "It's light," he commented as he followed the smooth, raised metal detail of the sheath with his fingers then trailed it down and up to the hilt. Such power traveled from his fingertips through his body. "Thank you. I promise I'll be careful." Braern attached the sheath to his belt on the other side of his water pouch and larger leather satchel filled with a few days of dried figs, *inoshishi* jerky, and bread.

The old dragon twirled his wrist as his robe fell to the inside of his elbow. A withered map flapped and floated to him, and he placed it flat on the table. "You will leave here, travel north through Lavendale Forest until the trees become a meadow, make your way over Ao River, and come to the Fire Wyrm Swamp beyond the crescent stones. There, you must extract seven scales from its hide." He followed the points on the map with his claw for Braern's eyes to follow.

"Why seven?"

"That is the amount I need, boy. Now, pay attention."

Braern studied the map and imprinted the old paintings of the landmarks into his mind as he mumbled the instructions to himself. "How do I retrieve the scales? Do I slay the wyrm?" Braern asked, imagining the slimy creature choking the life from him with its muscular body.

"As with all magic, taking a life comes at a cost. We all react differently when faced with defending our own lives. I cannot tell you what you must do. You choose the path you take. However, if you must slay the creature, retrieve the body for the rest of the village to harvest and use every part: scales, claws, teeth, even the eyes. This shows respect for the creature and for its sacrifice. Very important." Orastos softly shoved his son toward the door. "Now, off you go, and be safe! Travel through the sky as far as you can." Orastos placed his claws on Braern's shoulders. "After all, I didn't teach you to fly for nothing."

"I will not disappoint you." Braern stepped backward and bowed low in respect, adjusting the belt on his belly.

The elf turned and sprinted toward the library entrance, careful not to run into anyone. Braern slid open the doors and stepped outside into the bright, warm day. He located his tan boots and laced them, taking a deep breath.

Orastos leaned on his staff with both hands on the top and nodded. He forced a smile, knowing the fate of his son was no longer in his control. The dragon hoped he had prepared his son for what would come.

BRAERN

FIRE WYRM SWAMP

Welcoming sunlight beamed through the maple trees. Green-winged *hainu* yelped as their herd flew overhead. The lavender grass danced on either side of the stone path leading into the forest. The fragrant herbs covered the ground in a blanket of purple.

Braern never grew tired of the sweet, tranquil scent of his home. He drew a deep breath and closed his eyes, determined to appreciate the beauty all around him. As he smiled, his walk turned to a run, with his belt and sword flapping around his waist. Orastos, the only father he'd ever known, had done his best to protect him. In turn, it had taken many years to send him out on his own. Repressing the fear of solitude, he strolled on.

The stone path declined down a hill and faded into the ground. As the last of the lavender vanished, he stopped. He glimpsed back at his village with pride. Tall, earth-tone homes with thatched roofs, the library, and the community tower shimmered in the sunlight. Their bright emerald-colored roofs came to points, topped with swirled, wooden decor. As he slowed, a tightness churned in his stomach. He missed home, though it was still within sight.

Growing smaller in the distance, Orastos emerged from the library doors, his arm leaning on his staff, and waved goodbye.

A single flash of red streaked across his vision as Braern blinked. He frowned and blinked again. It disappeared. *What was that? Never mind.* Shaking his head, he straightened his posture and waved back. He decided it was too beautiful a day to be distracted. He nodded, spun around, and pushed onward.

The elf picked up momentum as he jumped with glee, levitating for brief leaps every so often, clutching his satchel of supplies to ensure it remained closed. He passed a grove of olive and tan ents as they braided each other's vines. They stood taller than the other trees around them, and their wooden facial expressions changed leisurely.

"Good morning, Braern," the oldest female greeted the elf as he passed, her gradual tone lifting as she spoke, and proceeded to braid her daughter's vines.

"Greetings, ents! It's a fine day for flying!" Braern cheered as he ran through the shrubs.

He accelerated, pushed off the ground for a moment, and propelled himself into the air. The forest and Lavendale grew smaller as he looked below. He remembered the instructions his father had given him: *"North through Lavendale Forest, over the meadow and the Ao River, past the crescent stones, and into the Fire Wyrm Swamp."*

He flew with ease, his arms outstretched before him. His clothing flapped at his sides, and his face cooled and warmed all at once. As the only elf in the realm who knew how to fly, he felt privileged. Flying was his favorite action he could do; a close second was learning powerful magic that Orastos taught him. He had moderate confidence in his sword fighting abilities. Now, he added traveling the world to his list.

Gazing at the ground, Braern witnessed the forest and land become painted swatches of various shades of green. He knew he was high enough in the sky. Any farther and he would have trouble breathing. He remembered the last time he flew too high. It had taken him days to recover.

In the distance, the blue trickling river came into view and parted the land as far as he could see. It was longer than he remembered since the last time he was here with his father. Minutes passed as he glided over the water. Vibrant greens faded into a darker gray land of twisted dead woods; uninviting bubbling muck covered the ground.

He descended, feet first, and landed on a broken, slanted stump. A rush of putrid, wet decay filled his nostrils. He forced his mouth to stay closed, biting his lip. No intelligent creature who valued their life ventured into this land, all except the swamp salamanders. They weren't too bright and often died shortly after hatching, forgetting to keep their own skin submerged in the swamp to protect it from drying up. They hid inside dead tree trunks, where they survived on insects and the remaining vegetation. The only sound he heard was the gloomy goop bubbling and popping as the swamp churned.

He searched for any sign of the wyrm. Nothing. He knew he would need to entice the creature out of the swamp, so flying would not be a sensible choice. From his studies, he hypothesized the vibration and noise of their prey attracted the fire wyrms.

Crouching low, he jumped from one stump to another. He placed his hands to steady himself and nudged forward, only to feel a pull behind him; he had snagged his satchel on a protruding branch. Rolling his eyes, he tugged with both hands on the straps. "Let go," he hissed, grasping and straining to free his belongings.

The tree branch broke with a snap and flung Braern into the swamp, covered to his belly and sinking fast in the sludge. As the mud filled his boots, he felt nauseated. He fought his way up and out until he climbed onto the stump. He wrapped his arms around his body and made himself as small as he could. Shaking, he freed as much mud as he could and levitated, disgusted by the grime seeping down his back. He hoped his supply of bread and fruit was still clean and edible.

A rumble sounded, and his ears perked up. He eyed his surroundings. It grew louder as he turned.

"The wyrm!" he shouted in terror as its immense size overwhelmed his senses. His heart beat faster, and he held his breath. He froze as the slithering creature lunged toward him with its mouth open, a thousand large, serrated teeth ready to pierce elven flesh. Foul breath made his head shake. He flew backward. A hard surface met his back as he slammed into a tree behind him. He pushed off with his feet to propel him into the air with his arms outstretched.

Catching his breath, his veins pulsing in his temples, he looked around as the thing disappeared under the swamp. Forcing his breath to slow, he calmed his spirit so he could listen for the slightest of movements. He floated down and grabbed a loose branch then threw it into the sludge. His attention focused as his vision jumped from every object he saw.

"Where are you, you slithering mass of scales?"

Large lumps of swamp protruded as the creature slithered toward the ripples. The wyrm's hide gliding in and out of the swamp surprised Braern, as he realized how big this creature was. Its girth was the size of an enormous tree trunk. Dirty, off-white, scaly skin made it easy to see but more terrifying. An oval, bumpy head and large eyes made it something of nightmares, and its crimson jaw opened wide, slobbering and screeching so much Braern's ears hurt. He forced his hands to stay where they were while he fixated on its upper body.

The creature followed him, half its body remaining submerged.

Braern zigzagged, swished, and flew in circles around tree branches, but the wyrm seemed never-ending in its pursuit, as if it hadn't eaten in weeks. Out of breath and fearing he would soon succumb to exhaustion, the elf flew as high as he could without losing sight of the creature below.

The wyrm followed as far as it could, then ceased its relentless chase and retreated.

If that thing could fly, I'd be dead by now. Braern paused. He took long breaths to calm his body and mind, his pulse aching in his ear lobes, toes, neck, head. *I need those scales.* He reminded himself of his quest as he forced his mind to focus, in between slowing breaths. *It's much faster than the books say.*

Moments passed, and he took one more deep, slow inhale and exhale to free his thoughts. As he felt his body resting, he scanned the vastness of the swamp. He studied the area: dead, black trees and stumps, flat stones of various sizes. There were very few places to hide. Staring at a charred tree, he realized it was about his size and shape.

He levitated downward but stopped before reaching the sluggish, bubbling surface. A nearby branch protruded from the goo. He grabbed it and threw it where he was levitating seconds before. It splashed and sank.

Moments later, a rumbling mound under the surface barreled toward Braern. Once again, the filthy wyrm showed itself and shrieked with a high-pitched, rumbling shrill.

The elf kept his focus on it but snuck a peek at the previous tree to his right. Time slowed as his attention grew. A dripping, slimy mouth lunged toward him. He imagined a shield as he conjured the blue magic from his fingers, and it appeared around his arm in a flash of light. Unsheathing his sword with one hand, a glistening shield in the other, he braced for battle, eyes and hands steady and sure.

The wyrm reared its neck and lunged in front of him, expanding its lungs and transforming into its protective crimson color that shone through its dirty, white hide in stripes.

Braern's eyes widened as his heart skipped a beat. "How did I forget the fire? They're called fire wyrms!" Angry with himself, he clenched his jaw, bracing his shield.

The elf bent his knees against the light as a wave of heat rushed toward him from the creature's throat. Orange and yellow flames roared, forcing him backward as he fought to steady himself in the air, grimacing and groaning. Several smaller bits of fire flew around his shield and landed on his shins and elbows. He winced, fighting to keep his focus through the sweat beads dripping into his eyes. Most of the flames spun around his body in spirals as he used his strength to push himself against the inferno, teeth clenching. The fire dissipated, and smoke surrounded them both.

His eyes burned. Blinking, he peered in all directions, unsure of what to expect next.

The air cleared. Braern screamed in sheer terror as the wyrm came from the side. It sunk its teeth into his left arm, sending searing pain up his arm and down his spine. The creature dragged his body into the swamp. Before it could pull his other arm under, he thrust his sword into the wyrm's hide. It released him and retreated again into the swamp, bloody ripples forming after its stumpy tail. The elf floated in the air, heart racing, gasping for breath. He fought the urge to hold his injury, knowing if he dropped his sword, he would die.

Braern watched. "I'm not finished with you," he taunted, his body shaking.

Moments later, the wyrm flew from the swamp and straight toward him.

While he swung his sword, his shield at the ready, a small circle of light no bigger than his hand appeared in front of him, and, for a split second, he plunged his weapon through. His weapon stabbed something difficult to pierce. The flash of a shiny, yellow metal surface appeared where he had stabbed. His hair blew backward from a small breeze welcomed in the heat of battle.

He retrieved his sword. The circle closed and disappeared, the wyrm unscathed. It happened fast. *"What?"*

The creature bellowed. It vanished into the mud but remained close to the surface as lumps of its body swooshed in circles under Braern, trickles of dark blood staining the surface.

"I cannot defeat this creature by myself. Or can I?" In seconds, he muttered the spell, *"Go ni naru!"*

Five illusion clones of Braern appeared all in a row, spaced out around the creature as it reared its ugly head, screaming and wailing. It grew impatient at how much work this meal was taking. Confused, the wyrm surveyed each of the six elves, unsure of which one to attack, as it blinked its terrifying eyes and growled. The wyrm attempted to bite the magic illusion, only to have it wither and fade into the thick air. Five left. It opened its mouth as the clones followed Braern's every move.

He swung his sword toward the beast as it barreled toward each one. The real Braern in the middle whispered another spell and disguised himself as the nearby tree he had been eyeing. He vanished, confusing the creature more. Four.

The wyrm stopped.

Braern blew a small puff of air out the corner of his mouth, careful not to move. The other clones vanished in a whiff of magic.

Raging and livid, its eyes glowed brighter, smoke formed from its nostrils, and saliva spilled from its mouth in chunks that fell to the swamp with a splash. As it released one last flaming, hot breath toward nowhere in particular, it slithered close to the burned tree.

Braern allowed himself to be seen once again, braced his sword backward, and plunged with all the strength he had left into the wyrm's neck below its jawline.

It closed its eyes, foul blood spurting every which direction from the wound, and surrendered. The weight of the creature dragged him down.

Acid rose from his stomach and up his esophagus as the bitter taste of the wyrm's blood found his tongue. He shook his head to remove several drops. He retrieved his sword, dripping with bits of flesh on the blade. With his left arm around the creature's midsection, he remembered Orastos's words.

"If you must slay the creature, retrieve the body for the rest of the village to harvest and use every part: scales, claws, teeth, even the eyes. This shows respect for the creature and for its sacrifice."

Braern murmured, *"Chijimu,"* and waved his hand over the deceased wyrm.

It shrank. Smaller and smaller, it became. Now the size of Braern's palm, it continued to shrink.

"Wait! Stop! Stop shrinking! What do I do now?" He panicked, shaking his head, and looked in every direction. He searched his mind.

The wyrm was the size of his little fingernail.

"Hidogaru!" he yelled, staring at the wyrm in his palm.

It grew larger.

"Owaru!"

It stopped.

He summoned a transparent orb from the air and placed the fire wyrm inside. It floated in suspended animation, unable to decay or move. He placed the orb inside his satchel and sighed.

Drained from battle, his body dangled downward as he floated to the nearest patch of land, his feet dragging in the mud. He scraped the blood off his sword on a stone, hearing the high-pitched sound of metal. The tattered elf bent his knees, attempting to propel himself into the air to begin his journey home. Instead, he found himself unable to muster the strength and magic needed. *Magic always comes at a price.* He reminded himself of his father's words. The spells he'd cast had diminished his energy. Braern's eyelids closed. He dropped his sword with a thud. His shield vanished. Unable to support his weight, he fell to the ground, unconscious.

*****

A few hours later, Braern awoke from the stench of death and decay. Still unable to fly, he spit out the vile taste and reached into his satchel. He devoured his soggy food, then washed it all down with water from his pouch. He lowered his head and smelled his own burning flesh, his wounds black and red. A magenta, navy-blue, and orange sunset appeared behind the far-off mountains. He blinked and felt too tired to appreciate the colors. The elf headed in the direction he hoped was home.

Each step was more painful than the last. He held his blood-soaked left arm with his right hand as he wobbled and limped. His boots sloshed from the grotesque liquid inside. The little orb rubbed his leg as his sword pulled with every step. The ringing in his ears stopped, his energy waning. He knew if he didn't keep going, he would fall asleep again, and who knew what would happen to him then. Hours later, he heard the trickling of the river as it drew closer.

Taking a step with closed eyes, he tripped and fell onto something hard and squishy. He saw a small circle of light with his foot and leg caught inside. *What is happening?* Exacerbated and unwilling to experience anything else out of the ordinary for the rest of the day, he lifted his leg and noticed his foot covered in some tiny creature's sausage-shaped excrement, with bits of wood pieces stuck to his boot. The odor reached his nose as he coughed and shook it off.

The light circle disappeared, and it left him with the remnants of something unknown still attached. He hobbled to the river and washed his weathered brown boots in its soothing current, turning them upside down to clean out the rest of the swamp sludge. Soft trickling from the waves soothed his throbbing ears.

I need to return home to my father. He will know what is happening to me, he promised himself, determined to move faster to get his questions answered.

Feeling a small, renewed energy about him, he leaped into the air, paused, and gained height. Unable to rise higher, he stayed at the top of the trees as he saw Lavendale Forest come into view once again. He forced a smile. Everything around him brightened. Everything around him brightened with the familiar and comforting sight of the lanterns lit around his village. The brightness shining through the library windows guided the beaten elf home.

He lowered himself and peered at his disastrous body as his feet landed flat on the walkway. Covered in blood, his hair a filthy mess plastered to his face, he hobbled to the library's twin paper doors.

"Father! I need help!" he called, holding his injured arm.

No answer.

Placing his hand on the wooden frame, his body gave in. Braern collapsed as an enormous circle of light appeared and enveloped his entire body, allowing him to fall for what seemed like ages. Colors of blue, gray, white, and purple surrounded him and glowed, blinding him. He squinted and floated, feeling a sense of relief from the weight lifted off his body.

The magic around him felt stronger than anything his father had shown him. The light encased and penetrated his body, but left him unharmed. He watched light surround his arms, then grasped at a cloud of blue as it vanished, leaving his hand cool. A tiny smile appeared on his worn-down face, and a sense of wonder overcame his fear. He relaxed enough to enjoy the ride for mere moments.

The circle of light closed as he landed on a hard surface. Grimacing in pain, he brought his knees to his chest and hugged his body then rolled over. He tried to lift his head, shaking, and looked around. Through tired eyes, he forced his eyebrows to do the rest of the work as his vision blurred.

Shocked, he saw a building made of an unknown material. It was smooth, with four large pillars, two spaced out on each side. A parcel with human language written on it adorned a large arched doorway. He remembered his extensive studies in learning one of the common tongues of humans. It read, *T-Rex, the Ultimate Predator,* and took up most of the front of the entrance. *What is a T-Rex?*

A set of twin transparent doors were nestled farther inside the precipice. Horizontal stairs led upward with thin, metal, cylindrical poles stuck in the ground with a top pole laid across each one. Four statues of humans dressed in various styles of clothing that he remembered seeing in books stood gazing onward on top of each of the four pillars toward the roof. *Truth, Knowledge, and Vision* were carved into the front in between. He read the words as best he could. Grasping the object next to him, he looked up and witnessed another statue, darker this time and at ground level, with a more-shaded gray of another human riding a horse with his gaze looking away from the larger building.

Where... am I?

MOIRA

MUSEUMS AND WATER BOTTLES

G oodbye, kids! Come back soon!" Moira exclaimed as she guided the group of twelve from the nearby elementary school to the gallery exit.

"Bye, Miss Moira!" A little girl with blond pigtails and a flowery dress smiled at her. She waved and skipped back to her classmates. Her little feet pattered on the marble floor while a Scooby-Doo lunch bag trailed behind in her grasp.

"Goodbye, Kayla!" Moira waved back as she watched the kids. "See ya next time!"

Chattering and giggling came from the children as they situated their backpacks, grabbed their empty lunch bags, then pushed through the large, golden-trimmed, glass doors of the front entrance. The chaperoned kids raced down the stairs to the bus that had arrived outside by the curb.

Moira waved again. A group of boys waved with both hands, with silly smiles, jumping up and down. Youngsters visiting the museum were the highlight of Moira's week. She always enjoyed giving tours to them and teaching them about all the most important portraits and sculptures she had grown to adore over the months while she ensured the safety of the grounds. The last rambunctious boy climbed onto the bus, and the sliding door sealed behind him. The bus drove off as she continued to smile through a closed mouth. Then the smile faded. She sighed.

Moira touched her hair to secure her long braids in her bun and out of her face. Her auburn skin and white uniform top glistened in the sun as it faded from the sky; brightened streaks escaped through the exits. Placing a hand across her forehead, she narrowed her eyes. She blinked as the light lessened, and a beautiful array of cerulean-pink and yellow shone through the clouds. She paused to enjoy the city view.

The street lights turned on. Shadows deepened, following pedestrians as they strolled by, while taxis and other vehicles slowed and drove past. This was a busy area of New York, but it slowed ever so slightly when night came. Many people of all ages sat and spoke to one another outside on the grand steps leading to the museum.

"Back to work," she murmured with a sigh, saddened the day was ending, but her shift had barely started. Her keys and radio dangled on one side of her black, polyester, ironed pants, and her safety-locked pistol sat on the opposite hip.

Moira began her boring routine of locking the doors at closing time. She walked to the far-left door, twisted the lock, then continued to the right—moving down the line, right to left, to keep things interesting. Preparing to secure the last door by the information desk, a blurred, dark figure floated toward her. It looked like a person, but she couldn't be sure. Something about the figure creeped her out, so she slammed the door and twisted the golden lock shut. She backed away from the door, blinked, and the figure vanished.

"What the hell?"

A scraping sounded behind her. She twirled around, her right hand hovering over her gun. Her heart raced as she frantically looked around. Nothing.

Then the figure appeared again, the tip of its feet squeaking on the floor as the rest of its body floated around the corner.

Is that guy flying? Naw, I must be imagining things. "How'd ya get in here? The museum's closed! You can come back tomorrow!" she shouted in aggravation as she ran after the thing, toward the enormous Apatosaurus skeleton in the main lobby.

The man was tall, skinny, and smelled of sewage and burned cloth. Horrible smell.

He must be homeless, but that doesn't explain why he's floating around like that. Am I dreaming? Moira shook her head and followed him into the Van Gogh exhibit. High crown molding ceilings continued above as her footsteps tapped on the floor. They curved around to the right into a room full of Russian-themed artwork, from paintings to pottery and glazed, female-form nude sculptures. Moira stopped as the squeaking grew silent.

"Stop! All right, where are you? I'ma escort ya outside and no harm done, but ya need to come out, now." She clicked on her flashlight.

No response, then a thud.

"Look, dude, I'm not in the mood for this. Come out now or I'm callin' for backup. I'm tryin' to do you a favor and not have you arrested!" She frowned, growing more impatient. She tiptoed so the intruder would not know her location, steadying herself with outstretched arms. Knowing the entire floor plan, she had the advantage. Unsure of any possible danger, she turned on her radio with one hand then unhooked it from her belt. She stopped walking before the Egyptian exhibit, the fifteen-foot statue of Anubis in front of her. The only way out was through the entryway.

"Can't believe I have to do this," she murmured. With a pit in her chest, she rolled her eyes and shook her head. She flipped the switch. "This is Moira Washington. I'm at the Museum of Natural History. I got a ten-sixty-four. Send backup."

"Ten-four, on our way," the man replied over the radio.

She recognized Brad from the NYPD. *What a tool.*

"Hope she doesn't break the dude's neck before we get there. Another waste of ti—" The voice cut out.

Moira frowned. *They're still laughing at me. Assholes.* She took a deep breath and ground her teeth, then licked her lips, stabilizing her shaking hands from hearing her ex-fellow officer mentioning such a painful part of her past. Swallowing the lump in her throat, she recalled her duty was to wait for backup. She remained where she was for several minutes, then caught a glimpse from the corner of her eye. She heard knocking and raced to the entrance.

Two officers, one heavy set and one medium weight, arrived at the front, with narrowed eyes and folded arms.

She unlocked the main middle door, and the men pushed through.

"All right, where's this *criminal?*" The rotund cop curled his fingers into air quotes. He tugged on his belt around his enormous belly and snorted.

The other man tapped his foot and raised an eyebrow at Moira.

"Well...?" Brad, the taller one, gestured inside with his hand.

"Last I saw, he was in the Egyptian exhibit. I'll show ya," she said, remaining professional yet determined that this was a genuine emergency. Pushing away thoughts of how her ex-coworkers had never taken her seriously, she returned to where she had lost the intruder.

The men didn't bother to walk quietly and instead seemed to step louder with their heels. They searched for a few minutes around each ancient pot and faded sarcophagus. However, the man they were looking for was nowhere to be found.

"Oh, look, he's not here. Shocker. Let's go get some dinner. I'm starving," the larger cop teased as he turned, securing his flashlight to his belt.

"He was right here! I saw him! I'm not making this up!" Moira snapped, spitting all over the two ignorant men.

"Why don't you go back to playing with your little statues? You're not a cop anymore. Call us when there's a real emergency." The other officer stood, feet apart, hands on his rotund hips, as he bent forward to challenge her to her face.

Moira clenched her fists, crushing her flashlight. She felt broken pieces of metal dig into her hand, her body shaking, livid with emotion. "I don't play with them! They're part of the exhibits! Get the hell outta here! I'll find him myself!" She waved her arm, pointing toward the door, her chest heaving.

"I told ya she was crazy," Brad muttered as the two of them strolled through the exit.

Why did I even bother? With tears in her eyes, Moira's face burned as her chin quivered, hands convulsing. Her flashlight echoed as it hit the marble and flickered off. The imprint of her hand had crushed the handle.

"Gah!" She threw her fist into the nearby door leading to a bathroom, splitting an enormous hole into it, with shards of wood flying in all directions. She paused with her arm halfway inside and welcomed the pain of a thousand splinters on her knuckles. Shaking, grinding her teeth, and taking short, useless breaths, her mind flooded with every hateful comment she had ever endured. She balanced herself against the corner of the wall with her other hand as sweat dripped down her sides. Moments passed, and she removed her beaten arm from the door. The cracked wood chunks clicked on the ground in piles.

"Wonderful. This'll come out of my paycheck." She shook her head, disgusted with her actions. "I'm better than this."

She refocused on the intruder who needed to be evicted. She wiped away her tears with her arm, adjusted her uniform, and grabbed her flashlight. With a frown, she sighed. *Oh, great. Does this thing still work?*

A soft murmur uttered behind her. Moira's eyes widened. She spun around, drew her gun, and pointed the barrel forward.

A thin, dirty man with burned areas on his unusual clothing hunched over before her, beaten and limping. He grasped his bloody left arm, and he tried to bow before her but lost his balance.

"Don't move." Moira stood her ground, a wad of snot pooling from her right nostril. She sniffed it back up, keeping an eye on the stranger. She shined her light on his face, and as it flickered, he blinked from the brightness. "Ya shouldn't be in here. The museum is closed. I tried to tell ya that several times." Getting a good look at the guy, her brain registered the dried blood on his clothes and face, and she felt an unthreatening aura emitting from him. "Hold up. Are you hurt?"

The young man answered in an unknown language, his voice shaking.

Moira lowered her gun and shook her head. "I have no idea what you just said, dude." Convinced he couldn't understand her either, she noticed the weathered man's pointed ears protruding from his light-colored hair. "You're an elf? Oh, you must be from the comic convention down the street. Let me help ya get back to your hotel, man. Why'd ya sneak in here as I was locking up? Were you asking for help? I guess the uniform could be confusing. I'm the security guard here, not a cop."

She questioned him as the duo headed toward the main entrance, supporting him while he grasped his left upper arm. A piece of wood fell to the floor from the broken bathroom door. Moira flinched. *I'll deal with that later.*

Without another word, Moira allowed the struggling man to support himself on her arm as she showed him out the door. She turned to check the museum once more with her dying flashlight and looked through the lobby, the several exhibits before her in the rooms across from the dinosaur skeletons, the information desk, and the bathroom. No sign of anyone, so she felt safe enough to escort this poor guy down the street to the convention hall.

Dirt and dried blood covered his medieval European and Eastern mixed clothing. His pants were torn, his boots caked in mud. He left a trail behind him as she helped him across the lobby.

Moira sniffed and scrunched her face, blinking and moving her head backward. He smelled like vomit, dirt, and decaying flesh, with a hint of burned toast. "You reek, man. You need to shower."

He eyed her as they scooted toward the front. The last of the sunlight shone on his face as she relaxed her expression. His piercing blue-green eyes seared right into her soul. His dirty hair had crusted onto his cheeks.

When they reached the door, she noticed he carried a tan satchel and wore a belt with a sword. A toy, she assured herself. "What'chu been doin', dude? Get in a fight over Sting here?" She gestured with her eyes to his weapon.

He regarded her with heavy eyelids. The man collapsed, but Moira caught him and supported his weight on her muscular arm.

She hardly felt his weight, which wasn't much of a surprise anymore. "All right, all right, take it easy. I'll get ya to the hospital." Moira hoisted him and heaved his body over her shoulder.

Moira helped the unconscious elf-man out of the museum and into her car parked by the ground-floor parking garage. No one noticed her carrying him. Her 2000 gray Prius had its own parking spot labeled, SECURITY.

As the man's belongings smacked into her back, she grasped her keys from her pocket and unlocked her car door. She placed him in the backseat, laid down his head last, and scooted him all the way inside before closing the door. She didn't want another mess on her hands, like the last man she'd almost killed when she'd put him into her patrol car.

Shaking her head, she suppressed the horrific memory that haunted her for the past eight months.

As she touched the sheath of his sword to move it away from his body, it gave off a shock. Retracting her hand with a frown, she pressed her fingers together and opened the door. She leaned across the driver's seat and tossed all the Starbucks cups onto the passenger floorboard. She pulled her cellphone from her back pocket before sitting and starting the car.

Glancing in the mirror, she noticed part of her braided hair had come loose from her bun. *No time to fix that now,* she thought, although the thought of looking so unkempt bothered her. The nearest hospital was three blocks away. As she drove out of the parking garage, the light inside the nearest steel lamppost shone through her windshield.

Moans sounded in the back seat.

She held her breath every few minutes to give her nose a break from the stench. *I'm gonna have to pay to get this car cleaned now, too.* Pausing to look both ways, she listened to his breathing. She relaxed her shoulders as she zoomed off. *I better hurry and drop this dude off and get back to work. I can't afford another mark on my record.*

*****

Several minutes later, Moira came upon the Manhattan Memorial Hospital and drove straight up to the front ER entrance. She parked out of the way and ensured she placed her law enforcement sticker on the window. She got out of the car and opened the back door to secure the tattered, beaten elf-man onto her shoulder once again and walked to the glass entrance as it slid open.

Another doctor in powder-blue scrubs glanced in her direction and strode over. "What do we have here?" The young, umber-haired man gestured toward the nearest empty hospital bed in the hallway.

She placed the elf-man on the bed. "I'm a security guard at the museum. This dude showed up after closin' time, covered in blood. His left arm's injured. He's been limping and has several burns. I think he's been in some sort of fight or something. I came straight here."

"Thank you. We'll take good care of him." He raised an eyebrow at the pointed ears. "Wait right here; someone will be with you to fill out some paperwork." He nodded toward the chairs on the opposite side for her to sit.

"All right." She watched a nurse wheel the man through the hallway and around the corner. "But... I don't even know his name," Moira said to no one in particular.

She collapsed, slouching on an uncomfortable green and brown chair. Taking a deep breath, she closed her eyes and scratched the armrests. The smooth hardness soothed her fingers. "Man, what a night..." She shook her head as she brushed off the dirt from her filthy uniform.

As she adjusted herself, a clang startled her. She turned and looked down the crevice between the chair and the wall. One peculiar item the man had brought fell with a thud. His satchel and brown pouch lay next to the long object. *Guess I better take these to him. It's made of plastic, but maybe he'll miss it.*

She grasped his belt from under the chair, trying to avoid scraping any of his items on the floor and drawing unwanted attention. The longer object was heavy—a sword. She retrieved the belt and laid it all across the arms of the chair. It resembled a weapon that could be displayed, alongside a painting of the dragon-slayer Saint George, in an actual museum. *Oh my god, this thing is real. Someone beat the crap outta him for this?*

Moira hovered her fingers over its artistry and noticed the shimmering designs of swirls and birds that flew between tangled vines. She grasped the hilt and unsheathed the blade a few inches, then a spark jolted her hand. She dropped it. *This has happened before... in the car.*

A janitor appeared and stopped his cart a few doors down.

Perfect. She ambled over as he entered a room to clean it. He whistled to himself, keyring rattling on his hip. She snatched one of his clean blankets and walked back to the sword, wrapped the fabric around the middle, and picked it up. No shock. She looked around, wondering if anyone else saw her. All the medical staff were busy hustling with papers, typing on keyboards, or chitchatting.

Moira grabbed the belt containing his other belongings. She spread the blanket over most of the sheath and handle. Carrying it at her side, she stiffened her grip. Knowing it would be difficult to hide such an enormous sword, she sauntered to the nurses' station, where a lady wearing pink scrubs worked on her paperwork with a phone between her shoulder and ear. She had blond hair, short bangs, and silver hoop earrings.

"That's correct. We will keep him overnight and monitor his vitals... Yes, thank you... You too," the lady told the person on the other line. She placed down the phone and spun her chair to Moira. "How can I help you?"

"Hi, I dropped off an injured man, and I wanted to return his... stuff to him."

"Oh, that fella? Are you family?"

"No."

"The John Doe got moved down the hall. Turn right. It's on the left. One-oh-three. They're checking him out now; you can leave it for him there. Since you're heading that way, would you mind filling these out?" She handed Moira a clipboard of papers with a pen attached under the metal clip. The nurse answered another phone call as she angled away.

"Thank you," Moira replied, taking the clipboard while attempting to juggle everything in her arms.

Moonlight shone through a nearby window. *I'm gonna be in so much trouble if I don't get back soon.* She hastened her steps. The floor was a neutral-colored tile, and the walls were a light brown. *Coulda sworn I heard somewhere that the colors in hospitals neutralize all the red blood. Seems peaceful in here.*

Paintings of flowers and multi-colored brushstrokes lined the walls every few feet—101... 102... 103. She stopped. The blinds were open. Two trauma physicians were still examining him as he lay motionless. She struggled to open the door and saw the guy's clothes cut open as the doctors checked his heartbeat with their stethoscopes and palpated his abdomen for injuries. Another doctor in blue scrubs with a ginger-colored ponytail and freckles placed a saline bag on the hook of the metal stand next to the bed. She inserted the IV and taped it onto his wrist, then secured a plastic bracelet with a barcode on his other.

Moira noticed the two doctors looked puzzled as they pried away his bloodied clothing and inspected his wounds.

"Are you family?" one doctor asked.

"No."

"Then you can't be in here. Please leave." Another doctor with blood-covered gloves signaled for her to scram.

"These are his. I'll leave them here." Moira set his belongings and the clipboard on a table next to a lamp. She didn't bother filling out the paperwork—not yet.

"It looks like a bear tried to eat him... or a lion. How is that possible in New York?" she heard the doctor ask as she looked up at her.

One cleaned his wound while the other examined his burns. "Was he in a fire?"

"I don't think so," Moira said. She turned and left the room, spying the man on the bed, as the doctors murmured to each other. Before she got too far, she felt something tug at her to return to the room. She turned to see the patient's hand reach for her, his bright eyes staring, unblinking. No matter how hard she tried, she couldn't look away. Her throat and chest ached. She felt heavy.

"Ma'am, if you're not family, you need to leave now or I'll call security." The tall doctor noticed her badge. "Er... I guess you are security?"

She reached out, confused by the plethora of emotions running through her. All the machines and medical equipment blurred. She touched his hand, surprised at how soft it felt on her fingertips.

He gazed at her and grasped her palm. He opened his mouth to speak, but nothing came out.

This is too much. I don't even know this guy. I need to get back to work.

The room illuminated, and everyone shielded their eyes. Swirls of blues, purples, and whites glowed with radiant light that consumed the rest of the room. Moira couldn't release his hand, even if she'd wanted to. An oval of blended colors surrounded them in a clockwise motion. Moments passed as the two floated; his sword and satchel flew around them over the table. They blinked and fell onto a crusty salsa-stained carpet with a thud. The colors vanished.

*****

Familiar blue curtains darkened their new location. Two couches and a chair formed a U-shape, while a cracked, solid oak coffee table, held together with peeling duct tape, furnished the space. Broken picture frames lay facedown on tables with minimal decor—or much of anything hanging on the walls. A large, ancient television with a DVD and VHS combo in the front stood on a narrow stand with two bookshelves on either side. Duct tape wrapped around the front left leg of the television stand. Broken things were strewn across the floor. Clothes were scattered everywhere, with takeout boxes on tables and countertops in the small, open kitchenette.

"This is my apartment," she said with a laugh and a cry all at once, placing her hand over her mouth, as she pushed herself up from her knee. "How'd we get here? This is freakin' me out."

The elf-man bent to unlace his boots. "I assure you, I am as confused as you are, milady." He grimaced as he rose to stand. With a frown, he released his laces and stared at the IV sticking out from his arm. He tilted his head and pulled on the tape with a finger. It budged. Then he peeled off the rest with one motion and flinched as he removed the needle.

"Oh! You speak English. Well, that helps. And... uh, sorry... that looks painful. You don't have to take off your shoes, by the way. Let me help you." She supported him and led him to her couch.

"Are you sure? It is customary to remove your shoes when entering someone's home."

Moira raised an eyebrow and scoffed. She realized she hadn't had a man over in months, let alone one who was bleeding. Usually, she was the damaged one.

"Yes, I have studied many of the human tongues for years, with my father." His eyes sunk as he exhaled, peering at his boots.

"Cool. Oh, and I'm no lady. Trust me. Now, what the hell's going on here? This is crazy. I must've taken too many sleeping pills last night, and I'm losin' my mind!" Moira clutched the sides of her head in response to seeing all the trash. She rarely had guests over, especially uninvited ones. Never having time nor energy to clean overwhelmed her, though she knew if she cleaned, she might not be so overwhelmed—a vicious cycle that had remained for years.

She helped him sit, then collapsed onto the couch next to him, slapping the cushions. "I was working. You showed up, then I took you to the hospital, then... we ended up here. How? Did I zone out at the wheel? And what were all those flashing lights? Wait, did I even see flashing lights? Oh my god! And who are you, and where did you come from?" *Let the man answer! Damn!*

"I apologize. Was that your home back there where we first met?"

"The museum? No, I just work there."

"I see. My name is Braern Yogensha of Lavendale. I come from Yumerion. I'm certain magic brought us here, as it had brought me to your world." He steadied his breath as he tried to get comfortable.

His voice soothed her, calming her fears for a moment as she relaxed her shoulders. "I'm Moira Washington of... New York, which is where we're at right now. Where is Yumerion?"

"Yumerion is my world, and this is... Earth, am I correct? I have read about this planet from my studies."

"Yes, this is Earth..." she said, raising an eyebrow at such a strange question. Moira outstretched a reluctant hand, hoping he would shake it to make the encounter less awkward.

"I believe I am familiar with this human greeting. I take your hand, like so..." he said as he took her hand and lifted it, then smiled.

She shook his hand and sniffed. Her nostrils flared as she leaned her head back and frowned; his stench hit her nose like a wave. She pinched her nostrils and scooted away.

"Allow me to make myself more presentable," he said as he peered at his body. He stood and closed his eyes. *"Kirei ni naru."* Braern waved his hand from his knees to above his head as the light-colored cloud of sparkles changed him. He stood, clean from head to toe, with no noticeable cuts in his clothing—no blood, grime, nor smell. His brown, shin-high boots were clean and had a hint of shine. His pants were loose, with a faded gray-green color. A cobalt-blue vest was laced up, while his long-sleeved, *kimono*-style undershirt reached his wrists. He sported shoulder-length, blond hair, while his pale skin and protruding pointed ears stood out most of all.

With a wave of his hand, his belt, sword, satchel, and water pouch floated over to him and fastened themselves onto his waist.

Moira eyed the objects. She rose and stepped backward, fists clenched. Against the wall, she screamed and pointed. "What the hell?"

He noticed her expression, removed the belt, and placed them on the floor next to his feet.

"I apologize if I have frightened you. That is not my intention." He cleared his throat and pulled away his sleeve to inspect his wounds. The gauze and tape held, but the pain remained.

Moira pulled the cord of her maroon lamp on the end table closest to her and stared at him with wide eyes and a gaping jaw. "Whew, are you for real? How'd you do that?"

"I cast a cleaning spell; although Orastos warned me not to use magic for minor tasks..." Braern's face relaxed as the light shone on Moira. She watched, leaning against the wall behind her, as the man checked her out from head to toe.

"Who's Orastos?"

Braern blinked. "He is my father and mentor. He taught me everything I know."

"Thats nice," she said, not paying much attention to his words. Moira threw her arms in the air. "I'm sorry. I don't know what's going on here. You're all clean, and I don't remember how we got here, and we were at the hospital, right? I didn't imagine that. We were at the hospital and—" Moira hyperventilated, unable to catch much of a breath. She placed her hand on her chest, looking all around, then back at Braern. "Your ears! You're a real elf? So, you're magical and... what? You fight dragons on your days off or somethin'? What's happenin'? I'm going insane. That's what's happenin'!" She forced her eyelids shut, unsure she wanted her mind to process everything she was seeing.

"I assure you I need answers as much as you do."

"Oh god, I'm talking to Legolas who's sittin' on my couch when I should be at work reading about Pharaoh Tut's mummification for the billionth time while I make my rounds. I shouldn't be here. I don't have time for this. I-I need to get back to work. You need to leave!" She pointed toward the front door. She needed something to be normal. Work. Back to work.

"*Legolas?* Eh... I apologize for any pain I have caused you. That was not my intention." Braern stood as he sighed and made slow movements toward the door. He fastened his belt with his belongings around his waist and avoided eye contact with her. "I will navigate this world on my own. I'm sure I can find the answers at your library. It must have books that would lead me in the direction of how all of this came to be. Could you point me toward such a place?"

"You mean Queens Library?" She gave him directions, avoiding the subway. "Good luck walking around like that at night."

"A library of a queen? *Yatta!* Thank you, milady. I will find my way from here." He nodded and bowed again as he inched away from her, grimacing from his wounds.

As he was about to touch the doorknob, racked with sudden guilt, she staggered over and reached for him. "Wait... I'll give you some water before you leave." She walked the few steps to her kitchenette with basic appliances: full refrigerator with a loose, brown and metal handle, toaster, oven, stove, and sink, with only enough room to stand, let alone cook in. She grabbed the fridge handle and pulled, causing the handle to fly off and land ten feet from her living room television.

Braern approached her, keeping his distance.

"I got it!" Moira exclaimed, annoyed. "Happens all the time." She bent to collect the handle and screws, then retrieved a screwdriver from a small drawer to the right of her sink. While she held the handle in place as she secured the screws into their holes, she opened her fridge as gently as possible and surveyed the sparseness inside. Ketchup, water, and an expired yogurt stared at her. She was afraid to cook at home, and for good reason. Everything she touched, broke.

Braern watched as she handed the crinkly, plastic water bottle to him. He nodded, stepped forward, and accepted the gift. Staring at it, he tilted his head in confusion. "How do I... drink from this strange cup?"

"Here, lemme help you." She reached for the bottle, then stopped. As she stepped backward, she retracted her arms. *I'll probably break his arms if I try to help. I better stay back.* "I'll explain. You take the lid at the top in your hand and twist," she instructed, twinging with unease as she watched him struggle to follow her directions.

Seconds later, Braern opened it on the first try and raised the bottle to his lips. He gulped the entire container and shivered. "Thank you. That was refreshing. What would you like me to do with this?" He held up the bottle.

"Throw it on the floor. I'll get it later," she said, knowing she'd forget about it for a few days.

He complied and looked to his left. A framed photo of a man with his arm around Moira sat on an end table next to the couch. The white frame was chipped, and the glass had several cracks, distorting the picture. "Is that a tiny person trapped in that... object?" Braern asked, gesturing toward it.

"Oh! That's a photo. It's not a person. And, uh, that's Adrian. He's my ex. I really messed that one up—but, oh god, he had great abs." Moira's eyes lifted as she sighed with a grin escaping her face. She stared at the photo for a moment with a vacant expression. Shaking herself, she blinked, her eyes watering for a moment. "But it's over now, and I'm single. Again. It is what it is."

"What's an ex?"

"Someone who you aren't dating anymore." Moira sighed again.

"I don't know what this dating is."

"It means... never mind. All right, I'm going back to work, but I need to pack some stuff and use the bathroom." She stepped through the hallway, undoing her bun with both hands, her elbows up. "Wait here and don't steal anything." *Not that I have anything to steal, anyway.* She narrowed her eyes at him, as if to dare him to disobey.

He nodded and turned to sit on her couch.

Moira padded to the bathroom at the right of the hallway and looked in the mirror. Rolling her eyes, she glanced at the mess of a uniform she wore, with a bloodstained shoulder. *Gross. I'll finish my shift and then change. My spare uniform ain't back from the cleaners.*

She went to her closet in her bedroom and removed her belt with her gun and crushed flashlight. She placed them in a locked, silver case at the back. She grabbed a large leopard-print messenger bag from the top shelf. She threw in a complete comfy outfit, including her favorite thick yoga pants, then ripped her phone charger out of the wall and placed it in too.

In the bathroom, she noticed her hair was a mess, with half of it still up and the other half still pulled back while the other parts frizzed out. She scanned her hair products in tubes and circular jars, chose her container of gel, and squeezed it onto her fingers, then smoothed it on her head so her hair would behave once again and stay out of her face.

As she was about to place it on her small counter, another light appeared in front of her toilet over her turquoise, fuzzy bathmat. It grew and changed colors, like the one that had appeared at the hospital. Her eyes widened, and soon, it became as big as she was, moving toward her. She felt a force pull her in against her will, as her screams echoed in her tiny bathroom.

She watched as Braern came to her aid, only to see a hand sticking out of the large circle of magic. "Moira!" he shouted and clutched her hand.

They fell together through the weightlessness and comforting forces. Still holding hands, the unlikely pair floated in an awkward circle as their clothes fell upward, along with Braern's satchel. Something unseen pulled them down and up, all at once. All around them was a vortex of cool hues mixed with electric currents of whites and yellows.

"Why is this happening again?" Moira panicked as she reached to touch a nearby swirl of electricity attracted to her fingers. The minuscule jolt shocked her and made her giggle through a closed mouth, retracting her hand to her chest. *I guess this isn't so bad. It's kinda cool, actually.*

The surrounding vortex disappeared, and green ground faded into view underneath through a spiral of circles.

ARADUK

THE DWARF

The dwarf meditated under his favorite tree in an attempt to train his mind to forget his violent past. With his body entirely in shadow, he felt protected by the great branches of the willow above him. Her tiny leaves tickled his cheek as he mustered a faint smile. He adjusted his arms and shoulders, the coolness of his metal flask touching his side from the pocket of his robe. His one and only vice, the flask was given to him by a witch who cast a spell, enchanting it to never empty. He worked five years as her servant for that spell. Inside, he asked for the strongest alcohol known between Yumerion and Earth—*gin whiskey.* The bitter, honey-colored liquid was 100% proof and the sole path to intoxication for the dwarf. For dwarves do not become intoxicated unless they have the help of magic. They could drink their weight in anything and hardly feel a thing. But why did he need such a drink?

Araduk Lightbringer used to be called by another name, a name he changed of his own accord because of an oath he swore to the gods. He swore to never harm another being as long as he drew breath, after he believed he was given a second chance for redemption when he suddenly found himself able to heal the sick and injured. His dead name, Araduk Ironspine, once inspired fear throughout the realms as one of the deadliest *kappurai* warriors of the world. As commander of the army of dwarves from Tetsu Mountain, he demanded respect and absolute fealty with no tolerance for insubordination. The lives he took over the course of his forty-five years of existence collapsed nations. Every motionless face of the dead never left his memories. In fact, they seared such a hole in his conscience that only his trusty flask brought him solace.

He scrunched his closed eyes, his hand shaking while his tongue begged him to drink. The dwarf listened to several groans that sounded from the sky, not far from him. *Flying visitors? I haven't seen another being in the weeks since I came here in solitude, except the creatures o' the lands. An' what was that strange oval o' magic that they fell through?* He listened intently, keeping still.

Is that an elf? Araduk thought, with one eye open. *And... a human?* He watched as the elf flipped in the air and landed on his side, despite trying to brace himself. His elbow hit the ground first. He scrunched his body into a fetal position, whimpering and scowling.

Oh, that must've hurt. Araduk winced, thinking about the sound he made when he hit the ground.

The human fell on her hands and knees with a thud. She rolled over onto her side, gasping, then glanced above. She touched the strap of her strange, animal-skin bag that had fallen with them. "At least I'll have a change of clothes," the human said as she sobbed, grasping her wrists. *Ah, she speaks the English tongue.*

She turned to the elf and saw his arm bleeding through the bandage. Groaning, she crawled toward him. "I need to put pressure on that so you don't bleed out."

The elf nodded, gulping.

She pressed down... too hard.

"Gah!" the elf yelled, fighting to grasp his arm, and recoiled.

Araduk winced, keeping one eye closed, watching their interaction transpire a few feet below at the base of the small hill he sat upon. *Sounds like they're in a lot of pain. Alas, I must wait for them to come to me. The lands will be able to tell if they're evil or not. I shall remain here, under m' tree.*

"I'm so sorry! I forgot..." the human cried as she scooted away.

The elf held his arm, gritting his teeth and curling himself onto his side.

"Are you all right? Again, I'm so sorry. I can't control myself most of the time." The human fought to get out the words.

The elf grunted in her direction as he shifted his head to her.

She rotated her gaze past her feet to see his face.

"I will be. You?"

She nodded.

They must have known each other for years. They seem to be close.

A minute passed as they both steadied their breathing, lying flat; the blades of grass tickled their exposed skin. Scratching and tiny chirps surrounded them. A flock of griffins flew overhead in an elegant shape toward the mountains. They called to one another as they disappeared over the horizon.

The human sat upright.

A beautiful sage hue covered the landscape. Trees with broad, twisted, dark branches dove into the earth, then crossed themselves up again, reaching for the suns. Two different sized overlapping spheres of oranges and violets filled a quarter of the sky.

"Whoa, two suns?" the human asked.

"Ah, yes. Our twin suns, *Izanagi and Izanami.* They created my world, and now their spirits rest in the sky for eternity, watching over their creation." The elf rose to a sitting position.

"Toto, we're not in Kansas anymore," the human said, monotone.

The elf turned to her and cocked his head as she faced away. "I am Braern, not this *Toto.*"

Ah, his name is Braern. Sounds vaguely familiar. Wonder what her name is?

"Oh! Ha! Never seen *The Wizard of Oz?* Yeah, I guess not, huh? It means we're in a strange place. Funny to think about ya watching an old TV," she snickered.

"I am not familiar with a *TV.* What is that?" he asked.

"It's uh... a box with moving pictures on it."

Braern nodded.

What sorcery is that? A TV? Strange name. He seems to be as confused as I am, Araduk wondered, continuing to listen to their conversation.

"I have not ventured far from my home, and I'm uncertain of our location, but we are close to the griffin kingdom. They seldom fly too far from their nests, from what I've studied. Perhaps, I can see where we are at the top of this cliff." Braern held his head with one hand and rotated his shoulders.

The two travelers craned their necks to see while pushing themselves to stand. Surveying the distance, they realized they were high up. A large navy-blue flowing river snaked through beds of large boulders far into the horizon. The ravine was rocky, and patches of yellow-tipped, pointed flowers protruded from several patches of earth, their leaves curving in tiny swirls. They turned their attention to the large, shaded willow that came into view before them. Its immense trunk stood taller than any of the other trees that overlooked the river. They walked closer to view a cross-legged figure who sat motionless underneath.

Oh! Here they come! Araduk closed his eyes and remained still, once again.

A loud scuffling sounded behind them while a dark shadow appeared and grew taller and wider on the grass. They paused.

Araduk peeked through his barely opened eyes to watch the plant life make their decision. He witnessed a family of kakusu grass sneak up behind them. The native inhabitants knew the hidden grass casually pried itself up from the ground to inspect travelers. Like all the other vegetation in the lands, it never harmed anyone, as long as they proved amicable.

The kakusu grass dropped back down to the soil and returned to its usual stance. Together, they turned around. Braern unsheathed his sword in one swift motion. He held it in a fighting stance, ready for action.

"That was weird. Did you see that?" the human asked, watching his confused expression.

"I thought something was behind us as well."

The two shrugged and refocused their attention to the figure on the cliff. The duo approached. Braern's weapon patted his leg as he walked.

The lands have made their decision. They intend me no harm, or anything here. They're safe. Araduk sighed with relief.

The dangling vines wobbled and brushed their arms. A soft breeze caressed their faces, chasing away any fears.

As they neared, the dwarf sat as still as a statue. Braern noticed his robe carried the peaceful symbol of the mountain monks—the same color as the surrounding lands. He wore a pale green cloth with long sleeves. He sported wiry locks of crimson brown with flecks of gray in his hair with a top knot braid, and a long, wide beard covering half his face. His wrinkled eyes remained closed. He did not move, nor speak.

"Greetings, Master Dwarf. We do not intend to disturb you, but my companion and I have been thrown here, and we are unsure where we are. Could you help us?" he asked in a calm and reassuring voice, allowing a sizable amount of space between himself and the figure.

The middle-aged dwarf opened his eyes, yawned, and stretched, pretending as if he didn't hear their entire conversation. Leaning his head forward, he narrowed his eyes, as if he had seen them for the first time.

"Ah, *konnichiwa!*" Araduk greeted them in Japanese, his native language.

Braern answered him, and they spoke for a few moments.

"Pfft! Oh, this is wonderful," the human said to herself with a sigh.

"I can speak English, if that will be easier for ye, lass," the dwarf said with a chuckle.

"That would be great. Thank you."

"In that case, naw need for such formalities. Am pleased to meet ye both. The name's Araduk Iron... uh... Lightbringer." *Am still not used to saying that out loud, nor do I much deserve such a hopeful name.* The dwarf placed his boots on his feet and took his time to stand from his kneeling position. His joints popped as he grunted. Stepping forward, he shook his feet to adjust.

"Nice to meet you, Ara... duk," Moira said, trying to pronounce it. She remembered the confusing altercation when she'd shaken Braern's hand and decided not to repeat such a gesture. "I'm Moira Washington, and this is Braern... Yo...?" She raised her eyebrows and narrowed her eyes, lowering her jaw. She signaled to Braern for him to finish.

"Braern Yogensha of Lavendale." The elf bowed in respect, wincing once again from the pain. The poor elf couldn't decide which injury hurt more. He collapsed to his knees.

Araduk rushed to his side and knelt. "Allow me to help ye, lad." The dwarf placed his palms over Braern's injuries and closed his eyes. A bright yellow and white light swirled around his hands.

Moira and Braern stared in disbelief, their eyes glowing.

"An elf and a human? I haven't seen such a pair in many years. I was thinkin' about how lonely these lands are. Then, ye both appeared out of nowhere. Strange coincidence. Only one to talk to is Lenleonette. She's the queen of these lands.

Quiet, most days, though." A swathe of branches brushed Araduk's cheek in response.

Braern's pain vanished. His wounds closed and healed. Blood disappeared, and he looked new once again. "You're a healer?" Braern asked as he inspected his body.

Araduk outstretched his arm for the elf to grasp. He helped him stand.

"Thank you, Araduk."

"Sure am. Unsure of why the gods chose me to carry the ability to heal, but here I am. May I help ye too?" *Especially after all I've done.*

"So, you can heal people, and Len... leo... whatever, is the tree? And she's a queen? A queen tree?"

"Aye," Araduk said, nodding.

"Uh, okay. This is too weird," Moira said.

"May I?" he asked.

"Sure, I guess?" she said, an eyebrow raised. He seemed safe.

He hovered his hands over her body as well. Her discomfort faded, and she felt gratitude toward this new man.

"Thank you."

The dwarf nodded. "Ye both are most welcome. What brings ye to the Ever-Changing Lands?" Araduk's kind, brown eyes wrinkled as his chubby, pink cheeks raised into a smile. He stretched his arms and looked in a circle at the vastness of beauty surrounding them.

"We don't know how we got here. One second, I'm in my bathroom, and then the next, we're flying through these circles of light and end up here. This is the second time this has happened," Moira answered, raising her voice and using her hands to gesture her words. She slapped them down by her sides.

"Am afraid I don't know what ye speak of, lass," Araduk said with a sigh. *Seems strange that they appeared here out of nowhere. Wonder what magic this is?*

"Wait, why do they call this place the Ever-Changing Lands?" Moira asked.

Before he could answer, they heard a rumbling on the horizon where the sun met the winding river. Araduk turned around. Moira and Braern met his gaze. The trio stared into the distance. A vast ripple appeared that stretched as far as the eye could see to the east and west. A deep rumbling shook the ground and grew louder. The wave of land rushed closer to them. A large mound replaced the river, topped with tufts of white. Everywhere, all around them, the land transformed from a forested ravine and into snow-covered hills.

Braern and Moira braced themselves against the tree and kneeled, terrified. Moira screamed, and Braern trembled, closing their eyes as the roar shook the earth beneath them, hurling toward the cliff.

The tree remained, draped with powdery fluffiness. The air cooled and sent chills through them. Braern and Moira opened their eyes; the sun beating onto the bright white surfaces blinded them. They shielded the rays with their hands.

Moira shivered and held her arms in her hands, watching her breath escape as she exhaled.

Braern bent and scooped some snow into his water satchel and drank a few gulps of the icy cold liquid. He also shook from the temperature change and flung his hands in the air, then bent and rubbed his legs.

"Friends, ye're safe. Naw need to fret." Araduk touched them both on the shoulder to not scare them any further. "Look." Araduk pointed.

Below, they saw a small rock with a bear-catlike creature sitting atop a stone and munching on something, surrounded by a small pool of water leftover from the river. The animal finished its fishy meal and ran off without a shriek. Through the change, it hadn't seemed to care.

"These are the Ever-Changing Lands," Araduk explained. "The lands decide when they want to change but never harm another in doin' so. They have a mind of their own. I rather enjoy the changes. As long as ye respect every being here, the lands will not harm ye."

"That's... cool." Moira sighed, unsure of how she felt.

"I've heard of these lands, though I've never traveled here," Braern said with his thumb and forefinger on his chin. His other hand grasped his opposite elbow. "There is much I do not know about my world. I've never been this far from my home for this long." A dull pain in his chest caused his heart to skip a beat.

"I should be used to the cold by now, growin' up in Brooklyn," Moira told them.

"Is that where ye're from, lass?" Araduk asked.

"Yup." She rolled her eyes. She had very few fond memories of her childhood and pushed them from her mind—no time for reminiscing.

"As ye were saying, about the magic that brought ye here?" Araduk turned to Braern.

"Yes, I battled a fire wyrm to retrieve its scales for an important potion for my father, and..." Braern removed the wyrm, suspended in its orb, from his satchel.

"Creepy. And tiny. That thing can't get out, can it?" Moira stepped backward, holding her wrist.

"No, no, I assure you. I cast a spell to shrink it and freeze it. It will not move until I say so. During my battle, strange things happened. I noticed circles of magic light on the ground. I made it back home, and as I was about to open the door to the library, I fell through to the human world and met this beautiful woman."

Moira bit her lip as her cheeks blushed. She looked away. It had been a long time since anyone had complimented her.

"She helped me and gave me a strange cup of water. Then we fell through another ring of magic and ended up here."

Could they be back? I've only heard stories as a wee one. "Am sorry to hear ye both went through such trouble to get here. Sounds to me like the portals found ye."

"Portals?" Braern and Moira asked in unison.

Braern remembered the portal wars from his studies. Such violence had led to the closing of all magic portals for generations. "Why are they back now?"

"Portals, dwarves, and elves?" Moira asked. "This is all too much. Wait, aren't dwarves supposed to be fighting in wars with axes and things?" She swung her arm, pretending to wield a sword.

"Ye're correct, lass." Araduk's smile disappeared, and his shoulders drooped as he closed his eyes. "I left that life behind me years ago." He turned from his new friends and gazed into the horizon. A bloodied face appeared in his mind, then vanished. A familiar pain rose in his chest. The dwarf retrieved a silver flask from his robe and took a sip, then stowed it in his pocket. He shook his head and faced his new companions, the strong bitterness soothing his throat as it traveled to his stomach.

"I'm sorry. I didn't mean to bring up painful memories," Moira reassured him.

Araduk cleared his throat and returned to his usual content expression. "It's fine, lass." *I vowed to help those in need. It's time to keep m' word. I need to go with them. Been here for two weeks and haven't made much progress with my meditation. My fellow monks will have to wait for my return.*

"Well, ye convinced me. I'm comin' along to help. Let's be on our way, shall we?" He beckoned as he began strolling down the angled, snowy cliff, anchoring his weight backward to keep his balance.

"You're coming with us? Where are we going?" Braern asked as the two of them followed their new dwarf companion, his hand on his satchel and sword.

"Sure am! We need to find out why the portals are back. I'm interested to know why m'self. Haven't had this much excitement in a long time. Come along, now." Araduk's arms bent at his sides to help stabilize himself down the rocks.

"Orastos would know. Do you know how to get to Lavendale?" Braern asked.

"Orastos o' Lavendale? The old dragon mage and keeper of the largest library to the north?" Araduk eyed the elf.

"He's my father."

"Yer kin? A dragon raising a wee elf? Very strange, indeed."

"Yes, I am aware of how strange it sounds. Whispers scattered about my village as I grew. Orastos is my father and mentor. I owe him my life." Braern flew into the air in a circle, smiling the biggest smile.

"Aye, I've heard much about his generosity. I'd be thrilled to meet him."

"Hold up. You can *fly*?" Moira stopped with her hands on her hips, frowning at him, wondering why he hadn't mentioned this before. "I guess I kinda knew that since you floated into my museum when we first met."

"Since I was an elfling! Being raised by a dragon has its benefits," he retorted, floating above them. He levitated on his back, his arms folded and leg on top of the other, as if he were reclining in a chair.

Araduk imagined a wee elf wearing a nappy in a high-chair. A dragon wearing an apron, holding a jar of food, breathing fire on it, then cooling it before handing it to the bairn with a spoon. He chuckled.

"A flying elf? Never seen one o' those before." Araduk chuckled. "Yer full o' surprises!"

"I know where Orastos lives, but I'm uncertain how to get there from here. How do we travel to Lavendale?" Braern asked as he circled the two of them, happy to have regained his strength and magic.

"Lavendale, ye say? It is north, like I said. I believe it's... several days' walk! This way!" Araduk beckoned for his new quest mates to follow.

Moira had a tough time weaving down the steep, slippery, snowy hills. She shivered and rubbed her arms as she climbed downward, fighting her instincts between staying warm or keeping her balance.

Braern didn't seem too affected by the drastic weather change, floating close by.

"Wish I could fly," Moira scoffed, annoyed by the elf's lack of sympathy for those of the group who had no choice but to walk. As her friends were out of earshot, she whispered, "Maybe this is my chance to do something good? To get outta my crappy situation and hang with these magic guys? Haven't had this much fun in such a long time."

Another portal appeared, small at first, growing large. A wind wrapped around the three of them, causing their hair to stand on its ends as their clothing ruffled.

"Not again," Moira said, trying to run the other way.

"Is this what ye were talking about?" Araduk yelled.

The magic pulled them in. The group flew through the many colors and circular arrays of lights. They found themselves on a stone floor as the portal disappeared from above them.

BRAERN

THE SEARCH

Braern's eyes watered as he exhaled in relief, peering at the shelves of books around them. Lavendale Library. *I'm home. The portal led us here. Did I control our destination with my thoughts?*

"How many times is this gonna keep happening? I'ma get jetlag from all this." Moira chuckled under her breath and beheld the vastness of the library. "This your home?" she asked without shifting her gaze. Her eyes widened and mouth agape. Tall wooden shelves filled with books and scrolls spread as far as she could see. The massive building's interior boasted natural wood ornamentation carved into staircases, as magical lights flickered above. The rainbow-colored stained-glass windows caught her eye.

For a moment, many of the creatures paused and stared at the group who had fallen through a portal and had appeared in the lobby. Every manner of being she read about in books stared at them.

The scuffling and turning of pages sounded once again as everyone resumed reading, as if people appearing from nowhere weren't very interesting.

"Well, that was different. I prefer to walk next time. Could use the exercise." Araduk patted his large belly. "Tell those portals to give it a rest." He brushed himself off and peered around him. "Nice place ye got here." Araduk nodded toward a group of hippocampi who swam in their interior stream toward their waterproof book section.

They acknowledged him and went on their path, splashing a few drops of water onto the floor near them.

"Always wanted to come here but never had the chance."

"We have no control over them," he said to Araduk. "And thank you. This is Lavendale Library." Braern shuffled his feet, remembering that they all needed to remove their shoes out of respect.

"Please, remove your shoes and place them outside the entrance. I shall return as soon as I can."

The group nodded and did as he asked. The elf scouted his home for any sign of Orastos. This was not like his father to disappear without warning, nor send him off without checking in. His mind whirled from the terrible thoughts that had tried to overrun his quest. He placed his hands on the sides of his head and closed his eyes to calm his breathing, forcing such negativity to leave his thoughts. He didn't have time for such things. "We need to find my father. He will know why the portals keep sending us to different lands. Let's head to my workshop, you two." He guided them toward the large, wooden and metal darkened entryway. He imagined the red smoke seeping from inside—one of the last moments he had with his father. Braern waved a hand.

"Who do we have here, Braern?" Chimon awakened, shaking his head, and greeted them with one eyebrow raised.

"They're friends," Braern said, giving them permission to enter.

"Whoa, your door can talk?" Moira asked, wide eyed.

"Of course, I can talk. I can sing too!" Chimon joked. He sang a few bars as his voice rose.

Moira clapped, smiling.

"This is Chimon. He guards our workshop and is rather amusing... *most* days."

"Pleased to meet ye, Chimon. Am Araduk." The dwarf bowed.

"I'm Moira. You're so awesome. Can I take you home with me? My neighbors would freak out," Moira said, bowing too.

"I'm stuck here, but I find the sights of the library comforting."

"He's so cool!" Moira said.

"Yes, he was once a prisoner. We found him in the King's dungeon and brought him home with us, but the magic on him was very strong. We allowed him to become our doorknocker, but he serves out his sentence for eternity here."

Moira stopped and stared at Chimon with widened eyes. "What did you *do?*"

The doorknocker sniffed and wrinkled his nose. He ignored her question. "I'm going to catch up on my reading," Chimon said as a book and a pair of spectacles floated to him. It turned to the right page, and he picked up where he left off.

"Well, okay then."

Braern signaled for them to move on.

They entered, and the door closed behind them.

"Be careful and touch nothing, I beg you. Many of these potions can be quite dangerous if handled incorrectly," the elf warned his friends, hearing his father's words in his voice. He hustled through the room, zigzagging around desks and shelves. He looked under and above the tables, searching for any trace of where the dragon could've gone. Everything was as it had been the last time he was with his father. The same half-cleaned messes and potions they'd discussed, remained. Braern stopped, observing his friends stare at him with concerned expressions.

"How can we help, lad?" Araduk leaned toward the elf. He lifted his chin to see, for he was not much taller than a table. "I can feel the good created here. Very soothing magic."

"Yeah, let us know what we can do. We're here for you." Moira plopped onto a nearby chair. She fiddled with her fingers, crossed her leg, and tapped her toes. Braern noticed she wanted to explore but controlled herself.

"He's not here." Braern's eyes drifted. "We must investigate the rest of the library." The elf opened the door and hesitated. "Follow me."

Moira's fingertips were inches from the base of a broad flask filled with a translucent substance. She stopped herself, donning a crooked smile. Placing her hands at her sides, she turned toward the elf and narrowed her eyes. "Coming!"

Araduk and Moira followed Braern from the room and into the library.

Chimon closed without a touch, once again.

"Have you seen Orastos?" Braern asked.

"Not since he saw you off the other day," Chimon answered.

Braern sighed. "Wait here," he instructed his friends. A sense of uncertainty overwhelmed him. He checked the loft landing.

Braern turned left and came to a large, wooden, curved staircase. The elf climbed with his left hand on the smooth, polished railing adorned with carved, floral designs and wooden vines that swirled into pointed posts at the beginning and end of the stairs. He reached the top and stood in front of two dark-brown doors with those same natural carvings on them. His pace quickened across the overhang and he opened the far-left door.

The room belonged to Orastos, and everything in it was larger. Even the pile of golden coins and jewels that he had shaped into a bed for himself was about the size of a small pond to fit his reptilian body. He looked around with the door open to give himself more light to see. A twinkle of brightness reflected onto the gold type of one of Orastos's favorite books on a shelf by the door—*The Age of War*. A few stray white hairs had fallen into the start of the third chapter. He supposed an old dragon constantly lost his hair.

Braern dashed out and to the second room that peered over the library and into his own safe space. His sloppy bed was exactly how he'd left it. The blanket called to him to rest. He resisted, knowing if he slept now, he would never wake until the next morning. Books were strewn across the floor, a few open, and his nightstand housed a small, twisted lamp, with a desk next to it with writing quills and ink on top. Parchment also littered the floor, and a few of his garments were in a heap in the corner by a bookshelf. He reminded himself to clean his room in the future. "Not here either." He closed his door and floated above to see who he recognized.

A dozen different beings spread throughout the enormous room in little groups. A familiar burgundy straw hat caught his eye by the ancient fighting scrolls former *kappu-*

rai warriors had written to chronicle their adventures. He longed to become one of them in the future.

"Rokado, my friend, it's been a long time," Braern said, forcing his voice to remain low to not disturb anyone around him.

The racoon-dog turned and looked up at Braern as the elf floated down to him. The two shared a glance and bowed to one another. Rokado adjusted his hat strings under his chin. His vest matched his hat, his busy tail twitching while he smiled.

"Braern, it's good to see you. How is Orastos these days?" he asked, holding his paws.

"That's what I wanted to speak with you about. I have not seen him in... days. Do you know where he is?"

"I'm afraid I don't. I have been busy storing food for my village. Winter will be upon us soon, as you know. I came here to borrow a book on sword fighting for my daughter. She's a spitfire!" he told him as his eyes crinkled.

"I have something that will help you." Braern raised a finger as he twisted his torso to reach his satchel. He removed the tiny orb with the fire wyrm suspended and frozen. "I want you to have this to feed your village. It's a fire wyrm that I slayed when Orastos sent me on a quest to retrieve its scales. If you wouldn't mind saving us a few of its scales for healing remedies, I'd appreciate it." He handed Rokado the orb. "The spell will wear off in a matter of days, and it will grow to its normal size. I haven't had the time to do it myself because of the portals."

"The portals? I thought they were a myth. What have you gotten yourself into this time?" Rokado chortled as he received the orb, then placed it in a fur pocket by his hip.

"It's a long tale, and one I will be happy to tell you soon. For now, I must find my father. It is of the utmost importance."

"Thank you for such a generous gift. This will provide us with meals for many moons. I wish I could be of more help to you."

The two bowed to each other once again, and Braern returned to his companions.

Moira jumped when Braern appeared at her side. "This is so pretty. We don't have anything like this in New York." She handled a shelf of books, their spines smooth with beveled stripes and writing in diverse languages. The vivid lights illuminated everything around her.

Araduk chatted with a unicorn near the staircase. The dwarf stroked his beard as he quietly laughed. He signaled with his hands as his low voice reverberated, even a decibel, above a whisper.

Moira sauntered to them with wide eyes. "Oh my god. Is that... a...?" Moira pointed at the pale, horse-like creature.

A shimmering horn on his head glistened in the light, with a flowing blue and silver mane and tail. He paid no attention to the gawking human. He bowed to Araduk and trotted to a nearby shelf with rows of smaller books. A wicker basket floated at his side. He guided it downward with a nod, using its magic to levitate chosen books inside.

"He's a unicorn. Very well respected in Yumerion." Araduk placed his arm on hers and mentioned, "It's not polite to point."

"That's cool," Moira said with wide eyes. "I can't believe this place. First, I meet a real, live elf and a dwarf, then I fall through some magic portals—not once, but three times—

and now I'm meeting a unicorn who's casually checkin' out books at a library!" She placed her hands on her head and spun around in disbelief with her mouth open.

Creeping closer, she found herself against the bookshelf while the unicorn stood yards away. With wide eyes, she placed her shaky hand in front of the books. The shelf crashed down, sending books flying in all directions.

One hit Braern in the head. He flinched, placed his hands on his head, and looked up at an angle with one eye shut. It bounced off his skull and zoomed away, squeaking.

Various creatures stopped and stared at her. She sunk her head into her shoulders, covering her face, as she peeked with one eye at the damage. Mixed emotions flooded her mind. "Damn it! Not again!" Her face heated as she pursed her lips.

Several books flapped their pages like wings, sending tapping sounds through the air. The ruin of shelves on the floor paused, then righted themselves, and all the books flew back to where they belonged as if nothing happened.

"I find myself rather amused at your lack of tenacity, milady." Braern laughed. "But we must continue our search."

"I didn't mean to! I'm so sorry! Are you okay? But how did that...? Were those books flying?"

"It's a magic library, lass. What'd ye expect?" Araduk said.

"I'm never gonna get used to this. What's next? Am I gonna meet a dragon?" she squealed.

Braern caught sight of a familiar white tail tuft disappearing behind the opened entrance. He pursued.

"Are you taking me to meet a dragon? For real?" She jumped up and down and clapped as her voice became an octave higher. Then she looked around the library and quieted her excitement.

Braern navigated through the busy entryway and outside, forgetting his comrades. He had only one thing on his mind: finding his father. They gathered their shoes and followed the elf. He touched the tall, thick trees as he weaved through them. The cool shade was a welcoming feeling from being indoors. He came to the tree where he was sure the tail had disappeared. The elf checked the tallest branches above him and peered out as far as his elf eyes allowed him to see in all directions. Not a sight of Orastos.

As he lifted his foot, he noticed a small white hair lying on the ground. He bent his knees to pick it up, feeling a surge of relief at the thought that his beloved father was close. "He was here!" he exclaimed, holding up the hair and shoving it into his satchel for safe keeping.

Araduk and Moira caught up to him.

"Let's try this way." He pointed toward the group of stones that lead upward on a hill, to the far right of the library.

The two followed the elf as the steepening brush became stones underneath. They climbed onto the flat surface of the entrance to a small cave with glowing lights shining through the opening.

"This is Yume Fountain. I used to play here as a young elfling and dip my fingers in the water. Oh, the memories I've had here," Braern educated his friends as they entered.

Moira nearly hit her head on the ceiling, for it was not very high.

Araduk, of course, had no trouble.

"Wow, this place is amazing too." Moira couldn't get over how different this world was from her own. "The only interesting creatures I ever see are stray cats."

"Bonnie cave, here. Love the colors," Araduk said, watching the twinkling rainbows reflected on the glistening wet surfaces of the walls, floor, and ceiling. The damp air sent a shiver down his spine. The dwarf closed his eyes and inhaled deeply. He rubbed his shoulders and shivered. "Brr!"

The glowing yellow light appeared, and the trickles of running water sounded in their ears. Turning the corner, the three arrived at the fountain. Large rocks surrounded it.

As they got closer, Braern noticed another white hair on the ledge of the stone barrier. He inspected the silky strands and rubbed them between his fingers. *Father. Was he sending me here? Was I meant to find this?*

"Where is he?" he asked the fountain, placing his right hand under the water as the falling drips splashed onto his hand and soaked part of his wrist. "He is always there when I need him. It's so unlike him to disappear and not sense that I... that we need help. He's never sent me on such a long quest. I can't do this without him." Braern's chest felt heavy as a sense of despair overcame him. A single tear escaped and trickled into the pool and rippled to the edges. He sobbed as more tears dripped into the fountain, sniffing back a wad of snot in his nose.

"Hey, hey. It'll be okay. We'll find him." Moira placed her hand on his shoulder. Her touch relaxed his tense muscles. He bent his arm and placed his hand on hers. For a moment, they shared a connection that ignited his heart. Araduk joined and placed his hand on his other side. "We are with ye, my elven friend. We will find yer father." The sparks in his chest disappeared.

As Braern bawled, his eyes closed, and his lips parted in a tensed form, showing his teeth.

More tears fell into the water, and their echo became louder as the water reflected onto the ceiling in colorful waves. Another portal appeared small and expanded, this time with no one falling or being pulled into it. As the magic light cleared, the three gazed inside.

Braern wiped his nose with his arm and sniffed back any tears he had left, blinking the blurriness from his eyes.

Inside, a wavy picture became clear as a male human watched them with only his shoulders, arms, and head visible. He had brown hair and a white shirt, with a thin neck and tired, red eyes behind his black-framed spectacles. His fingers moved on top of a rectangle of lights and symbols as one of his hands moved back and forth between an oval-shaped device that lay flat on a surface in front of him.

Braern placed a fingertip into the water, disturbing the ripples.

The human male jumped backward and disappeared with a thud as he screamed in shock.

Braern scrambled onto the flat surface and eyed the three of them in disbelief as he wiped drops of water from his face.

A finger from the other side came through and touched Braern's. For a second, two beings touched fingertips.

"Is that a human? Is this another one of yer portals?" Araduk asked, taken aback.

A large circle of light brightened around the entire tiny cave and nearly blinded them.

Braern found himself unable to pull away from the other side as he felt forced into the portal. "When will this end?" he asked himself, trying to recoil backward with his other hand holding firm to the side of the fountain, his knees against the stones. Moira grabbed his hand as he disappeared and outstretched her hand for Araduk to follow. Without a sound, the three vanished, the ripples faded, and the light dimmed.

TIM

THE NERD WITH THE BLUE CAT

Timothy fell out of his black, leather computer chair onto the water-soaked tan carpet. He scrambled backward on all fours, doing some embarrassing crab-exorcist walk, climbed onto his bed, and smacked his head on the post as he became squished between the wall and the bedframe. Panting, heart beating out of his scrawny rib-visible chest, he pulled his green and black striped comforter over his head and adjusted his black-framed glasses. He sobbed in the darkness, various bodily fluids pouring from his face.

"This is not real. This is not happening. I'm dreaming. I'm dreaming. I'm dreaming. Wake up, Tim! Wake up!" He banged the back of his skull on the wall corner, feeling the pressure on two points on the back of his head, cramped and uncomfortable. Afraid to move or get up, he sensed the crushing of his sides and legs and wondered if this was what a pretzel must feel like. Through his erratic breathing, scuffing and soft footsteps sounded around him.

"What should we do? The poor kid is terrified," the woman whispered as she shook her body.

Water dripped onto the carpet in splatters. Through the thin fabric covering his eyes, he saw one of strangers ring out their clothing. He heard his computer spark and shut down as the fans turned off.

Oh no, my new keyboard is probably ruined. I mowed yards for weeks to pay for that thing. Tim sobbed.

"Did it have to be water? Never gonna dry off at this rate," the shorter one said in a Scottish accent. His feet sloshed on the floor as he ambled around the room.

"I apologize for the intrusion, young human. We had no control over how we traveled here." The tall one with light colored hair took a step toward Tim.

He flinched backward, his heart beating faster. His earlobes throbbed as he fought to catch his breath. "Don't tou— come near me! My guard cat will eat your eyeballs out of your so-sockets! Blue! Sick 'em!" Tim called to his kitty friend.

Blue meowed during a yawn that moved back her ears. She was lying in her cat tree by the computer desk, annoyed the noise had woken her from her catnap. She sat upright, stretched, and yawned, then went back to sleep. Her soft gray striped fur looked like a loaf of bread as she tucked her arms and legs underneath her and faced away from all the ruckus.

"You're no help, brat." Tim glared in her direction, even though she couldn't see him. He took deep breaths, with his hand on his chest, and simmered down enough to listen, knowing his feline friend was close by.

"Well, that was a ride! Nice moggy ye got thir," the short one said, ringing the water out of his robe. He noticed the boy.

"You... understand me? What's a moggy?" Tim asked. Goosebumps rose on his legs, his socks soaked from the moisture. He craned his neck to see through his thin comforter he'd had since he was ten.

The short one peered at Blue.

"Oh, her. Yeah, thanks. She's my kitty soulmate." Something about these strangers seemed less threatening. He felt as if he had met them before, but that was clearly not possible. *Who are these people? How did they crawl out of my computer screen and splash water everywhere? Am I hallucinating from staying up too late, playing WOW again?*

"Well, young human, we don't mean to impose on yer dwelling here. We, uh... Where are we, exactly? And where to begin?" the short one stuttered. He gawked at the walls of the boy's room with wide eyes.

"I will try to speak with him again," the tall one assured the group and stepped forward. He brushed himself off; his clothing dripped onto a small puddle on the floor. He made small, deliberate steps toward the lump of blanket-wrapped Tim, beholding his unique room, and stopped in front of the bed. "We mean you no harm. You see, the three of us fell through this magic portal, and we were led here. We don't know why."

"This seems to be a repeating pattern for them. First time for me though," the short one said.

"You can say that again," the woman agreed.

"We seek answers, as I'm sure you do as well," the tall one said. He sat on a nearby bright orange, sleek and soft bean-filled apparatus and dared not go any farther. He sunk into the strange mound, rubbing his fingers on the cool, slick surface, and scooted his butt side to side. "This is pleasant. What do you call this contraption?"

"It's a beanbag," Tim muffled. The teen pulled the covers off his head as his greasy, unwashed hair stuck straight up. His cheeks shivered from his sweat hitting the air. "You all came through my computer screen. And now my floor's wet. I was flying my mount over a lake when I was playing WOW. Wait, are you WOW characters come to life?" he asked with wide eyes and a gaping mouth, stifling his excitement. He'd always dreamed of being sucked into an adventure, like in his games with his raid group. His scrawny arms shook, and his room smelled like a damp cave.

The woman shrugged and eyed the two other strangers. They shrugged back.

"Never heard of this WOW," the short one said.

"Neither have I," the tall one said.

"*World of Warcraft*. It's a game."

The tall and short ones looked at one another with raised eyebrows.

Returning to a semblance of reality, Tim widened his nostrils and caught a whiff of his own body odor. He nearly knocked himself unconscious right then and there, as he could almost feel the weight of his own stench pulling down his nasal passages. His eyes watered. "Note to self, take a shower." He gagged and pulled himself upright in his bed. After all, he had been playing his MMORPG for almost twenty-four hours straight, with hardly more than a few bathroom breaks, let alone a shower.

"Let me help you." the tall one stood and offered a hand, his knee on the bed, using his weight to help pull out the boy. "I am Braern Yogensha of Lavendale. These are my companions: Moira Washington and Araduk Lightbringer."

Lightbringer? There's a paladin in my game with that name. Cool! Tim paused and rubbed his shoulders. His bed creaked as he sat on the edge. "Uh... Timothy. My name is Timothy Rodriguez... but you can call me Tim." He remained uneasy as he struggled to untangle his body from his blankets, keeping an eye on the strange people in his room. He used one hand to grab his sheets and reluctantly gave his other to Braern.

The elf shook his hand, then bowed, stood, and stepped backward to give the kid more space.

"It's a pleasure to meet ye, Tim," Araduk said as he bowed, staring at the teenage human.

Tim noticed his computer screen and keyboard still dripped onto the desk, his mouse upside down on the floor. They soaked his clear, plastic chair mat where years of wheel indentions caved and cracked. He thought of his mother and how long the lecture would be once she found out what had happened here. "You all really came through my computer screen while I was playing WOW and... here you are? Why are you wet?" He couldn't believe the words coming from his mouth. It was like a real, live video game had come to life in his bedroom. Part of him longed for the truth, while the other was terrified and unsure if he was asleep or awake.

"Oh, kid, it's a long story, and I don't know how many more times I can tell it. Y'all can step in anytime," Moira said with a sigh. She eyed a dragon and knight figure on a wall shelf. Refusing to turn around, she waved for one of the guys to take over and explain, then wiggled her fingers in Tim's direction. "Hi, by the way. Nice to meet ya and all that."

Tim noticed Braern's pointed ears. "Dude, you... you're an elf! Are those real?" Tim's eyes widened. His gaze turned to Araduk. "And... you're a dwarf! Wait, is that rude? I'm sorry. And you..." He regarded Moira. "Wait, what are you supposed to be? A cop?" Tim raised one eyebrow and cocked his head, pursing his lips. The temperature of his head rose; a knot formed at the base of his skull. The only females who had ever been in his room were his mom and sister.

"I'm a security guard—or, well, at least I was before this dude showed up." Moira gestured a hand toward Braern. "Suppose I'm fired now, but oh well." She eyed her tattered uniform, feeling holes and rips where there shouldn't be. "I need to change, but I keep getting thrown through these damn portals and haven't had a chance to!" She shook her head and tossed up her hands.

Tim held his breath as he forced his eyes to stay focused on her face. "Oh... uh... the bathroom is down the hallway, to the left," he squeaked. He pointed toward his door; his arm shook as his lips quivered.

"Before you go, I'd like to answer him and be of some assistance with this calamity in your room," Braern said. Moira paused at the door. "Yes, I'm an elven mage, and Araduk is a dwarven healer. I do apologize for the mess we have made here. If you'll allow me, I will clean it all and dry everyone and everything off."

With wide eyes, Tim nodded. *How is he gonna do that?*

Braern rose from the beanbag and took the few steps to the middle of the room. He raised his arms and closed his eyes. *"Kaze o tsukuru. Kirei ni naru,"* he said. Facing his palms close to the other without touching his hands together, a breeze blew through the room. Everyones' hair moved as the air sucked all the moisture from their clothing. The wind grew stronger while drops from the carpet and computer screen rose up and floated in the air. The drops flew toward Braern into a swirling ball of magic between his palms. He moved his hands further away as the magic grew larger. Tim watched as his computer, mouse, and keyboard righted themselves and floated back to his desk, where he left them. Everything that was once wet, dried quickly.

"How did you... do that?" Tim fought the urge to hide again, but was too amazed.

"My father taught me to harness the power of the wind during our flying lessons. I find it most useful, indeed. I do, however, need somewhere to place this," the elf said, grimacing to control the spinning ball of watery magic in his grasp.

"Oh! Uh... here..." Tim stuttered and ran to the floor by the cat tree to retrieve a large, empty metal water canister. He opened it and pointed the top toward Braern. Braern guided the water as it floated over to him. It curved its path through the air and ended inside the canister. Tim looked inside for a moment, then closed the lid. "That was... so cool!"

Braern bowed for his audience.

"Thank ye. It feels good to be dry again," Araduk said with a shiver, patting his chest.

Tim opened the lid again and blinked, peering at the water inside. *I can't believe that happened. Is this real?*

MOIRA

MOMS, MUFFINS, AND PTSD

Thanks for drying us off, man. I'm gonna go change now. Don't fall through anymore portals till I get back." Moira nodded and headed out of Tim's bedroom and toward the bathroom. She adjusted her bag, the straps rubbing her shoulder through her shirt.

She walked down the hallway past the awkward family photos in golden frames. A much younger Tim stared at her from behind glass, who didn't quite know how to smile without looking like a total creep.

His sister, mother, and father appeared picture perfect. He had braces and looked skinnier than he did now. The hallway desk lamp illuminated the crucifix on the wall.

Pale-pink stripes lined the walls, adorned with golden fixtures everywhere. A large painted lily hung on the pastel shower curtain. An array of essentials—from toothpaste, palettes of eyeshadow, to a plugged-in purple curling iron— covered the double sink vanity. "They have good taste. Oh! I love that color." Moira surveyed all the makeup organized in a little stand.

She placed her bag on the counter and rummaged through her things, then removed her clean clothes with a sigh. She took off her dirty uniform then stuffed it in the bottom of her bag. Moira stared at her reflection. "What if I fall through a portal in here... all alone? I could end up in the tundra of Siberia, freezing to death." She shivered, clenching her jaw.

As she put on her yoga pants, a knock came from the door.

"*Mijo,* dinner is almost ready. Your mother made tamales," a man's voice sounded from the other side.

She pursed her lips and stood still.

"Are you in there? Tim? Can you hear me?" he asked, raising his voice.

"Just a minute!" Moira tried her best to sound like a teenage boy. She pulled up her pants.

When she tripped the few feet to lock the door, Tim's dad barged in on her wearing only a bra and her pants.

"What the hell?" she screamed, throwing her arms across her chest.

"*Who are you?* What are you doing in my house?" he yelled, slamming open the door with a wrinkled brow.

Moira struggled to put on her shirt and tried to push past him.

"Timothy! Why is there a woman in our bathroom?" he hollered down the hallway.

The veins popped out of his neck as his mustache twitched, his eyes wide open as he let her pass. She raced to the bedroom as Tim ran out of his room and held onto the doorframe.

Inside the room, Araduk spun around in the computer chair.

Braern stretched on the bed, watching Tim's family.

"Papa, I can explain!" Tim cried out.

Soon, his mother ran up the stairs with a look of terror on her face, wiping her hands on her apron. She joined her husband, and the three of them argued in Spanish loud enough for the entire house to hear. They waved their arms and yelled at one another.

Tim sunk his neck into his shoulders after a few moments as his parents overpowered him with their harsh words. He looked at his feet, with his hands in his hoodie pocket, becoming smaller and smaller as the screaming continued.

His parents yelled while pointing to the bathroom and his bedroom.

Araduk, Braern, and Moira stood motionless in silence. They dared not try to intervene.

"Are you"—Tim's mother gulped—"dating my son?"

"Hell no! I promise. I just met the kid today," Moira said, raising her voice and shaking her head. She frowned at the thought. *Me and a sixteen-year-old? Yuck.*

"Language! I'm relieved to hear that," his mother said.

"Sorry," Moira whispered.

"He knows what would happen if he snuck a girl into his room," his father said in a deep, unwavering voice. He folded his arms and looked inside Tim's room, past his son standing in the hallway, to stare at her.

Moira averted her gaze from him and sucked on her lips, afraid of saying anything.

Araduk's chair squeaked inside the room as he twirled in a circle, munching on some Cool Ranch Doritos left on the desk. Moira giggled under her breath as she watched the hairy dwarf drop crumbs on his beard and try to lick them with his tongue.

Braern lay on the bed, throwing a ball above his head and catching it, his sword draped over the edge, touching the carpet.

Moira stood on the opposite side of the doorway.

Tim remained against the wall in the hallway, his hands in his pockets, with his head down and hoodie covering most of his face.

"Pardon us. We are not used to seeing our Timoteo with... friends over," his mother said. "I'm Isabella, and this is my husband, Miguel." She gestured to him at her side.

The sweet scent of cinnamon-sugary goodness filled the air as everyone relaxed their shoulders, sniffing in the direction of the kitchen.

Isabella smoothed her apron with her hands and heard a beeping downstairs. "Why don't we all go into the living room? My churro muffins are done." She descended the stairs, looking back at the rest of the group.

"Muffins?" Braern shot from the bed and to the doorframe, nearly knocking over Tim as he leaned forward, hands on the frame, with a drop of drool escaping his lips.

"They smell delicious!" Araduk joined him, pushing the elf out of the way with his strong, stout body.

The two men raced down the stairs, followed by Miguel, who stopped halfway, watching Tim and Moira, who remained.

"Hey, you okay?" Moira asked Tim, out of earshot of his waiting father.

"I... I don't know. I've never seen them so mad."

I'd better not touch him or his dad will go berserk, Moira thought, refraining from placing a hand on his arm to comfort him.

"I know this is a lot to take in. It was for me too. But, these are good guys and it's been fun hangin' with them. Dude! You should've seen the unicorn at Braern's library!" Moira excitedly pinched fingers and made a horn gesture from above her forehead.

"What? Really?" Tim asked, pulling the cover off his head.

Moira quickly explained all that happened up until the point where they met.

"Wow, that's crazy. I wonder why you guys came here?"

"No idea, but maybe you're important somehow. I think we owe it to ourselves to find out."

Tim paused for a moment, staring at his feet. His eyes darted back and forth.

"I know my parents will be pissed if I leave, but when is the next time I'm gonna go on a quest with real life WOW characters? This is all so weird but something is telling me to tag along. Guess we should go before Papa gets mad." Tim said.

Moira and Tim ambled down to the main level. The rest of the house was an open space layout. Gold colors shimmered on vases and lampshades, with white carpeting. A large fireplace held a mantle, with family photos and a few knickknacks. Tim's sister sat on the large family sofa in front of an enormous television playing Animal Planet as a cheetah chased a gazelle through the African plains.

Braern and Araduk stood by the oven, salivating, licking their lips, and twiddling their fingers, awaiting their treat.

Isabella used her oven mitts to place the muffins on the top of the stove. Steam rose from the two-dozen plump desserts.

"Thank you for your generous hospitality." Braern bowed to Isabella. He inhaled and sunk his neck into his shoulders, a smile on his face with his eyes closed.

"Aye, thank you," Araduk said, bowing too.

She retrieved plates and a spatula and served the two of them. "Such polite gentlemen. I approve of your friends, *mijo*. Though I must say, next time give us more notice of their arrival." She peered at her son, then at the men drooling all over themselves in front of her. "You're very welcome. I hope you enjoy them. They're a family recipe. You may want to wait a few minutes till they cool off."

They stuffed the muffins into their mouths in unison, blowing air from the heat in their mouths and fanning their hands over their faces. *"Mmm,"* the two sounded simultaneously as they devoured their treats.

The sounds of pots and pans clanked and water ran from a faucet from the kitchen where Isabella cleaned.

Everyone else sat in the living room. The chairs and sofas were soft and comfortable without a stray hair anywhere—perfectly clean. A golden leaf sculpture, hanging on the wall in whimsical curves, adorned the room.

Moira noticed the glass coffee table. Her heart skipped a beat. As her breathing increased, her hands itched. She blinked, and they were covered in blood, shaking while her mind took her back to her apartment. A rush of panic overcame her senses. To be sure, she turned her palms upward. She covered her face with her hands, and her arms shook. She covered her eyes and forced her arms to stay where they were, terrified of touching anything in the room. Flashbacks of her boyfriend filled her mind.

"*I can't marry you. I'm not ready! Why do you gotta keep bringing this up? Can't we take things slow?*" Moira begged.

"*It's been three years. How much slower we gonna go, Mo?*" Adrian rushed to face her.

His breath warmed her nose as he spoke. With his usual, gentle touch, he placed his hands on her shoulders. "I'm ready for the next step. I love you and I want to move out of this dump and start a life with you, maybe even have a few kids later."

Moira stepped back and gazed into his eyes as she fought to calm her breathing. Time slowed as he released his grip, reaching for her. Each moment felt like a metal box was closing in on her, growing smaller and smaller until she would be nothing but a cube of meat.

He reached into his pocket and pulled out the ring she had grown accustomed to seeing. And each time, she turned him down. With one more step, his hopeful eyes met hers again. He raised his eyebrows with open arms, tilting his head toward her.

"*How many times do I have to tell you I'm not ready?*"

"*Oh c'mon, baby ...*"

"*No!*"

She pushed him, and everything happened so quickly, it was a blur. He fell onto the coffee table and shattered glass everywhere. The ring flew in the air and landed under the TV stand. His screams. She never forgot the sound of his screams. And the blood... so much blood. Next thing she knew, flashing blue and red lights appeared through her balcony window and the sound of sirens filled her ears.

"Are you all right?" Miguel asked, leaning forward, holding his drink.

Moira shook her head. Then she blinked again, and her hands were clean. In Tim's living room, their coffee table was whole. It was just a memory. "Uh... yeah, I'm fine." She sunk into the chair and decided she wouldn't speak for a while. She didn't trust her own voice to not reveal more about her past.

"Would you like one too, dear?" Isabella offered Moira a plate.

She smiled and took it. The sugar was a shock to her jaw as she chewed, forgetting about everything. She closed her eyes and enjoyed its soft gooeyness. "Thank you," Moira said in between a bite.

"Where did you say you met your friends?" Miguel asked.

"We fell through his picture box in his room," Braern answered.

"Aye, an' it's been quite the journey." Araduk began. "Ye see—"

"No! No! That's not what they meant. ComicCon. We all... uh... went as Stormtroopers and wanted to hang out," Tim said, his voice shaking. "This is... uh..." He couldn't remember their names.

Braern stood and bowed. "My name is Braern Yogensha. This is Araduk Lightbringer and Moira Washington. We're companions of Tim's. We are truly sorry for barging in unannounced, but we needn't stay long. In fact, we must be on our way."

"Surely, you'll stay for dinner," Isabella pressed.

"Dinner?" Araduk asked. "What are ye—"

"They have to go. Right now," Tim interrupted as everyone but Miguel stood.

Tim's mother offered the men another churro muffin. "For the road?"

"Yes, please! These are delicious! Thank you," Braern accepted, smiling.

Araduk nodded.

Isabella entered the living room and sat in the recliner next to her husband and crossed her legs. "It's nice to see our son making friends. He spends so much of his time in his room these days."

Blue pattered down the stairs and joined them. She jumped on Tim's lap as his shoulders relaxed, and he petted her soft fur while she purred.

"Blue always knows when Tim's distressed. She's been a wonderful cat," Isabella said. "I remember when I was pregnant with him."

"Ugh," Tim's sister groaned, threw down the remote, and went upstairs, rolling her eyes.

"Maria, Tim's sister," Isabella said, raising a palm in the girl's direction as she disappeared down the upstairs hallway.

"Mama, we don't need to get into this," Tim begged, sucking on his lips and narrowing his eyes.

"Don't interrupt your mother, son," Miguel told him.

"We had a dog before Tim was born, Freckles, and I could feel that he spoke to her when he was in my belly. She would bring all manner of things to me when I was pregnant: treats, toys, and little animals she found outside. I always felt Tim was instructing her to bring them to me. He kicked whenever she was near me. It was so cute." Isabella smiled and gazed at the ceiling with a sigh.

"Where can I put this?" Moira asked, holding up her plate.

"Oh, I'll take it," Isabella said, reaching for it.

Moira's hand shook, and the plate shattered in her grasp.

Blue spooked and scratched Tim's leg, her fur on end. She ran behind the couch to hide.

"I'm so sorry. I didn't mean..." Tears welled in the corners of Moira's eyes. She stared at her hands as her brow furrowed. *I don't want to hurt this family. Why does this always happen to me? I hate my strength!*

"It's all right. These are our everyday plates." Isabella hurried to the kitchen to fetch a broom and dustpan.

Moira sighed in relief, seeing no one was hurt. "We need to go now," she told the group.

Tim nodded in agreement. "I'm going to say goodbye to them. I'll be right back, and I'll help with dinner."

Miguel nodded as Isabella cleaned the mess.

Another pain in Moira's chest rose again as she held back any offers to help Isabella clean up. She knew she could easily make things worse if she didn't leave. It was time to go.

Tim led the group down a wide hallway with crown molding and to their front door.

"We can't leave without ye, lad. Ye're part o' this with us now," Araduk said.

"He's right. We all need to find out why we have all met and what this magic is that brought us all together," Braern said.

Tim paused for a moment. "All right, I'll meet you outside. Give me a bit to pack some things and take a quick shower. I hope my parents don't catch me, or I'll be grounded for a year."

"I can cast an invisibility spell on you, though it will only last for a minute," Braern told him.

"What? Seriously?" Tim asked with wide eyes. "Okay, that's dope. Remind me to ask about that later. Uh... can you cast it from outside?"

"As long as I can see you."

"Wait outside, and when you see me at the top of the stairs, then do it." Tim pointed at an angle behind him.

The group nodded, and he opened the door for them. They waited outside and watched through the glass window as Tim rushed up the stairs. They saw him travel from the bathroom to his bedroom, wearing only a towel around his waist. He disappeared inside for a few minutes, then reappeared at the top of the stairs. He adjusted his backpack over his shoulders and gestured a thumbs-up to them.

Braern whispered and wiggled his fingers toward the boy. Moira pushed Braern's head aside to watch as Tim widened his eyes, looking down at his increasingly invisible body. Soon, he was completely gone. They waited another minute and heard the rustling of the doorknob and watched it rotate. Tim opened the door slowly as his invisible body shoved them backward.

"Dude, you're so cold," Moira whispered, shivering from his touch.

Tim's head appeared with the same wide eyes as before... then his shoulders, torso, hips, and legs.

A wave of spiced scents hit Moira's nose. Tim's hair was wet and his body was clean. He wore a dark blue hoodie, white undershirt, jeans, and red Converse.

"You smell nice," she complimented him.

A slight smile formed at the corner of his mouth as he stared ahead.

"How ye doin', lad?" Araduk asked, leaning forward.

"Meow!" Blue said, rustling around in his backpack with a convex window for her to peer out of at the back.

"The moggy's comin' with us?"

Tim nodded.

"Uh... that was cool and all... but I don't think I want to do that again."

BRAERN

PORTAL RESIDUE

The back of Braern's neck ached as he shuddered, feeling the energy to stand drained from his body. *Magic always comes at a price.* He had used too much magic the last few hours. Not the best choice. His legs wobbled while the sight of Tim's village blurred.

They walked past the cars in the driveway and curved around to the side of the house, into the shadows, then rested for a moment to collect themselves.

Braern bent his knees and plopped to the ground, trying to catch himself with an arm extended. He welcomed the scent of grass.

"Here, you need to cover up those ears, dude." Tim retrieved the blue hoodie for Braern and handed it to him. "Put the hood over your head."

Braern tried, puzzled at first about how to wear such a garment. He figured it out and put one sleeve on each arm over his satchel and pulled the hood over his head, covering his light hair. His ears made two little bumps on the side of his head through the fabric, while parts of his hair stuck out in front.

"Where are we goin', lad?" Araduk asked, scanning all the strange-looking houses.

Tim checked his phone. "I saw an article online about some kids finding something like a portal at a park nearby. Moira caught me up on what happened when you guys ran downstairs."

"A park? What's that?" Braern asked.

"Uh, it's a place for families to have fun outside and stuff." Tim opened Google Maps.

"I need a moment longer, please. Haven't completed an invisibility spell in ages," the elf said, placing a hand on his chest to feel his lungs expand with air.

They waited a few minutes while Tim kept checking his front door.

"Ye ready, lad?" the dwarf asked.

Braern nodded and rose to his feet with the help of Moira's powerful arm. He gazed at her face as she smiled back at him. The two nearly touched noses, then quickly took a step away from one another.

She's so beautiful that I feel I'm unworthy of her presence. I've never met a woman who looked like her. Most of the elves I know back home were as pale as the afternoon sky in winter. Her dark braids dangled across her cheeks and those lips. *Those full lips...*

He involuntarily leaned his torso toward her.

Moira caught him gawking at her mouth and frowned.

He flinched and stared at his feet. His face burned.

As she turned her head away from the group and folded her arms, he sensed much pain behind her sad eyes. *I wouldn't want to cause her anymore pain.* Braern sighed, pushing away his thoughts of her.

Tim raised an eyebrow at the sight of their embarrassment.

"These are houses, correct?" Braern asked. "They're as large as castles."

"Yeah, my dad owns a factory. This is a pretty nice neighborhood. All right, the park is about seven blocks... uh... that way." Tim pointed toward the street to their left, lined with neutral-colored houses, like Tim's, with perfectly manicured yards without leaves on the ground in this warm, spring weather. "I'll call a ride share. I don't think we should walk that far, and my mom won't let me drive till I'm forty."

"What's a ride share?" Araduk asked, as the group followed Tim to the sidewalk in front of the street.

"Oh, it's a big car or SUV that can fit all of us. I pay money from my phone, and the driver takes us where we need to go," Tim answered with a raised eyebrow. "Forgot I'm talking to a dwarf and an elf. You'll see when it gets here... which will be in two minutes. Perfect!" He tapped send on his app as they waited.

Minutes passed, and a large black SUV pulled up to the street and stopped by them. Araduk and Braern stood motionless, braced with arms bent at their sides with focused gazes, their mouths agape.

"What is this metallic monster? It devoured a human! I'll free you, good sir!" Braern drew his sword in one swoop and pointed it at the vehicle.

The driver, sipping from his Red Bull can, didn't notice someone threatening his ride.

Moira stifled a laugh, covering her mouth.

"You guys sure do have a lot of questions... uh... understandably." Tim raised an eyebrow with his mouth open.

"Is it alive?" Araduk sidestepped toward Braern and hid behind his back, peering around his arm.

A mom with kids playing in the front yard, a few houses down, saw Braern holding his weapon. She gasped and hurried her family inside.

"Dude! Put that away! It's a car! It's not alive, and it won't hurt you. Now, get in, both of you." Tim opened the door, looked back at his house as he sucked on his lips, and rubbed his arm.

Moira climbed inside and sat in the far back. Araduk took a seat behind the driver. Braern paused for a second, then sat next to Moira.

Tim closed the doors and sat behind the passenger seat, next to Araduk. He laid down his backpack and hushed Blue. She settled in silence.

"Where to?" the driver asked, tapping on his phone that was secured on its vent holder.

"Midtown, please," Tim answered as he sat his backpack on his lap. He looked inside and whispered, "Stay quiet, Blue."

The driver accelerated slowly, but that still unsettled Braern and Araduk. They both clenched their seats with their hands.

"Put on your seatbelts, like this." Tim demonstrated.

Moira had already buckled herself in. The dwarf and the elf obliged. They buckled themselves in as well, taking a few tries to click the belt.

"This is the weirdest car ride ever," Moira said, staring at her restless companions.

They stared out the windows as they passed buildings, trees, and stoplights.

"This is rather soothin'," Araduk said, relaxing his shoulders, kicking his feet.

"I agree. I'm enjoying this... *ride*... *share*. The human world is very different from ours," Braern said as he fiddled with the lights above his head.

"This your first time in an Uber?" the driver asked, adjusting his mirror as he stopped at a light.

"Yes, it is. Araduk and I do not have such things in Yumerion."

"Oh yeah? Where's that?"

"It's in—"

"Australia!" Tim interrupted. "Good ole' Down Under."

Moira shook her head.

"Quite extraordinary. Look at this!" Araduk screamed with a wide smile. He pushed the switches up and down to lower and raise the window. The breeze blew in their faces as they giggled.

"Y'all are hilarious. It's just the window." Moira shook her head and giggled along with them.

Tim rubbed his neck, watching his house fade from view. He tapped his toes and scratched at his arm. Tightening his grip on his legs, his face paled as he took deep breaths through his open mouth and exhaled through his nose. He reached to pet Blue, as she looked up at him, but stopped when he heard the driver clear his throat. The boy retracted his hand.

They arrived at the park, and the SUV stopped on the side of the road.

Tim thanked him and tipped him on his phone before exiting the vehicle. "Here we are," Tim said as he unbuckled his seatbelt and shuffled toward the door. "Push the red button to release the seatbelt," he instructed the guys.

Araduk and Braern took a few seconds longer to push the button hard enough to release themselves. Then the group exited the vehicle and stared at the large trees before them, as well as the children's playground.

"Never seen anything like this before," Braern commented, gazing at his surroundings in awe.

"You've never seen a park before?" Moira asked.

The group stopped in front of the playground.

Tim swiped his fingers over his phone. "'Children Discover Mysterious Light Circle at Midtown Park,'" he read the online news article headline. "From the photo in the article, it looks like it happened... over there." Tim pointed toward a larger tree, about fifty feet from them.

They walked over there as the sun became brighter and warmer on their backs and heads. Blue jumped from the backpack, stretched her legs, and walked next to her human.

"Stay close, Blue," Tim told her, and she stayed by his feet.

The afternoon heat felt hotter and a little uncomfortable as they looked skyward and blinked from the light. They passed the fenced-in dog park on their left, but no dogs were around today. Only a few children played on the playground as well. It was quiet.

"Maybe no one wants to come here so soon after an unexplained event," Moira suggested. She stepped over a yellow and black caution tape strip that was blowing around in the wind at her feet. "Guys, I have a bad feeling about this," she warned, walking faster to catch up.

"I see nothing different here, but somethin' feels funny about this place," Araduk said.

"I agree. Something happened here. I can feel the dull magic that was left." Braern circled the tree, searching for any clues.

"Hey, guys, I see something metallic over there." Moira pointed at the roots of the tree where a shimmering, tiny pool of something became visible. At the right angle, the sun shone down and caused a reflection.

Braern bent his knees, touched the substance, and sniffed it. The scent was bitter and metallic, with a faint smell of burnt wood. It felt cool and almost looked like a spot of spilled dark silver and blue glitter mixed with paint.

As Tim searched on his phone again for any information about this unknown substance, Blue ran over and sniffed the liquid. She swiped at it with her paw and tried to shake it off.

"Oh, Blue, let me help," Tim consoled her and dug in his backpack for a tissue. He wiped her paw, but he noticed it started turning red.

Blue howled as the liquid burned her paw. She shook it, scooting backward while growling.

Tim grabbed a water bottle from his bag, dumped it on her paw, and wiped vigorously. His brow raised in an arch as his eyes watered. He caressed her head.

Braern blinked, wiping away the strands of hair from his eyes, as he watched Tim care for his cat. Then he felt a debilitating and sharp pain in his head. He closed his eyes and held his head in his hands. Collapsing to the ground, he could hear the voices of his comrades standing over him.

With closed eyes, he saw a disturbing array of colors, from reds to blacks and blues, swiping around his mind in every direction. He saw a younger Orastos hiding behind something as figures in front of him fought each other, one slaying two others. He couldn't decipher who the figures were or anything about where they were located. Everything was blurry and erratic. The coolness of tears traveled down his cheeks as he clenched his teeth in pain.

"Braern..." a voice called through the noise in his head as the picture faded.

"Braern! Are you all right?" Moira slid over, knelt, and touched his shoulders with both hands.

Braern's mind slowed, and the sounds and colors vanished. Her long black eyelashes blinked as he lost himself in her breathtaking eyes. "I... I'm fine." He tried to reassure her and relaxed, allowing himself to breathe deeply. He sat upright as he scanned all the worried faces.

"Dude, that must've been a killer migraine. You okay?" Tim asked, still tending to Blue's burn.

"Would ye like me to help, my friend?" Araduk offered, outstretching his hands.

"No... no. I'm fine. Help the cat." Braern looked at Blue, still mewling in agony. "I had a strange vision, and I'm unsure of what it means. So much uncertainty." Braern felt himself again and spoke to the group. "I saw a younger version of my father hiding from a great evil that slaughtered others in front of him. I can't make sense of it."

"Ye're seein' visions, and the moggy is now injured. I think we should leave this place at once." Araduk waddled to Blue and stroked her head for a moment to calm her down.

"Mew!" she screeched as the dwarf placed both hands on her tiny paw, and a warm yellow-white light appeared around the wound. As it vanished, her red burn healed, and

she stopped making noises. The poor kitty buried her head into Tim's arms as she planted her body on his lap.

He stroked her fur, and she purred. Tim picked her up and headed toward the entrance to the park.

Everyone else stood and followed him.

Tim's belly growled. "Let's go somewhere. We can make sense of all this and get something to eat." He lost his balance a bit when he stepped down from the curb of the parking lot.

"I'm down! Could go for a burger or a burrito right about now," Moira exclaimed, trying to lighten to mood.

"I'm *down,* as you say." Braern gestured toward Moira.

"Am followin' ye youngins'. I could eat a whole horse!" Araduk exclaimed, rubbing his belly.

"Didn't you guys just eat Tim's mom's muffins?" Moira asked.

"Aye, but am still hungry!" Araduk answered.

Braern nodded.

"Awesome. I know a great place we can go," Tim said.

NOZOMI

THE KITSUNE

Nozomi Hayakawa had no time for anyone's bullshit. She often traveled in solitude, living out of hotels, and made a career out of chasing down fugitives who refused to appear in court. As a shape-shifting *kitsune,* she preferred to be alone.

After years of eating at restaurants as a party of one, she ran into a red-haired girl at her favorite café. The two parted ways, only to run into each other again. They clicked. One thing led to another, and they moved in together into a tiny studio apartment in Boulder, Colorado.

*****

A year later, a swirling oval appeared above Nozomi's head. The purples and blues sparked in a clockwise rotation. The colors reflected on her eyes as the movement mesmerized her.

"Hey, you okay, hun?" Danielle asked, looking up from her glittery, flower-encased phone. Her dangling bracelet clicked on the smooth table. Nozomi sat in front of her at their usual booth in her teal, wooden chair. They often visited Le French Café. After all, that was where they first met.

A small metal caddy with sugar, salt, and pepper sat in the middle of their tiny table.

Nozomi blinked and shook her head. Her girlfriend's voice shook her out of her trance.

"Yes... I thought I saw something on the wall. Do you see anything weird?"

Danielle turned her head and peered at the wall next to them. She saw nothing but a painting of the Eiffel Tower with French-themed knickknacks on the little black boxed shelves above.

"I don't see anything." She placed her phone facedown and reached her hands across the table.

Nozomi sighed and gently clasped her hands in hers.

"Noz, you seem distracted. Are you worried about your next assignment? Your boss has been working you to the bone lately. Where are you off to this time?" Danielle asked.

Her long, wavy, ginger-colored hair illuminated from behind as the afternoon sun shone through the wide restaurant window. The place was busy, but everyone spoke in hushed tones. Mouth-watering smells of baked goods and peppered omelettes filled the room.

"I'm not sure yet. I will check with them tomorrow at the hotel."

"I hope you catch the criminal quickly so we can actually spend a weekend together. Tomorrow's Saturday."

Her girlfriend's touch melted all her troubles away. The confusion that plagued her thoughts for weeks disappeared. She caressed her soft hands and rubbed her thumbs over her palms.

"Oh Danny, what would I do without you?"

"You'd be a boring loner, grow old, and die alone."

The woman laughed.

"*Kuso!* Thanks!"

Nozomi stuck three fingers into her water glass and the ice jiggled against the side. She threw a few drops in her hand at her girlfriend. Danielle yelped with a huge smile across her face and flinched backward.

"Oh yeah?"

Danielle, wearing a playful frown, fished for an ice cube and threw it at Nozomi's face. The coldness smacked her cheek.

"Ow!"

A nearby family of four coughed in their direction with narrowed eyes.

They sucked on their lips, trying not to laugh.

The women stacked the dishes on top of each other, placed all their trash under their silverware, and left their bill with a generous tip on the table for the hot waitress who served them.

They walked outside holding hands, their shoulders touching.

Soon, an older couple walked by them.

The man with a balding head and white, wispy hair tufts above his ears glared at them with a stern expression.

Danielle stopped and pulled Nozomi close to her, reached her hands to her cheeks, and pulled her to her lips. Nozomi tasted her fruit-infused lip gloss that moistened both their lips. They heard the man scoff and mumble something under his breath.

Once the couple disappeared into the restaurant, the women burst out laughing and ran down the street, holding hands.

They stopped at a bustling crosswalk. Flickering light from Nozomi's side caught her attention. Another portal.

"What is it?" Danielle asked. The few people in front of them crossed the street as soon as the pedestrian light turned on.

"Hey love, you go on home. I'll meet you there soon. I'm gonna go check something out first," Nozomi said.

"All right, I need a nap anyway. Feel free to wake me up when you get home," she said as she smacked Nozomi on the butt, biting her bottom lip.

"I most certainly will. I'll be home soon. Love you," Nozomi said with a smile, showing her upper teeth. She noticed the worn pocket of her skin-tight jeans. Several stitches came loose, and that made her butt stand out even more. She waited as Danielle disappeared down the road.

Such a hot mess. How did I get so lucky? she thought.

Nozomi turned her attention and gazed upward to see the portal floating above, fifty feet off the ground. No one noticed except for her.

Something wants me to go in there. I can feel it. These portals have been appearing all over the place for weeks now. It is time to go through one.

She rushed around the corner of a building into a dark alley where she wouldn't be noticed. With a wave of her arm, she shifted into a pigeon with gray and white wings and a green neck. She watched as the world around her grew bigger. Her tiny bird body felt light as she flapped her wings. Nozomi, the pigeon, flew in front of the portal.

With a deep breath, she zoomed through and vanished to the other side.

Inside was a blue, clear lake filled with purple and green salamanders scattered about on the rocks and in the shallow waters. She lowered herself down to observe them. They carried tiny webbed areas on the insides of their arms and legs that looked like the wings of a flying squirrel.

Unusual creatures. I wonder what they need those for?

Then she saw a pair of them shoot out of the water and dive back inside with a tiny splash. The little amphibians flew above the water as high as twenty feet in the air.

Nozomi smiled. "That looks like fun. I haven't had a relaxing break in forever."

With a smile on her face, she dropped down onto the bank of the lake. The sun warmed her tightened cheeks and neck, where she often held much of her stress. The woodsy scent filled her nostrils as the quiet brought her long-awaited serenity.

Once again, she waved a hand over her body, but this time she transformed herself into her sleek, dark gray and white fox. She danced on her paws and rustled her fur to find comfort in her favorite form. She ran forward as her fur blew in the breeze. With a tongue over her snout, her mouth opened and arms outstretched, she leaped into the lake.

A rush of coolness soothed her body as she waded in the water. A scent of fish caught her attention as she splashed around. She paused. Several feet away, she spotted some delicious looking trout-like fish and decided to go swimming.

Nozomi inhaled deeply and dove under the water. It was much clearer than she thought as she noticed an entire school of fish swimming around one another.

With narrowed eyes, she swam to them and lunged forward. Several splashes and wriggling fights later, she grasped one in her jaws.

She headed toward the shore.

A sudden wave of bitter cold surrounded her. She shivered and peered around in all directions. Another portal appeared, adjacent to the one she had arrived through. Inside were several icebergs.

Nozomi dropped her fish. The frozen wasteland inside the portal spewed inside her lake. Hot and cold mixed as steam rose from the water. The lake cracked and froze as the ice hurtled toward her.

She yelped and hurried to the bank. Mid-stride, the ice froze around her, trapping her.

The little salamanders fought to swim out of the water, but a few also became trapped. They squealed and squirmed, trying to break free.

She stared at the portal as a green swathe of magic appeared next to it.

"What is that?"

Her teeth chattered.

With a frown, she roared and transformed into a grizzly bear. The ice broke and split all around her as she pushed down on her paws. She finally freed herself and made it to the shore.

After she caught her breath, she slammed her bear fist into the ice and cracked it so the salamanders would break free. They quickly scampered to safety in the trees.

What is happening here? she thought. *I do not know, but I better head back home. Danielle will be waiting for me.*

The second portal closed and the green light vanished.

The first portal awaited. She turned back into a pigeon again, flew through, and landed in the alley. As a human again, she adjusted her leather jacket as she walked home. It wasn't far... no more than a few blocks.

She reached the familiar apartment complex with neutral-colored doors and square-cut bushes out front.

With a hand on the doorknob, she called, "Hey, love, I am sorry I took so long. I was resting at a lake for a few hours and I lost track of time."

The door creaked open as Nozomi's eyes widened. Her heart skipped a beat. She dropped her keys onto the hardwood floor.

Chairs were overturned, papers thrown about, posters ripped off the walls, and porcelain trinkets lay shattered on the rug.

"Danielle!" she screamed so loud she thought her throat might be ripped to shreds. Her face heated and reddened as she raced to their bedroom.

Two legs stuck out of the open window, the teal curtains blowing in the wind.

She heard muffled screams. That's when she saw him.

A figured half-encased in shadow floated outside their second-story window wearing traditional, Japanese samurai attire in green, white, and black. The glowing green caught her eye. It was the same menacing color that appeared by the iceberg portal above the lake.

He tried to freeze me and now he's after her. Why?

Nozomi sneered, showing her teeth, and grasped Danielle's legs. She pulled as hard as she could, staring at her girlfriend's smeared makeup with a red, bruised face.

With one hand on one of Danielle's legs, Nozomi reared her right hand back, transforming it into a tiger's paw.

She slashed at the man, barely missing Danielle's cheek. He flinched and groaned, falling backwards.

"Gah!" he yelled, showing his teeth. Blood soaked through his clothing and pooled from the holes in his fabric.

Nozomi watched in horror as the man waved a hand behind him in a circular motion. A portal appeared like the ones Nozomi had seen earlier that day. He floated backward with Danielle in his grasp as they disappeared inside.

"No!" Nozomi lunged after them. A second later, the portal closed.

They all arrived in the middle of an unknown warehouse. Sunlight beamed through broken cracks in the multi-framed windows. Their footsteps echoed on the concrete as the breeze blew hanging chains as they tapped on metal.

Listening to her own erratic breathing, she watched Danielle kick and flail her arms, struggling to get away from him. The man conjured a glowing, green, magic dagger from his fingers and held it to her throat. His other hand cusped her mouth.

"What do you want? Let her go!" she demanded through gritted teeth.

Danielle wore nothing but her tank top and matching shorts. Her bare feet had brown, dusty stains on the bottoms. Nozomi's chest ached, seeing her exposed like that.

"Come get her, my little fox. Damn, you're beautiful. I know what you are, and if you surrender to me, I will let her go," the man said with an American accent.

Nozomi peered at her face as tears streamed down her cheeks. Danielle shook her head with a furrowed brow.

"Fine! I surrender! Let her go!"

Nozomi raised her hands in the air, her chest heaving. She walked toward them as sweat dropped down her back. Her body temperature rose.

He will not honor my wish. I know it.

She sneered and ran after him again. He tossed Danielle over to his left, opened a portal with his palm, and shoved her inside. She screamed, reaching her hands for Nozomi. The portal vanished. It all happened in a split second.

"Where did she go? I'll kill you!" Nozomi lunged after him, screaming as she pushed off the floor and ran toward him.

"You didn't think it would be that easy, did you?" he asked with a chuckle.

He made a half circle gesture with his arm and disappeared through a separate portal without saying another word. She ran after him and flew through the swirling oval.

He tightened his fist, and the portal closed behind them.

They appeared in a different place. It looked like any city, but she didn't know where they were. And she didn't care. She had one thing on her mind.

Nozomi and the man wearing the *kamishimo* stood feet apart. He raised his chin as if he challenged her to make the first move.

Wiping the tears from her eyes, she nearly broke her teeth from how tightly she clenched her jaw.

"Tell me where she is!" Nozomi yelled. She ran toward him.

He floated up with his hands behind his back, peering down at her, and zoomed off in the opposite direction.

She ran after him. With a wave of her hand, she transformed into a falcon and screeched. She dove in between buildings, swooped through busy streets, zigzagging around lampposts and palm trees.

Finally, out of breath, she sat atop the corner of a building, still in her falcon form. She inhaled as her spotted chest rose and fell with her beak open. His glowing green magic appeared a building away on the other side of the street.

She watched him. His attention was no longer on her. She stood, staring through the window of a Chipotle. She watched him from afar as he stared inside the restaurant at a table of four. An elf, a dwarf, and two humans ate with smiles on their faces.

I do not know why he took her. But he carries the same look on his face that he had when he was pulling her out of that window.

He thinks they are important. Maybe he intends to hurt them too. I need to find out why. Maybe they know the key to capturing his sorry ass so I can force him to release her.

As the thoughts raced through her mind, she watched him wave his arm again.

A portal appeared. Half of the oval stuck out of the top of the restaurant, while the other was inside.

Oh no. That cannot be good. The same thing that happened to me at that lake could happen here. I have to warn them.

BRAERN

FLOODING BURRITOS

Braern stared with wide eyes as they came upon a gray and tan, modern, cube-like building with an outside patio and large black-trimmed windows. Tim held his cat and rubbed her paw. She hissed in his arms, tensing her body, and fidgeted closer to him. A white dog walked past with its human. Blue growled and retreated to the safety of Tim's backpack, peeking out her window.

"Hey, it's okay. I won't let that dog hurt you," Tim told her.

"White," Braern whispered as he stared at his feet. *Is my father leading us here?*

"I love Chipotle," Moira said, breaking Braern's trance. "My grandma used to take me here all the time! I'm starving." Moira opened the transparent door and entered.

Signs advertised food on the windows while customers enjoyed their meals at their tables. Tim followed Moira and peeked back as the dwarf and elf stood outside, gawking at the restaurant.

"I've never been to a place like this. Is this a tavern of some sort?" Braern asked, surprised to see such an establishment.

"My fellow monks and I harvested the only food we ate over the years. I haven't seen a place that prepares food like this either," Araduk countered.

The two men kept staring and didn't notice they were blocking other people from entering the store.

"It's not a tavern. It's a restaurant, and you're in the way," Tim said.

"My apologies." Braern bowed and stepped aside. The elf held open the door for other humans to enter. He sucked in his stomach to avoid touching a larger man coming in to dine. His hood fell from his head as he backed against the wall. He exhaled with a sigh and returned his gaze to his friends.

"It's rather busy," Araduk commented, still unsure of everything.

They waited in line. Moira was already at the front.

"Holy mother of... Is that a sword?" a nearby teen whispered, staring at Braern's weapon. They peered at his face and saw his ears.

His cheeks flushed.

"Dude..." Tim hissed, eyeing his ears. Tim and Braern pulled their hoods back over their heads.

"My apologies. I'll put that away." He waved his hand over his sword and it disappeared, but he tapped his weapon at his side.

"Wait... What? Where'd it go? It was just here—"

The clanging of dishes interrupted him from the back room. The teen investigated and left the group alone, frowning.

Meanwhile, Tim crouched, trying to hide his face under his hood again. "Keep that thing hidden, okay?" he hissed, eyeing the spot at his side where the sword had vanished, then back at Braern.

"I can only make it invisible for a short time, as I did with you."

"Do what you gotta do. We wait in line here until we get up to the front. Then you can pick what you want on your burrito. They have tons of options, from meats, cheeses, vegetables, sauces—all kinds of stuff. You tell them what you want them to make for you and they make it."

Braern wasn't paying attention and kept looking everywhere and taking in all the sights of the restaurant.

Araduk winked at a child. His eyes crinkled as he smiled.

The boy kept staring at his short stature and pointing, then smiled back. His mother instructed her kid not to stare.

Moira asked the crew members to add extra cheese and guacamole with her chicken.

A family waited in front of Tim, Braern, and Araduk. The next few people ordered, and it was their turn.

Braern stared at the black painted pipes and tubing on the ceiling. Metal lights hung down, and wood and metal chairs were scattered about. A few families at the tables were eating and talking. Sculptures hung on the walls and the sounds of several conversations filled the room. He licked his lips as he stepped forward to the three people in charge of preparing the food, with a glass shield in front of them. The elf got a little too close and banged his invisible sword on the counter at waist level.

"White or wheat?" the young sandy-haired teen asked with a smile and an apron on. He pointed his gloved hands to his tower of tortillas.

"Pardon me?" Braern squinted his eyes at the black-background menu with white lettering and bright pictures of ingredients and products that came in the burritos.

"Thank you. May I ask what that is?" He pointed to an orange pile of textures.

"What? Oh, that's cheese. Would you like to add extra to your burrito?"

"What is that?" he asked again, pointing at something else.

"That's a tortilla," the boy answered, narrowing his eyes and sighing.

"I see. And what is that?" Braern asked again, pointing to guacamole.

"Dude! It's stuff that goes on a burrito. Have you never been here before?"

"No, I'm afraid I have not."

"All right, would you like a wheat or white tortilla?" the teen asked, staring at the antsy customers behind him.

"I've never seen a bird prepared in that way."

"Dude, that's chicken." The boy's smile vanished as he narrowed his eyes. His eyes closed, and he pressed his lips together, sucking them in.

Customers behind them murmured about them taking so long.

"You start with a tortilla," Tim interjected with a slight tremor in his voice, "which goes on the outside, then you tell this guy what you want on the inside, like chicken, cheeses, and sauces."

"I'll have a wheat tortilla with chicken, cheeses, and sauces!" he exclaimed as the other customers glared at him.

Tim slapped his hand over his face, shaking his head.

The boy passed the tortilla on foil to the next person, and they made the burrito he had asked for. The boy gestured with his eyes for the next customer to come forward.

"That enough?" the next lady asked as she put a spoonful of steaming-hot, seasoned, chicken chunks on the top of the tortilla.

"More, please." Braern watched as she added more. "A little more. More ... one more." His burrito was nothing but a pile of chicken with a skosh of tortilla sticking out the bottom.

"You do you, man," the girl said, chuckling, as she passed it to the next guy.

He added the cubed tomato salsa and cheese as requested and passed it along. The next guy tried to fold the burrito three times, then gave up, piling the meat into a paper bowl, and handed it to the cashier.

"A'll have what he's havin'," Araduk cackled, standing on his tiptoes as he peered at the yummy-looking concoction Braern had ordered.

The crew obliged, and Tim ordered his own food and handed out their cups the cashier had given them.

"What thin cups," the elf said, touching the paper between his fingers. Braern dug into his satchel and handed him three gold coins with holes in the middle. "Will this be enough?"

The cashier collected the coins and inspected them close to his face, squinting. "What currency is this?"

"It's *mon,*" Braern answered, cocking his head.

"Okay, I got this," Tim interrupted. He paid for the three of their meals and checked the receipt for the extra charge for the chicken. With a sigh, he reluctantly handed over his card from his wallet.

The cashier handed Braern back his money, blinking and still confused.

Tim led the guys to the soda machine, where they had multiple options. Tim pushed the Dr Pepper button to fill his own paper cup, while Araduk and Braern's eyes widened.

"Holy mother o'... what sort of ale is this? That's grand!" Araduk exclaimed with delight.

The elf and the dwarf pushed buttons, giggling, as more soda came out in synchronicity.

"It's not ale. It's soda. All right, guys, c'mon. Moira is waiting for us." Tim narrowed his eyes and groaned.

They grabbed their food and sticky cups from the spill-age and walked to the table where Moira was already eating, waving between bites with her mouth full. The group sat at the round table with a half-circle, pleather, black seat. Everyone dug in, but Tim picked at his burrito bowl and barely touched it, his head down.

"Thank ye for the meal," Araduk said, food spilling from his mouth.

"Yes, thank you." Braern nodded and took a huge bite of his burrito as bits of meat fell to his lap. *"Mmm...* that's delicious."

"All right, what do we know so far about all this?" Moira asked.

Everyone listened, continuing to feast.

"We've been thrown through portals, not knowing where we'd end up. I'm surprised we haven't fallen into the middle of the ocean or somewhere."

The entire group imagined the worst in sync, with blank stares on their faces.

"My bad. Let's not go there," Moira corrected herself.

"We're being pulled between our worlds. We don't have any choice but to let the portals take us where they want us to go," Braern said.

"Yeah, I guess the universe wanted you all to meet me?" Tim asked.

"Also, we now know the moggy was harmed when she touched the substance left from the portals," Araduk said.

"But not us. Why?" Tim asked. He peeked in his backpack and saw Blue catnapping, purring to herself in a ball at the bottom. "Here, Blue, for when you get hungry." He dropped a piece of chicken into the bag and looked around to see if anyone had noticed.

Braern peered out the window and saw a dark-haired woman outside, dressed in a black leather jacket and ripped jeans. He watched her as she ran down the street to the restaurant, pushing people out of the way. She seemed distraught but focused, looking behind her as if someone were chasing her. The woman entered and shoved through the crowd.

"Hey, get in line like everyone else, lady," a patron demanded.

"Good feelings gone," Tim said as his eyes widened, seeing her push toward them.

"Who's that?" Moira asked, then finished her burrito and gulped a drink of Diet Coke. She put her hands on the table and raised herself to get a better view of where the lady was headed.

Crew members and customers murmured, then resumed what they had been doing.

"I don't know, but she seemed like she needed help," Tim added, then took a bite.

"The lass did seem distraught," Araduk said.

"Perhaps she's very hungry? I'd be happy to share my meal," Braern suggested.

They kept their eyes on her as she weaved through the tables to theirs.

Out of breath, the woman placed her hands on the table and addressed the entire group. "There you all are. We need to get out of here, now!" Her long black hair with blue highlights fell into her face as sweat beaded on her forehead.

"Wait a moment. Who are you?" Braern asked as the group stood.

"There is no time. We need to leave, now!"

The entire restaurant stared at her with frowns and whispers.

Braern sipped at his strange, bubbly drink with a raised eyebrow. His feet suddenly felt cool. With a hand on the table, he peered at the floor. Brown water surrounded his boots. With wide eyes, he lost the grip on his drink and it splashed onto the floor. The water rose. Everyone shivered from the cold temperature. Chunks of ice scattered, coming from the back of the restaurant. Soon, everywhere was soaked. People raised their feet, and a few escaped in time for the doors to lock themselves, and all the lights went out. The sunlight through the windows was the only light source. Dinners were abandoned on tables as screams filled the room. Others swished through the waters and beat on the doors and windows to escape. As it rose, it turned into a greenish-brown color. People cursed and groaned with disgusted looks on their faces.

"This is bad," Tim said, hyperventilating. Blue stirred in the backpack and meowed. "I got you, Blue. Stay there."

"Look!" Moira yelled over the loud chaos and pointed out the window.

A dark figure stared at them from the corner of a building across the street. They appeared to be about the elf's build: tall and thin with similar attire to Braern's. The unknown figure waved an arm in their direction in a half circle as the water rose to their stomachs. A pang rumbled Braern's stomach. He squinted his eyes, peering at the creature outside. *Something about them seems familiar. But why?*

Araduk struggled to climb on the top of the seat.

The rest of the customers joined and climbed as high as they could, along with the staff, who stood on the counters and tables closest to them. Screaming and wailing sounded through the flooding restaurant.

"I knew this would happen! We have to get out of here!" The strange woman pushed her arms as she swam toward the nearest exit that had the fewest frantic humans clawing at the door.

Araduk fought to keep his head above water.

Moira grabbed his hand and held on tight.

The group swam to the nearest exit and pounded on the door.

Moira was in the back with Araduk as the water rose higher up to their waists.

"What the hell is going on? Did the pipes burst?" Moira asked over the screaming of people around them. She waved her arms through the flood.

"I don't know! We need to get out!" Tim yelled.

Braern pulled out his sword, but lost his grip under the water. It was too murky to see where it landed.

"There goes that plan," Araduk said, his beard spreading out across the top of the surface.

Several customers pounded on the nearest door as water splashed in their faces.

Tim's backpack filled with water. Blue escaped and swam as quickly as her little legs could carry her, trying to keep her head above water. Tim grabbed her and pulled her close to his chest. Her claws dug into his skin through his shirt. "I got ya."

They stayed close together.

The strange woman gasped, lifting another person out of the water who needed help.

The water rose higher and higher. Then it was a foot from the ceiling. Everyone pushed with their hands above them, frantically trying to keep their mouths and noses free.

Muffled sounds of glass cracking pricked Braern's ears as he gasped for breath, peering at the breaking window.

Moira followed his gaze. "We're not dying today!" she hollered as she pushed herself off the wall and swam backward. "Clear out!" She kicked the ceiling and punched the door. It didn't break. As the building became completely filled, she held her breath and punched with all her force at the window.

The glass shattered, and everyone spilled outside in a giant mess of wet clothes and soggy appendages, gasping for breath. It all happened in a matter of seconds.

Lying in heaps of exhausted bodies, they coughed and groaned. The group waited several minutes before anyone spoke a word.

Braern raised a shaking hand with his palm open. Raven shook underneath a dripping table and floated over, flipping around for the elf to grasp the hilt. He rolled onto his side and sheathed his sword.

"Is everyone all right?" Araduk staggered to stand and ensured they were all breathing.

Tim gave a thumbs-up, then plopped his arm back down.

Blue was soaked up to her neck and jumped off her human to shake her body as drips flew off her fur. Tim flopped over to his side, coughing and spitting the disgusting tasting water out of his mouth. "You okay, Blue?" She growled while licking herself. "Yeah, I hear ya."

Through the blurriness and the water dripping into his face, Braern saw the shadowy figure standing in the same location, watching the entire disaster unfold. Purple and green salamanders wiggled to free themselves from underneath burrito bowls. Fishes jumped around in the street, gasping for breath, and various other amphibious creatures ran off. The figure walked in the opposite direction as Braern tried to push himself up to stand.

"Who's... that guy?" Tim asked.

Coughs and wails were audible as Araduk hovered his hands over anyone who was unconscious, reviving them.

"This is what I get for mentioning the ocean," Moira joked, gasping for breath.

"We need to find out who was watching us. I sense they had something to do with this," Braern said, his face heated as he frowned. "Whoever they are, they will pay."

The elf paused and stared behind him. A pain erupted from Braern's chest. *Now we have the added burden of evading this evil. How can I keep my friends safe when I cannot keep myself out of harm's way? Father! Where are you? Why have you left me? I cannot feel your presence in my mind, and it pains my heart.*

"Is everyone okay in here?" Moira asked in a shaky voice.

Piles of soaked and exhausted people lay all over the floor as water dripped from the ceiling and walls. Glass pieces cracked under her feet as she flinched. In the distance, the whooping of sirens grew louder.

Inches of mucky water covered the sidewalk as Moira climbed over the shattered door and window fragments. She hobbled inside, gagging from the smells of soggy burritos and animal droppings.

An elderly man with white hair, brown pants, and a gray sweater in the far corner caught her eye as she rushed to him. He lay motionless on the floor, his face paling, his lips turning purple.

She alternated between mouth-to-mouth and chest compressions on the unconscious man, remembering her training: tilt head up, pinch nose, breathe into mouth twice, place two hands on chest above the two middle ribs of heart, press hard at each count of one-one thousand, two-two thousand, three... She repeated the steps for a minute until he coughed, spit up a sizable amount of water, and breathed on his own.

"You're gonna be all right. The ambulance is on the way. Don't move." She placed a hand on his chest as he mouthed, *thank you,* and his eyebrows raised with a hand on his chest. Pushing off the floor, she looked around.

Araduk healed who he could. Three ambulances and two fire trucks arrived with flashing lights. Several EMTs with stretchers and equipment bags ran inside and treated the most critical patients first, placing oxygen masks on them. The firefighters helped people who could exit through the broken doorway, letting everyone know they needed to get outside as quickly as possible in case the ceiling collapsed.

Moira and Araduk stopped and walked out. They spotted paramedics carrying the elderly man on a stretcher.

He locked eyes with Moira for a moment as he smiled through a closed mouth, with who appeared to be his young grandkids following close by.

They watched as the dark-haired woman distanced herself from the wreckage, peering in all directions while shoving her hair out of her face. "I lost him!" she yelled, dropping her arms to her sides.

"Lost who? Who was that shadowy man watching us?" Tim asked, checking to see if his phone was still alive. He shook off the remaining water and sighed as he placed it in his bag.

"Mine appears to be okay," Moira said, holding up her phone. "Thanks, waterproof technology."

The woman walked through an arbitrary street.

"Blue! C'mon!"

Blue paused for a moment to lick her fur. She hated being ungroomed, but she stopped and ran to her human with a sneeze.

Tim scoffed. He bent and scooped her up to place her in his back, then adjusted the straps over his shoulders.

"Wait, please! What's your name?" Braern rushed to catch up to her pace.

The rest of the group followed.

"How many more times are we gonna end up soaking wet? Yuck!" Moira yelled, flinging the water off her hands.

Araduk hobbled behind everyone else with his arms bent, swinging at his sides, his weight leaning backward. "Ye tall lads and lassies are fast! Phew!" he said, catching his breath.

"My name is Nozomi Hayakawa." She stopped at an intersection to wait for a few cars to pass, then continued onward.

"I hope everyone will be okay back there. That was insane." Moira glanced back as the last bit of the flooded disaster disappeared behind another building as they turned.

"I have been tracking him. He opened a portal and allowed a lake I swam in to spill through into this world. I work alone."

"So ye know about the portals?" Araduk asked.

Nozomi nodded.

"Why does he want to kill us?" Tim asked.

"*Wakaranai.* I do not know, but I will find out. The portals have been appearing for me for a while now. I cannot explain it." Nozomi raced onward without looking back, squeezing the water out of her hair behind her.

"Who is he, and why is he after us?" Braern asked.

Nozomi pivoted her body. "An elf and a dwarf? You are not from here, are you?"

"No, we are both from Yumerion. Portals sent us to the human world," Braern said.

"Eh, there you have it," Nozomi answered, leaning forward at an angle.

"Now, don't get ye britches in a twist," Araduk said. "Let's find someplace dry and talk this through."

"I do not have time for this. He could be worlds away by now." Nozomi waved an arm with a groan. She turned and took a few steps forward.

"Hey!" Moira yelled at the top of her lungs, frowning with a stiffened jaw. "This is the first scrap of info we've heard since the first portal. You're not going anywhere until you explain what the hell is happening to us and why we're targets cuz of some psycho!"

Once again, Nozomi turned to face the group. She closed her eyes and exhaled. "I do not know everything. I saw him staring at you. You all looked the part when I saw you through the window at Chipotle. I was not sure I was in the right place or had the right people. It appears I was correct."

Moira sped up to walk in front of Nozomi; the rest of the group followed.

"What do you mean, 'looked the part?'" Tim asked.

Nozomi raised an eyebrow. "An elf, a dwarf, and humans? You stand out like a black eye."

Araduk and Braern shrugged.

"That's fair," Araduk said.

"But that doesn't explain the portals throwing us from place to place," Moira said.

Tim adjusted his shoulders and placed his backpack on the ground by his feet. Blue peeked out through the window.

"Why do you have a cat? Never mind... fine! I will tell you but only if we keep going." She headed down a familiar street with taller buildings on each side. Cars raced by as they came to another intersection. Nozomi pushed the crosswalk button and waited, tapping her foot. "I do not have time to babysit you all. I need to catch up to him to make him pay for what he did to... someone close to me." Blinking, she shook her head then shoved Moira aside and hurried down the sidewalk, scoffing.

"We need your help, milady. Please." Braern caught up to her.

"You all are going to stalk me until I give you answers, are you?" Nozomi stopped and turned around with her arms folded and one eyebrow raised.

"Yes!" they all said in unison. Even Blue meowed at her.

Nozomi paused to stare at the cat, then at the group, shaking her head to get back to focusing. "About three months ago, I was with my *kanojo* when a tall, dark man appeared outside my window. He showed up and, well... let's say, he took her, and I believe he did it to get to me. Now he will feel my wrath if it is the last thing I do." Her strides elongated over the pavement.

The group crossed as well, and poor Araduk continued to have a hard time keeping their pace.

"*Kanojo?*" Tim asked.

"I forgot that most Americans do not speak Japanese. My girlfriend."

Tim stopped. With wide eyes, his face blushed as he placed his hand over his mouth, stiffening his neck. He turned away from her.

"Can we slow down? Am not as spry as I once was." The dwarf stopped when they reached the other side to bend down and touch his knees. His back rose and fell as he struggled to catch his breath.

Nozomi stopped and used her outstretched arms to remember which way to go. *"Gomen*—or, I mean... sorry. No time, dwarf." She turned left past a brick store with white mannequins in the display window wearing ripped jeans, button-up shirts, and winter knit hats. "Keep going this way," she murmured to herself. "I'd been tracking him down, then I sensed you guys in that restaurant back there. You all have some sort of magic power, don't you?"

"What do you mean, *magic power?"* Tim asked, straightening the backpack on his shoulders.

"You do not know?" Nozomi asked again.

"I think she means Braern and Araduk. I don't have any powers." Moira felt sure of herself as she walked to Nozomi's side, watching her. "Wait, do I?"

"I know what I felt. And one or all of you possesses great power. I could feel it from a distance. I have seen the mess this man can make, and it is disastrous. He has destroyed an entire town with the help of the wind and froze a pond in the middle of the hottest day of the year. I followed him to your restaurant and saw you all were sitting inside. I knew you were the ones he was after with one look. That is why I tried to go in there and warn you."

"Warn us about what?" Tim asked.

"Hate to break it to you, kid, but this guy wants you all dead. I am like you, and he has been after me for months." Nozomi stopped and stared at Tim.

His head cocked as he raised his eyebrows at her. His lips quivered. "Wait, what? *Dead?* What do you mean, dead?" he yelled, becoming small after raising his voice at her. "I'd never hurt a fly. Why would anyone want me dead?"

"Because you are a threat. To what? I do not know. He probably wants power or money, like everyone else does, and feels that you all intend to take that away from him."

"Wait, hold on. No one's gonna die," Moira claimed. "Not while I'm here. I kinda like you guys now."

"I can't die. I've never even had a girlfriend," Tim whispered to himself.

"What?" Nozomi raised her voice, looking back.

"Nothing!" Tim uttered.

"A threat from what? And does he not know we don't have money?" Araduk spoke up, tapping his fingertips.

"You all are a threat to his plan to take over the world, I guess. I told you I don't know what it is. I just know he is snatching up creatures and humans, opening portals, and spilling environments into each other. Who knows what he is doing with them." Nozomi closed her eyes and stared at her feet, placing a hand on her temple.

"You mean, *worlds?*" Braern corrected her. "I'm not from this world. There is my world and this world."

"Enough with the worlds! You all better not get in my way. I have a job to do."

They passed several more stores as the sky darkened. The lights around the city turned on, one by one, and car headlights did the same. Hundreds of nails secured various colored flyers to lampposts.

One caught Tim's eye as they strode on; a hockey game was coming to the American Airlines Center in Dallas. "I wanted to go at some point. Never got a chance here in Houston. We don't have a hockey team," he whispered.

Before long, they reached an old, brick building with lights strewn about in front. A line of people were waiting to be let in as a large, burly man checked their IDs. They felt bass-heavy music in their stomachs and feet as they walked closer.

Nozomi led the group around the back, lit by a single flickering, cracked light with a door underneath. A dumpster sat on one side, and a stack of dirty, wooden pallets lay on the other.

As they got closer, a light appeared in front of the palettes.

"There it is!" Without hesitation, Nozomi walked through the portal and disappeared.

For a moment, the remaining part of the group stood still.

"Are we really going in there? Who knows where we could end up?" Moira puzzled.

"Is this what you guys were talking about? I don't think so..." Tim said. Blue poked her head out of his bag. She meowed and purred as Tim scratched her chin. "Blue says we should go through," Tim said, looking back at Araduk, Braern, and Moira.

"Well, if it's good enough for the moggy, it's good enough for me! Here goes!" Araduk walked through the glowing palettes.

Moira and Braern went next, followed by Tim and Blue. As the six of them passed through the portal, the familiar cool colors swished and swirled around them, and gravity seemed to disappear.

Tim held his cat, keeping his eyes closed, scared out of his mind. This was all new to him. Blue pawed at the purple light that swooshed by her face, her irises wide with curiosity. Tim opened his eyes, gazed around, and was in shock at the world around him. He turned upside down and stretched his arms, allowing himself to spin in circles.

The group rather enjoyed being suspended in magic light, but soon the light ended, and they landed on the ground with a thump.

*****

The portal took them to a different location. Warm sand was almost too hot to the touch. Everyone scurried to rise off their hands and dusted the sand off their arms and faces.

"*Kuso!* This is not where I came through before!" Nozomi yelled, looking around.

"Where are we this time?" Moira asked, surveying the gloomy, gray, wispy sky. She walked a few feet and stopped at the edge where the sand and water met. She turned and walked the other way and, in only a few feet, stopped again at the shore. "An island?" she shouted, placing her hands on her head and spinning around. "We're trapped on a tiny, little island! Are you kidding me?"

"Eh, this place moved. Last time I came through here, I ended up in a lake," Nozomi said with her hands on her hips, gazing into the distance.

"I, for one, am a wee tired o' water." Araduk was unamused at their current predicament, continuing to twist his robe as drops pattered on the gray sand at his feet. He frowned, dipping his foot into the sea. "Brr! Well, we're not swimming anywhere!"

"Look!" Braern pointed westward through the mist. "There's a strip of land over there! I see it!"

"Cool. How do we get over there?" Moira narrowed her eyes.

"We need a boat or..." As Tim spoke, Nozomi raised her hand from above her head to her waist.

She transformed, from top to bottom, into an enormous owl with brown-and-cream-spotted feathers. Her large yellow-green eyes glistened from the sun peeking through the clouds. She stretched and stomped, getting used to her new body. Her talon feet were a darker brown and shook the ground when she stepped. "Hop on," Nozomi said with her new beak, bending a wing to the sand.

"The symbol of my family, the owl," Braern said, bowing.

Nozomi nodded.

"What the heck? How did you do that?" Tim raised his eyebrows in disbelief.

Blue sniffed the air and climbed onto his back to stare at the enormous bird. She hissed and pulled closer to her human.

"It's all right, Blue. It's Nozomi."

"What is the matter? You have never seen a *kitsune* before? I am a shapeshifter. I told you I possess power too. I prefer a fox, but this will have to do for now."

"Ya know, I really am too tired to be shocked by anything anymore. Damn, what a day." Moira shook her head and took a deep breath. "Guess I'll be the first." She climbed onto the owl's back and grabbed handfuls of feathers as she situated herself on top of her neck.

"Tim, Araduk, Blue, you climb aboard. I can fly myself," Braern urged as he raised himself into air above them.

Araduk and Tim climbed onto Nozomi's soft, feathery back.

Moira wrapped her arms around her neck.

Araduk held onto Moira's waist.

Tim zipped his backpack with Blue inside and ensured his bag was secure on his back. He held Araduk's waist and rested his head on his back. He squinted his eyes closed and his teeth chattered. "Don't look down... Don't look down... Don't look..."

Nozomi raised her wings. She pushed off the ground and launched into the air. Her shoulder blades undulated underneath her passengers.

Araduk loosened his grip and hollered with glee, "Relax, lad!"

Tim's scrunched his face and held his stomach with one hand.

Blue peeked her head from Tim's backpack, squeaked, then sunk back inside.

"It'll be over soon, Blue. Hang in there," Tim reassured her, trying to reassure himself too.

"We're getting closer." Braern flew up beside the giant passenger owl and pointed toward the enlarging land mass. Clouds flew in their faces as the mist smelled like rain. Braern felt the coolness touch his face as he placed his arms at his sides again, resting one on his sword and the other on his lumpy satchel.

Minutes later, they arrived on another sandy shore. Braern landed feet first, while Nozomi flapped her wings and descended to the ground.

"Everyone, time to get off," she said.

Tim was the first to collapse on the ground. He opened his bag and freed Blue.

The little feline took a moment to clean herself and press her messy fur back down. She had to look presentable for whatever this new world was they landed on.

Araduk and Moira slid onto the beach.

Nozomi raised her right wing and lowered it as she became a young woman once again. Her blueish-black hair blew in the breeze, and she placed her fist on her hips and looked onward.

"I feel drier now, at least," Moira said.

"Where are we now?" Tim murmured incoherently. He remained in a fetal position with his arms over his face. As he decided to stand, he surveyed the beach leading to a dark, thick forest.

"This place gives me the creeps," Moira said as she stepped backward.

"Are we going in there?" Tim asked.

"It appears that way," Araduk commented as he walked toward the trees.

"I do not know where we are. The portal led us here for a reason, so let us go." Nozomi walked past Araduk, and the group followed.

A shrill cry sounded in the distance. Then that cry became two... then three. Soon, the sounds of dozens of shrieks and high-pitched hollers grew louder. In the distance, a flock of creatures rose from the trees and flew toward them. As they got closer, their features became recognizable.

"Are those harpies?" Tim yelled, tensing.

Blue ran between his legs in terror.

"Wait, what are those feet? And that bill! They look like floppy platypuses! Platypusees? Platypusai?" Moira screamed, shaking her head.

"Flying harpy-platypuses?" Araduk exclaimed.

"Platypies?" Tim said, his voice shaking, as they were nearly on top of them.

Moira, Braern, and Nozomi formed a barrier with Araduk, Tim, and Blue in the middle. Sword raised, fists up—they were ready.

TIM

THE PLATYPIES

Platypies swooped down in waves with talons out-stretched. One dove on top of Tim. He gasped, covering his head with his hands, ensuring Blue was close.

Braern removed Tim's hoodie that he wore and leaped into the air to meet the creature, catching it off guard. He hit its deformed beak with the butt of his sword, knocking it several feet away before it took flight again.

Moira bent her knees and punched one before it slashed her arm. The thing landed on the ground beside her feet, wriggling and crying, attempting to right itself.

Transforming into a sleek, dark, two-tailed fox, Nozomi jumped and landed on the back of one that was seconds from reaching Tim and Araduk. She hissed and locked her jaw around its neck as it frantically spun in circles, shrieking in pain.

Araduk and Tim knelt with their arms over their heads, not allowing themselves to look above. Tim freed a hand and lifted the bottom of his shirt. Blue scampered onto his belly and curled into a ball, terrified, as he placed his arms above him once again.

"These things are hideous! And they're so loud!" Moira yelled through gritting teeth as she whacked another one down from the air to join her growing pile of the injured. The creatures next to her feet were clumsy and had a difficult time righting themselves, so much that they snapped at each other.

Nozomi snarled in between filling her mouth with platypie feathers. After releasing her latest victim, she jumped from wing, back to tail, all while remaining in the air. She kicked and clawed with ease at any creature that came near her. The others below could barely see her in action—nothing but a blurry dash of fur racing through the flock.

Braern swung his dark sword with one hand and freed his other to conjure glowing fireballs in his hand. He placed his hand on the blade of Raven as it engulfed in flames, but it didn't burn him. His blade's steel sliced shoulder blades and cut feathers from wings while he set several platypies on fire as they fell to the earth.

Cries and bellows sounded everywhere as Tim squeezed his hands tighter on his head, his ears and heart throbbing from the surrounding violence. Rivers of sweat dripped from his armpits down his sides as he shook and struggled to take solid breaths, while he rocked back and forth with his knees up against Blue.

"It'll be over soon, lad. Hang in there," Araduk tried to comfort him while staying as low to the ground as he could. The dwarf shielded his friend and scrunched his eyes, shaking his head. He rotated and snuck a sip of his flask.

Blue jumped out from under his shirt, scratching his belly. He ignored the pain, clenching his fists. "Stop! Shh...

shrawk!" he involuntarily screeched, covering his face with wide eyes. *How am I doing this?*

The creatures stopped charging and stared at him, bewildered.

Nozomi, Moira, and Braern, with Raven lowered, ceased fighting and spread out. Moira relaxed her fists at her sides. Nozomi's ears perked as she spit several bloody feathers from her mouth, coughing.

Tim peeked through one eye, surprised he had single-handedly stopped the battle. A strange sensation tingled in his throat, as if he had used a distinct part of his vocal cords than he usually did during speech. Once again, he felt confused as he uttered several clicks, shrieks, and hollers as the platypies paid close attention to him with cocked heads.

With a battered wing, one pattered forward, bill open. It walked right up to a confused and terrified Tim.

Araduk stepped away, and Blue regained her place between Tim's legs, puffing herself up and hissing.

Tim, still shaking, braced himself as the clumsy creature stared at him. He giggled at the platypie's goofiness and relaxed his tense shoulders and jaw. It had feathery large wings, forearm clawed fins, black, sharp talons, an oval, umber head with a mane, small, dark, beady eyes, and a rounded beak. It sounded like a goose honking, and Tim spoke its language.

"What is happening?" Nozomi asked as she returned to her human form and approached Moira.

"Your guess is as good as mine, girl." Moira raised an eyebrow with one hand on her hip.

"He speaks their tongue," Braern said, shaking drops of blood off of his sword, extinguishing the flames, then sheathing it.

Several screeches and honks later, Tim walked to Braern, half-smiling. "They said some dark magic had fused them together. They didn't ask for this, but they have adapted in the days since this happened to them. The evil who had done this to them returned and they felt threatened, so they attacked," Tim educated the group while Blue flattened her fur. She took a moment to clean herself after her fright.

"*Days?* He was here *days ago?* Did you ask them which way he went?" Nozomi placed her hands on Tim's shoulders and gently shook him.

He stared into her eyes, his body paralyzed. "I..." His face turned bright red, and then white. *A girl touched me. What?* His eyes stiffened, and he fainted onto the sand, knees first.

As his face smashed against the grainy ground, Araduk rushed over and placed his hand on the kid's back.

After a moment, he jolted awake, curling his fingers and seeing the concerned faces above him. Even one platypie managed to sneak a glance over his head. "What... happened?" he whispered, his face burning.

Moira grabbed his hand and helped him stand, ensuring he was steady before letting go.

Tim brushed off the sand and stepped backward as he remembered Nozomi was the last one who'd touched him. He felt woozy, and his knees gave out.

Moira placed her arm in front of him to lean on as he regained his composure.

"Kid, look, I will stand over here," Nozomi muttered as she walked several feet away, still within hearing distance.

She folded her arms, looking skyward, while tapping her boot.

Tim shook his head. "Sorry."

"Quite all right, Tim." Araduk chuckled as he rose to his feet.

"I told them we didn't mean to hurt them and that you might try to help them, Araduk," Tim said.

Araduk nodded and healed the creatures, one by one.

"They told me the one who did this to them went in that direction two days ago." Tim pointed toward the vast forest before them, where faded mountains lay far in the distance.

The one who had spoken to Tim slowed and looked back at him.

Did that actually work? He rubbed his eyes.

The platypie nodded.

Tim nodded back at him as he disappeared into the thick gray clouds with the rest of his family.

"He must have portal jumped because he cannot be that far ahead of us," Nozomi groaned, brushing the sand off her clothes. She wiped a drip of blood off her lip and hurried toward the trees. The sand only allowed her to go so fast, as her feet sunk in from the moisture of the beach.

"Would ye like me to take care of that scratch for ye?" Araduk offered.

"Do not touch me." Nozomi frowned and waved an arm in his direction, looking away.

"Hey, you don't talk to Araduk like that! He was trying to help," Moira inserted herself.

"Nobody asked you!" Nozomi said to her.

"Girl, I outta take ya down a notch!" Moira clenched her fists as her face became hot. Her nostrils flared, and her heart raced.

"I could kick your as—"

"Enough!" Braern ran over and stood in front of the two women. "You are not her enemy, and she is not yours!" He panned back and forth between them. "Now, our worlds have been threatened, and who knows how many lives have been or could be lost because of all this chaos. We need to find this evil and stop him before he destroys everything! And then we can all go back to our homes." He clutched his chest as his brow arched, gazing at Moira.

Tim stared at Braern and Moira. *I may not have much experience, but there's definitely something goin' on with those two.*

"I know we're all on edge here, because so much is bein' thrown at us all at once, but we've got to keep our heads about us," Araduk advised.

"You're right. I'm sorry." Moira relaxed her fists.

"I do not know how many more ways I can say this. I have no time for this nonsense!" Nozomi scoffed and kept going.

"Well, she's a touchy one, isn't she?" Araduk asked to no one in particular. "We better get a move on."

"Hey, thanks, Tim, for saving us back there," Moira acknowledged the boy as his gaze stayed down while the group headed toward Nozomi.

"Uh... it... was nothing," he murmured.

"Ye've got a gift, lad." Araduk walked alongside Tim.

"How long have you been able to talk to animals?" Moira asked.

"Oh, uh... since forever, I guess. Blue and I kinda talk in our minds. It's pretty cool." He giggled at his kitty friend walking alongside with her tail raised.

"My father and I speak to one another in our minds, as well," Braern whispered as he turned away from his comrades. He closed his eyes and gazed into the distance, rubbing his arms.

"Braern?" Moira asked.

No response. He seemed lost in a trance.

"Braern!"

The elf blinked, shaking his head. His friends came into focus as he blinked.

"Did ye have another one of those... what'd ye call em?" Araduk asked, bewildered.

"Sounds like he has recurring visions," Tim answered. He knelt in front of the tormented elf. "I've seen this before in the MMORPG I'm playing. That main character keeps having visions of his past, and it unravels his next steps in his journey. Maybe that's happening to you."

Blue approached Braern and placed her forepaws on his knees. She regarded him with her big, green-yellow eyes, gently raising a paw so he would pay attention. Her tail was up and swaying at the tip.

"She wants you to pet her." Tim smiled, proud of his little friend for knowing what to do. "She can sense you're upset."

"She... said that? I didn't hear her speak." Braern quivered as he felt a tiny rumble on his legs. It came from Blue.

"She doesn't have to talk to be understood. Cats are great at communicating with their body language. They know when someone needs help." Tim showed him Blue's preferred way to be stroked, in the direction of her fur growth.

Braern stared at her head and scratched his hand down her neck and back. "She's so soft. That's strangely comforting. Thank you, Tim. And thank you, Blue." He motioned toward the happy feline as he stood.

Blue looked up at him and slowly blinked her eyes.

"She trusts you," Tim told him.

Braern smiled.

"She's sweet, but we better get a move on," Moira reminded them.

The rest of the group stood and walked quicker into the forest.

"I think you're right about what you said, about the possibility of my visions holding clues to why all this is happening," Braern said to Tim as they walked side by side.

Blue jumped over fallen logs to keep up.

"Yeah?" Tim felt a little shocked that he could be right about one thing. That rarely happened.

"I need to find out what these visions mean. I see my father in them."

"Then we must find him," Araduk said.

"I think we lost Nozomi," Moira announced as the sand stuck to their feet while they trudged forward.

Rustling of leaves and broken twigs filled their ears as they walked along. Moira stepped over large branches in her way. They snapped as her legs contacted them.

Braern hovered nearby and swerved around the thick, coniferous trees.

Araduk walked beside Tim as Blue jumped over or squeezed under protruding roots and vines.

They all stayed close to each other.

"Anyone else think this is weird that this forest has sand this far from the shore?" Tim asked, gazing down, and looked back from where they'd come from.

"That seems odd," Araduk commented as he lifted his foot in mid-stride. He surveyed the trees as well. Their leaves blocked most of the sunlight, but a small amount shone through to the forest floor.

"Can we be sent somewhere that isn't creepy, for once?" Moira asked, unamused, as only the crunching of their steps were audible. No animals chirped or rustled in the plants.

"I see something!" Braern pointed ahead as he flew a little way in front of the rest of the group. He lowered himself and gently placed his feet on the ground next to his discovery. "You all should see this." Braern waved them over.

The group quickened their pace and stopped in front of their elf friend.

"Oh... my... god. The poor thing." Moira placed her hand across her lips as her eyes widened and watered, blinking.

"I'm gonna throw, uh..." Tim covered his mouth as stomach acid mixed with his lunch traveled up his esophagus. His cheeks puffed. He walked two steps from them, bent down, and vomited onto a pile of leaves. The drops splashed on the ground.

Blue walked over and sniffed his pile, scrunched her face, and backed away. She headbutted his leg and rubbed the side of her body on him.

Tim reached down and scratched her head.

Braern shook his head with his hand on his chest. At their feet was a harpie-platypus hybrid, but unlike the ones who flew at them earlier, it was horribly deformed. A platypus head protruded from its belly, with its oozing mouth and black eyes open. Its wings were broken, with most of its feathers fallen off beside it. A talon protruded from its harpie head and through its long, dark hair. Two legs shared the same base, one with a fin and one like a bird's. Another leg was crushed behind its back, hardly visible underneath its hide. A beaver-like, brown tail stuck halfway out of its chest. Bulges and lumps covered its body—a disfigured mix of two creatures.

"I hate to add more bad news, but look down thir." Araduk stepped a ways away from them and stood at the top of a steep, rocky hill, peering down. He gestured for them to follow.

Braern and Moira raced over.

Tim lost his balance at first, but stood and ambled to his friends.

Moira gasped, while Braern closed his eyes and looked away with a long exhale, feeling the cool tears stream down his face.

"What could be worse than"—Tim peered over the edge at the carcasses below. Hundreds of platypus-harpie hybrids lay on the forest floor, mangled, deformed, and lifeless—"this." Tim vomited again.

A groan sounded.

"What was that?" Braern squinted to catch any movement.

"Look! One's alive down there!" Moira skirted down the hill as sand kicked up behind her in a dust cloud. She stepped over numerous bodies and slid to a barely moving creature several feet from her.

Araduk followed as Tim regained his composure, scooped Blue into his arms, and descended.

Braern flew over. When he landed, he carefully placed his feet to not disturb the bodies.

Tim reached the bottom and placed his cat friend in his backpack. He tiptoed over, wiping his mouth with his forearm. He knelt as a platypie with two heads lay gasping for breath. "Who did this to you?" Tim asked in the creature's native tongue.

The malformed animal screeched back as blood pooled from its mouth. It spit out a few sounds, pointing its clawed fin past the group. The poor creature gasped with wide eyes, taking its last agonizing breath.

The group hung their heads and sighed, their bodies becoming heavier with despair.

Araduk's throat tightened. If he had been there seconds sooner, he could've healed the poor creature. Angry with himself, he looked in the direction where the platypie had pointed.

"Then that's where we're goin'."

MOIRA

SANDSHOE CRABS UNDER THE STARS

Moira stood slowly and gazed at the lifeless creatures scattered over the forest floor. "I don't know about y'all, but I'm startin' to get so angry I can't even think straight." She clenched her fists as her chest hardened with knots. Her head ached as she tightened her shoulders. Her fingers turned a lighter brown while a drip of blood formed from her nails, digging into her palms. She focused on the tops of the trees rustling in the wind as she let out a piercing, agonizing scream.

Moira wiped her tears with her forearm, as she sniffed. She closed her eyes, and the world around them was silent for a moment. The repugnant smell of decay filled her nostrils, causing her to scrunch her expression and shake her head. She placed a hand over her mouth and held her breath, then moved her fingers down to her neck, gulping. Moira exhaled as more tears stained her cheeks.

"Those poor things..." Moira kept her eyes closed.

"If anyone ever hurt Blue, I don't know how I'd survive," Tim commented. He pulled off his backpack with one arm, picking up and placing his cat inside. "Stay in there, okay? I don't want you to get sick?"

Blue meowed and blinked slowly at him to show her appreciation. She fidgeted inside his bag.

"Not a single one's alive," Araduk told the others as he stepped over the creatures to search for any movement or noise. "I could've helped 'em if we were here earlier. I feel so helpless." He lowered his gaze and collapsed to the ground in an empty space with dead platypies surrounding him. He arched his back and sobbed, his hand over his eyes.

"We cannot let this happen to any other beings." Braern placed his hand over his heart, shaking his head. He gritted his teeth with eyes closed, his pulse visible in his neck. "Let's channel our energy into finding our enemy and stopping him."

"Ye're right. No sense in sittin' around mourning their deaths when we can do somethin'." Araduk rose, wiping sandy leaves from his robe and boots.

Everyone dried their tears and adjusted themselves.

They walked, with Braern in the lead, around the trees and over branches and piles of sandy leaves, their feet crunching on the forest floor. Blue hopped out of the backpack and trekked close to her human, despite several scents of nearby rodents catching her attention.

Tim heard a growl in his belly. He paused to rummage through his bag. "Anyone want a snack?" he asked as he found granola bars in an outside pocket of his backpack. "They're kinda smashed, but they'll do, for now." Tim distributed red-and-white-wrapped goodies to his friends.

The group gladly accepted his offering as they stopped in a clearing. Moira unwrapped hers and placed it in her mouth. The sweet, chocolate goodness sent a shock through her teeth. The chewy oats and peanut butter satisfied her hunger. When she finished, she threw her trash behind her without looking.

Tim stopped and picked it up, frowning, but said nothing.

Araduk pulled on both ends but couldn't figure out how to open his snack, scoffing. He huffed and handed it back to Tim. "Would ye mind... uh...?" The dwarf placed the plastic wrapper in Tim's hand.

"No problem." Tim pulled off the wrapper with ease and handed it back.

Araduk devoured his treat in a few bites, burped, then licked his fingers. "My apologies. That was delicious. Thank ye, lad."

Braern fiddled with the wrapper, frowning. He huffed, squinting, then managed to open it. He took two bites before it disappeared into his salivating mouth. "Yes, thank you," Braern said with a mouthful.

"Granola bars. Interestin' name for such food," Araduk commented. He licked the last crumb off of his index finger.

"Here's your food, Blue." Tim slowed his pace and picked up his kitty friend. He pulled out a bag of small, brown, rounded kibbles for her. Tim placed her inside the backpack. Then she munched from the bottom of the bag after he poured a handful inside. The bag was big enough for her to turn around in. He grabbed several water bottles from his other pocket and passed them out to his friends. Before moving on, he adjusted the bag over his shoulders to not bother Blue while she ate.

Everyone drank as they walked.

Araduk handed his garbage back as well, but Braern held onto his half-empty bottle and placed the remaining water container in his bag. "Hold on, guys. Blue needs water too." He stopped and removed a collapsible, blue, polyester bowl with paw prints on the sides. He grabbed his cat as she was still munching and held her with one arm under her belly. She adjusted herself and placed two front paws on his up-turned hand as he offered the water bowl to her. She lapped happily and purred.

Once again, he saw Moira throw her garbage on the ground. He walked the few feet to pick it up. "C'mon now, this isn't the human world. We already destroyed our world, but we should treat this one better."

"Hmm?" Moira turned around and watched him place her trash in his bag. "Oh, I'm sorry. You're right," she said with a nod.

"Could you all give me a hand?" a familiar voice with a twinge of pitch came from farther ahead.

They parted the branches before them and stepped into a clearing.

A gray fox was stuck in the sand up to its chest. Its large ears were upright with sand over its snout, screeching.

"We should help it!" Tim pointed.

"Stop staring and get me out!" Nozomi's voice came from the fox, a frown on her face.

"Nozomi!" the group hollered in unison.

"Get me out of here!" Nozomi demanded, her black paws slapping the surrounding sand.

Braern stood on the edge of the solid sand, reached in, grasped her under her arms, and pulled her out.

Nozomi stretched and shook herself to loosen the sand from her fur. She shook her bushy tail, then transformed into her human form. Inspecting herself from head to toe, she rotated her arms and legs, checked her back, and fluffed her hair to get out the last bits. She pulled her hair into a ponytail with the band from around her wrist.

Moira began, "How did you—"

Nozomi raised her hand and shook her head, closing her eyes.

Moira narrowed her eyes at her. *The least she could do is thank Braern. So rude.*

"Maybe ye should stick with us next time, lass," Araduk suggested with a half-smile as he trotted by Nozomi.

She frowned in silence and snorted with her arms folded.

Braern flew above the trees for a moment, scouting the terrain. The forest continued to the far-off mountains that were little more than desaturated, gray bumps. The landscape appeared clearer on the horizon. He turned his gaze behind him and saw the ocean.

"The ocean is behind us and the mountains are several days' walk from here! I believe the best way is to continue north!" Braern shouted to his friends below and pointed in the direction they needed to travel, with his other hand tickling the hilt of his sword. They peered up at him through the trees.

"Islands behind us and mountains ahead of us," Araduk said. "If I remember my maps, we're headed toward the Shiro Peak Mountains."

"That sounds correct," Braern said, lowering himself.

"My monastery is located atop the highest mountain. They have an impressive collection of ancient scrolls an' books on the history o' our worlds. Very quiet, peaceful place. It's where I've been for the last few years after I... chose a different path for m'self," Araduk educated the group as everyone continued on, adjusting their clothing and bags.

"Ah yes, Shiro Peak Monastery. I've heard wonderful things about the head monk, Artemis. He and my father used to train together. Perhaps my father is there. If not, we can benefit from answers that their collection could give us as to why our journey with the portals has been so taxing," Braern said.

Moira nodded. "Sounds like a plan. We could use a change of pace from all this insanity."

"What do you think, Tim?" Braern looked back at the silent boy.

His kitty climbed up and settled herself on his right shoulder, facing forward while her head bobbed as her human walked. Her tail swished as she chittered at the tiny creatures flying nearby.

"Oh... uh... sounds fine to me."

"I guess I will tag along with you if it means getting closer to this enemy," Nozomi grunted as they spread themselves out. "But you better keep up."

As the words escaped her lips, the ground vibrated beneath them. Sand swooshed as all five fell from their standing positions, unbalanced and confused.

"What's happenin'?" Araduk sat watching the ground rise from underneath them.

Braern drew his sword and pointed it downward with two hands grasping the hilt.

Moira knelt with one foot and one knee on the ground, both hands poised and ready.

Tim held Blue and tried to brace themselves.

Soon, a hard, smooth, cracked shell of an enormous creature appeared from the earth. Braern, Moira, Tim, and Blue sat atop. A second creature became visible, with Nozomi and Araduk on all fours. The pair of giants moved, causing the group to lose their balance once again. Soon the ride became smoother as the sounds of creeping feet underneath scurried along the sand at a slow pace. Little clicks resonated as the group relaxed their tense bodies.

"Looks like we're catching a ride!" Araduk laughed, open-mouthed, as his eyes crinkled. He made himself comfortable and sat with his hands behind his neck and his legs spread out, enjoying the steady motion of the wind in his beard.

"They look like giant horseshoe crabs." Tim peeked off the edge of his creature to see the tiny swooshes of insect-like legs busily walking.

"In Yumerion, they're called sandshoe crabs. I believe they migrate south every year, from what I've read. They seem harmless." Braern sheathed his sword and loosely wrapped his arms around his legs.

"Suppose they are not so bad." Nozomi joined in the relaxation.

"Maybe you could ask them to take us to the monastery?" Moira suggested as she giggled, lying flat on her back with her arms behind her head.

"Okay!" Tim said as he comforted a terrified cat that had jumped in his backpack and retreated quickly to the bottom, her body crouched in a ball. Tim placed his hands on the creature's smooth back and closed his eyes. He remained silent for several moments as everyone stared at him. "They said they're on their way to their breeding grounds, but they'll take us for as long as they can before they need to go in a different direction."

"Great! Wake me up when we get there, lad!" Araduk yawned, stretching his arms. He took a sip of his flask, then stowed it in his pocket. His bones creaked as he settled down and snored with his mouth open, drooling.

"Such loud sounds coming from such a small man." Nozomi chuckled.

"I know! Right? Wonder what's in that flask of his. Whatever it is, it must be strong enough to knock him out in a second." Moira laughed, watching a pool of drool escape Araduk's bottom lip and disappear into his beard. "Men... *pfft.*"

"I'll take the first watch." Braern eyed his friends, smiling at the tranquility of the night.

"I'll stay up with you," Moira said, smiling through heavy eyes. She yawned, patting her mouth.

Tim lay curled up as Blue emerged from her bag. She baked biscuits on his arm for a few moments, then snuggled up to her human with his hand on her paw.

Moira sat next to Braern with her knees to her chin, her eyes lowered but not quite asleep. She noticed Braern sat upright, alert and watchful.

"You can sleep. I don't mind keeping watch." Braern nodded to her.

"Nah, it's all right. Sleep is for the dead. I don't wanna miss anything. This whole journey has been a trip," she told him, knowing she was exhausted, but her mind was too busy.

Braern and Moira giggled, then stargazed. A dark navy-blue blanket of white sparkles were scattered across the sky.

"The stars in your world are the same as mine," Moira said. "They really are beautiful, no matter where you are."

"Yes, they are," Braern said.

Merely a foot lay between them. As her gaze lay on the twinkling stars, his was on her. Her long, dark braids tickled her skin as they waved in the cool breeze. A few strands fluttered from her face across her ear. She shook her head, bent her knees, and sat cross-legged. She gracefully gathered all her braids into a bun on top of her head and secured them with a hair tie from her bag. Then she lowered her arms, her hands lying flat on the crab's back.

Braern inched his fingers toward hers. He stopped, looking up, his face blushing as he averted his eyes away from her. The dark of night made it much easier to disguise his red-hot cheeks. He took a long breath, his chest and the sides of his head pounding, and placed his fingertips on hers.

Moira flinched for a moment, redirecting her gaze to the elf beside her. "Oh, Braern. I can't. I—"

"It's all right, milady. I apologize if I overstepped." Braern gulped and retracted his hand.

"You didn't. I... don't want to hurt you." She closed her eyes for a long moment as her eyes watered, her lips quivering. She blinked several times as tears streaked her face. Her mind filled with images of broken picture frames of her ex-boyfriend, bloody with shards of glass embedded in his arm as he slammed her door shut, leaving her. She cried, distracted by her thoughts, with a painful lump formed in her throat. Gazing at the stars soothed her.

"You won't hurt me. I hate to see you cry. I did not intend to upset you." Braern sat on his hands and stared at his lap.

"No, it's not you. I... my ex-boyfriend said the same thing. He said it didn't bother him... until it did. The last time I saw him, he was walking out of my life forever. We were arguing about something stupid, like marriage. I barely touched him and... he fell on the glass table. I didn't... wasn't..." Her chest ached as she fought to say the words.

"I'm sure it wasn't your fault," Braern said in a soothing tone, biting his lip, his arms trembling.

"It was. I can't control myself. I use most of my energy every day to keep myself from hurting any of you. It's exhausting." Moira paused and gazed at her friend. "I especially don't want to hurt you, Braern. You're the first... elf I've met here, or anywhere, and you've showed me more kindness than I deserve."

"You deserve more than you give yourself." Braern sighed and studied her agonized face.

"How do you know what I deserve?"

"You saved a man's life yesterday. You deserve happiness."

"I don't know if I believe that anymore. Maybe some people aren't meant to be happy. I've hurt so many people. I've hurt you. That book fell on your head and..." Moira buried her head in her arms, pulling her legs closer. *There's no way I can let myself have feelings for this guy. I met him days ago. But those eyes...*

"I'm fine. Look at me. You will never hurt me again. I'll ensure it." He mumbled incoherently to himself in another language, fumbling inside his satchel with one hand.

"What'd you say?" She wiped tears from her eyes as she sniffed, meeting his gaze once again.

Moira heard silence. Araduk's snoring stopped. She looked over Braern's shoulder to the other crab. Their friends had vanished.

Braern's head shot upright as he followed her gaze. Empty. He stood, bracing himself with his legs spread apart as the undulating movements continued. "Where is everyone?"

"Where'd they go?" Moira echoed as she scooted on her hands and knees to the back of the crab's shell. She peered over as the moonlight reflected onto the sand tracks.

Braern stretched his body to look over the edge at her.

"I don't see them!" the duo shouted together as they surveyed the area in the dark.

The clouds parted as a speck of light appeared in the air a short distance from them.

"Wait! What's that?" Moira pointed. A shimmer of light reflected in a half circle above their view. Moira jumped down and ran toward it, followed by a flying Braern.

They looked back as the enormous sandshoe crabs vanished down a hill.

The shimmer stood above them, three times their height.

"Do you think that's another portal?" Moira asked.

"Only one way to find out." Braern grabbed her hand and leaped into the air.

This time, Moira didn't pull away.

TIM

THE HOCKEY GAME

A deep horn sound resonated through the air. Tim rubbed his arms while the lower temperature tickled his ears and nose. He exhaled, watching a mist escape his mouth. Blinking, he saw a white light blur through his eyelids as his vision focused. The stench of sweaty men surrounded him as several players wearing large jerseys in blue, yellow, and white, skated around a stadium, full of gawking people. The opposing team wore green and black. He heard someone cough. Four enormous televisions hung at the top, each facing a different direction. Two goals with nets lay on each end of the rink.

"Where the hell did you guys come from? What was that weird light circle?" A player slid to a halt, flinging ice shavings onto Tim's face. The bitter cold made his shivers shiver.

"You appeared out of nowhere!" another player hollered, his hand on his stick. He offered Tim a thick-gloved hand. "What was up with that light?"

"Oh no, how did we end up here?" Tim asked, sinking his neck into his shoulders from all the people staring at him. His face heated and cooled all at once.

Braern eyed the players' strange footwear. "Why do you all have blades attached to your boots? What purpose does that serve?"

"They're skates." The man removed his mouthpiece and sucked back some drooling saliva.

"What are *skates?*"

"You're a funny dude." The player laughed without answering. "But y'all really need to get off the ice. Game's gonna start."

"Am I dreaming?" Tim blinked again and rubbed his eyes as he stood with help. He watched the rest of the team help Araduk, Nozomi, Braern, and Moira to their feet. He ripped open his backpack, severing the zipper—empty. *A hockey game? I was thinking about this place yesterday. That can't be a coincidence.* Tim's eyes widened, and his heart raced as he turned in circles, holding his head. "Where's Blue?" he screamed in agony, his voice breaking.

They led the group off the ice and through the low-swinging, white door as the crowd returned to their seats.

Tim whipped his eyes in every direction. The ruckus had ended, but his mind was cluttered with his worst nightmares. *Is she hurt? Is she hungry? Is she trapped?*

"Hey, are ye all right, lad?" Araduk placed a hand on his shoulder.

"I need... my cat. I can't... breathe." Tim gasped, his hand patting his neck. His entire body convulsed as he lost his balance and fell from a seated position to his side with his cheek on the hard floor. His eyes narrowed; sweat poured from his forehead and dripped into his mouth. He tasted the warm salt. The excruciating pain in his skull silenced any coherent thoughts.

"We need to help him!" Moira ran to his side and her legging rubbed his arm.

For that second, he forgot. Then that second ended. Several hands rubbed his back, which distracted from his attack. His arms and legs were paralyzed, but he could hear and see everything going on around him. He couldn't react to anything. His erratic breathing continued as simply blinking his eyes felt exhausting.

"Tim?" Braern reassured him as he pulled his arm over his shoulder and dragged him up the cement stairs, his knees scraping against the corners of the steps. "We're gonna get you out of here, okay? Hold on."

"B-Blue!"

"Yeah, we'll find her. I promise," Moira said.

"Guys? You need to come look at this," Nozomi warned.

"What else could go wrong?" Moira shook her head and turned around to where Nozomi was pointing.

A rumbling, shadowy figure flew through the rafters. Every eye but Tim's gazed above at the creature. Shocked whispers and gasps echoed through the arena. With a shrill cry, a blinding bolt fell from above. Right in the middle of the stadium was an orange circle, bleeding from its center and growing larger and brighter. Beneath it, the ice melted as the temperature in the room rose. Stiff bodies were no longer cold. Then the flames grew from its center, melting the entire ice rink, leaving a shallow pool of water. The top half of the creature glowed an orange hue as it expanded with a bellowing roar. By now, terrified people were wailing, and the players were speed-skating off the ice, screaming at one another and ripping off their skates to scurry to the exits.

"Dammit! I hate being so right all the time!" Moira yelled.

The flying figure shot a flaming projectile toward the stairs where they stood.

"Let's move!" Araduk hollered as he and Nozomi shoved the rest of their friends out of the way, seconds before the blast hit underneath them. A crater appeared where it hit and smoke overwhelmed their senses. Coughing and gasping for breath, they waved the smoke from their faces. An intense heat wave rushed over them. Blisters formed on their feet.

They climbed the stairs with Moira and Braern carrying Tim, wiping sweat from their brows. The boy looked back in time to see the fire swallow a Zamboni and several rows of bleachers. The nearest television came crashing down as electric wires flung about with white sparks shooting everywhere. Tim thought of his beloved feline friend engulfed in flames, sending tears dripping from his eyes that instantly evaporated.

They reached the top of the stairs. Nozomi looked back to see if anyone else needed help to get the hell out of the inferno. No one did. The humans had left in time.

"Alright, there's the exit. We need to get outta here, now!" Moira screamed as the flames reached above.

The second television crashed to the ice and exploded into millions of pieces while the ceiling collapsed in an ear-piercing mesh of wires and metal scrapings. As they reached the top of the stairs, a familiar meowing approached them.

"Blue!" Braern yelled as the little gray cat bounded toward them, meowing through the roar of the flames.

She stood in front of them for a second, then ran off a few yards, stopped, and meowed again as loud as her little lungs could.

"What are you trying to tell us, cat?" Nozomi asked, watching the flames roaring closer. "We need to snap Tim out of it so he can talk to her!" She slapped Tim's face, to no avail.

"That was harsh!" Moira frowned.

"We do not have time for this!" Nozomi transformed herself into a flaming phoenix and flew above Blue. "This way!" She motioned with her bright wings.

"Follow that moggy and the bird!" Araduk shoved them toward the nearest hallway, and the flames clawed at their heels as they ran to the exit.

They arrived on the second floor of the stadium. Nozomi flew above. Blue scurried away to stop at a bathroom, keeping her ears and tail down. Screams came from inside as several people banged on the door. She perked up her ears and tilted her head as she sneezed. A metal beam had fallen in front of it, blocking them inside. The flames crept even closer as they wiped sweat from their eyes with shirts and arms.

"Someone's in there!" Braern hollered as the fire reached closer.

They moved as far out of the way as they could while still being within reach of the door.

"Help! Let us out!" several voices sounded at once from inside.

Moira placed Tim on the floor, while Braern held the unresponsive teen by himself. She grunted and pushed the beam. The metal shook, but it didn't budge. With her bottom lip out, she aimed and blew air upward so the sweat would fly out of her eyes.

Nozomi screeched and Blue scratched at the door so the victims would know they weren't alone.

"Gah! Okay, this isn't working. Watch him. Stand back." Her skin glistened with excessive perspiration. She took a deep breath and shoved her bag out of the way. Then she wrapped both arms around the beam and bent her knees, positioning herself under the metal. The sound of sizzling flesh filled their ears. She groaned in pain as she lifted the beam from the door then threw it away from her friends. It slammed on the floor as their feet vibrated. The door was free.

Araduk flung it open, and three young kids and two adults fell onto them. Blue ran out of the way to avoid being squished.

"Thank you!" the man screamed, his face shining with sweat. He looked up and shielded his family behind him. "Is that a flaming bird? What is happening?"

"No time for questions! We need to get outta here, right now! This whole place is coming down!" Moira urged, ignoring the bubbling burns on her hands, and stepped on a flame that reached her boot. She grabbed Tim and flung him over her shoulder once more.

"There's the exit! We need to leave, now!" Braern shouted as the roar of the flames crept closer.

Clothing caked to their skin as their tongues lost all moisture. Beads of sweat dripped into their mouths. The group ran as fast as they could with the family close behind. They came to the top of the elevator. Ear-piercing rumbles and cracks sounded from above.

"Look out!" Moira pushed the two kids out of the way of a falling air duct. She fell onto her side, wincing while holding her arm. She dropped Tim as Blue ran over to her human.

"Wake up, human! You must get up!"

Tim heard her cries in his mind and willed his muscles to move, but they didn't. *Why can't I move?* Her little head rubbed his hand. Still, his body and mind seemed separated, even after feeling her touch.

"I got you," Moira groaned as she heaved him over her shoulder again.

The air duct blocked the elevator. "We can't use the elevator in a fire! Let's try the stairs!" the dad shouted, pointing in the right direction. "Hurry!"

They followed him as the inferno consumed the entire ceiling. No one could see where they were going from the smoke that filled the entrance.

"Get down to the floor, like this!" the mom ordered. She crouched on all fours, coughing and spitting, her clothes covered in ash.

They obeyed as the cat ran ahead and stopped as the open area for the stairs appeared. Moira adjusted Tim as she walked on her hand and both knees. Her other palm held Tim in place on her back, her elbow outstretched at the side of her head.

"Right here!" Nozomi hollered through her beak. She pointed with her wings once again, but the smoke inhibited their vision from seeing most of her fiery body.

"Why is that bird talking?" the dad asked, panting. Everyone ignored him.

The ceiling shook. Cracks echoed through the walls as the roaring inferno followed them to the stairwell. Crouching low and coughing, they crossed their arms over their necks, bracing for impact.

BRAERN

BATTLE OF THE DRAGONS

Braern's hands sparked; his face twisted as he conjured a white pearlescent convex shield around everyone.

"Wow! I didn't know... you could do that!" Moira coughed through her words.

"I don't know how long this will hold." Every part of him shook as he clenched his teeth, spreading his fingers to hold the shield in place.

"What the hell is this?" the father yelled as his family inched away from the glowing elf.

"No time for questions! We need to move!" Nozomi ordered, flicking her tail toward the way out.

Blue and the group followed, crouching on their hands and knees.

Wonder if I can take this shield with me? Braern struggled to shift the magic from one hand to the other. His biceps ached from the mental and physical anguish of moving through such a sweltering environment while protecting his friends. Soon, he rejoined the group as they pulled themselves along the floor. He held the shield in place over the top of his friends while limping along like a three-legged dog.

"It's holdin'. Keep movin'!" Araduk coughed.

Another crash. Metal shards fell onto the shield and splintered it in half. The roar of flames continued as the ceiling had pockets of writhing waves of fire galloping along. Everyone hacked, gasping as the air thickened.

"Meow!" Blue screeched, pawing at the air in front of her. She found a door that was labeled, ROOF ACCESS.

"Going up!" Moira hollered, her lips cracking. On the balls of her feet, she crouched with bent knees and tested the doorknob, moving her shoulder under Tim's belly. "Ow!" she hissed and recoiled her hand, shaking, as her fingers reddened. She shook her injured hand, grimacing from the pain. She laid the catatonic Tim on the floor next to her, his vacant eyes staring at nothing. "It's... locked!" She stuttered and wiped the sweat from her forehead with her arm. "We need to get up there. We're running out of time."

"Can ye break down... the door?" Araduk asked, panting.

Moira shook her head. "I barely... have the strength to carry this dude." She gestured toward Tim.

"Let me try." Braern outstretched his arms and squinted at the doorknob, attempting to unlock it with a single hand of magic. A spark of white formed as he concentrated on aiming the energy toward the doorknob. The magical energy transformed into a key shape, floating in the air, and slid it inside the lock. He imagined the inside components moving out of the way of his magical key that he had formed.

Another crash.

"Ceiling is cavin' in!" Araduk placed his palms above his head, crouching to the floor.

The windows shattered from the heat and threw glass shards in all directions.

Braern blinked, and the energy vanished.

"I'm sorry... I almost had it," he whimpered.

"Mommy, are we gonna die?" the little girl asked as her parents held her, studying the unwavering shield above them as more pieces of the ceiling fell and splintered off to the side.

Blue climbed over the array of bent knees to the girl and put a tiny gray paw on her lap to comfort her.

"No, we're going to get out of here. I promise," the mom's voice wavered as a tear ran down her cheek. She held her little girl's head, kissed her, and pulled her hair out of her face. Her tears instantly evaporated.

"You cannot promise the kid that!" Nozomi, in phoenix form, scolded her.

"Why is that bird talking?" the mom screamed. "I think... we're hallucinating, sweetie."

"I will go under the door," Nozomi growled. The *kitsune* transformed into a tiny, dark lizard, squashed herself under the door, then unlocked it from the outside. She flung it open and motioned for everyone to get up and follow her. Then she was human again in a matter of seconds.

Braern grabbed Blue as she yelped, lifting her into his arms. He knew Tim would never forgive him if anything happened to her. The smoke snaked through the stairway to the roof, but it was not as thick and toxic. Braern waved everyone through the doorway. Araduk was the last. The elf released his shield as a large beam crashed down, blocking the other side of the door. He slammed it shut with a thud. "Let's move!"

They ran up the stairs as fast as their legs could carry them. Up, up, up, three flights of stairs, they reached the roof.

Braern looked down the stairwell at where they had come from. The gray smoke had thickened so much he couldn't see anything past a few feet in front of him.

Moira, with Tim still over her left shoulder, crashed through the door with her right arm and collapsed outside the door onto the concrete roof, skidding her arm. The cool, night air soothed everyone as they fell down, coughing in a heap of exhausted bodies.

"We made it... all of us." Araduk's arms and legs had never had such a workout in his life. His muscles ached from such exertion. He forced his shaking head up to witness his friends breathing heavily.

As soon as they were safely outside the roof door, sounds of sirens resonated from the ground. Dozens of police cars, ambulances, and firetrucks parked by the entrance of the hockey stadium. Blue and red lights reflected on the sides of the building as shouting sounded from down below. Firefighters connected their hoses and sprayed gushing water onto the still burning building as the air filled with more smoke that reached the clouds. People scurried to contain the fire.

A deep rumble bellowed in pitchy tones that sounded like a creature had swallowed a metric ton of gravel. The stadium trembled as a dark figure loomed over the edge of the roof: the same creature from inside who started the disaster. Ebony claws grasped the edge as it pulled itself upright. Glowing yellow eyes pierced their souls as smoke rose from its nostrils. Pointed horns sat on its enormous reptilian head, and it locked eyes with the group on the roof.

Their eyes widened and mouths opened in pure terror.

A dragon.

It spread its large wings and inhaled a huge breath.

The group watched, coughing and unable to stand, backed up, and scooted in the opposite direction.

"You're the one who set this stadium on fire!" Moira yelled in horror, watching the dark blue beast scramble onto the roof. "I finally meet a dragon, and he's tryin' to kill us! Figures."

"Mommy! It's a dragon!" the little girl hollered to her mother, struck with fear and paralyzed, as her skin turned white.

The family's eyes widened, lips quivering.

The mom held her breath as the dad spread his arms, attempting to protect his tiny family from such a shocking creature. "It is a dragon!" he screamed.

Moira dragged an unresponsive Tim by his arm. Everyone soon reached the edge of the roof and could go no farther. A brave Blue refused to leave her human's side. The terrified feline arched her back and fluffed out her fur, hissing at the enormous beast as it crept closer, acid dripping from its gnarled jaws.

"I will move you humans to safety. This isn't your battle." Braern wiped the gray ash off his fingers and wiggled them to free his mind. He formed a cocoon made of wind big enough to fit the family. His hair blew backward from the breeze. "Climb in! It'll float you to the bottom!" the tired elf ordered, still unsteady about his newly developed ability.

The father complied, grabbing the hands of his stunned family inside with him.

Braern placed his hand out flat and blew, as if it were a tiny bubble mere inches from his lips.

The family drifted slowly down to the side of the building and disappeared.

Braern felt confident they would be safe.

The dragon looked over the barrier. He pressed his claws into the concrete, ready to prey on the unsuspecting humans below.

Araduk whipped his gaze at the beast. "Yer qualm is with us! Leave them alone!" the dwarf yelled with his lips drawn.

Braern stood up at lightning speed and drew his sword. "Back, dragon! You don't belong in this world!" the elf said, stifling any wobbliness he may have felt, and renewed adrenaline overcame his body. *Neither do I.* His muscles tensed; his breath came fast as he tightened the grip on his sword, causing his fingers to turn white.

The dragon lunged its long neck straight at the elf, who led it away from his friends.

He sidestepped to the opposite area of the roof, kicking up dusty gravel in his path, his attention unwavering. He knew dragons were notoriously quick and witty. Any slight mistake could cost him his life.

The beast followed, lashing its spiked tail and slamming it with various thuds. The dragon inhaled as its chest glowed orange through its dark scales.

Radiating light formed all around them, nearly blinding the elf. *He means to cook me.* Remembering his spell, he quickly conjured a magical shield that appeared in his left hand's grasp. With his sword prepared to make its mark, he readied for the beast to make another move.

The dragon bellowed and hissed as its chest grew twice its size. It paused, then opened its mouth and blew a wave of fire at the elf, forcing him backward against the gravel, his boots leaving marks on the roof. He stumbled by the edge, but he regained his balance, ready for its next move.

"We've gotta wake up Tim! He's the only one who can talk some sense into that dragon." Moira wiped the sweat from her forehead with her arm and shook Tim's shoulder.

His head bobbed, but he did not move.

"Wake up, Tim! We need you!" Nozomi yelled in his ear.

"I'll handle this, lass." Araduk slapped Tim across the face.

He woke up instantly. Tim looked all around, frantic and boiling hot, his cheeks flushed rosy-pink.

"Rrrow!" Blue greeted her human and stood with her tail raised. She rubbed her head on Tim's side.

"Blue! I'm so glad you're safe!" He hugged his cat, then felt a sting on his left cheek. He rubbed it with his dirty hand; a swatch of dirt appeared. He blinked to force his eyes to see through the blur.

"What is... is that a dragon? It's a dragon! We need to get outta here!" Tim backed up and knocked a loose piece of concrete onto the ground below. He twisted his body to look over the edge, then back at the chaos before them.

"Stand yer ground, lad. Braern can handle this." Araduk nodded toward the poised elf.

The dragon swiped the sword from Braern's hand with his tail, sending it spinning in circles across the roof, and it landed several yards from the elf.

"Or not."

"I'm going." Moira pushed herself upright from the dirty roof and ran off to help. She stumbled, caught her balance with one hand on the roof, and rose again. She surveyed the dragon as it crept closer to Braern.

He held out a hand, quietly begging his sword to return and forcing his eyes to stay on the dragon. Out of the corner of his eye, he witnessed Moira heading toward the creature. A twinge in his chest, he imagined her body inside its jaws as it clamped down. He shuddered at such a thought and forced it from his mind.

Moira laid eyes on the dragon's spiked tail thrashing around and narrowed her eyes on her target. As she inched forward, she tripped over a hammer left on the roof and fell to the ground with a thud.

The dragon shot its deadly gaze her way, hissing.

"Shit!" Moira pursed her lips and stood quickly. She readied her curled fingers as she held her hands in the air.

The dragon clawed its way toward her, mouth open as it snarled, ignoring Braern as he ran to grab his sword. As it reached Moira, its jaws were nearly upon her.

She reached and grabbed its top tooth with one hand and bottom with the other, forcing its enormous mouth to stay open. As it thrashed, she felt its mighty power overcome her as she channeled all her strength into remaining in position.

Filling with rage, the dragon inhaled, throat open, as its chest glowed once again.

"Damn." Her eyes widened as her brow raised, her jaw loosening, shaking uncontrollably. Moira closed her eyes as the orange light from inside the dragon's throat blinded her. Acid spilled onto her arms from its saliva, burning her flesh. She clenched her teeth, ignoring the searing pain.

Braern came from the side and slammed his magical shield onto the dragon's head at an angle, as Moira released its fangs from her grasp. Braern's force slammed the dragon's mouth shut as flames oozed from its nostrils and teeth.

The dragon grew more out of control, its back legs kicking frantically as its tail smacked the roof every which way. It recoiled its head from the duo, then lashed its snout toward them, sending them both flying over the nearest edge of the roof.

Moira screamed.

Before they were about to hit the top of a white police car, Braern's shield disappeared as he tightly wrapped his arms around Moira and took off toward the dragon, through the air. She stared at him, chest heaving, with her arms around his neck.

Several people in uniforms, as well as civilians sitting in blankets, looked up to see the two flying. Shocked expressions overcame the people on the ground.

Braern flew them up and above the dragon. For a moment, it was bliss—even through the stench of burned fabric and their bodies drenched in sweat. Then the moment came to a halt as the dragon narrowed its glowing yellow eyes and leaped into the air in hot pursuit.

"It is my turn now." Nozomi shook her head and opened her mouth, sighing. She still ached from the fire, but she had no choice now. She hurried a few feet in front of Tim, Araduk, and Blue and transformed herself into an ebony, Eastern dragon with a slender, scaled body and long, black hair around its horns. Her eyes shone blue and bright, with a feminine crease on her lids. She lashed her tail, getting used to her new reptilian body for a moment, as she lifted each hand and twisted herself in a circle. She jumped into the air and headed toward the Western dragon.

"Is that Nozomi?" Moira shouted, looking down, as another dragon hurled toward them, growing bigger by the second.

Braern saw and zipped in a different direction, confusing the blue dragon.

It stopped in time for Nozomi to crash into it, claws outstretched, roaring.

Braern flew Moira to the roof and toward Tim, Araduk, and Blue. Exhausted, they collapsed as they watched the night sky.

The dragons intertwined as flames flashed through the air. Nozomi struck the dragon with her vicious teeth as it breathed fire in a veiled attempt to fry her. The two reptiles flew toward the group as the dragon growled.

Tim's eyes panned back and forth as he tried to make sense of what the dragon was saying. "I don't want to be here..."

The reptilian duo clashed and flew higher into the night sky, swiping claws and lashing tails.

"Is that what ye heard? What else did it say?" Araduk asked.

"I don't think it came here willingly. I think it's defending itself against us."

"It tried to burn us alive!" Moira shouted from the flat of her back, catching her breath.

"It's scared, and maybe it didn't know what it was doing."

"I have an idea, but I need help." Braern turned his head to face his friends.

"Whatever ye need. No tellin' how much longer Nozomi will last up thir," Araduk reassured him.

A glowing light filled the sky again as bright flames illuminated a patch of clouds. The two dragons shrieked as smoke engulfed their bodies. Soon, smog permeated the entire sky as the Western dragon breathed fire in every direction, twisting and turning as its flames narrowly missed Nozomi.

"I hope I can replicate this spell again. I've only done it once with a fire wyrm. That dragon didn't ask to be thrown into the human world. We have no right to kill it. However, there is one problem."

"What?" Araduk asked.

"I've never completed the spell on a moving, living creature before, especially not one that's flailing around up there."

"Seriously? Well, you better learn fast, man!" Moira shouted as the clashes in the air became more prevalent and louder.

They heard deep growls and shrill cries as the two dragons clawed at each other, hissing and spitting. A fireball flew down from the sky and landed right next to an ambulance, shaking the ground. Several car alarms sounded as the building beneath them shook. The fireball dissipated, leaving an immense crater on the dark asphalt.

"We'd better hurry before anyone else gets hurt," Araduk urged.

"I have a plan, but I'll need all of your help."

"Whatever you need. We're in this," Tim agreed.

"Tim, I need you to translate what the dragon is saying."

"What about me?" Moira asked.

"I need you to hold down the dragon long enough for me to cast the shrinking spell."

"You got it."

"Alright, I'm going to go entice the dragons to come this way." Braern nodded to his friends and leaped into the air toward the clashing beasts. Braern kept his distance for a few moments. *How did I do this last time? I remember imagining the wyrm shrinking. I had already killed it, though; this will prove to be difficult.*

Nozomi and the dragon clawed at each other while zooming through the air.

The blue dragon whipped free from Nozomi's grasp and bit her neck.

Screeching in pain, she lashed her tail and wrapped it around its neck. She pulled with all her strength as its jaws dislodged from her scaly hide. Yellow acid penetrated her skin and dug deep into her wound, mixing with blood.

Snarling and hissing, the blue dragon batted its wings, sending waves of wind at Nozomi, and knocked her backward.

She thrust forward and zipped her body around the dragon, like an anaconda squeezing its prey. Rendering the blue one flightless, the two dragons plummeted toward the ground, their faces cold from the night air.

"Now might be a good time for a plan!" Nozomi screamed at Braern, who zipped down to meet them.

The blue dragon snarled and writhed, trying desperately to free itself.

Nozomi held tight, unsure of what would happen next.

"I need it on the roof!" Braern yelled.

The entangled mess of dragons rotated and stalled their descent while Nozomi guided them back.

The blue dragon took a deep breath to breathe fire again, smoke seeping from its nostrils.

Nozomi gasped and quickly used her free claws to clamp its snout shut.

It swallowed the lump in its throat and grimaced from the pain; its belly returned to its navy-blue hue.

Braern slowly flew backward to the roof where his friends were waiting, keeping a sharp eye on the duo before him.

The dragon snarled and mumbled to itself. As the dragon softly lay onto the roof, it succumbed to its hold, thrashing less. The tired creature bellowed through a closed mouth.

"I think he said something about missing his family. He's a *he,* by the way," Tim said.

"Don't wanna know how you figured that out." Moira raised an eyebrow, pushed herself upright, and stumbled over to the action. "Did you lift its tail when we weren't looking?"

Tim shook his head. Araduk and Blue stayed behind. The cat hissed, then huddled behind a nearby black, metal trash can with its paint peeling off, revealing rust underneath.

"Could use some help!" Nozomi hollered.

Moira climbed on top of the dragon and held its mouth shut as Nozomi released her claws from its jaws.

"Wait, let him talk." Tim approached carefully with one hand out. He stopped right in front of the fire-breathing beast, who stared at him.

They paused as their bodies reflected in each other's eyes. The dragon blinked as he placed a hand on the top of its snout, then rubbed his smooth, cool scales.

The boy bellowed, finding himself speaking in the strange tongue of dragons, flinching with a raised eyebrow from the deep ways of his voice.

"You sure you wanna risk him tryin' to fry us again? This ain't McDonalds," Moira said.

"Let him talk," Tim reiterated.

Moira slowly released her grasp.

Nozomi sighed as she ached from keeping the dragon steady with her body, her tail flat on the roof.

Tim spoke to the dragon, in guttural, inhuman tones, as he placed a hand on his belly. The two conversed for what seemed like ages.

"What are you two talking about? Get to the point! Tell him what your plan is!" Nozomi yelled. "What exactly is your plan?"

"We'll shrink him into an orb and release him back in Yumerion," Braern answered.

Nozomi rolled her eyes and nodded.

The bellowing dragon speech ended, and Tim faced his friends. "This is Telzraug. He has a mate and two hatchlings and would very much like to return home. He only set the stadium on fire because he was forced through a portal and got caught in some nearby power lines, then flew inside. Nearly killed him. Tried to free himself, but then spit fire to burn the wires off of him, which reached the ice and... yeah."

"So, why'd he come after us? We didn't do anything to him," Moira asked, staring at the dragon's enormous tail.

Tim turned and spoke to Telzraug once again. "He said he could sense our magic and felt threatened by us."

"We're threatening? Am not threatening. Look at me! Ha!" Araduk joked.

"Let's stay on task, everyone. Tell him we intend to send him home if he will allow us to shrink him. We can't bring him with us in his current state," Braern urged.

Tim relayed the message.

Telzraug relaxed his tense muscles as Nozomi's grip loosened.

"He says, 'Anything to get back to my family.'"

"Wonderful. You can release him, Nozomi. Thank you."

"As you wish, but if he eats us all, it is on you." She snorted, letting her body go. She turned herself into a human and stepped away.

Moira stood next to Nozomi.

The dragon shook his body and fanned his wings. He crouched for a moment, as if he were about to jump into the air, but stopped himself. He approached Braern and nodded.

"Alright, here goes! Everyone else stand behind me. Don't want to shrink any of you," the elf beckoned.

The group obliged.

Telzraug faced Braern and bowed.

"You know, I've read in books that dragons have a very hard time trusting anyone, except other dragons. Please don't hurt him," Tim shrieked quietly, unsure if Braern heard.

Braern blinked, imprinting Tim's words in his mind. *My father must've spent years learning to trust me, then.* Braern took a deep breath and stared at the dragon in front of him. It occurred to him that he had never been so close to another dragon in his life—such beautiful creatures with such underappreciated elegance and intelligence. His father was the only one he ever met. He exhaled and shook his arms to relax, rotating his neck to the left and right.

"What was it? That's right... *hidogaru!*"

The dragon shook as it watched its wings and legs grow larger.

"Wait! No! That's not right! Stop!" Braern yelled, extending his hands.

The dragon grumbled as it inspected its body, unsure of what to do. Soon, its enlarging body forced trash cans and pillars out of the way.

"Braern! Make it stop! It's going to take down the entire building!" Moira screamed, feeling the roof shake, as cracks formed and headed straight for the group.

"Yameru!" Braern shouted.

The dragon stopped growing. Now it was nearly twice its size as the roof began to cave in.

"Chi... chijimu!" he shouted again, closing his eyes, unsure if he wanted to see the aftermath of his spell this time. Forcing his right eyelid to peek open, he saw the dragon shrinking. He heard relieved sighs behind him as the dragon flapped its wings. *"Owaru!"* Braern said again.

Now the size of a small mouse, the dragon squeaked and ran to Braern. Blue appeared from behind her human and wiggled her butt, ready to pounce on the tiny creature.

"No, Blue! Stay back!" Tim warned her. She growled and swished her tail back and forth, remaining at his side.

The elf scooped the tiny creature into his hand as the dragon exhaled a breath of fire to relieve its uncomfortable belly. Braern barely stepped backward, then summoned another orb from the air. He placed the dragon inside.

Once sealed, it froze in suspended animation, like the fire wyrm. It would need neither food, water, nor sleep until Braern awoke the creature when they returned home.

Araduk, Tim, and Moira rushed over to witness the tiny frozen dragon in the orb before Braern placed it in his satchel for safekeeping.

Nozomi passed out nearby, snoring.

"Wow! That's so cool!" Tim gasped, wide eyes twinkling in amazement.

"Ye did good, lad," Araduk reassured him with a pat on the shoulder.

"It's cool... I guess," Moira said, stifling a smile.

"What are you talking about? That was really something," Braern retorted playfully, watching the creases of her mouth as she released the white smile.

"It was so cool! Can you teach me sometime?" she begged, grinning. Moira placed her hand on Braern's arm, gazing at him.

"Of course, milady."

The two locked eyes. Braern felt her touch radiating through his body. Time froze. His arm shivered from the urge to caress her dark braids. He remembered her wishes and remained motionless.

Then she walked back to the others.

Braern relaxed his shoulders and soothed his mind with a few long breaths; his eyes closed, listening to the sounds of the sirens. *Will I ever have the chance to tell her? Perhaps, when we aren't fighting for our lives...*

A flash of red appeared across his vision, once again. *This has happened before.* He froze as a new vision flooded his mind. With one eye shut, he struggled to keep the other open. A weight pulled on his body, begging for him to sleep. His legs wobbled as he touched every available surface in their path to try to keep his balance. The elf placed a hand on his head. He saw a large white fist and a misshapen mound of a face without eyes. *A white fist? No eyes? What? I don't understand what my mind is telling me.*

"Braern?" Moira asked, leaning closer to him. He felt her hot breath on his shoulder.

"I saw something... but I fear I'm too exhausted to put it into words. I need... rest." he answered.

"We all do."

BLUE

THE CAVE

Lights flashed and high-pitched wails hurt Blue's flattened ears. The air smelled of burned metal. She wiped a paw over her sensitive nose as the stench left soot in her nostrils. She sneezed. Puffy humans, wearing black and yellow, shiny coats with strange head coverings, ran about like they were chasing the infamous red dot, but there was no dot. Water spewed from hoses to calm the last of the dancing heat. Her human's friends coughed, stepping over broken pieces of gray rock and loose wires, their feet crunching over the uneven, unnatural ground. The burning smoke stayed in the air, but it was much easier to see. The entrance to the big building stood several tail-lengths ahead of them. Blue stayed close to her human, ensuring her tail tip touched his leg at all times.

The strong one nearly tripped over a long beam, trying to climb over.

The pointy-eared one reached for her arm and caught her as she was about to hit the ground. They eyed each other for a moment, then brushed themselves off and looked in the opposite direction. Silly creatures. They should lick each other and get it over with.

The short one watched the puffy humans carefully move bits of black, burnt, building parts outside in a heap. He gazed around to see if any other humans were injured. Blue liked him more than the others, but certainly not more than her beloved human who fed her. Her mouth filled with saliva.

"When will we eat?" she asked her human in his mind.

"Not now, Blue. We need to find somewhere to rest, first," he said, looking down at her. She lowered her tail. Cats were not known for their patience.

The puffy humans urged the group outside while a dangling wire sparked above them. They ducked their heads. Tim bent and picked up Blue, holding her close.

"Thank you. I don't want to injure my pads on any of these sharp things."

Tim nodded.

Finally, they reached the nighttime smoky air. Dozens of humans sat wrapped in blankets on the ground and on the backs of roaring monsters with colored lights on top. Sleeping humans with black faces lay on moving beds. Humans wearing dark colors came in and out of the building, checking with one another to ensure no others were inside. Others wearing white tended to the ones who often coughed and placed curved devices over their mouths to steady their breaths.

"That could've been us," the strong one mentioned, placing her hairless paw on her chest. She shuddered.

"Do you see anyone who needs my help?" The short one surveyed all the exhausted, soot-covered humans. He approached each one, spoke to them, and offered a comforting

hand without getting in the way of the white-topped work-
ers.

"He's such a good guy." The strong one watched him
heal a family of four who were in shock, shaking, and hardly
noticed the lights emitting from his hands.

"He is indeed. Glad he's on our side," the pointy-eared
one replied.

The short one finished healing various humans and
headed back to the group.

"I want to get as far away from here as we can. And I'm
starving," the strong one said.

"Me too," Tim agreed.

Everyone nodded.

Blue meowed. *Me too!*

"I could eat," the angry one said.

"First, we almost drown, and then we're almost roasted
to death. What the actual hell is happening to us?" the strong
one screamed, throwing her hairless paws in the air.

The short one healed his friends as the group walked
through the busy monster lot to the street. The lights were
too bright and caused the group to blink several times before
continuing onward. Somehow, they found food, and then a
small dwelling after discovering their money vessels had remained intact through the fire.

"Is this pet friendly?" her human asked.

"Yes," the human behind the counter said. She watched
with wide eyes and asked if she could do anything to help.
She handed them the dangling metal toys, her mouth open.
They settled into their rooms—the angry one and the strong
one in a room and Blue, her human, the short one, and the
pointy-eared one in the other.

"Where is my litter box?" Blue asked, meowing.

"I'll set it up in the bathroom for you," he answered.

Her human set up her litter box and food and water bowls, ensuring they were separated, the way she preferred. She did her business, munched on her kibble, and lapped up her water. When she finished her delicious meal, she curled up next to him and purred. Soon, Blue fell asleep, warm under the blanket.

*****

Several hours later, Blue jolted awake from the short one snoring. She narrowed her eyes in the darkness. Every time he made a sound, Blue winced; her ears screamed. She rolled over and snuggled closer to her human, trying to return to sleep. The cat yawned so wide her ears pulled back. *How can my human sleep with all that noise?*

After the thousandth snore wince, Blue closed her eyes. The darkness under her eyelids lulled her into complacency. Sounds of the wheeled monsters outside dulled, and soon, she heard nothing but her own purring that vibrated her tiny body.

She watched as the pointy-eared one gripped his sword in one hand. He used his other to stretch and feel for anything. Tiny dripping sounds rang in their ears. He winced. Scooting inches at a time, he stepped with one foot and stretched out his other, tapping the ground.

"Hello!" His voice's echo was so loud he startled himself, scrunching down with a sudden lapse of terrifying sounds. "Is anyone there?" he shouted again, loosening his tense shoulders. He only heard his voice.

He tapped and scooted, then turned around and felt nothing but cool, moist air. He perspired and blinked, unaware of where he could be. "Where am I? It's freezing in here," he said, giving into the terror, hoping for even the squeak of a mouse or the sound of something, anything, to show him where he was.

"Braern?" a soft familiar voice sounded close by.

"Moira? Is that you?"

"Why's it so dark in here? Turn on the light... and it's so cold," she said; her voice sounded scratchy.

"We're not in the hotel anymore."

"What do ya mean? I'll turn on the lights." The strong one fumbled and patted the cold, hard surface underneath her. "All right, where the hell are we?" she asked. "Gettin' so tired of asking that." She rubbed her arms and exhaled.

The pointy-eared one opened his mouth, and the cold air traveled down his throat, drying out his tongue.

"Where are the others? Araduk! Tim! Nozomi!" the pointy-eared one shouted to his friends.

"Are you guys here? Wake up!" the strong one yelled as their echoes filled their ears. Still nothing but darkness. No answer.

"Follow my voice so I know where you are," the pointy-eared one said.

"Marco!" the strong one shouted.

"What? Eh, I'm Braern. Don't tell me your memory has gone," he said, exasperated.

"No. It's a saying from my world. I say, 'Marco,' and you say, 'Polo,' and we find each other. It's supposed to be a game, but there's nothing funny about this. Never mind.

Keep walking toward my voice. I'll keep talking until you come... to my voice... keep walking toward my voi—"

The pointy-eared one found her and touched her shoulder.

She wrapped her arms around him, and the two stood silently together for a moment, holding one another.

"Braern? Moira? Is that you?"

"Yes! Tim! Over here!"

"Why is it so dark in here? Did the power go out? Did you not pay for the hotel?" the angry one asked, annoyance in her voice.

"No. We are somewhere else," the pointy-eared one answered with a sigh. Having to explain everything several times aggravated him.

"Araduk?" the pointy-eared one asked, rotating his head to hear.

They didn't hear his snoring.

"Where's Araduk?" the strong one asked, panicking.

"I don't know. He was in the room with me," my human answered. Blue meowed while she stretched.

"I'm glad you're still here, Blue."

I am too. Who else would feed me? I'm not interested in chasing any vermin in here! Blue thought.

"Great. We have the cat but not the dwarf," the angry one said.

"We need to find him. Can you follow our voices? We're afraid to move," Braern said. He repeated the same saying until my human and the angry one eventually found the duo.

They touched all their arms and heads to ensure they were there.

"I'm glad everyone is all right, but we need to find our healer."

Drops of water pattered on the floor as the air remained static.

"Give me your hand," the angry one demanded. *"Kimoi da ne!* Wipe that on your pants or something. That's disgusting."

"Who's hand?" the pointy-eared one asked.

"Not mine," the strong one said.

"Tim?" they asked in unison.

"Uh... yeah, sorry, it was me. I sweat in my sleep! Don't judge me!" my human said.

It's fine with me as long as you keep me warm, Blue thought.

They heard swiping noises.

"Are we in a cave?" the strong one said, her voice echoing.

"A cave? What makes you think that?" the angry one asked.

"It's cold, damp, and dark. A cave," the strong one answered, her voice shaking.

A loud rumble sounded as a few drops of water fell onto their heads.

"What was that? Stand behind me!" the pointy-eared one shouted.

No one moved as he pointed his sword toward where he thought the noise had come from. It reverberated through the cave as it grew louder.

"Wait. I know that sound; that's Araduk. He's snoring. Kept me up half the night," my human said.

Yes, he was so loud, it hurt my ears! Blue thought.

"Everyone, go toward the snoring dwarf," the angry one said.

The pointy-eared one led the group as everyone touched arms and shoulders to keep together. They grasped each other's clothing and held on as they shuffled toward the noise. He scooted, bracing his feet every few inches to ensure the ground was stable. Closer, they crept, inch by inch, until his foot reached a lump of the short one still asleep on the hard ground.

"How can he sleep like this? It is freezing here." The angry one shivered.

"He's a dwarf. They're supposed to be well-suited to mountains and caves," my human answered.

The pointy-eared one nudged the short one as he rolled and shifted.

His snoring stopped. "Five more minutes, lad." The short one chortled.

"Araduk, wake up. We're in a cave." The pointy-eared one nudged him harder.

"What?" The short one shot upright, and his shuffling sounds resonated as he stood. "A cave? We woke up in a cave?"

"Looks that way. Well, not really *looks,* because we can't see anything, but you know what I mean."

"Oh. Well, I'm not afraid of any cave. I used to call Tetsu Mountain my home, many years ago," the short one said.

The short one's body pressed against the pointy-eared one's side.

"Why can't we go back to the Ever-Changing Lands? That place was dope... and we could see," the strong one said, chuckling.

"Ever-Changing Lands?" my human asked.

"You weren't with us yet, kid," the strong one answered.

"Can't you cast a light spell or something?" my human asked.

The pointy-eared one sighed. "I can try." He opened his palm as a spark appeared. A tiny fireball formed, illuminating a small radius around them. A drop of water fell and landed on his hand, extinguishing the light.

The angry one frowned. "Eh, so much for that idea."

"Can ye use yer healing powers as a light?" the strong one asked.

"No, we are all well at this moment. Am afraid it doesn't work that way."

"Well, I guess we're out of ideas." my human sighed.

The group huddled in the cold, dripping cave. The eerie whistles of the faint air filled their ears. There was nothing but darkness in every direction.

"What is it?" the strong one asked.

"Now that I've had some rest, I feel that I should explain what I saw in my mind last night," the pointy-eared one said.

"Go for it, lad," the short one said.

"I heard echoes ring in my ears. I blinked and I couldn't see. I blinked again. Black. Sitting upright, I reached for my sword and searched for anything familiar. A cold hardness crept up under my legs. I wondered if I was dreaming, but part of me knew I was still awake.

"I cried out. No answer.

"Then I heard a low grumble near me. I unsheathed Raven and circled around, unsure of where the noise was coming from. Hot breath warmed my neck, and I turned to gaze upon an enormous blurry figure in front of me, white as snow.

"It towered over me... with that same deep rumble as before and regurgitated saliva as it looked down on me. I saw no eyes atop its large, lumpy head with enormous ears and wrinkled, layered skin. It carried two enormous fists with bulging muscular arms, bigger than its head, that touched the ground. A large burlap wrap tied around its low waist covered its bottom.

"The giant beast leaned forward and tried to grab me with a groan.

"I jumped sideways, dodging its lethal grasp.

"The creature was slow for its size and did not seem at all very intelligent. It wondered where its victim was. I jumped the other direction as it turned its ear to the ground, listening.

"I cannot rid my thoughts of its hideous face. No eyes. I remember placing a hand on my chest as something dragged me across the ground and into a bright green and colorful forest, filled with many large flowers and chirping birds. I blinked, and that forest became a desolate wasteland of deserted grays and browns. All color had vanished as my vision once again became blurry. That's when a flash of red appeared as I saw a tiny creature with two long ears lying motionless before me. A crown of vines lay next to it. The red grew until it consumed my entire view. Everywhere, red. All directions, red.

"I screamed, sweat dripping down my face into my mouth. I remember its bitter, warm taste."

The pointy-eared one paused.

"I don't remember anything from after that vision, until I found myself in a soft bed at the... what do you call it?"

"A hotel," my human answered.

"Yes, right... then I woke up here, in this dark, cold cave," the pointy-eared one finished.

Strange words, Blue thought after listening to him speak. *How could a creature without eyes see that I am the most beautiful cat that ever lived? How terrible for them to not be able to experience all that is me!*

"Wow, that was a lot. What do you think it means?" the strong one asked.

"Is it a premonition?" the short one questioned.

Blue licked her paw while the others muttered to one another. She watched them and pitied her human's friends for having such poor eyesight in the dark.

"Enough of this. I will lead everyone out of here," Blue said to her human as she spoke to him in her mind.

She struggled in his arms to free herself, pushing her paws on his chest. He let go as she jumped on the ground and rubbed on his legs. She mewed, and he couldn't feel her headbutts any longer.

Blue scurried a few steps, then paused. "Meow rrrow!"

"What's that moggy sayin'?" the short one asked.

"She... she wants us to follow her," her human replied.

"We are going to put our lives in the hands of a... cat?" the angry one groaned with displeasure.

"I don't know about this." The strong one seemed worried.

"Yeah, I'm not sure how I feel about this either," the pointy-eared one retorted.

"Guys! Cats can see in the dark!" Tim exclaimed. This was one topic he was well versed in. Blue felt his confidence for the first time in a long while and he stood with a straight back and took a breath. "Look, she can see in the dark. I'll translate what she says. She can guide us out of here. I know her, and I know she will keep us safe."

"Alright, we trust you... and her. Lead the way, Blue," the pointy-eared one announced.

"Okay, everyone, keep close and make sure you are holding the arm of the person in front of you. We will find our way out of this cave."

"Mewow mew."

"Keep going straight," her human translated.

"I will join Blue again and get us out of here faster." The angry one transformed into a bat and screeched signals that bounced off the wall and returned to her. Blue forced her predatory instincts to remain calm, as much as she wanted to leap into the air and catch the creature.

Pointed rocks hung from above that dripped water to tiny pools beneath them. Puddles formed on either side of their path. More pointed rocks rose from the ground in small clusters, some even touching the ones above.

"This place is beautiful," Nozomi commented as she nodded to Blue below her. The cat and the bat continued on-ward at a slow pace so as not to leave their clan behind.

"Mrrrow meoww."

"Blue says something is coming up ahead. Keep going forward."

They obeyed, shuffling their feet along as the sounds of their flat feet echoed through the cave.

"This is all too freaky, you guys. I'm never taking my sight for granted again." The strong one attempted to add some humor, with all the uncertainty.

"You humans have such poor eyesight. I imagine this is what you see, normally."

"Blue! That was rude and not true."

"What was rude?" the short one asked.

"Nothing. Blue is being snotty."

"Didn't know moggies could be *snotty.*"

"Anyway, I hear ye, lass. These old eyes are going places after this." The short one chuckled.

"I must tell you all that I had another vision, but this time was different. I-I'm not sure what it was," the pointy-eared one said.

"What'd ya see?" the strong one asked as they continued at their sluggish pace.

"I saw this darkness. I'm sure it was this cave we're in now. Pitch black, like this. I couldn't figure out where I was. Then the cave lit up, and a giant white creature stood before me. It tried to grab me, but it was too slow. The thing was enormous, and it didn't have..."

"It didn't have what?"

"It didn't have eyes. I can't form the words to explain such a terrifying creature. Where there were supposed to be eyes, there... wasn't. It had giant hands. It was horrifying. I escaped and found my way out of the darkness. Then I came upon a beautiful forest full of flowers and dancing figures with a pair of tall ears. Then I blinked, and..."

"Ew," the strong one said.

"Mewow!"

"Blue says to stop."

Blue turned around to ensure they had stopped.

"I blinked, and all the beauty vanished, and there was a streak of red. It washed over everything, and all the colors vanished. I felt such sadness overcome me, and I'm not sure why. I awoke here, with you all."

"Is that like some kind of premonition?" the strong one asked.

"Sounds like ye had a foreboding vision. Ye saw into the future."

"Yeah, that's what it sounds like to me too," her human said. "I've heard of seers carrying the same gift you have."

"A seer? I'm not—"

"The gift of sight is rare, indeed," the short one told him.

"It comes with such burdens, I'm afraid. It's difficult to quiet my mind these days. I hear voices."

"Well, we're all here to help you through this," the strong one reassured her friend.

I like her. She's pleasant and knows how to stroke my fur properly.

"Curve around to the left to avoid the wall," the angry one told the group in her squeaking bat voice.

Ahead, a tiny speck of light appeared.

"Light! I see light!" Nozomi gasped, excited.

"I see it too!" Tim shouted.

"Mewow meow!"

"Blue says we still need to be careful and watch for uneven ground."

"I did not say uneven ground. I said bumps," Blue corrected him.

"Kuso, I am getting out of here," the angry one retorted as she flew toward the light.

Light. It illuminated the path, leading to the exit.

"Watch out for this lump on the right," the angry one screeched.

"Got it. Avoid the lump on the right," the short one repeated.

The group shuffled along. The pointy-eared one kicked his hind paw on the lump that she warned him about. "Gah!" he groaned. Shifting his body, he pulled the group to the left.

"Ye ran into that bump, didn't ye?" the short one asked.

"Yes."

Everyone continued onward, and the light blinded them. Sheltering their eyes with their arms, they blinked. Blue's eyes were especially sensitive as her irises shortened to adjust to the new surroundings.

"It's so bright!" the angry one said as she transformed into a human again. She ran outside and vanished through the tall grass into the sun. "It's all right. You can come out!"

"Yes! Finally! Oh, light, how I missed thee!" the strong one laughed as she exited the cave with wide eyes.

"Thee?" Braern quirked.

"What? I was trying to sound all Renaissance."

"Good one." The pointy-eared one chuckled, smiling at the sight of all the surrounding greenery.

They heard a faint rustling from inside the cave as they all emerged into the daylight.

Blue pricked up her ears and flinched, rotating her body backward. Her fur stood on end. She growled and ran between her human's legs.

"Did ye hear that?" the short one looked back inside, only to see nothing but the darkness from the shadow from the sun.

"I heard nothing. Let's be grateful we made it out of there alive," Braern admitted, rubbing his hind paw.

"See, yer premonition came true but without that thing attacking us." The short one walked over as the rest of the group emerged and patted him on the back.

Everyone spread out, enjoying the lush green grass and the feel of the breeze on their faces.

Raising her hands in the air, the strong one closed her eyes and enjoyed the sounds of birds chirping and flowers brushing against one another, rustling through the vast, beautiful greenness of the forest before them. "I will never get over how beautiful this place is... well, most of it, anyway." She smiled, collapsing onto the grass as the tall blades tickled her face. "I never wanna go home."

Blue flattened her fur and relaxed her body. She peered upward, then averted her gaze to not burn her eyes.

The sun. I think I shall have a nap in the warmth, Blue said.

"You go take that nap, Blue. I'll keep an eye out," her human said with a smile.

TIM

RAINBOW RABBIT BURROW

Tim turned on his side with his palm on his cheek, watching Blue. The cat chased little jumping kasa-obake umbrella demons with single eyes and legs through the grass. She pounced on one, her tail twitching. Lifting her paw, it stood and licked her, then bounded away. Tim's energy waned while his eyelids grew heavy.

"The air is so much cleaner here than in New York," Moira said. She inhaled, with closed eyes.

They smelled the woodsy fragrance of the world around them.

Araduk rustled through the greenery as the blades tickled his hands. He grinned as the warm rays beamed onto his face. For the first time in days, he did not reach for his flask.

Braern floated around in figure-eight patterns above his companions at a relaxing pace. His arms were propped behind his neck while his back faced the ground. With the chill breeze in his hair, his tired feet had a much-needed rest.

For a few minutes, Nozomi relinquished her vengeance. She settled with her arms outstretched behind her, leaning on them, as she glanced at the luminous sky filled with painterly, wispy clouds. A faint smile escaped her lips as even she enjoyed herself.

After such darkness and uncertainty, they appreciated their precious time to rest.

The grass rustled, then two tiny lumps of white hopped toward the group, pausing every so often. A tiny, pink nose sniffed the air above the flowers as a pair of eyes peeked about.

Moira sat upright and leaned forward as it gasped and hid back inside its shield of nature. "I think we have a little visitor, guys." Moira smiled as she motioned with her head toward the small creature.

Blue crouched, wiggling her butt as her irises widened.

"Oh, no you don't, Blue." Tim grabbed her as she leaped halfway into the air, pulled her back to himself, and stroked her fur to calm her instinctual nerves.

Blue let out a low growl and flicked the tip of her tail in annoyance, knowing she wanted nothing more than to capture such an easy meal.

The little white lumps became two fluffy ears as Braern floated to the ground several yards from the little nose that peeked up again.

"It's a rabbit. I wonder if he can talk?" Tim asked.

"I beg your pardon, of course I can *talk!*" he yelled, frowning with a paw over his chest. The bunny hopped closer to them. Everyone raised their eyebrows at him as he adjusted his clothing and pricked up his ears. He sat upright, wearing a bright green vest with carrot designs embroidered on the front with orange thread.

"You can talk!" Moira's eyes widened as her mouth hung open. "I don't know why I'm so surprised. Magic is the new normal here." She giggled to herself.

"Greetings, uh... whoever you all are." He paused and leaned on his forepaws, twitching his nose as he sniffed the strangers. "My name is Thistletail, and I live nearby. My village adores visitors. I heard you coming and would like to escort you to my king, if you would oblige." He bowed, speaking in a cheery voice.

"Hello, uh... Mr. Thistletail. I'm Moira. This is Braern, Araduk, Tim, Nozomi, and Blue," she introduced everyone as they nodded in acknowledgment.

Blue dug her claws into Tim's lap, waiting for him to release her.

"A cat! Oh dear, oh dear! That will not do!" The bunny lifted a leg and leaned away from Blue, outstretching his paws in fear.

"Don't worry. She won't hurt you, I promise," Tim assured him.

"All right, we just met, but I trust you," he said happily.

Nozomi huffed with an eyebrow raised.

"My king would very much like to meet you all. If you would follow me, I can escort you to Rainbow Rabbit Burrow." Thistletail bowed and gestured his paw toward the dirt road that led into the lush forest.

"Of course! Pleased to meet you, Thistletail." Braern knelt and bowed.

"Pleased to meet ye as well, Thistletail. Am Araduk." Araduk bowed too.

Nozomi narrowed her eyes, crossing her arms.

"Psst," Moira hissed at Tim.

The two bowed.

"You all as well," Thistletail said politely. "All right now, let's be off!" He hopped to the path and waited.

The group looked at one another, then followed.

"Do keep that cat under control or the entire town will be in a frenzy," he warned Tim, who was still clutching Blue.

Her ears were down, and her eyes remained wide while watching the rabbit's every movement as it hopped along.

"I will. I promise," Tim assured him. "Blue, chill." He stroked her fur and pressed gently on her head to try to calm her instincts again.

"I've never met a talking rabbit before." Moira chuckled, curious to see where he would lead them. "Feel like I'm chasing the white rabbit with the big watch in *Alice in Wonderland*. How cute," she whispered.

"How far is this place?" Nozomi asked, raising her eyebrows and eyeing the trees on both sides.

"These are the Niji Woods. You're quite safe. Do watch out for the kitsuka. They like to trip unsuspecting travelers."

Every color imaginable shimmered on every leaf and flower petal. Blue lilies as tall as a man swayed in the wind. Tree trunks looked smooth as silk, with stripes of varying complementary hues that reached to their branches. Florid, sweet smells filled their noses. They heard chirps and rustling all around.

A creature emerged from the ground that looked like a dolphin with fur and a fluffy tail. Its fin-like paws came to tiny points. Dirt flew upward as it jumped in and out of the ground like it was water.

They watched as a few more joined as they chirped and dove into the ground.

"There's one now. This way, please! We're almost there!" Thistletail said happily in a high-pitched voice.

"Oh my god, this place is beautiful! So many colors!" Moira squealed, her hands together, touching her lips as she gawked at all the plant life.

A few minutes later, large fruits and vegetables appeared ahead. As they approached, windows, doors, and little chimneys attached to each house came into focus.

"You live in fruits and vegetables?" Braern asked, stretching his neck to get a closer look.

"Why, yes, our mage cast a spell on several carrots, turnips, apples—any fruit or vegetable you can think of. He ensured us they would never rot as long as we never tried to eat them. We live privileged lives in Rainbow Rabbit Burrow. We have everything we could need in our quaint little village."

"Wow, that's amazing. They're so big!" Moira exclaimed, her eyes wide as she beheld the whimsical, colorful village.

"I couldn't keep that promise. I'd eat m' house in a day if it looked like one o' these!" Araduk joked.

All the bunnies emerged from their homes and stood outside, watching the strange visitors. Flowerpots lined windowsills. Yards housed gardens with smaller plants growing in the well-tended dirt. The rabbits came in various colors: black, brown, tan, white, gray. All had even more colorful and elaborate clothing of all sorts, with designs that coincided with their gardens. They wore dresses with swirling vines and turnips and carrots, as well as hats, pants, and blouses. None of the rabbits donned shoes. They sniffed the air as the group passed. A few ran inside to the safety of their vegetable homes after noticing Blue.

"What is a cat doing here?" a whisper sounded from be-hind them as they continued onward.

"Who are these folks?" another whisper sounded.

"I don't think we're all that welcome here," Moira stat-ed.

"Yeah, it doesn't sound like it." Tim's head sunk into his shoulders as his face reddened with so many eyes staring at him.

Blue struggled to free herself from his arms as he squeezed her harder.

"Blue, you gotta chill. You can't chase these rabbits," he calmly told her.

Blue growled as the tip of her tail flicked.

"I'm sorry. I'll find you proper prey later, but not in this place."

"Here we are! Wait out here, and I'll announce your presence to the king." Thistletail bounded along with a smile as he disappeared into the large, multi-carrot-shaped dwell-ing in front of them.

This carrot was much larger and wider than the other smaller houses. The windows were larger, with shining sin-gle panes of glass. Various colorful flowers and plants grew outside, reaching the windows on either side of the door, which was also carrot shaped.

"These bunnies sure love their carrots," Araduk chuck-led quietly, patting his belly. This was the first time he'd felt tall in his life. He held his head high with a smile.

"Greetings, travelers!" a voice sounded as three rab-bits emerged from the castle. The first wore a crown of vines around his tall ears and a long purple robe with vegetable designs in gold. His long whiskers wiggled as he hopped over, amazed by their tall statures.

After a moment, another rabbit with sleek, gray fur emerged, wearing a bright yellow dress with a pastel pink flower around her ear. The third wore an orange robe with light gray fur and glasses over his eyes.

"This is Master Kabu, my seer and healer, and this is my daughter, Princess Plum. I am King Carrot."

The onlooking rabbits hopped over and bowed their heads in respect for their king, intrigued by the visitors.

Braern knelt and bowed as well. Araduk, Moira, Tim, and Nozomi followed his lead. Blue relentlessly kicked and scratched her human's chest. Tim held her tighter as she grew more agitated.

"Greetings, King Carrot, I'm Braern Yogensha of Lavendale. This is Moira Washington, Araduk Lightbringer, Nozomi Hayakawa, Timothy Rodriquez, and Blue."

"Who's Blue?" Master Kabu asked as he gestured with his head.

"Oh, she's a cat," Braern answered softly, feeling uneasy.

"Oh wonderful, a cat... a *cat?*" King Carrot jumped into the air, flailing his paws about in a panicked frenzy.

The whole village erupted with screams of fear and little paws scampering in all directions. Flashes of colorful clothing zipped by as they stood still, afraid to move in such chaos.

A rabbit ran into Tim's leg, nearly knocking him over. Blue seized the opportunity and jumped from his arms to chase one wearing a dress and a flower hat.

She dropped her basket of celery and darted in the opposite direction, her fluffy tail jumping behind her as Blue gave chase. Everywhere, screams of "cat!" sounded as the ruckus ensued.

Tim ran after Blue, but she was too fast, whipping around and cutting off the bunny.

She pursued several rabbits but stopped right in front of the dress-wearing one, licking her lips as she salivated, her eyes wide and claws extended.

The terrified bunny's chest quickly rose and fell, its eyes wide with panic. The bunny jumped into the air above Blue, startling the cat as she crouched down, watching her plaything escape.

She whipped around and pursued the bunny at top speed.

"Blue!" Tim yelled so loud his throat hurt. He bunched up his eyes and mouth, forcing himself not to bite his lips. "Blue! Get over here! This is not how we act!"

The cat halted and crouched, her tiny chest heaving. With her ears down and her tail dragging across the ground, she sauntered to Tim.

"Blue, you can't chase these rabbits. They're not like the rabbits at home." He squatted to face her as she chittered at the tiny, scared fur balls. Tim spied the terrified creatures peeking from behind their homes.

King Carrot and Princess Plum creaked open the large door to their castle, sniffing and blinking.

"My cat apologizes for her actions, and she will never again chase any of you. I'm really sorry about this," Tim said, his head down, frowning at Blue.

"Are you sure it's safe to come out?" King Carrot's twitchy nose peeked out of the door.

"Yes, she will behave herself or..." Tim met Blue's gaze. "I'll never feed her... again."

Tim heard what his cat was thinking in his mind. *"You'll never... feed me... again?"* she asked him telepathically. Blue swallowed hard, staring at her human. She imagined an empty bowl growing bigger, never filling with food, as she cried alone in darkness with no chin scratches from anyone.

"That will be your doom if you don't listen to me!" he told her telepathically.

His cat glared at him, swooshing her tail.

"Hm..." King Carrot began. "All right!" He hopped to them and looked up at Tim. "In that case, I invite you all to dinner this evening. Our cooks make delicious carrot and bean soup." King Carrot's nose twitched.

At the mention of food, Tim thought of his mother's enchiladas and how she'd always put too much sauce on top—but that was fine with him. He missed her. He felt a sense of guilt, knowing his family was at home worrying about him, but he pushed away the feeling, knowing he had to see this quest through to the end. After all, this was what all those years of playing RPGs had prepared him for.

Princess Plum walked forward and welcomed them all into her kingdom.

"Food!" Araduk exclaimed. "Got any whiskey?"

"Uh... we have ale."

"Thank the gods!"

"Wow, you rabbits sure do forgive fast," Moira pointed out, half-giggling under her breath.

"We don't believe in grudges or anger, really. Too many negative emotions help no one, I always say." King Carrot pointed in the air as he spoke, to make his point.

By now, the entire burrow had relaxed their tense, little bodies and hopped behind the group, sniffing the air to inspect the strangers.

The bright sky soon filled with magentas and yellows as the vine lights tied to the trees glowed, illuminating the area. The royal rabbits led the group to the clearing. Rows of curved half-logs lay in large circles as King Carrot gestured with his paw for them to sit.

"We're sorry for the cramped quarters. We're not used to having guests of your... size." Princess Plum clapped her paws as the other rabbits swarmed around, carrying food in pots and wooden, painted dinnerware.

They placed trays of fruits, vegetables, and grains onto little tree stumps on the opposite side of the seats.

The group refrained from touching anything from the display of friendship the rabbits gave them.

King Carrot and Princess Plum pointed their paws at where they wanted the feast to be placed, as the townsfolk reluctantly sat down.

One brown rabbit with a feathered hat and a brown vest sat next to Tim with Blue on his lap. He scooted an inch from Blue as she sneered at him, imagining him inside her mouth.

The cat groaned under her breath.

"I heard that," Tim whispered to her with narrowed eyes.

"Behave yourself, Blue."

She raised her head and turned away from him, flicking her tail.

"Tonight, we feast in honor of our guests from the cave!" King Carrot announced with his paws in the air as his crown adjusted on his head.

"Thank you, King Carrot." Braern nodded. "You are most gracious."

The last of the trays of bright, sparkling food vanished into the castle. The smell of warm, cooked vegetables and juicy sweet fruits filled the air as everyone realized how hungry they were. Their stomachs growled and mouths watered.

"Please, eat!" King Carrot smiled, holding out an open paw to them.

A second round of rabbits appeared with wooden pitchers of various juices and ales. The smells of fermented fruit filled the air to join the scents of delicious foods. Several rabbits distributed other wooden cups and poured their contents into the vessels for the guests first, then served the rest of the burrow.

"You didn't have to go to so much trouble for us." Moira took a bite of a luscious whole pear with one hand and grabbed a slice of wheat bread with the other.

"Oh, it's nothing. My cooks are the best in all of Yumerion!" King Carrot beckoned with his paws to a group of younger bunnies. He introduced them as his other children.

"How... many children do you... ahem, I'm sorry. I don't mean to ask." Moira coughed, her cheeks reddening as she sunk into her seat, munching on a stalk of celery and looking away from the king.

"Oh, one hundred and ninety-seven, last time I checked. My wife, Queen Rose—"

"Queen Rose! How we miss thy sweetness!" the whole town exclaimed in unison.

The king and princess joined, raising their wooden cups. "Yes, my late wife and I produced many offspring. We rabbits are not ashamed of such things."

"Wow, one hundred and ninety-seven..." Tim said and took a tiny sip of his drink. Immediately, he spit out its contents all over a nearby rabbit maiden who was filling more cups with her pitcher. Tim had soaked her dress as she stood motionless with droopy ears for a moment, her eyes closed.

"I'm sorry, but what was that?" He looked into his cup full of a tan, thin liquid.

"It's ale, lad. Have ye never had ale before?" Araduk burped, patting his belly as he finished his fourth cup that lay on the ground beside his feet.

"No, I haven't," Tim answered softly, still smacking his lips to try to get the bitter, aromatic taste out of his mouth. He coughed, scrunching his face as his nostrils hurt from the powerful smell.

"I don't think Tim needs to be drinking anything at his age." Moira glared at Araduk, who clearly had no sense of when to stop.

"May I have some water, please?" Tim asked, not wanting to draw much attention to himself. "And I'm sorry about your dress," he said to the rabbit.

She nodded and smiled and didn't seem to mind her current drenched state.

Everyone feasted, and soft murmurs and conversations sounded all around the town as the sky turned a navy-blue. Twinkling stars showered the sky through openings in the tall trees. Strings of carrot-shaped glass lights hung across the entire village, tied to the branches above. Moving, tiny creatures floated inside each light that caused the illumination of the burrow. The wires swayed in the gentle breeze.

"Now then, tell me about how you came through that dreadful cave. We never venture there anymore—not since so many of my subjects have never returned," King Carrot asked.

"We didn't see anything, thankfully. As we were sleeping, we must've been forced through another portal," Braern answered after he swallowed his bite of steaming hot carrot and potato stew. He sniffed his bowl as he put another spoonful in his mouth, peering at the king.

"Where did you say you came from again?"

"We're from the human world. Braern and Araduk live here in Yumerion," Moira answered, gesturing her hand between herself and Tim.

"The human world? I thought you three were elves or fae folk." He pointed to Nozomi, Moira, and Tim.

"You mean, I could be a fairy?" Moira's eyes lit up as she smiled an enormous smile, giddy with excitement.

"You came from the human world? I can't believe it." The king rose and bounced onto his seat with wide eyes. He placed his paws on the table and leaned forward.

The entire village stared in disbelief.

"Well, this is awkward," Tim whispered.

MOIRA

THE DANCE

Moira leaned toward the rabbit king with an eyebrow raised. "Yes, Tim and I are human. We're from... Earth," Moira said. *It's so weird saying that. 'Hi! I'm from Earth!' What?*

"I've never met humans before. Years ago, my great-grandfather said that your kind used to roam freely in our world. Now, I've only heard of you in stories. In fact, I finished one the other day. I believe it was about how you only use a small portion of your brains. What a mockery!" The king chuckled.

"Yeah, that sounds like a lot of people I know." Moira sat down as she shook her head and raised her eyebrows, recalling all the stupid humans she had come across in her lifetime—too many to count or remember by name.

"Speak for yourself," Tim muttered quietly enough to avoid most everyone hearing him. He hid behind a cup of water that a rabbit had recently served.

"Tell me, are you all staying here for a while?" King Carrot asked as he munched on an apple, his mouth full.

"We're on our way to the monastery atop Shiro Peak. We're traveling there for information," Araduk answered.

"A monastery? Hmm... I believe I know such a place. Never been there myself, of course. I heard tales of all manner of folk traveling there for the gift of knowledge. What are you hoping to learn there, if you don't mind my asking?"

Braern finished his drink. "We seek answers of our intertwined destinies and why we have no control over where the portals have taken us."

"Portals, you say? I know not what you speak of. I do, however, know that mountain you seek. I believe it's a few days that way." King Carrot pointed toward the north. The trees hid most of the mountain range many miles away, but the shaded gray was visible in the distance.

"Thank you, King Carrot. We appreciate the help. If you'll have us, we intend to stay the night and leave in the morning," Braern announced kindly.

"Of course! You are all welcome here! In fact, we have not had visitors in a long while. Let us celebrate our friendship with a little music!" King Carrot clapped his paws as his ring sparkled in the light.

Several rabbits of varying sizes and different clothing emerged from the castle doors, holding instruments. They played a soft, whimsical melody in the corner by the king.

Araduk blinked and shook his body. He poured the contents of his flask into his cup to not arouse suspicion. "This rabbit ale does nothin' for me."

One of the nearby rabbits sniffed him and toppled over, coughing for a moment, then fainted. Araduk peered down at him and shrugged.

Nozomi stared at her feet, hunched over, and picked at her food with her fingers.

"You okay?" Moira asked, looking at the king, then back at her.

The king started a new conversation, asking everyone to raise their cups in a toast to the visitors.

"I am fine. *Demo...* Danielle loved bunnies. We used to go to petting zoos all the time. I even got her a big stuffed white bunny. She loved him and slept with him every night," Nozomi spoke with heavy eyes as she spread her fingers over her full cup. Her elbows rested on her knees as her long hair covered her ears.

"And you have no idea where she is?" Moira placed a hand on Nozomi's back.

"Taken. I do not know where, but I will find her once I get my hands around the neck of the one responsible," Nozomi sneered, her nostrils flaring. She placed her cup on the ground, stood, and stepped over the log to walk in the opposite direction of the festivities. She disappeared into the trees until the light of the hanging lanterns no longer reached her.

Moira closed her eyes and sighed, feeling a heaviness in her chest. She knew exactly what it was like to lose a loved one. *I need to find a way to help her.*

At the party, Araduk told jokes, sloshing his cup. Tim spoke to the rabbit folk around him, smiling, his anxiety fading. Braern grinned and sipped his cup, while the king and princess giggled at the nonsense that the drunk dwarf was speaking. His speech became increasingly indiscernible.

As the soft night breeze moved Braern's thin hair from his ears, Moira peered at the profile of his face. Too often had she averted her eyes when he noticed her, her thoughts conflicted. She watched as the light trickled across his cheek, his blond hair covering half his ear. *He's actually pretty damn cute.* She blinked, shaking her head out of her trance.

Moira watched the rabbits dance in circles with their arms around one another, twirling happily. Flutes and soft drums played as they patted on wooden instruments and tapped their long feet on the dirt ground. King Carrot clapped his paws, while the other rabbits followed in his actions. Soon, numerous paws clapped as everyone moved to the beat.

A bunny wearing a green dress moved toward Braern and offered a paw, mid-dance, requesting silently for him to join her.

He accepted her paw, bent down, and swayed to the music as best he could with an arched back. They danced until the song ended. Braern laughed, his smile crinkling his eyes as he straightened his back with a groan. He approached Moira, bowing with one hand behind his back, his other outstretched. "Dance with me," he gently requested with a smile.

A new melodic song began. Moira's eyes widened as her face heated. With a shaking hand, she placed her fingers across his palm.

The two danced as he tried to teach her, without much luck, to dance like an elf. She tried to teach him to dance like a human, even going so far as to teach him how to do The Robot. She explained and demonstrated, then laughed at his attempt to straighten his arms and pivot on the beat.

The rabbits stared at them, confused.

The clumsy pair laughed, stepping on each other's feet.

Araduk raised his glass to them, then downed another.

Tim watched and offered Blue some freeze-dried fish crackers from his backpack.

She happily gulped them, her tail relaxing. After she finished, she licked her lips and paws and rubbed them over her ears.

Tim watched everyone dance as he sighed, slouching in his chair. "I'll never get a girl like that. He makes it look so easy," he muttered.

The dwarf's voice increased as he couldn't keep his head still, swaying his arms around and cheering on the dancers. He blinked at Blue as she approached, drooling. Narrowing his eyes, he saw the blurry fuzzball before him. "What're ye doin' here, moggy?"

Blue leaned forward and sniffed the drunken dwarf. Her nostrils moved. She sneezed. Blue backed away, nearly closing her eyes as she felt the burn from his whiskey in the air, with her ears and tail down.

"Back to ye boy, ye go," he said as Blue ran off.

Soon, the music slowed, and the rabbits paired up. The king and princess danced together.

Braern placed his hand on Moira's lower back, sending chills up her spine as the two held hands. Caught in the moment, she gazed into his piercing blue-green eyes. "I never realized how tall you are," she said with her arms around his neck. She ran her fingers through his light, thin hair that had a bit of curl to it. Moira caressed his ear all the way to the tip. Something about his ears called to her. She yearned to kiss them but restrained herself.

"Yes, elven folk are fairly tall." He closed his eyes and smiled.

Moira sensed he never wanted the moment to end, like she did.

For a moment, elf and human heard no other noises and felt nothing but their touch as they danced. The world around them vanished. Braern floated them off the ground, observing her and only her. She looked down at their floating feet and smiled with a soft giggle. Braern smiled back, exposing his perfectly straight, whitened teeth. She had never noticed them before that. *I wonder if elves have some form of braces.*

Braern pulled her closer by her waist and tightened his other hand around her fingers. He lowered his rounded jaw and licked his lips to moisten them. "I would very much like to kiss you now, if you would let me," he whispered. Their noses touched as she smelled the bit of ale on his breath. She didn't mind it. Moira's pupils dilated as she leaned in. Their lips tickled one another's and their breathing increased.

She blinked and Braern's skin and lips changed. They were darker and not his. Moira flinched and leaned backward, eyeing the man before her. Her ex-boyfriend appeared over Braern's face. A jolt surged through her heart as if she had woken from a nightmare. *Adrian. I've caused so much pain to everyone I love. I won't do that to Braern. He's kind and genuine, and I'd never forgive myself if I hurt him. Why do I keep lettin' myself get so close to him? Stop it, girl!* She blinked again and Braern returned to normal. Her eyes glistened as she bit her bottom lip. "I'm sorry. I can't," she squeaked, her throat constricting.

Braern closed his eyes, and they reached the forest floor once more. She turned and hurried to her seat, averting her gaze as she felt her breaths become erratic.

The elf said nothing, but held his head low and sat next to her. He scooted over to give her more space. Without looking at her, he whispered, "If I have hurt you in some way, please know that I would rather pierce my heart with my own sword than cause you any harm."

"It's not... you."

Moira placed her head in her hand and closed her eyes, trying not to let the tears escape that pooled at the corners. "I..." she began, looking at him.

He saw her from the corner of his eye but focused on the rabbits. "It's all right. I understand."

Moira stood and walked toward where she'd last seen Nozomi. Braern disappeared from her sight behind the trees. She turned her attention to where Nozomi had vanished. She fought the painful urge to be close to the elf she had grown fond of. Her temples ached. Sighing, she decided comforting her friend was more important and headed to where she had vanished. *Why is this so hard?*

NOZOMI

THE TROLL

Nozomi leaned against a nearby tree with her face half lit by the light. "There you are," Moira said as she approached.

The shapeshifter stood with one bent leg against the bark and her arms folded, watching the commotion with an unamused, vacant expression. "I am still here," Nozomi answered in a monotone voice. *Much to my surprise. Cannot seem to get away from them.*

"Braern danced with me," Moira opened up to her.

"Yes? How did that go?" Nozomi placed both feet on the ground and faced Moira.

"It really didn't go anywhere. I walked away... again."

"Again? Are you in love with him or something?"

"No, it's nothing like that. I care about him but... I don't know."

"I heard you hurt your ex and you are scared to get close to anyone again."

"So, you do listen."

"Sometimes." Nozomi laughed.

The women giggled for a moment, then watched the festivities.

"You know, you're not as cold as everyone thinks you are." Moira smirked.

"And you are not as tough as you think you are." Nozomi tilted her head back and forth with a smile.

The music continued. Araduk was still waving around his drink, drenching himself in his drunken state. He laughed loudly while Tim smiled, enjoying the rabbit dances. Blue sat at his feet, unmoving, while her tail twitched.

"Such a sweet little village. The rabbits have been so kind to us. I hope nothing happens to them." Moira sighed as she watched several rabbits raise their iridescent sleeves in the air while they danced.

"What do you mean?" Nozomi asked.

"We seem to bring trouble everywhere we go."

"Did you ever think maybe we arrive before the trouble comes?"

Moira paused. "Never thought of it like that. I'd like to think we're doing the right thing, but I'm not sure what that is anymore. All this moving around is making me forget where I belong—if I ever belonged anywhere." Moira lowered her gaze to her feet with a sigh. She tapped the ground with her boot and watched the grass spring back up after moving her foot.

"Maybe we are like this grass." Nozomi's gaze met Moira's feet. "They pushed us down, then we rise again."

"How very poetic of you." Moira eyed Nozomi, who smirked at a passing rabbit that leaped into the air like a ballerina. "I think this is the most we've talked since I met you."

"Yes... eh, do not let it go to your head." Nozomi laughed through a closed mouth.

They sipped their drinks and enjoyed the upbeat music. Then the ground shook. Ripples formed in Nozomi's drink.

"What in the *Jurassic Park* shit is this?" Moira asked, feeling her heart beating faster as she looked all around.

"Did Araduk fall over again?" Nozomi tried to lighten the mood.

"That's definitely not him. Look." Moira pointed toward the trees and moved out of the way as something large bounded toward them.

The music stopped. Braern leaped over the log to Moira and Nozomi, watching as the giant thing split trees in half, sending them crashing and splintering to the forest floor. The cracks of wood echoed in their ears. A wave of panic swept over the group as the rabbits all ran to their homes, squeaking in terror.

"Where'd eberbody go?" Araduk slurred as he spit all over himself. He shook his head and tried to regain his composure as the log underneath him vibrated.

Tim stood, looking toward the moving trees.

Blue's fur bristled as she hid in a ball behind her human.

"That sounds big. Really big. What is it, Braern? What's happening?"

"We don't know yet, but we'd better be prepared to fight," Braern answered.

Nozomi caught a glimpse of its skin reflected in the moonlight as she heard the last slam of a door behind her.

The creature's pale hide looked as if it had not seen sunlight in its entire lifetime. It emerged from the forest and stopped outside the burrow. An enormous squashed, bald, oval head sat atop its muscular shoulders with large, round ears. Its fists touched the ground, dragging behind, leaving dirt and leaves stuck to its hairy fingers. Shorter, smaller legs looked as if they couldn't possibly support its weight, but they did. A loose fabric covered its legs and groin area, while its chest warbled with uneven, disheveled, bumpy skin. One feature stood out the most of all–it had no eyes. Its ugly nose sniffed the air as its upper lip moved.

"The troll from my vision," Braern said quietly to himself, his eyes widening as he drew his sword. "It's the troll from my vision! I saw red! He will kill everyone here if we don't stop him!" Braern warned the others.

"I got this!" Nozomi transformed into a bear mid-run as she attacked the giant, eyeless troll.

It swung its fists, unable to see where its enemy was coming from, perking its ears to listen. The troll swung its fist with a whoosh.

Nozomi ducked before it impaled her and darted under its nose, her thick, brown fur rippling as she ran on all fours. Growling loudly, she pushed off a tree with her hind legs and ran behind it, then climbed onto its back. She tried to wrap her claws around its neck, but it was so thick and slippery she could not get a grip.

The troll reached behind with one arm, rotating to grasp the nuisance on its back.

Braern flew over and thrust his sword toward the troll's chest.

It sensed his movements and tried to grasp the elf in the air.

He quickly dodged out of the way.

Moira ran forward, fists ready, with her feet apart. "You're not touching these rabbits!" Moira punched its shin so hard her arm went all the way through. Slimy muscle and blood sprayed all over her face and body. Afraid to move, she felt shredded bone scrape against her skin.

The troll lifted its giant fist above her. It swung toward her and ripped her from its leg, howling in pain. It threw her face-first into the bark of a tree.

She fell to the ground, and her nose throbbed as she covered it with her hands.

"Moira! Look out!" Braern yelled, spit flying from his mouth.

The troll swiped its free fist straight through the tree behind her. She rolled a few feet out of the way in time for the troll to lunge its mighty hand, inches from her. The creature ripped the tree out by the roots and chucked it in the opposite direction. Bits of dirt and grass erupted and hit her face, landing in her mouth. She coughed as she pushed herself to stand, resisting the urge to place a hand over her aching head. Running to the other side, she watched Nozomi struggle to get a grip.

Nozomi, the bear, bit the troll at the back of its neck. *You will not escape my grasp, troll!*

It bellowed a deep scream in pain as it raised its arms, pulling on Nozomi's fur, with her teeth deep in its skin. *Gross.* Her mouthful of troll tasted like rotten fish that was bathed in sewage. The thing grasped her so tightly, piercing her muscles, that it knocked her unconscious for a second and ripped her teeth from itself, sending chunks of flesh falling. The troll threw her past the entire village, and she slammed into a stone.

*****

A minute later, Nozomi was awakened by water splashed

onto her face. She shivered and quickly rose to stand, smacking drops out of her face with a frown. She morphed into her human form, coughing and holding her chest as she fought to catch a breath. Her muscles ached as her spine felt bruised.

"Apologies, Miss Nozomi. You looked as if you needed some assistance," Thistletail said, looking up at her with his ears down. He stepped back to give her room, clutching his empty bucket.

Nozomi gave him the slightest of nods, then turned toward all the ruckus. Moira and Braern continued to battle the beast.

"Where is that damn troll? I will rip its throat out!" Nozomi yelled, clenching her fists. Her vision blurred as her knees wobbled and gave way. She leaned against the tree behind her with one hand on the bark and the other on her forehead, peering at her feet.

"You going back out there?" Tim asked from beside her.

"Yes, once I catch my breath and I can see straight. Damn thing knocked me into a tree."

Tim watched the battle with wide eyes and a quivering chin. With his hands on his reddened cheeks, he ran to Araduk and attempted to relocate him to the safety of the castle side. Barely moving an inch, he collapsed on top of him, out of breath. "You have to help me get you somewhere safe! You can't stay here!" Tim wiped his sweaty forehead with his arm.

"Sure t'ing, lad," Araduk answered shakily. The dwarf narrowed his eyes, seeing blurry figures swarming around a lighter, larger one in front of him. He tried to stand but fell again, chuckling to himself.

Blue stayed close to Tim and stayed hidden.

"Yes, you need to get him out of here," Nozomi demanded with a wave of her hand.

"They always do all the fighting without us." Tim frowned.

"I wiss I waz that strong," Araduk slurred.

"I can't stay here and do nothing again. You wait here; I'm going to help them," Tim told Araduk and watched Blue curl her tail around her eyes, shaking in a ball. Tim pushed himself off Araduk's shoulder and stumbled toward the giant troll as it grasped the air at Braern, flying quickly in circles around it, sword swinging.

The troll bounded toward Tim and Nozomi until it was several feet away. She looked up at its monstrosity of a face and stared at the large lump where its eyes should be. "You are ugly," she said, barely audible.

Tim surveyed his surroundings. The yelling and bellows continued. He kicked a rock beside his foot. He bent, grabbed it, and chucked it at the troll. Tim hit him square in his chest.

"Nice one, kid," Nozomi said, narrowing her eyes at where his rock landed.

The creature froze and opened its filthy mouth in a loud roar, facing Tim. Its curved teeth became more visible as green saliva spewed from its mouth in a rage. It slowly accelerated toward Tim, waving its head around.

The troll whipped its head around and turned its attention to them. Thistletail leaped into the air and zipped away back to his home at the burrow.

"I'm gonna try to lead it away from here," Tim said. He ran off around the beast, yelling at it.

"Hey you! Over here!" he yelled.

"That's my cue!" Nozomi forced herself to straighten her posture and raced toward the troll once again. *What could I possibly turn into that would bring down this thing?*

As if Tim heard her thoughts, he hollered, "Nozomi, try a snake!" toward her. Tim ran past his friends, the troll following close behind, wailing.

Seeing the troll grow larger as she drew closer, she transformed into a hawk and flew overhead, screeching. When she was high enough, she turned into an anaconda and landed on its shoulders. She shuffled to wrap her immense body around its neck and squeezed with all the muscles she had.

It ceased moving and frantically clawed at her, staggering and gasping for breath. The ugly creature ripped at her flesh, sending searing jolts through her body.

Braern levitated and rushed toward the creature, watching his companions fight with all their might. He pulled back his sword and thrust it into the creature's side. He quickly ripped out Raven.

The troll hissed, still trying to grasp the snake wrapped around its neck with one hand and holding his injury with his other. Spitting saliva everywhere, the troll flailed, growing more agitated. Heaving itself toward the rabbit village, it punched and swiped with its mighty fists through homes, crushing them and jettisoning little rabbits.

Tim hollered and waved his arms. He tried to lure it away from the burrow, to no avail.

The creature refused to contain its destruction.

Moira caught up and thrust her hands into its legs, causing enormous red patches to appear on its flesh. They heard the crunch of its muscle and bone as she avoided its slow stomps around her.

The troll fell to the ground, collapsing onto the abandoned trays of food and musical instruments, causing little sound to escape. A launched flute landed on the castle roof.

The creature fell, headfirst, right before Araduk's feet, awakening him from his deep snooze.

Araduk opened his eyes to see a large, blurry figure in front of him, hearing its sounds of angst. "Is that ye, Nozomi? Wha id ye turn inoo?" Araduk slurred again, blinking to try to see. He clumsily kneeled and immediately fell over, his arm meeting the troll.

The creature writhed and kicked with both hands on Nozomi's body, attempting to pry her off its neck as she squeezed even harder. She screamed from its tight grasp around her upper body.

"Araduk! Get away from it!" Tim warned.

Araduk squinted again, focusing on the blood over its body. He outstretched his hands as they glowed, healing its wounds with a swathe or white light. It was too late.

"No! Araduk! That is not me!" Nozomi screeched through her snake mouth.

The troll awakened, fully healed.

"We can't let it stand!" Moira screamed as she ran over and grabbed its ankle to pin it to the ground. "Braern! Do something, quick!"

The troll tried its best to push off the ground and stand. It flailed its arms, and its mighty fists smashed the castle to bits and destroyed several nearby houses. Vegetables flew as rabbits fell from their windows.

Braern placed his free hand on his blade and uttered, *"hidogaru!"* His sword glowed and grew ten times its size. Braern wielded the enormous weapon with ease and swung it behind him. Nozomi released her body and pushed backward, seconds before his blade sliced through the troll's neck, decapitating its ugly head in a gush of spraying arteries and saliva. "You're not coming back from that."

She transformed back into her human form, with her hands on her knees.

Everyone collapsed where they were, exhausted and drenched in blood. Their chests rose and fell, coughing and panting. Muscles ached and hearts raced. They wiped blood from their eyes and mouths.

The troll's head rolled away and stopped in front of a nearby pear house.

Nozomi watched as a rabbit peeked out its window to witness the ear of the troll before her. She squeaked in terror, then scampered to her bed and buried half her body underneath. She kicked her legs to hide as much of herself as she could. Her fluffy tail stuck out, shaking in sheer terror.

From the corner of her eye, Nozomi looked back to where the troll had come from and saw a green swoosh of light travel through the air. She narrowed her eyes as drops of sweat fell onto her lids. Blinking, she wiped her moist hair away from her forehead. She watched the light vanish into the dark gray clouds. *Was that him? The one I am after? I recognize that color of green.* She turned to hear Braern speak.

"*Chijimu,*" he said quietly between breaths. His weapon shrank to its normal size and clanked onto the ground. Raven's glow dispersed as Braern stared at his weapon. "My father would be proud of me. I slayed a troll. We all did."

"Damn straight," Moira said.

Blue ran to Tim as he lifted his weary arm to scratch her ears.

She lay purring next to him, relieved he had survived.

A muffled shrill cry pierced the silence as Princess Plum pushed large pieces of wooden debris off of her furry legs, staring at a lifeless body at her feet.

With only a few remaining pillars still standing, the carrot castle lay in a heap of colorless rubble. Bits of wood and carrots lay strewn about in piles as smoke rose from the dead fireplace that was once inside.

She cried, with tears streaming down her dirtied face. Her dress was covered with soot, and her shoulder was torn, with various scratches on her arms and face. She ignored her injuries and collapsed to the ground. "Father! Wake up! Please, wake up!"

Princess Plum placed both paws on King Carrot's chest, trying to wake him. His crown had fallen off.

The other rabbits emerged from their hiding places. They helped each other make their move to the beaten castle. Soon, all of the burrow surrounded the king and princess as they all hung their heads with heavy grief. No one spoke, except the princess. The king remained still as the color faded from his fur.

Master Kabu ambled over, knelt by the king, and placed a hand over his heart, shaking his head with closed eyes. He rose and climbed to the princess. He placed his loving paws on her shoulders. "We must let him go, Princess. Come now," he said, gently.

She sniffed as more tears streaked her face. She turned, stumbled over debris, and fell into Master Kabu's arms, crying.

He held her, staring at his beloved king with heavy eyes and drooping ears.

MOIRA

THE SEED

The next morning, Moira and the others walked with the rabbits as they carried their king to a special place in the forest where they brought their dead. No one spoke. With vacant expressions, the rabbits used their paws to dig a hole in the ground within an open clearing.

Braern and Moira helped lower him into the hole, deep enough for other animals not to exhume the king while he rested.

Princess Plum was at the front of the crowd of rabbits as they all stood in a semi-circle around the burial site. She carried a small brown bag and walked to the edge of the hole with her head down. Peering at her father's lifeless body, she dropped a single tiny seed, then stepped backward and nodded.

The other rabbits kicked and pawed the dirt to cover their fallen king. They stopped with a small bit of room left at the top. The others appeared around the mound, carrying small vegetable-shaped containers.

Moira imagined many more rabbits in their final resting places beneath each of the surrounding trees. *Maybe every tree grew from the body of one of their rabbit ancestors? So sad*

and yet so amazing! What a beautiful way to honor their dead.
Often, she reminded herself that she was in the presence of
a funeral and it would be rude to appear too interested in
the process. She pursed her lips as she watched, holding her
mouth with a furrowed brow.

After the rabbits poured the water, Princess Plum
kneeled, dirtying her purple dress even more. She didn't
mind. She placed a paw on the mound of earth and kissed
the spot where the seed was buried. "I know you'll grow into
a fine tree. I'll never forget you and everything you taught
me. The burrow will be fine. I'll take care of them. Goodbye,
Father."

As the princess lumbered back home, the group followed.

"Thank you all for stopping that troll. More of us would
have surely perished if you had not taken it down," she said.

"I apologize for not slaying the beast in time to save your
father," Braern said as he swallowed and stared at the grass,
bowing his head low. "I foresaw this in my vision. I should
have warned the rabbits. This is all my fault," he whispered.
Braern's face reddened as his eyes watered while he placed
his hand on his chest.

"No, please don't feel guilty. You did all you could. You
have our thanks and are welcome here in Rainbow Rabbit
Burrow anytime." She forced herself to show a tiny smile at
the tall elf.

He kneeled next to her as she took his hand in her paw.
Braern bowed once again. Then they all arrived, through the
trees, at the burrow.

Rabbits had already cleared the debris, and several others hammered away with their handmade tools. Every rabbit

worked to rebuild the burrow. No one slept or stopped. Tim, Moira, and Braern remained to help rebuild, even as exhausted as they all were. Master Kabu treated Nozomi's wounds.

"Now, I'm starting to miss taking showers," Moira murmured, half-joking, as a bead of sweat dripped down her back. She lifted her arm to sniff her armpit. *Gross. I smell like I haven't showered in a week. Wait, has it been a week? Really?*

"Me too," Tim said as they carried stacks of wood to the designated pile offsite.

"A bath sounds heavenly."

"I smell nothing," Braern joked as he sniffed under his own arm.

"Men are gross." Moira chuckled.

Numerous rabbits hopped over and spoke to one another to devise a plan to lift the troll's carcass.

Moira noticed them and offered to help.

They thanked her and scurried to their duties.

She bent and grasped its cold skin, feeling her stomach acid rise in her throat for a second. She looked skyward and took a deep breath. *This is the least I can do to help.* Balancing its huge body above her, she hobbled over, threw it off a nearby cliff, and returned. *Blech!* She shook her body, as if to rid of herself of the experience.

One unlucky rabbit made a scornful, disgusted face as it dragged the troll's severed head by its ear over to where Moira stood. The stiff expression of the deceased creature seared the image into Moira's mind. Its mouth remained open as its skin was covered in dirt. Its disgusting, long tongue dragged across the rocks. She bent her knees and met the rabbit's eye level with hers. "Let me help you with that." He wiggled his nose and leaned towards her. "Very well, thank you!" he squeaked, then hopped back to the village, wiping his paws on his tan pants. Moira watched as his fluffy tail stuck out of the back.

Her mind forced her to take one last look at the thing, but her hands encouraged her to release it. She rotated the head toward her and stared at its ugliness for a moment. Her body shuddered. She imagined what would happen if the troll rampaged around New York City, like in one of the *Godzilla* movies, roaring and punching buildings until they collapsed, with people screaming and running for their lives. Then it finally hit her. *What if the others and I are supposed to prevent something like that from happening? Naw, that's insane.* How could a troll make it to her world? She paused, staring off into the distance.

*****

Hours later, the sun disappeared behind the mountains as the sky painted a swathe of warm and cool colors that blended together, leaving the horizon a deep, magenta hue. *Did I really stay out here that long? It's almost night! Wait a minute... the portals. If Braern could magically travel through a portal to her world, without even trying, then what would stop other monsters from doing the same?*

She walked back to the burrow. Her friends were already asleep in a circle outside under the stars. They all had been through so much that she didn't want to burden them with any of her anxieties. She reached into her bag and placed her head wrap over her head. She ran her fingers over the smooth, silky fabric and pulled her blanket over her shoulder. Her head pounded from thinking of every possible scenario that could go wrong. The sounds of her friends snoozing soothed her mind. With a deep breath, she closed her eyes. The last thing she saw that night was the back of Braern's head. Her arm shook, yearning to run her fingers through his hair again. Tim, Blue, and Araduk lay between her and the elf. *I think Braern placed them there on purpose. Every time I turn him down, he gives me more space than I need. What the hell am I supposed to do with that?*

Moira rolled over and stared at the stars that peeked through the openings in the tips of the trees, her blanket up to her neck. Her thoughts jumbled in a chaotic mess of recent memories. She kept Braern at arm's length. The portals, nearly dying at every turn, and having little control over her life anymore caused her to miss the simplicity of going to work and coming home to an empty apartment. A second later, she shook her head. *Hell no, I'm never goin' back. As much danger as we're in, I'd rather be here with all of them than go back to barely living my life... but I've almost died so many times! Ugh!* She went back and forth between wanting to stay in Yumerion with her friends and going home. Then, her eyelids grew heavy like anvils and sleep finally took her.

*****

Another day passed. The rabbit's spirits lifted as their home looked more like it had been before the troll's destruction.

Master Kabu hobbled over with a basket over his arm. Everyone stepped backward as he carefully placed a tomato, then a stalk of broccoli and three large carrots on the soft dirt ground where the houses and castle used to stand. He scooted backward and waved his cane as a swirl of magic came forth and enlarged the vegetables. They grew big enough to replace the houses. Then the trio of carrots grew fat and wide and took the form of the castle once again—pillars and all. The elder nodded and walked away to allow the other rabbits to hollow out the new castle and their homes with their teeth, spitting out the remnants as they worked.

They remembered they could not eat their homes or Master Kabu's magic would vanish. Soon, builders came forward and added windows and doors. Not long after, the burrow looked new once again.

"I guess we should wake Araduk and be on our way," Braern announced.

"Wait, a moment!" Princess Plum ran over, lifting her new clean dress off the ground. Her silky fabric made soft whistling noises through the grass. She stood before Braern. "Come sit with us for a moment. We have some gifts for you all."

"Princess Plum, that's very generous of you, but I don't believe we deserve much after we allowed your king to die."

"Please, sit."

Braern, Tim, and Moira sat on the same logs as before and waited for the princess to sit on her nearby tree stump.

"Thank you again for stopping that beast," Princess Plum spoke kindly, making a point to look each of the travelers in the eyes.

"My father would not want us to mourn him, only remember the great joy he brought us all, so that is what we'll do. I know you all are exhausted from your battle, and we appreciate you helping us to rebuild our great burrow. Please, let us fill your bellies and give you a comfortable place to stay. You can leave for the monastery tomorrow."

A series of rabbits brought more food for them as everyone felt at peace once again.

The group ate slower, aching as they lifted their arms to their mouths.

"We don't want to intrude," Braern said.

"Nonsense. Stuff your weary faces, then you may leave in the morning."

"Very well. We accept your hospitality, and we thank you, Princess." Braern rose and thanked the rabbit who brought him a delicious-smelling plate of vegetables, fruits, and grains.

"Now then, the gift." Master Kabu placed his palm up, and a triangular object with a small circular glass in the middle appeared. The elder handed it to Braern, who stepped forward.

"Thank you, Princess Plum and Master Kabu," he said. Braern showed it to Tim and Moira.

"What is it?" Moira asked, inspecting it in her hand.

"It is called a yakusha. *That,* you must discover on your own once you reach Shiro Peak Monastery. I hope you find the truth that you seek," Master Kabu answered.

"Thank you both. You're very kind even when we feel we don't deserve such a generous gift," Braern said, bowing.

Tim and Moira nodded.

Araduk snorted and woke up, looking around from the side of the castle, rubbing his eyes.

Moira craned her neck to see him and chuckled. "Can't imagine being so wasted that you sleep for two days."

"Yeah, for real," Tim said.

"Should we tell him what he's done?" Braern asked as he swallowed a delicious bite of warm yams.

"I'm not sure. Maybe he already knows?" Moira said.

"After thirty-seven pints of ale, I'd forget my own name, if I was still alive." Braern shook his head as he noticed the dwarf jiggle his body and try to stand.

A dozen rabbits carried Nozomi from a larger house with bandages around her waist, her jacket laid on top of her belly. The little paws stabbed her back.

"I'm fine, thanks. You can let me off here," she told them.

They carried her for another few feet before she grew hot with annoyance.

"I said I'm fine!"

The rabbits dropped her on the ground and scurried off.

She winced in pain and held her stomach as she stood to rejoin the group.

"Glad you're back," Moira said with a faint smile.

"Thanks."

They stayed the night and pushed away recurring thoughts of the troll returning to finish the job. It took them all a long while to sleep, despite their exhaustion.

The fire blazed, and the rabbits gave them all blankets to sleep on, made from their discarded fur. Even on such hard ground, Araduk curled up on his side, spreading out his beard over his arms and under his chin. Tim pulled his knees to his stomach as Blue snuggled against his chest. Braern couldn't keep his eyes open, falling asleep with the hilt of his sword in his grasp. Nozomi sighed, shaking her head. She rolled over, away from everyone.

Moira was the last to sleep again. She watched everyone, afraid another danger would appear. *So much death lately. We'd better not wake up somewhere different tomorrow. I've had about enough of these damn portals.*

Braern

Fishes, Faeries, and Friends

Golden rays of sun warmed Braern's eyelids. A wave of memories from the night before hit him like an anvil. He pondered, allowing himself to forget such events, if he could be stuck in a purgatory inside his mind for a little while longer. For he knew, when he opened his eyes, his memories would be real and no longer could he convince himself it was all a dream. Another died because of their actions—or lack of action.

With a reluctant sigh, he tapped his sore fingers to awaken them on his soft blanket and opened his eyes. Birds chirped as drops of morning dew fell onto the elf's face. He shivered from the coolness that traveled down his torso. He spied his comrades still sleeping.

"What a feat to be able to sleep that long," he whispered to himself.

The tranquil sounds of a nearby river pricked his ears. *I think I'll go fishing while everyone is still snoozing. I haven't had a scrap of meat in days.*

Braern quietly moved his blanket out of the way and slipped on his boots. He fastened his belt, satchel, and sword at his waist. Sliding by his friends without waking them, he treaded on the balls of his feet to not make a sound. The tranquility of the water put his mind at ease. Braern welcomed the peace. He came upon the rocky bank and watched the sparkling fish flap along the waves, their little tails splashing drops of water everywhere. The elf smiled.

The birds and fairies of varying colors filled the sky above the river with a magical tint as they scattered about.

He grabbed a long branch on the ground beside him. *"Yari ni naru."* It transformed into a spear with a solid wooden handle and a sharp steel head at its tip. He carefully placed his footing, determining the best path to descend to the water without falling in or disturbing the fish.

He spotted a plump one as he lowered his legs into the water at knee level. Remaining still, he took a deep breath, his lungs expanding to breathe in the fresh, woodsy air.

The fish became curious, swam to his boot, and nibbled on his laces.

He stabbed it with lightning speed and flung it onto the bank.

It wriggled for a moment, with a hole in its gill, gasping. Then it stopped.

A few more for everyone else. We will be grateful for fish on our long journey ahead.

About to pierce another, he saw a two-tailed fox leap into the water with outstretched claws and catch three fish with its jaws. Several wet black strands reflected in the water atop its head. The fox swam to the rocks and bounded onto the grassy shore with its mouthful of fish.

Braern stabbed the nearest fish and tossed his second next to his first.

The fox noticed Braern and ran to the village. The elf followed the swift creature with his eyes.

Several feet away, Tim had arrived at where Braern was, beholding the river once again. The two were almost out of sight from the rabbit burrow. Blue had followed her human through the grass and chased a tiny, winged, yellow and orange creature.

"I wouldn't do that if I were you, cat," Braern turned to Blue. "Faeries are notorious for holding grudges and cursing those who wrong them."

"Huh? I thought fairies granted wishes and things?" Tim raised a curious eyebrow as he watched his feline friend try to catch it as it fluttered about.

"Not everything is what it seems here. I am certainly not," Braern answered in a monotone voice and returned to the burrow with his head down. *I thought I could complete this quest without him, but I can't. Father, where are you? This has become so much bigger than I ever expected. I need you!*

"Blue, cut it out!" Tim hissed at her. "First the rabbits, now faeries. You're gonna get us all in trouble."

She heard his words and immediately stopped. She released the tiny fairy from her paws, and it squealed and flew away, leaving a trail of magic through the grass.

Tim followed Braern to the burrow, ensuring he left space between. He gulped as he arrived, sat where he had slept, and wrapped his blankets over him, hiding his head.

Moira and Araduk stirred.

The fox ran right by Tim's legs, then transformed into Nozomi. Her bushy tail remained for a moment and then vanished.

"I thought that was you," Braern said.

"You did not think I would let you have all the fun catching our breakfast, did you? After all, the fox is my most comfortable form. I thought I could put it to use here," she said, hugging her fluffy tail. Her soft fur put her at ease. With a wave of her hand, her fox tail vanished and she became fully human again.

The fish fell to the ground as Braern threw his two fish beside Nozomi's three.

Araduk stumbled over with his hands on his head to fall next to the rest of the group. "M' head..."

"That's what you get for drinking yourself into a coma," Moira said.

"What happened?" Araduk belched a disgusting foul gas from his opened mouth.

The group cringed and held their breaths, waving their hands.

"Sorry..."

"Araduk, we need to tell you something." Moira sighed with heavy eyes.

Braern blinked with a slightest head shake toward her. *Not now!* the elf thought.

"After you had your... fill of ale, a troll came into the village and attacked us and the rabbits. We..." Moira swallowed hard.

"We fought it off, but you healed it, thinking it was me. The troll killed King Carrot. We attended his funeral and helped them rebuild their village," Nozomi finished without remorse for her words. She narrowed her eyes, gesturing with a hand for someone else to continue.

Braern placed his hand over his forehead, lowered his head, and shut his eyes.

Everyone sat in silence, picking at their hands and rubbing their skin. Braern buried his head in his arms with his knees bent to his chest. Araduk returned and sat with his back away from everyone. No one spoke a word.

The rabbits were busy harvesting and preparing for their breakfast and paid no attention to their guests. The pattering of their little feet and the flow of the river drowned the deafening silence.

Blue climbed over Tim's legs and made herself comfortable, tucking her arms and legs underneath her to keep them warm. She became a kitty loaf.

Nozomi was still in earshot, working on the fish at a table a few feet away. She swooshed her fox tail behind her, then it vanished with a flick of her wrist.

Araduk, Moira, and Braern faced away from one another.

ARADUK

THE HANGOVER AND THE GLUE

The dwarf sat in silence, staring at his boots.

"It cannot be..." his brow furrowed as his eyes watered. A sharp pain traveled from his throat to his belly as his stomach acids began to dissolve his tongue. He placed a hand over his mouth, stood quickly, and ran clumsily a few yards to the nearby bushes. He vomited all the contents inside him as his mouth filled with a repulsive, bitter taste. On his hands and knees, he sobbed and wretched putrid stomach bile. It burned his tongue.

He heard the others talking about him.

"Should we... help him?" Tim asked, hearing him wretch over and over.

"No, leave him be," Braern told them. "We all have many regrets from this journey. Now, Araduk is no different from the rest of us." Braern looked up at Moira, her eyes glistening in the morning sun.

"I will gut these fish. You all can stay here and feel your feelings," Nozomi said, folding her arms. She caught a glimpse of Blue, who buried her gray, furry head in Tim's arm before she collected the fish and walked away, scoffing.

"Braern... I..." Moira reached a hand, but before she could touch his arm, he rose.

"He didn't need such a burden on his heart. Not now." Braern turned and walked through the trees.

"You go to Braern. I'll help Araduk," she told Tim as they both stood. Their blankets slid off their legs onto the ground with a tiny thud.

Moira went to Araduk and placed her hand on his back as he sobbed.

"I thought m' days of killing were long gone. I took an oath..." he spoke between coughing and tears.

Moira remained silent. She knelt beside him, sniffed, then stepped backward, gagging.

The dwarf closed his eyes, his hands over his face. *I can't bring m'self to tell them... that is the only way... the faces of the lives I took with m' own hands will vanish from m' thoughts. I shouldn't have let m'self go that far. I allowed m' mind to be clouded from all rational thought, and an innocent was killed. M' fellow monks would frown upon m' actions.*

"Hey, you should drink some water. You must be dehydrated," Moira offered.

Araduk nodded, rummaging for his water pouch, and drank a sip. He stared blankly at her, unblinking.

The group silenced themselves once again. Only the faint breeze and trickling of the nearby river were heard.

"Alright, enough!" Tim yelled in a faltering voice as he rose. Blue mewed at him, then walked away in annoyance.

Everyone turned to face him.

Nozomi stopped mid-cut and peered at him.

Tim's breathing became erratic. His mouth shook as he forced himself to speak. "Araduk, you made a mistake. We all make mistakes. Quit beating yourself up over it. Your jokes are sometimes the only way I can get through the day. Braern, you're the glue that holds us together. You need to accept your role in this and that it will never be perfect. We like you the way you are—weird visions and all. Moira, you're strong on the outside, but you must let yourself feel strong on the inside too. And, you two, just kiss already! Nozomi, you're the most rude, difficult woman I have ever met, but I'm glad you're with us. The changing into animals thing is awesome.

"Now, I don't know what my role here is, and I've been feeling pretty useless lately. I stay in the shadows while you all fight, and it makes me feel terrible, but I'm willing to keep going with you all. And I'm hoping I can figure out why I'm here. So let's get to this monastery and figure out why we keep falling through all these stupid portals!" He paused. "Now, if you'll excuse me, I'm gonna go throw up." He hurried off with moist armpits with his hands straight at his sides, his entire body tense.

He stopped and collapsed against a tree. His legs gave way, and he sat hunched over, panting. Through his aches, he managed a smile. "Can't believe I did that," he whispered.

"The kid's not wrong." Moira chuckled to herself as she eyed the group.

"*Baka,*" Nozomi said.

Braern retrieved a flint rock from his bag and scraped it against his metal sword. Sparks fell onto their pile of wood. The elf carefully blew on the flames as they grew.

Nozomi cut the fish on a flat piece of wood and cooked them.

"I think that's the most we've heard Tim talk this whole time." Araduk laughed as he swung his legs to face the group.

It's true. I did make a mistake... as I've done so many times before. Somehow, my new companions give me hope that I can heal from this an' make amends for what I've done. The fates knew I needed 'em. Where they go, I go. Araduk thought the words to himself, peering at all the faces he had grown close to on their journey the last few days.

Everyone sighed and faintly laughed as their bodies relaxed.

Two gray ears appeared next to Nozomi as she cooked, then a little paw. Blue sniffed and patted at a piece of the fish's tail.

"Blue! Don't be rude!" Tim yelled, looking back.

She quickly chomped the tail and ran off with a mouth full of fish.

Tim chased after her. "Blue! Don't eat that. You'll barf it up later. Gross!"

She growled as he bent to take it away.

"Fine, don't come crying to me when you start hacking."

Braern remained silent as Moira peered into his eyes. She sighed and then stared at the ground.

The elf looked on, afraid to meet anyone's gaze, without blinking for a while longer. Absorbed in a trance, he patted his lips with his fingers. The softness of his skin soothed his nerves.

The aroma of smoky, cooked fish filled the air and made everyone's mouth water.

Nozomi beckoned them to fill their plates with fish and food as the rabbits said nothing of the strange meat they cooked over their fire.

Tim found his way back and sat next to Araduk, his chest out with a straightened back.

The dwarf brought him a plate full of fish, fruits, and breads. He placed a loving hand on Tim's head and tousled his hair before sitting again.

Tim smiled as he stuffed his face.

Everyone else ate, enjoying their meal.

"This is the best fish I've ever tasted in my life," Moira said through her mouthful of food.

"You are welcome. I am glad you like it." Nozomi nodded. "It could use some *ponzu* sauce, and some jasmine rice would make this perfect."

"Well, maybe we'll fall through another portal and end up in your country. Then we can taste all that awesome sushi and stuff," Tim joked.

Everyone stopped and stared at him with eyes wide and mouths open.

Araduk's food fell from his mouth. He caught the drops on his plate. He didn't want to waste any of his delicious meal.

"I'm kidding!" Tim said and continued eating. He dropped a few pieces of fish for Blue.

She gobbled them, then cleaned herself by licking her paw and rubbing it over her ear. She purred at such a delicious treat.

They finished their plates and helped the rabbits clean up. They packed their blankets and the gift and bade farewell to them. One by one, they thanked the princess and all her family for their gracious hospitality. Everyone felt a renewed sense of adventure and remembered the kindness and motivation of Tim's words. Walking on with their belongings on their backs and the extra food the rabbits had prepared for them and had dried, they waved goodbye to Rainbow Rabbit Burrow. Their colorful clothing and quaint vegetable and fruit homes soon grew smaller in the distance through the trees.

Araduk passed Tim and gently nudged him. "I believe *ye* are the glue now," the dwarf said with a smile, comforted by his friends walking on either side.

Tim stopped and watched them trek onward.

Araduk noticed the boy was no longer by his side and looked back, gesturing for him to follow.

Smiling, Tim hurried to catch up.

BRAERN

PORTALS AND TRANSPORTS

It had been over a week since Braern and his friends started their journey together. As he walked behind them, he stared off into the distance, his heart so heavy in his chest that it felt as if it could rip through his body and drop into the grass. He thought of his father. *Did he feel the weight of my absence? Was he hurt? Was some force keeping him from me?* The elf knew that it would take seconds for Orastos to find him, since they were linked telepathically when he first came to live with the old dragon. One single thought and they'd be reunited. *Why did he not come to my aid?*

Araduk ambled in front of Braern. He appeared to be lost in thought as well. Still dizzy from his alcohol excursion, the dwarf lost his balance often. Then he sang a guttural, Nordic tune as he found a large branch on the ground to help him walk.

Moira looked behind her and exchanged glances with Braern. She looked away as soon as he met her gaze.

Tim periodically checked on his feline friend as she was mesmerized by the creatures of the valley, perking up her ears at the fleeting wisps flying by.

Keeping her distance, Nozomi strode on.

The travelers listened in silence, only their footsteps resonating as he sang.

"Where is that music from? It's interesting," Tim asked.

"It's Viking. Used to hear it as a young lad," Araduk answered with his head up.

"Thought the Vikings were violent people?" Moira asked.

"You informed us that you are distancing yourself from that part of you as well," Braern replied.

"Aye. Those who run from thir past are doomed to repeat it. I simply keep it at arm's length for when I need to remind m'self that am no longer that killer. Plus, it's rather catchy."

"Well said, my friend."

Nozomi stopped for a moment as the others continued. She stared at her feet. "What if I never escape this thirst for revenge? What if it consumes me? What, then, will I become?" she whispered.

"Hey, Nozomi, you comin'?" Moira stayed behind and approached her.

Nozomi shook her head and spied her friend from the corner of her eye, keeping her head low. Without meeting her gaze, she answered, "Eh, yes." She rejoined the rest of the group and walked beside Araduk and Moira.

More silence.

About to open his mouth and say something, Braern stopped. His pupils dilated, frozen. First, his knees gave way, then his torso fell forward. He did not brace himself or outstretch his arms. Instead, he simply fell onto the short, burned grass of the rolling hills. His satchel's contents spewed out and rolled an arm's length away.

Everyone crowded around as whispers of his concerned friends faded. He could not move his mouth, talk, nor respond in any way. His body froze while his mind took control.

Thoughts clouded his brain with swirling colors surrounding him. A rectangular door appeared in front of him—or rather, a doorframe. He floated through the doorframe and ended up on the other side of another world of different colors, much more subdued than the last. He heard various scraping noises, like metal on stone. A small pit of darkness appeared below him. It enlarged as it approached the panicked elf.

Two black reptilian claws emerged from the pit below toward him, sharp talons growing closer.

He reached up, trying to grasp the air and free himself from its pull. Flying was useless. His muscles tightened as he fought his way up, his breath quickening as he placed his shaking hand on the doorframe, then his other. The elf willed himself up. He fell back through the entrance and returned to the more welcomed colors floating around him.

The claws retreated into the void.

A moment of peace overcame him as he watched the doorframe and the darkness sink away, enveloped in the light. Braern shot awake, as if he had taken his first agonizing breath after nearly drowning, his throat opening wide. He hyperventilated as his shaky arms pushed himself upright. He bent his knee and placed an arm to rest on his thigh. For a moment, he held his head down, forcing himself to inhale deeply. A feeling of being submerged in water overwhelmed his senses, but he was dry. The coolness faded and was replaced with his own body heat.

"Braern..."

He did not respond. Closing his eyes, he tried to make sense of what he had seen.

"Braern! Talk to us! What happened, lad?" Araduk bent to meet Braern's vision. He watched the color return to the elf's face.

"I-I think I had another... vision. I-I need to stand. My legs are tingling."

Nozomi and Moira bent down, and each took an arm to help him stand. Moira stood quicker than her friends, and Braern went flying several yards away.

The group gasped.

Braern stopped and floated at an angle before his head hit the ground. His eyes opened wide, and he braced his hands on the grass and righted his body to a standing position.

"What was that?" Tim asked, rushing to his side.

"Are you okay?" Moira asked, her hand over her mouth as she ran over and hovered her hand over his shoulder from behind.

"Yes, milady, I'm fine. Truly." He peered into her brown, worried eyes and saw his own reflection.

Her lip quivered.

"Do you want to wait here for a bit and recover before we press on?" Araduk asked, concerned.

"No, I will explain on the way." *I want to fly, but I'm not sure I have the energy.* He hated not being able to fly. Ever since his father taught him how to concentrate his magic to lift him into the air, he felt it difficult to calm his mind on the ground.

Moira blushed, then slowed her pace as the others continued.

They walked for a minute without saying a word to give the elf a chance to calm his nerves.

"Ye're all right, lad. Now, about that vision of yers..." Araduk said, breaking the awkward silence.

Braern explained as best he could, placing his hand on the side of his head. "Only my father would know what it all means: the claws and the darkness. It pains me that I've been separated from him for so long."

"Perhaps yer answer's within those walls," Araduk added, his hands in the air. "Ha-ha! Thir it is!"

The monastery appeared, still far off, halfway up the mountain. Its green thatched roofs and tall pillars were now visible. It faced east.

"Is that it? We're so close," Moira pointed out.

Everyone walked along for a few moments, quickening their pace with renewed smiles on their faces. Even Nozomi stifled a half-smile.

Blue meowed and weaved through the group, pawing at their legs.

They stopped.

"What is it, moggy?" Araduk asked. He bent his knees and outstretched a hand to the cat.

After a moment, Braern felt a pang in his throat and turned around.

Nozomi caught his attention and did the same. "Where is Tim?"

Araduk and Moira spun around.

"Tim!" Moira screamed, her veins in her neck popping as she cried out.

Blue ran to the portal, meowing louder. Tim's glasses lay on the ground. She crouched, searching for her human companion right where Tim disappeared.

On the ground, Braern observed the familiar ripples he had seen in his vision. He dove into the ripples and submerged himself in a cool atmosphere once again. He heard the muffled sounds of Moira's scream, but he pressed onward. His body temperature lowered as he saw a petrified Tim falling from him, arms outstretched. Braern swam through the thickness of the portal, and the doorframe appeared; only this time, it was circular.

The same claws of smoke swarmed like a rush of wind. The dark void appeared, barreling closer, ready to engulf them both.

Braern frowned, determined to save him. He flew at Tim and grabbed his hand before the darkness could swallow him whole.

It was on their heels.

He flew through the portal opening to the other side with Tim's hand in his. The brightness of the day shocked his eyes as he and Tim collapsed onto the ground, cold and exhausted.

The rippled oval on the ground disappeared in a reflective swathe of light.

Tim shivered from the cold he had felt and rolled into a ball, grasping his knees as he lay on his side. "Let's not... do that... again." He tried to find the humor but couldn't.

Moira removed her blanket from her bag and placed it on Tim.

Braern refused a blanket from Araduk. He sensed something bitter inside him. Something told him he didn't deserve to feel comfort. He had almost allowed his friend to be lost to a portal—another portal. *I can't even keep my friends safe. The one dragon who could ensure their safety had vanished. How many more must we fall through? How am I deserving to be with such people when they have knocked on death's door far too often?* "What good are these visions if I am never given enough time to do anything to change the course of our fates?" Braern yelled, throwing his arms at his sides.

"Braern, you ain't alone. Can't expect to bear the burden of everythin' we've been through by yourself. It's not your fault. You saved Tim," Moira assured him, coming closer.

"No!" Braern held up his hand to gesture for her not to come any closer. "What good am I?"

"Hey, I'm still here. You... saved me from falling through that portal. It was... weird in there," Tim said between breaths, rolling over to watch him. He bent and picked up his glasses, then situated them back onto the bridge of his nose. His chest heaved as he wiped the sweat from his hairline.

I cannot do this, Braern thought. Tim watched the elf dig his fingers into his legs to torment himself further.

"Braern, please, lad. Breathe for a moment. Ye must realize ye did something we have never done. Ye gained control o' that portal." Araduk attempted to sound cheery and hide his concern under his voice.

"That's right! You rescued Tim. Then the portal disappeared. Whoever is doing this to us didn't throw us into some other world when we're so close to our goal. Look." Moira pointed at the mountains with the monastery in sight.

"I did? Why? How?" Braern narrowed his eyebrows as he gazed in all directions, bewildered by the sudden series of events.

"We might survive all this, after all," Nozomi said.

"What she means is, we have a chance." Moira frowned at Nozomi.

"Do ye need to rest for a while? We can take a break," Araduk suggested with a half-smile.

Braern looked up, catching his breath, as he saw the clouds part away from the monastery. "No, I will be fine. We're so close to getting answers."

Araduk helped the exhausted elf stand on his legs.

Moira stepped over and took his other arm in hers and helped him walk forward as he placed his weight on her. She made slow movements, likely to refrain from throwing the elf again.

Guilt swept over Braern. He could feel it in his chest. "Try not to throw me this time," Braern joked.

"I'll do my best."

Braern kneeled and gathered his belongings that had fallen from his satchel. He grabbed the strap with one hand and reached with his other, then paused before touching the orb with the frozen tiny dragon inside. He placed his satchel over his shoulder. Grasping the smooth surface of the orb, his fingers felt a sense of tranquility with such a cool touch. He placed all his other belongings into his satchel and carefully stood, so as not to upset his still aching head. Braern stared off in the distance at the mountains and gauged the time it would take to get there, then eyed the dragon orb.

"We are still half a day's walk from the mountain." He looked back at his weary friends, then spun around to witness the vastness of the valley surrounding them on all sides. The elf kneeled to place the orb on the ground again, then stood and stepped backward. "And we cannot make camp here. It's too unprotected and open."

"You aren't leaving him behind, are you?" Tim asked.

"No, I intend to free him."

The group stood back as Braern chanted his enlarging spell. *"Hidogaru!"*

The orb shook and glowed purple. It opened from its center crease, and the sphere vanished into the grass as the dragon emerged. In his tiny state, he also vibrated. The dragon grew larger.

The group walked backward, giving way to his massive body and long tail.

When he had returned to his original size, his stiff muscles relaxed. His tail lay on the ground as he swished it across the rough grass. He whipped his long neck around to gaze at his marvelous wings and fanned them out. The dragon turned the other way to look at Braern, who freed him.

"Hope he doesn't try to fry us this time," Moira muttered.

"Thank you for freeing me, young elf. I am Telzraug. I could not move nor speak inside your orb, but I did hear the tongue you and your friends speak," Telzraug said in a deep rumbling voice, bowing his head.

"You are very welcome, my friend." Braern bowed back as a sign of mutual respect.

"I want to sincerely apologize for trying to cause you harm in the human world. How can I thank you for bringing me back to my world?"

"We accept your apology. If you don't mind, would you fly my friends to the monastery of Shiro Peak? We are all exhausted and would be forever grateful to you." Braern pointed up at an angle toward their destination.

Telzraug eyed each of his passengers, then nodded, blinking slowly. "It would be my pleasure."

"Thank ye, my friend," Araduk said.

"Wow, we're gonna ride on a real dragon! Wait... we're gonna to ride a *real dragon?*" Moira's smile vanished as a look of terror took over.

Telzraug bent to the ground as everyone except Braern situated themselves on his back. Moira sat in the crook of his neck.

"I should not shift so soon after my injury. I will join you," Nozomi said. She climbed up next, clutching her injured side that was hidden under her jacket. Then Tim, Blue, and Araduk situated themselves.

Tim placed Blue in his backpack and zipped it all the way. He secured it over his shoulders.

Looking forward, the dragon rose as he felt his rippling muscles move under his thighs.

"This is so cool. Wait till I tell the guys in my raid about this!" Tim suppressed his squeal, smiling. He scooted back as Nozomi sat in front of him. He gulped and averted his gaze away from her.

She turned her head to see him from the corner of her eye.

He sunk his head into his shoulders in embarrassment, his face turning pink.

"You ready, Tim?" she asked.

"Yes!" he squeaked, then cleared his throat. "I mean, yes."

"Everyone, hold on tight," Telzraug urged.

The group obeyed.

Tim placed his shaky hands around Nozomi's waist.

The dragon crouched for a moment, then leaped skyward.

Braern flew alongside the rest of his friends.

Araduk laughed, watching the fluffy clouds above them.

Moira held on tight to the dragon's neck. She closed her eyes, scrunching her expression. Opening one, then the other, she beheld the beautiful cool sky flowing around her. Moira loosened her grip and flew her arms in the air, smiling.

Braern caught himself staring at her chest, then looked away. *Don't be rude. She's enjoying herself.*

Nozomi placed her hands on the dragon's scaly hide.

Behind her, Tim held on for dear life with his forehead pressed against her back. He adjusted his arms as his body temperature rose. The boy tightened his grasp.

"Kid, you are squishing me. Loosen that monstrous grip of yours before I pass out," Nozomi demanded, her voice muffled in the wind.

"Sorry," Tim whispered. He loosened his grip a bit and moved his hand upward. He touched the bottom of Nozomi's breast with the tip of his finger. A rush came over him as his eyes widened. Holding his breath, he retracted both his hands.

"Really?" Nozomi said, unamused.

"I'm sorry! I'm so sorry! I didn't mean to!" Tim released Nozomi and raised his hands in the air, as if to act the part of an innocent bystander. Soon, the ripples from Telzraug's muscles sent Tim flying over the side of the dragon's hide. He screamed, grasping for something to hold on to.

Telzraug stopped in the air and peered back at where Tim used to sit.

"I got him!" Nozomi leaned to the side and dove into the sky, arms at her sides. She transformed into a giant hawk with black-speckled feathers and a white-spotted chest. She lunged after him.

I shall pursue them, in case they need help, Braern thought as he zoomed after them.

The elf watched Tim sob with his mouth open. The ground drew closer as the boy's tears welled and floated above him in little droplets in the air. His glasses flew up and off his face. The fierce wind dried his eyes.

Blue moved around as her claws dug into his back through the fabric, wailing in terror.

Nozomi lunged at them with her large black-tipped talons open. She snatched his glasses in her beak and grabbed Tim before he was about to smack onto the ground, then flapped her wings to return to Telzraug's side.

"You have him?" Braern asked through the wind. He followed her.

She nodded with a mouth full of plastic and glass.

"Ye all right thir, lad?" Araduk asked, bending his torso over the side of the dragon.

Tim clenched Nozomi's talons without uttering a word. Blue pulled her claws out of his back.

"I will fly us over. Meet you guys there!" Nozomi said through her hawk beak and zoomed toward the monastery. "So much for taking it easy."

Braern flew alongside the dragon as they launched once again. "I hope he'll be all right."

Nozomi, Tim, and Blue reached the base of the mountain.

She gently released Tim, as his weight lessened when he touched the ground. She turned into her human form and brushed her long black hair out of her face.

Tim couldn't look at her.

She collapsed, holding the bandages over her belly as she winced. "Look, kid, it's no big deal."

Blue clawed her way through the bag. She shook herself and ignored the need to clean her disheveled fur. Her human needed her. She padded to his lap as she adjusted her furry body, purring to help him feel better. The cat headbutted his arm, hoping to entice his hands into petting her. It was a mutual benefit to them both.

Still shaky, he stroked Blue's soft fur. He did not look at Nozomi, nor did he speak.

Braern was seconds behind and lowered himself onto the stone path, adjacent to the grass. His boots clicked on the hard surface. He hurried up the steps to a petrified Tim, squeezing his cat while huddled on his side, shaking.

Telzraug and the others landed a few feet away in a gust of wind. He crouched and allowed his passengers to slide onto the grass.

Nozomi handed Tim's glasses back to him.

He nodded. "That cannot be comfortable. Are you all right?"

By now, Moira and Araduk had crowded around Tim with concerned eyes.

"Ye took quite a fall, lad." Araduk placed a cool hand on Tim's shoulder.

"You okay, dude?" Moira asked.

Tim uttered a high-pitched, tiny groan without moving. "I think I've had enough... almost dying... for today."

"He needs some space," Braern said.

"Thank you for transporting my friends here. We are forever in your debt, Telzraug." Braern bowed.

The Western dragon swooshed his tail and smiled, nodding. "You are most welcome. I am heading home now. I believe my home is several days' travel to the east of here. My mate must be anxious. I will never forget your kindness. When I return home, I shall make it known that the clan of Braern the elf are allies of Ryu Valley." He bowed once more, crouched, then took off in the opposite direction. Soon, his shadow disappeared into the gray clouds.

Nozomi pushed herself off the steps and stood. "Let us move on. Tim can join us when he is ready."

"Shiro Peak Monastery. I've heard of this sacred place in my books. Such a marvel to be here now." Braern stepped closer to the entrance.

A rush of colors pushed him backward as his friends disappeared. His body froze while his mind sharpened. He saw inside the monastery—bright colors in every room. He whizzed past the chanting monks and came upon a room full of ancient books and scrolls. A voice sounded in his head, "Find the scroll with the red, satin ribbon." He focused on a shelf that glowed at eye level in the corner of the library. A single scroll illuminated far more than the others surrounding it. A red ribbon vibrated before him.

As he was about to reach for the scroll and touch it, a rush came upon him once again, and the mountain and his friends came back into sight. He'd had another vision of the future.

"What'd ye see?" Araduk asked, becoming familiar with his actions surrounding his visions.

"I know what scroll we need to find in there."

They nodded, staring at the mountain above them.

"Then, let's be off," Araduk said. "I want to see what m' old friends have been up to in m' absence."

ARADUK

SHIRO PEAK MONASTERY

A m home again. The dwarf smelled the crisp, mountain air as he looked above at the tall, wooden gate before them. The emerald-green-thatched roofs with golden trim connected several layers at the top. He placed a hand on the smooth surface of the crimson pillar.

"Is this the entrance?" Moira asked.

Araduk nodded. "Aye, this is the *torii* gate, symbolizing the passageway from the mundane world into this sacred land. Once we cross the threshold, we must be open in our minds for all the knowledge an' power here. Many find that they're not the same as before they arrived."

"It's beautiful," Moira said.

Araduk, Braern, and Nozomi bowed in respect. Nozomi flinched, holding her wound around her belly.

Tim and Moira watched their friends and repeated the gesture. They walked through the gate with ease and paused a few feet away to wait for the rest of the group.

"I feel it already," Tim said with a smile.

The dwarf stayed behind for a few moments, reaching a hand to touch the gate. Inches away, he blinked.

The world around him was dark and red, his arm covered in blood. On the ground lay hundreds of armored corpses.

He blinked again, and it all vanished. His arm shook as he tickled the side of his flask in his pocket. *That last war haunts m', still.*

Araduk reminded himself that he could not drink his whiskey once he was through the threshold. His fellow monks frowned upon such things. Memories came of how he traded five years' work with a witch for his never-ending flask. He requested it be filled with the strongest alcohol known to any creature between Yumerion and Earth. The dwarf coined the drink worldswide as *gin whiskey,* or "golden whiskey." The dwarves had a heavy hand in creating it, for they were one of the few beings who were largely immune to most alcohol. A single drop on the tongue could send an ordinary man to the hospital with alcohol poisoning.

With a sigh, his head up, he caressed the smooth, crimson wood of the gate. He silently walked through and felt a wave of serenity overcome them as their fears and burdens dulled in the back of their minds. The fresh smell of mountain air filled his lungs as his breaths slowed. He closed his eyes.

Together, they reached the first step and surveyed the hundreds more that led to the monastery and above to the snow-capped peak. The steps carved into rock were wide and steep. On either side, large trees grew that intersected in curves at the top. These continued halfway up the mountain.

Moira grabbed a hair tie from her bag and pulled her hair into a ponytail. "Want one?" she asked Nozomi.

"Sure."

She handed a second to her as she repeated the hairstyle.

Tim adjusted his glasses, gulping.

"Let's get a move on, shall we?" Araduk said.

"How many steps are there?" Moira asked with wide eyes, her hand touching one of the trees on the side and feeling the bark's roughness.

"777," Araduk and Braern said in unison.

"So, you've both been here before?" Moira asked.

"I have lived here for years," Araduk answered.

"I have only heard of this monastery from my studies."

"Can't you turn into something and plop us on the last step?" Moira asked, facing Nozomi.

"What do I look like, a bus?" Nozomi spat with a raised eyebrow and folded arms.

"Sorry, I guess your transformy thingy has spoiled me," Moira said, chuckling. "I'll meet you at the top."

Nozomi transformed into a hawk as Braern floated to the first step. They both crashed into a springy, rippled barrier that sent them flying backward.

Nozomi turned back into her human form. "What the hell was that?" she yelled with a frown, forcing herself to stand.

Braern managed to stay airborne, moving his crossed arms from his face.

"Forgot to tell ye. Magic's forbidden on the great steps. The monks cast a spell long ago. They feel that in order to gain the powerful knowledge here, every traveler must be equal and prove yerself worthy by completing the strenuous task before ye. The monks lift the spell at the door. Ye'll have to walk like the rest o' us," Araduk explained.

Braern sighed. "Very well."

The group began the tiresome trek up the stairs.

Blue walked a ways up before meowing for Tim to carry her the rest of the way.

He placed her in his backpack as she watched through her little window, enjoying the clouds as they whisked by.

Braern whined under his breath, no doubt because he wasn't able to fly.

Nozomi stopped now and then, panting, with her arms propped on one knee.

*****

An hour later, with a few breaks and groans from their exhausted bodies, they finally reached the top.

Braern leaned on the outside wall, his head against the stone as his back moistened through his clothing from perspiration. He slid to the floor.

Nozomi crawled the last few steps and fell onto her back, arms outstretched as she placed a hand on her injury.

"Ye know, lass, I can heal that for ye," Araduk offered between breaths.

"I do not need help," Nozomi whispered, panting.

Suit yourself. I tried to help, ye stubborn woman, Araduk thought with a shrug as he panted.

"That wasn't so bad." Moira laughed through grimacing teeth as she plopped on the last step and hung her head between her knees.

"I've made the climb multiple times, and it never gets any easier," Araduk said as he sat next to Tim.

Tim gently placed down his backpack with Blue inside and collapsed, his chest heaving. His body vibrated as he shivered. "Why couldn't Telzraug drop us off right here?" he commented, gasping for breath.

"For real..." Moira said, panting.

The cold air pricked their skin where they sweated. After a few moments, the fragrant scent of agarwood overwhelmed their senses. The low, soothing hum of chanting monks sounded. They looked onward at the enormous double door that lay mere yards away. They staggered over, staring at the iron knockers on either side that had the faces of friendly demons.

"What business do you have here at Shiro Peak Monastery?" the left doorknocker asked through his iron mouth. The rest of his face moved as he spoke, but his eyes were unwavering.

"My name is Braern Yogensha of Lavendale. My friends and I seek meditation and knowledge of portals."

"Very well. You may enter. All who come to learn and release their burdens are most welcome here," the right doorknocker said. Again, his eyes did not move.

The doors opened.

Moira narrowed her eyes. She sidestepped out of the way as the doors stopped moving. "You're not related to the door in Braern's library, are you?" she whispered, reaching to touch the right's ears.

"I beg your pardon! No, we are not!" the right shouted.

"Sorry!" She quickly retracted her hand.

"Araduk, is that you?" the doorknocker asked.

"Am back! It's been a while."

"Welcome back! How was your meditation retreat? Do you feel that your mind has healed?"

Araduk nodded. "Aye, as much as I could until I met m' new friends. I believe they are my new path to healing," he answered, gesturing toward the group with his head.

"Aww, Araduk," Moira said in a high-pitched voice with her hand on her chest. She smiled as her eyes glistened.

They arrived in the courtyard. Reds, greens, and golds shone in the sunlight. Scribed paper tassels with vertically written calligraphy hung from wooden beams. Little tower sculptures lay on either side of the entrance. A trickling fountain soothed the throbbing in their ears. Incense burned as their heart rates slowed.

Moira rushed to meet her friends. She gawked at the tall, colorful ceiling. Large wooden pillars were painted with bright colors that reached to the top. She noticed the absence of ladders. "How'd they paint the ceiling?" Moira asked, softly.

"With magic," a deep, friendly voice sounded toward them. A large, white alicorn approached them with a silver horn. His wings were folded neatly on his back, with a large green cloth across his chest. The golden stars and swirls stitched on his clothing shimmered in the sunlight.

Araduk stepped from behind the rest of the group. "Artemis! M' old friend! It's been weeks." Araduk bowed to the alicorn.

"We wondered where you ran off to. Your meditation retreat must've been very relaxing, indeed." Artemis chuckled.

The pair ambled on through the main hallway, catching up.

"You all are welcome here. My name is Artemis. I am the guardian of this monastery. I ensure we create a diverse culture here and keep the books and scrolls in top condition. You must be frozen from climbing all those steps. Please, do come in." The alicorn gestured with his head for them to follow.

"Greetings, I am Braern of Lavendale. This is Moira Washington and Timothy Rodriguez and Nozomi Hayakawa of Earth and Blue the cat. I see you know Araduk."

Blue walked in front of Tim's legs and meowed up at the alicorn, then sniffed the air. She walked over and rubbed Artemis's thin leg, then returned to Tim with her tail in the air.

"She likes you." Tim chuckled, scanning the monastery's vastness.

"An alicorn is a mythical creature that is a combination of unicorn and pegasus. They're one of the rarest ones from any magic world," Tim whispered, leaning toward Moira.

"Oh, cool," she said with a nod.

"Allow me to give you a tour." Artemis nodded toward the newcomers, turned around, and trotted through the enormous main hall.

"That is very kind. Thank you," Braern said.

Several satyrs in golden cloaks were busy writing on scrolls on the left. A group of fairies huddled around a series of books on a top shelf by the ceiling. Their magic from their wings trickled and disappeared into the air. The ground shook as a stone giant stomped to their right and pointed at book titles, squinting at the tiny, vertical silver letters in various languages on their spines. A lone griffin dressed in a purple cloak with a golden headband around his feathery ears sat humming and chanting, while several others joined in meditation.

They passed a dining area with pillows and short tables filled with metal and wooden basins of food. A prayer hall became visible with a large shrine on their left, surrounded by more calligraphic parchments, with a small fountain to the side. A giant statue of the sun goddess sat in the middle back of the room.

Araduk heard Moira as she spoke to Braern. "This reminds me of your library."

"It does."

"All creatures are welcome here, and all knowledge is here for the taking," Artemis said to the group. "Our only rule is you must remove nothing from this monastery, only to leave your stresses in life here." He turned his head for a moment to pause.

"We won't. Promise," Moira assured him.

"Yeah, it's pretty cool. Nothing like what I have back home in Houston," Tim said as Blue padded by his feet. He periodically looked down to ensure she was still following him. "Stay close, okay?"

Blue meowed, staring at him.

"No, I don't know where you can poop. Go outside and do your business, then come right back."

Artemis cleared his throat as he watched the little feline patter down the hallway with her tail raised.

"Can we find our answers and get out of here?" Nozomi asked with narrowed eyes.

"What answers do you seek?" Artemis asked.

"We must find information on portals. My friends and I have involuntarily traveled from Earth to Yumerion and back, and we don't know why. We also fear a great evil is hunting us," Braern answered.

"Portals? Someone is after you?" Artemis frowned and lifted his head with his gaze on each of the group.

They nodded.

"I believe you seek the history of the *verndari.* No one has spoken of the famous council in years. Strange that you mention this now. Come this way, please." Artemis turned a corner and traversed an open corridor to another room containing smaller windows covered with black curtains. "Not many alive know the truth of the council from the last thousand years." He led them to a room with shelves filled with parchments and books. "This is where we keep our ancient scrolls and artifacts. The sunlight damages them, so we keep this room dark and cool." Artemis lit his horn and it turned a purple-blue hue.

"Find the scroll with the red satin ribbon..." the elf whispered.

"I know which one we seek." Braern scanned the room until he saw the light from the alicorn's horn illuminate a red ribbon. He reached out a finger to touch the scroll.

"Please do not touch. The oils from your skin can damage the paper and ink."

"Yes, my friend here is patient with many things, but certainly not when anyone touches the scrolls," Araduk chuckled.

"My apologies."

Artemis called the scroll to him, and it hovered over a nearby table. He rotated his head as his horn glowed with magic that carefully untied the knot without touching it. Four floating paperweights that resembled miniature stone towers floated to the corners of the unrolled scroll to flatten and secure it.

Braern perused the unfamiliar writing. "I can't translate this."

"Which one of you brought a cat in here?" the steady voice of a minotaur came from behind for them.

"That would be me," Tim answered as he reluctantly raised his hand.

"Come with me."

Araduk craned his neck to see around the group.

"I'll go with the lad to ensure he doesn't get lost," Araduk offered.

"Be right back, guys," Tim said.

Tim and Araduk followed the minotaur, studying his tall stature and dark, cloven hooves. They reached a room with only large windows. Without a pebble out of place, a large zen garden was meticulously raked with even swirled designs in the sand.

Blue scratched a corner of the sand over a small mound before her.

The room smelled of fresh excrement.

A young, dark basilisk floated behind the cat, his wings slowly beating to not disturb his sand designs. With his paw on his head, he groaned in frustration, a rake in his grasp. His mouth opened and eyebrows raised.

"Did you *poop* in this zen garden?" Tim asked, his voice raising as he spoke.

"Marrow!"

"I told you to go outside! Not in here!"

"Oh, no..." Araduk began, his hand over his nose, stifling a laugh.

Blue lifted her head and tail and said nothing more. She walked back toward the scroll room.

Tim followed. "I'm so sorry! How can I... clean it up?"

"I will... take care of it," the basilisk said, huffing as he dropped his rake.

"At least she covered it up. She doesn't do that at home, stinks up the whole hallway."

"Your moggy has a mind of her own!" Araduk burst out laughing.

"Yeah, she really does."

Araduk turned around, shaking his head. He peered at the poor basilisk monk. *"Gomen nasai,"* he said with a bow. He turned to face Tim. "Let's get back to the others," the dwarf said, still chuckling under his breath.

When the trio made it back to their friends, Braern was still struggling to translate the scroll.

Artemis only understood a few words.

Tim perked up. "What about the *yaku*—whatever that thing is, that Master Kabu gave us?"

"Aye, he said we would figure out on our own how to use it here," Araduk said.

Braern pulled the yakusha from his bag; the smooth wood soothed his fingers. He placed it before his eye and bent forward to read the page. The letters rearranged on the page before him into the language he understood.

"It worked!" Moira exclaimed.

Braern translated, "Long ago, Earth and Yumerion co-existed together in peace and harmony. Humans and all manner of creatures traveled between their worlds through portals that spread across the planets at different locations. Some portals lay dormant, while magic could summon others. Years passed, and the greed of men and power of Yumerions became too great. Wars ravaged the lands and nearly wiped out entire civilizations on both sides. A council came together, naming themselves the *verndari,* and used their combined magic, cunning, and strength to close the portals, pushing everyone back to their respective homes, forever. They sealed the portals, protecting their secrets." Braern unfolded more of the parchment with a wave of his hand; the rest had been torn.

Artemis frowned and snorted as he peered at the paper.

Braern flashed a disgusted expression. "What is—"

"How could this happen? The rest of the scroll was ripped out!"

"Maybe someone beat us here and did not want us to know where the *verndari* are or anything else about them," Nozomi said.

"Artemis, do you know anythin' else about the *verndari?* We need to find info about them before our worlds become more unstable." Moira peered at the alicorn pounding his hoof into the floor, still frustrated.

"What do you mean, 'more unstable?'"

"An evil has followed us," Braern answered. "We don't know who it is or what this creature wants. They seem to know where we go and where we've been. They've opened portals to kill us on our journey so far and have caused several environments and even creatures to bleed together from both worlds. We've seen beaches blend with forests and harpies blend with what the human world calls a platypus. We're not sure how we are all still alive."

"Then you must go find the council and speak to them yourselves," Artemis answered. "Last I heard, their castle lies beyond a waterfall in Reykjavík, Iceland on Earth."

"Then to Iceland, we shall go," Araduk said with a nod.

BRAERN

THE AVALANCHE

Several minutes of concentration later, sweat dripped down Braern's back as a wave of heat enveloped his body. The moisture tickled his skin. He adjusted his shoulders and looked around to see where it was coming from. Without much luck, he forced his attention back to Artemis.

Tim fanned his shirt collar. "Is it getting hot in here?" he murmured loud enough for everyone to hear. He fanned his face as it reddened.

Everyone ignored him and faced the alicorn, staring at the scroll.

"Not now, Tim." Moira brushed her hand in his direction behind her.

"It would take several weeks to travel there by boat if you landed in... Europe, I believe, is what they call the continent in the human world. I wish I could accompany you, but I must protect this place," Artemis said.

"Is thir a way to open a portal to Iceland?" Araduk asked.

"No one has seen or heard of the portals in years. I'm afraid that's not possible, though you have explained that they have appeared for you. Strange." Artemis said.

"Thank you for your help." Braern bowed in respect, his discomfort growing.

"Do you know anything else that might help us?" Moira asked.

"Something about an old, important relic in the home of the *verndari*. I cannot understand this last bit." Braern squinted through the yakusha eyepiece.

Moira felt it next. "Hey, I think Tim's right. It's gettin' crazy hot in here." She fanned her face as her mouth dried.

"Why would a monastery on a snowy mountain be hot?" Araduk asked; his body temperature rose as well. He pulled his robe from his chest and shook it.

Soon, the entire group fanned themselves, their faces reddening. Moira wiped her forehead. Araduk frowned and spread out his legs to air his body under his robe. Tim cleaned his glasses for the third time, while Nozomi lifted her arms and pulled several stray hairs back out of her face. She exhaled, shaking her head, and removed her jacket. Tim averted his gaze so he wouldn't stare at her exposed arms and chest. Blue didn't react and continued to lick her legs as if nothing were different. *How can that cat not be boiling hot with all that fur?*

"Master Artemis, you need to see this." A small satyr came to the doorway with a furrowed brow and terrified eyes.

"I'm coming," the alicorn said as he hurried through the door. He joined the rest of the monks outside in the stone entryway.

"We better go see what is happening too," Nozomi urged as she ran outside.

The group followed.

The monks looked skyward, shielding their eyes with their hands from the intense light source above them.

"What is it?" Braern asked, meeting their gaze. He blinked as his eyes burned. Sweat pooled in his eyebrows and dripped onto his lashes. His vision blurred as he rubbed the perspiration from his face.

An oval portal, nearly the length of the monastery, appeared in the sky with glowing white light surrounding it. Inside was a desert with sand dunes, sparse trees, and high winds. Everyone could feel the moisture sucked from their skin, thirsty from the scorching heat. Water droplets trickled onto the ground before them. Puddles formed from the melting snow. Behind him, a crash sounded as an enormous pile of snow fell from the roof of the monastery and drenched a group of unsuspecting minotaurs.

Braern walked a few yards to the edge of the building as the mountain shook. He heard a long rumble in the near distance. The elf watched in horror as the large snow drifts on the nearest mountain shifted, and enormous pieces cracked, filling the air with echoing sounds. A large mound of snow fell onto his shoulder and soaked his clothing. He trembled from the extreme opposite temperatures and shook his arms to rid himself of the liquid. "Look above!" He pointed as he walked backward, mouth agape.

They followed his stare. Huge cracks dislodged glacier-sized snow banks as they slid down. A piece the size of a horse hurled toward them. They jumped out of the way as it slammed into a stone statue, knocking it over into several pieces.

"We need to do something or we'll all get trapped under a mountain of snow!" Moira's eyes widened as the veins in her neck throbbed.

"Braern! Can you make a shield over the monastery?" Tim shouted, adjusting his glasses from the sweat on the bridge of his nose.

The group rose quickly.

"I'll try!" Braern struggled to spark his hands as they illuminated, his face grimacing. *I've never made a shield big enough to cover an entire monastery. Is this possible?* With fingers like trembling claws, he willed the magic to come. He clenched his jaw so hard it nearly broke his teeth. The scrapes of his molars grinding together hurt his ears. "Gah!" the elf yelled. The shield appeared above his palms. The magic drained from his body to the shield as it grew bigger.

"Everyone! Let's move!" Artemis hollered as he reared on his hind legs, spreading his mighty wings. The alicorn pivoted and pushed off the ground and into the air. He lunged towards the snow mounds. His mane flowed in the breeze while magic rays shot out of his horn and blasted them to bits.

Many creatures stood side by side and used their abilities to help stop the avalanche from shifting hundreds of feet above them. An enormous mass of snow barreled toward them, nearly deafening any other sounds.

Braern flew to the portal and spread his arms with his shield floating above one hand. He tried to remember what he had done when he'd rescued Tim from the portal. *Perhaps I could do the same to this one and close it. But how can I be in two places at once and shield the monastery and close this portal at the same time? I could clone myself, but I fear I could not concentrate on everything all at once to keep everything sustained.*

"This is exactly like I saw that bastard do to the lake, weeks ago." Nozomi yelled, eyes fixated on the surrounding chaos.

"You say this might be the evil creature who pursues you?" Artemis asked.

"Appears so. Wait until I get my hands on him..."

Every monk and available creature filled the courtyard. Various magic spells of light and color shot toward the rush of snow. The mountain quaked as the roaring of the snow continued. The avalanche grew larger and wetter while their magic suppressed it. Jaws clenched, groans sounded, and bodies trembled from keeping the avalanche at bay.

"What can I do?" Nozomi asked loudly.

"Can you turn into something big? Something that can hold the mound before it caves us in?" Tim answered.

"I know!" Nozomi turned herself into a giant *kasa-obake* umbrella demon and flew to the mound of snow as it dripped from melting. She opened her top, covering the monastery in shadow, and held herself steady as best she could. Resistance from the snow pushed her thin demon legs down the slope as she grimaced in pain. "Gah!" she yelled.

Soon, one monk, a golem, climbed the mountain and placed himself in front of the falling mounds with wide, muscular arms. Now, several creatures fought to keep the snow from consuming the monastery.

A glowing green light appeared in the air as a figure shone in the middle, facing the struggling travelers.

Braern knew it was the one after them. He did not know the creature's name, but he knew they had caused this. The air filled with a cackling of laughter as the glowing light flew off in the distance. Braern had a decision to make. He could fly off by himself and try to defeat this enemy who has caused so much pain and suffering for everyone around him and the worlds they have been to. Or he could stay and try to save the monastery from being destroyed by an avalanche or all the inhabitants being killed from the devastating heat, including his friends.

Braern watched as the glowing light disappeared into the sky. *I'm saving my friends and the people here.*

Steam filled the air as hot and cold mixed, creating a massive cloud of moisture. Through the steam, they struggled to see where the next pile of snow would land.

Braern blinked as the sweat dripped down his face and into his eyes.

"What can I do? I feel so useless," Tim said, pulling his hood over his head, sinking his neck into his shoulders.

Blue huddled inside the monastery doorway, shivering from fear, and crouched into a ball.

"I don't know what to do either!" Moira yelled. She punched away several snowballs that hurtled towards her and Tim. With a deep breath, she threw her arms around, breathing heavily and stomping her feet. She bit her quivering bottom lip.

"At least you can do that."

Araduk held the side of his palm over his forehead as he peered above, warning the others when a heap of snow was hurling towards them so they could safely move out of the way.

Tim stared at his feet for a moment, then shot his gaze to the elf. "Braern! I have an idea!" Tim shouted skyward.

"Tell me!" Without turning his attention from the portal, it began to shrink.

"Fly Araduk up there to the snow and have him keep your shield in place. Maybe he can hold it for you since he can do magic with his own hands. Then Nozomi can fan her body to create wind resistance, and the snow will fall off onto the other side of the mountain!"

Braern noticed the portal had only shrunk a small amount. "I agree! Artemis! Fly Araduk to me. I'll give him my shield. Then head back to the snow mound and keep his it steady!"

"You got it, elf!" the alicorn shouted. He stopped his magic trail and bent for Araduk to climb onto his back. The winged horse flew to Braern as he floated the shield over to Araduk's hands.

The dwarf had a much easier time carrying his magic than Braern did. "I got!" Araduk steadied his hands as the shield increased in size as they returned to the courtyard. Then, Artemis plunged down underneath the dripping melting snow as Araduk readied himself.

Nozomi fanned her umbrella body, opening and half-closing herself, as gusts of wind swooshed and swayed. Soon, all the snow from the top had fallen off the side, and it crashed to the base of the mountain.

"Quick thinkin', lad," Araduk said to Tim, wiping the sweat from across his eyes.

The boy smiled and removed his glasses. He stared at his feet while he wiped the condensation from the lenses with his shirt.

When all the snow had melted and disappeared, the monks and group of friends flew to the courtyard, except

Braern. He stayed in front of the scorching, hot portal with the desert on the other side.

Nozomi became a human once again.

"How are you doing up there?" Moira hollered at him, her hand over her eyes.

"I don't know how to close this!" he screamed, feeling his tongue crack as his hair plastered to his face.

The same flash of green appeared across the sky. It vanished as quickly as he saw it. The portal closed before his eyes in a split second.

Braern lifted his chin, drenched in sweat, as he tried to catch his breath. He peered at his hands. *Did I do this? I couldn't have.* He floated to the monastery inhabitants and his friends. "I'm unsure if I caused it to close or not. I didn't feel like I did."

"Maybe it was on some sort of timer?" Tim said.

"Or the one who has been tryin' to kill us saw his plan thwarted and he escaped again," Araduk said with a frown, gazing at the spot where the portal had been.

"You saw that too, didn't you?" Braern asked.

"Aye."

"All we can do now is find this *verndari* council and ask them to help us fight this enemy."

TIM

THE QUEST OF THE INSIDE JOKE

Tim admired the golden gifts and bags of food and clothing that Artemis and the monks had given them. "It's like saving people has made us rich or something."

"Tim!" Moira taunted him with a shoulder nudge.

They laughed.

Braern was in front, bowing to Artemis and speaking of their next moves.

Moira and Tim cleared their throats as they bowed as well, joining the others.

"'Am goin' with them," Araduk said. "'Am invested in this an' I want to see it through to the end."

"Of course, my friend," Artemis said with a nod. "We hope to see you all again."

"Thank you. We truly appreciate all you have done for us," Braern said.

The monks helped them fasten their belongings, sleeping blankets, water, and food supplies on their backs, waists, and shoulders.

"You'll never drink such water as pure as you have from here," a satyr said as he trotted to the group, eyeing their water pouches the monastery had given them.

"It is time for us to be off. Thank you again, Artemis." Braern looked back as the monks opened the doors.

The weather had cooled. Some of the snow remained. Sounds of drips echoed on stone from the rooftops. The air was thick and steamy. Moisture accumulated on Tim's glasses. He wiped them clean for the second time and squinted at the vast stairs in front of him. The scent of agarwood incense was faded.

"Oh no, not the stairs again," Tim said with a sigh.

"Oh, c'mon! We could all use some exercise. Some, more than others," Moira joked and jogged down the steps, wheezing as she went.

"Speak for yerself, lass! Am in the best shape o' m' life! Ha!" Araduk chuckled. He placed his hands on his head as he nearly lost his balance, staring at the steps.

Everyone descended through the fog. They spread across the breadth of the decline; Araduk trekked behind the others. Moira was in front and broke a sweat. "I'm gettin' my steps in today again."

"I'll meet you at the bottom," Braern said as he passed her with a smile.

"Oh no, you don't! I'ma see *you* at the bottom!" Moira yelled, panting.

The two raced as the rest of them staggered down at their own pace.

Blue followed Tim with ease. She stopped periodically to take a break, meowing for Tim to pick her up.

"C'mon, you lazy cat. You sleep sixteen hours a day. Time to get some exercise!" He laughed at his feline friend. He could feel Blue judging him with her sharp eyes piercing his back. *I bet she's plotting my death right now.*

Blue caught up and continued down with her human and the dwarf.

Nozomi traveled at the back.

After a long while later, Moira was the first to reach the last step, and the same muscles ached as the last time. She panted, trying to catch her breath with her hand on her chest. She leaned against the torii gate with her blanket strapped to her back, but the hard corners still pierced through and stabbed her spine. She winced, fanning her face.

Braern appeared next to her.

"How did I beat you? You're losing your touch, man," she joked.

"I let you win." He chuckled.

Nozomi came next, then a few moments later, Tim, followed by an exhausted Araduk.

"Never... again..." Tim panted and fell on the last step against his backpack.

"I suppose we can rest here for a while. The stones will keep us safe," Braern said.

They moved to the side of the steps between several large stones. It was much warmer than it had been on the mountain. The thick air was still making it more difficult to breathe. The smell of the mountain trees filled their nostrils as they looked out over the hills.

After many groans from the dwarf, Moira dragged Araduk over and helped him feel more comfortable on a slanted rock.

"So, where are we headed from here?" she asked, rubbing her leg muscles as she stretched on the grassy ground.

"Where are we? Ah, yes. So, from the steps of the monastery, we are facing east. We need to go... well, I'm not sure.

Artemis spoke of the *verndari* making their home in the human world in Iceland. Do you know where that is?" Braern asked Moira.

"I know where it is from New York. It's an entire ocean away. We would have to take a plane or a boat."

"I don't know what a plane is. Is it fast?"

"Hell yeah, about 600 miles-an-hour fast." Moira raised her eyebrows as she waited for Braern's expression.

"That is fast. I could not hope to come close to that speed, even at my best flight time. Now, we need to get back to the human world—your world."

"How are we gonna do that?" Tim asked, sprawled on the ground. He plopped his head onto the grass.

Blue found a dry spot to curl up next to him and licked herself.

"I don't know. I suppose we need to open a portal," Braern answered.

"We could sit here and wait for one to swallow us whole again," Tim said, mimicking the shape of a circle with his fingers.

"Hell no!" Moira replied.

Araduk and Braern shook their heads.

"You have never done that before, have you?" Nozomi asked Tim, her hand on her cheek.

"No, I haven't, but I have all the time in the world to learn."

"Do you though?" Moira said, her voice raised. She sighed.

"I suppose you are correct. Time is of the essence. We could be thrown through another portal at any moment." He paused. "Well, maybe we should press on? I can try to open a portal on the way." Braern stood, watching the others still having trouble as their chests rose and fell.

"No!" everyone said in unison. Even Blue meowed, as if she were agreeing.

Braern smirked, knowing full well his friends needed a much longer break. "If you insist. We can stay here a while."

They situated themselves in a circle, the boulders shielding them from the wind.

"Wanna see something funny?" Tim stifled a laugh as he relaxed his muscles and sat upright.

"Sure, kid," Moira said.

"Cats always do this. Watch." Tim pointed a finger at Blue.

She trotted up and touched her nose to his finger.

Tim turned his head, as if he didn't see her.

Blue looked up at him and meowed.

He pointed again.

She responded the same.

A few more times and he burst out laughing. "I don't know why it's so funny and cute, but it is. Oh, Blue, you're so silly." He picked her up and hugged her till she squeaked to be released. He let her go.

She shook her body and licked herself, as if to tell him she did not appreciate her fur being messed up like that.

"She's pretty cute. Can I pet her?" Moira asked while the others watched.

"Sure! Cats are excellent judges of character. She will be very happy to get belly rubs or chin scratches from you."

Moira placed her hands at Blue's level.

The gray striped cat switched her attention to her and rolled over, exposing her cream-colored and spotted, round belly.

Moira stroked her fur and smiled. "I've never liked cats, but she's honestly making me change my mind. Maybe I'll get a kitten from a shelter when I return home." She paused. "If I get home again."

Braern turned and met her gaze, but she glanced away.

"Blue does that. That's what I love about her." Tim crinkled his eyes as he smiled. He felt a sense of pride overwhelm him, knowing if everything else in his life went to shambles, he always had his kitty friend to comfort him.

"Silly moggy. C'mere." Araduk chortled as he tried to play with Blue a little too rough with his hands.

She bit him, growled, and ran to Tim with a thrashing tail.

"Oh, you pissed her off now," Tim told him. "I'd keep your hand away if I were you."

Nozomi scoffed, tapping her right foot. "Enough of this. Where are we going?"

"We need to get to the human world first. Problem is, I don't know how to summon a portal, and I have no idea where we would end up on the other side, even if I managed to summon a portal." Braern sighed, waving his arm in the air. He let it flop onto his knee, with his other hand cradling his head.

Tim watched him. *He's clever. He'll find a way.*

"Seems like an impossible task, lad," Araduk said.

"Yeah, but I'm sure you can figure it out, somehow," Tim said, trying to comfort him.

"The only way I know was back outside that misty island with the platypies. Do not see that happening anytime soon. What do you need from us to hurry this along?" Nozomi asked, removing a few snacks from her pack. She munched and stretched her legs.

"I'm not sure. I need some time."

"Time? We don't have time! We need to get this guy who keeps trying to kill us and rid ourselves of him!" Nozomi threw her arms in the air in frustration.

"Girl, I know you're anxious, but we have to be careful. There's nothin' we can do until we can get back to Earth," Moira said.

"I'll get some firewood. It's getting cold," Braern said.

"Why'd you have to be like that?" Moira asked, frowning.

"I did nothing. I think we are wasting our time sitting around."

"Braern is doing all he can to get us where we need to be. Learn some patience, lass," Araduk urged her, watching the elf walk toward the nearby woods.

"I think I'll go with him to collect firewood," Moira said.

As soon as she was out of earshot, Nozomi teased, "Figures. Those two are ridiculous. Get a room, already."

"Get room for what?" Tim asked, leaning forward.

"Nozomi! Well, ye right about one thing, lass. To be tied down is a big mistake. I was married once. One o' the worst choices o' m' life. Woman tried to kill m' more times than I could count. We had some great times too. She was a ravenous lover in bed," Araduk admitted, looking skyward. He shook his head.

"Ew…" Tim scrunched his face. "You were married? That doesn't sound like you at all."

"Aye, I was. She died years ago. Sometimes I can still smell her horrible cookin'."

Tim and Nozomi giggled under their breath.

"I've never even had a girlfriend," Tim muttered with his head down and blinked as he sighed.

"Shocker," Nozomi whispered.

Tim rolled his eyes, ignoring her.

"It's not like I didn't try. Asked out Jess from geometry class… but she laughed at me and went to prom with some blond jock. My mom made me go anyway, by myself. Never been so nervous about anything in my life."

"Well, ye have plenty o' time to find yerself an attractive young human. Take yer time. Whatever ye do, don't marry them unless they can cook."

"My mother says that same thing." Tim chortled as the dwarf patted his shoulder a little too hard, knocking off his glasses.

He readjusted them on his nose.

"What are those two talking about?" Araduk pointed to where Braern and Moira were chopping down several smaller trees that grew at the base of the mountain.

"Maybe they're finally confessing thir love to each other," Araduk said. "'Oh, Braern, I've dreamed m' whole life o' a lad like ye. Take me now!'" Araduk did his best female impression, but his hoarse dwarf voice hindered his impersonation.

"Araduk!" Tim scolded him.

"No, no, I got this. 'Oh, Moira. Your hair is as soft as silk. Marry me!'" Nozomi chimed in, giving her best manly impression.

Araduk and Nozomi laughed with their entire bodies. He fell over. She wiped a tear that escaped her crinkled eyes.

Tim put his hand over his mouth to try not to laugh, but he couldn't help it.

This is the first time I've ever heard Nozomi laugh. It's cute... and she's so hot, Tim thought with a smile.

"'What pointed ears you have, Braern. Can I touch them?'" Nozomi continued in her Moira voice.

"Better to... hear you with?" Tim added with a raised eyebrow, afraid he hadn't quoted the famous fairytale very well.

Nozomi and Araduk burst out laughing again, this time even louder.

"That was good. Wait, I got one. 'O' course, m' love! I grew them for ye!'" Araduk couldn't do it any longer and let his voice return to normal, laughing hysterically. He retrieved his flask.

"What is that? I want some!" Nozomi snatched his flask from his fingers before he could get a drop.

"Are ye crazy, lass? This stuff could kill ye!" He snatched it back with a frown.

Nozomi scoffed.

"No one is to drink my flask but me."

"Maybe *you two* should get a room," Tim mumbled, pleased with his comeback. He was a little sad that no one could hear him. He always thought of the best things to say after the conversation was over.

Nozomi scoffed.

Braern and Moira returned with arms full of chopped, thin, wooden logs. "What are you all up to over here? We heard laughing," he asked, unsuspecting and smiling.

Tim began, "Oh, they were—"

"Nothing! Simply jokin' around!" Araduk answered.

Nozomi spit out her water and laughed again.

"I think we missed an inside joke." Moira chuckled, watching the rest of the group falling over.

"What is 'inside joke?'" Braern asked her, facing her ear.

"It's a funny thing between certain people that others don't understand."

"Oh. Enjoy your inside joke," Braern said, nodding.

They laughed even harder. Araduk looked as if he were about to burst, his face reddening.

Braern raised an eyebrow and tilted his head. "I still do not understand."

"Let it go, hun," Moira said as she patted his arm, and their laughter died down.

Tim wiped his eyes under his glasses as he felt his belly muscles hurt a bit. It was a good pain. He hadn't laughed like that in weeks.

Nozomi took a deep breath and went back to her drink.

Araduk giggled to himself.

"It's lunchtime. Who's hungry?" Moira asked as she sat next to Nozomi.

"Aye, please! What did m' friends give us?" Araduk asked, his mouth watering.

"Looks like some type of dried meat and some bread." Braern unfolded the fabric from his satchel, revealing a small piece of dark-colored meat and a browned, crispy, tiny loaf. He sat next to Moira.

Everyone ate, taking occasional sips from their tan water pouches.

Braern finished his meal and lit his hands. He stared at his palms, looking as if he were willing a portal to appear. A few sparks later, he stopped. "I will keep trying."

"It's okay. You'll get it," Moira assured him with a half-smile.

"I wish I had your confidence, milady," Braern said. He shrugged and uttered a number of spells he knew off the top of his head.

He stopped.

"Do not drink the tea," the elf whispered.

"What did you say, Braern?" Moira asked.

"I... I don't know." He raised an eyebrow and moved his head back.

"Oh, okay." Moira shook her head and took a sip of her water.

Braern tested his magic again and again.

Tim stared, relaxing his shoulders as he shook his head. He raised the corner of his mouth in concern. *This is exhausting, watching him try to do this.*

As the day darkened, they became restless. Each took several walks throughout the day to amuse themselves. They threw rocks, hummed to themselves, and discussed silly things. They agreed not to go anywhere else and waste their energy until they found a way to summon a portal and return to the human world.

Soon, Tim knocked over a rock that housed a glowing light underneath. He leaned closer to inspect. "Hey, guys, look at this."

It pulled him inside.

Not again! Why am I always the damsel in distress?

"We're coming, Tim!"

He heard a muffled voice above him as the others joined.

They fell through a cloudy sky. Minutes passed. Still falling. All the while, they screamed and wailed, their tears floating above them.

Blue tried to place her feet underneath her but couldn't balance herself, howling.

Tim grabbed her, placed her in his backpack, and held her close.

Still, no land was in sight.

Panicking, Nozomi turned into a giant hawk and flew under Tim, Araduk, Blue, and Moira. She fluttered in circles toward the ground at a moderate speed, with her beak in the center.

Braern slowly flew down with them, knowing his friends were safe with Nozomi.

"We've been falling for a long time. When are we going to stop?" Moira yelled loud enough for Braern to hear her.

"I do not know. I have experienced nothing like this before!"

Tim could feel her warm body rubbing against his chest, shaking and terrified, so he patted her foot through the rough fabric. "It's all right, Blue. We will be out of the sky soon."

"This is ridiculous. We should be on land by now. Where are we?" Araduk asked, catching his breath. "And why am I always out o' breath with the likes o' you all?"

"I don't know," Braern said.

Finally, land. They slowed to a halt and quickly dismounted.

Nozomi turned human again.

"Thank ye, lass. I don't know what we would do without ye," Araduk said, his body trembling.

"Don't mention it, dwarf."

"Seriously, though, where the hell are we this time?" Moira placed her hand on her chest as she tried to catch her breath. She developed a hoarseness in her throat from screaming for her life. "Are we on Earth or Yumerion?"

"I guess we're about to find out," Tim said.

BRAERN

THE TEA GARDEN

With a blinding headache, Braern heard a staticky voice in his mind. Through squinted eyes, he ensured his friends were safe around him. All the traveling back and forth between Yumerion and Earth had left him drained and confused. He knew he wasn't the only one.

"I'm gonna get jetlag or something from all this." Moira shook her head, her heartrate returning to normal. "We're never gonna get used to these *damn* portals."

"Why is everything so foggy?" Tim adjusted his glasses and wiped them with his shirt. "Okay, it's not me."

"I can hardly see anything. This seems to be a common thing with us," Araduk said.

"You hear that?" Braern asked.

"What?"

"Water. Let's see what's over here."

They had to put one foot in front of the other and test the ground before taking another step.

Braern walked in the lead. He took another step and heard a clunk beneath his boot. He paused, holding up his closed-fingered hand to the group behind him for them to stop. Looking down, he saw, through some cleared mist, a curved, tiny bridge that crossed a small, peaceful creek. "It's a bridge."

"Should we cross?" Tim slouched his shoulders, scanning for any glimpse of something familiar. He rubbed his arms, adjusting his backpack, as Blue stuck out her head to sniff the air. "This place gives me the creeps."

"I'll go first and see what's on the other side. You all wait here." Braern hovered his hand over the hilt of his sword. He walked on the balls of his feet, but his weight made the bridge creak. Expecting something to happen, he winced with each noise. Waiting a few seconds, he continued. Each time, he felt afraid, then it subsided.

Tim paused and looked over the edge at the trickling water. The creek was the only place clear enough to see through the mist. Large orange and white fish swam around, narrowly missing each other. Their whimsical tails created ripples on the surface as they swooshed away.

"It's safe. You can come over now," Braern called.

"The water isn't deep," Tim said, relaxing his stiff shoulders.

"That's all I need to hear," Moira said.

They reached the other side, and Araduk stomped across the bridge.

"Could you be any louder?" Nozomi hissed, and figures of cypress trees appeared through the mist. Nozomi frowned and lifted her nose, wiggling her nostrils.

Braern saw the blurry figure of the shifter and followed what she was doing. He smelled scents of mint and jasmine in the air. The elf exhaled. *Such soothing scents. Reminds me of home, though we grow lavender.* He longed to wade through the purple tipped grass, if only for a second. His pain lessened as he thought of home.

"Hey, guys, did you see the koi fish?" Tim whispered.

Everyone stopped and peered at several more fish that came to greet them.

"Oh, how pretty," Moira said.

"I've never seen such fish like that. Let's catch them for dinner!" Araduk said.

"No!" Nozomi placed her arm in front of the dwarf, who licked his lips. "These are not for eating. They are symbols of good fortune and prosperity."

"How do you know so much about these fish?" Braern looked from the creek to Nozomi.

"I know because we have landed in Japan. This is a tea garden."

"Japan? Cool!" Tim squeaked, jumping and shaking his fists in the air. "I've always wanted to visit Japan. Never had the money or time. Well, thanks for saving me the airfare!" Tim looked skyward through the mist.

"At least we know we're back on Earth," Moira said.

"Yup, one step closer to Iceland," Tim said.

"Well, I'm happy to hear we are somewhere familiar. Where should we go from here, Nozomi?" Braern asked as he placed a hand on Araduk's shoulder.

The dwarf tapped the bridge with his fingers.

"But they look so delicious. Can I eat one?" Araduk begged Nozomi.

"No, dwarf. We will stop to eat soon," she said.

"Wow, I've never been to Japan, and I've always wanted to travel here too." Moira crouched and watched the fish for a little while longer. She rested her elbows on the railing and kneeled on the wood.

Braern bent to sit next to her. The coolness of the moist bridge soothed his legs and sent a shiver up to his back.

"Are you all right?" he asked, offering her a hand.

"Yeah, I'm fine. A little cold."

He rotated his torso, reached in his bag, and pulled out his thick blanket the monks gave him. The elf placed it around her shoulders.

"Thank you."

They stared at one another for a moment.

"Can we go find an anime shop somewhere? I still have my wallet. I'm dying to buy some new merch. Of course, my parents would find me and freak out when they saw me in Japan." Tim clapped his hands, and his eyes widened. He pushed his glasses onto his nose, as they had fallen.

Braern and Moira looked away and rose.

"We need to find somewhere to shelter. This mist is making it difficult to see anywhere," Braern urged the group. "We must stay together or we'll be lost."

"I agree. Let's head where the bridge is pointing and see what is over there, without losing one another," Nozomi answered.

"I think we should go toward that. I smell somethin' good that way." Araduk pointed across the grass to an exposed straight, colored top of a building standing through the grey.

"Very well. You lead the way, Nozomi." Braern nodded and gestured with his hands for her to move to the front.

"*Hai.*" Nozomi nodded.

The group followed her, taking small steps, and watched the backs of their friends. Few birds tweeted softly in the serene atmosphere. A deafening silence rang in their ears.

"It's too quiet here. Like... too peaceful," Tim said, rubbing his arms from the cold.

"It is a place of peace," Nozomi said. "That is why people come here, to escape the stresses in life. I should have visited tea gardens like this more often, especially after..."

"I'm sorry," Moira said, walking alongside her. "Hey, I'm here if you ever want to talk, okay?"

"Yes, *arigatou.*" Nozomi took Moira's hand with a grin. "This way."

Braern paused and pressed his hands to his temples. He rubbed his head, for the pains that anguished his mind had returned.

"Hey, you okay?" Tim asked Braern.

"I don't feel well. I need to sit."

"There is a shelter ahead. Can you make it that far?"

"Yes, I think I can."

The voice. It was incoherent, even more so this time.

"What about tea?" Braern asked.

"What? We didn't say anything," Moira replied. "I'll help him." She bent her knees and pushed herself up and under Braern's arm as she lifted him over her shoulder. With ease, she walked toward the shelter.

"Your strength is most appreciated, milady."

"It's nothing."

To drown out the whispers in his mind, Braern watched Nozomi's gleaming leather jacket in front of the two of them. The leather crinkling and rubbing against her arms as she moved soothed his ears. For a second, he lost sight of his friend, but those sounds brought him back.

"Almost there," Nozomi said.

"We're following ye, lass," Araduk said, grasping Braern's dangling hand.

Blue rustled inside Tim's backpack.

They walked the few wooden steps to the door that only contained a doorknob. A hand met the door with a thud. Nozomi opened it, and a bell rang when she entered. The sounds of their multiple sets of feet on the wooden floor were now the loudest thing they could hear.

"*Irashaimase!*" a friendly, soft female voice sounded at a higher pitch.

Moira lowered her elven cargo onto the bench by the door.

Nozomi gestured for them to sit, so they obliged. She bowed and spoke Japanese with the shop owner, who dressed in a simple gray and white kimono with red and blue painted brush strokes. She was short, with gray and black hair in a bob. Her glasses were tiny for the frame of her face. She scooted short steps across the floor, wearing *tabi* socks and *geta* sandals.

"Do you know what they're saying?" Moira asked. "How's your head?"

"Yes, and it's improving. I have this strange feeling that I'm supposed to remember something, but... I'm sure it's nothing."

Nozomi faced the group after speaking with the shop owner. "She says we are welcome to stay in the backroom for a while to rest. She is making us some tea right now. This is her shop."

The little tea shop was exquisite inside. Delicate, artistic pieces covered the walls, from jewelry to carvings of dragons, beautiful fan sculptures, and smaller figures of various animals. Meticulously placed shelves displayed many tea sets with cups, saucers, and handmade tiny teapots. Baskets organized an array of snacks by the cash register.

The shop owner appeared again and asked them to follow her past the *shoji* screen door. The back room was smaller, with pillows on the floor to sit, as well as a few chairs and a table. It was immaculate. She carried a metal decorated tray with several tiny teacups full of a green liquid. The steam rose above each tiny cup as the scents of herbs and spices filled their nostrils.

A faint cough sounded. The shop owner paused. Everyone looked at each other to figure out who made the noise, then shrugged as the shop owner handed each of the group their own cup.

Braern watched Tim. He sat on the edge of his seat to not squish Blue behind his back. He heard little movements as the cat adjusted herself. Tim tried hard to keep a straight face. Braern imagined he did not release his feline friend because the shop owner would not think too kindly about a cat entering her store with such fragile and valuable items on the shelves.

"Arigatou gozaimasu." Nozomi bowed to the shop owner.

The shop owner returned the bow, then walked through her door, her *kimono* swiping her legs as she walked.

Braern couldn't ignore an even stronger nagging feeling.

"Does your head still hurt?" Moira placed an arm on his shoulder.

"Yes."

"The tea will help. Drink some. Tea is always an excellent remedy for headaches."

"Yes, especially tea that tastes this good." Tim gulped his tea.

Araduk turned his body away from his friends and watched as his flask filled to the top again. He poured half the contents into his tea and drank it. "Interestin' flavor," Araduk commented and faced the front again.

Braern sipped his tea. The intense warmth traveled down his throat. His belly temperature changed as he smiled at how delicious and full of spice the tea was.

Moira took her time and sniffed her tea before taking a sip.

Blue pushed out of Tim's backpack as he let his body fall against the curved wooden seat. She did not care to be crushed, so she tried to free herself, but her back legs became stuck. She pulled and squeezed, pushing off the back of the chair with her forepaws, elongating her neck. With one last pull, she was free. She scampered to her human's side, her claws clicking on the hard surface. She watched her human's eyes grow heavier.

"I'm really sleepy all of a sudden, guys," Tim slurred. He slouched again; his legs moved outward, scooting across the hard floor. His human shoes squeaked and skipped until he fell asleep.

"I feel okay. Wait... oh..." Moira tried to speak. She dropped the cup, and it shattered on the floor as she fell.

"What's in that... tea?" Araduk fell on his side into his seat, leaning against Tim, with his mouth hanging open. He drooled and was no longer coherent.

Do not drink the tea.

Braern's mind whirled as darkness covered his eyes, no matter how hard he tried to keep them open. Up and down, his eyelids went as he felt himself fall to his knees and drop the teacup on the floor. It shattered into several pieces.

They were so drugged they didn't even notice the sharp sounds of shattering porcelain.

Nozomi was next. She dropped her teacup on the counter as its remaining liquid spilled over the side. The cup bounced on the surface before rolling onto its side. Its handle stopped it from falling onto the floor. It came to a tiny clink of a stop. Trying to hold herself upright, she could no longer support her own weight. Her hand slid down the wall, her fingernails scraping against the surface, as she tried desperately to grab hold of anything to stop herself.

She transformed into a dog, then a sheep, then a cow as the floor cracked under her hooves. Then, delirious and unsure of what she did, she turned back into her human form. Her knees gave way. She collapsed with a thud, her cheek bouncing for one second onto the floor, before she remained motionless.

"That's what... the voice... was..." Braern was out.

BLUE

DEMONS AND EMPTY BELLIES

Blue was the only one left. The cat clawed out of the backpack and ran to one of the teacups and sniffed its contents. She jumped back at the scent. The feline pawed at her face as the odor burned her sensitive nasal passages. Shaking her head, she wondered why humans liked such a taste. She sat to watch the others sleeping and sprawled out before her. Her human companion snoozed with his mouth open, half fallen off the chair by the window. *I must protect my human.*

She quickly hid under the chair as the shop owner returned. The echoes of her shuffled on the floor while her removable fur dragged behind her. The cat ducked her ears as the human approached. She curled herself into a ball and lifted her tail over her face to hide herself more in the shadows.

The female human nudged the group with her hind paw to see if they were still conscious. She made her way through everyone and over to her human. As she stared at them, the back of her black hair parted to reveal rows of teeth. A second mouth opened, and its tongue licked its lips, spilling saliva onto the floor. She stroked the tongue. Then the mouth closed and smiled.

She bent, the tightness of her clothing making it diffi-cult to do. She lifted her human's hind paw and dragged him backward.

Blue growled and unsheathed her claws. A rage en-gulfed her as she felt her body grow, watching as her eye lev-el raised from the floor. The chair rolled off her shoulder and crashed to the floor. She licked her lips and ran her tongue over her enormous fangs. Pricking her ears, she glared at the woman with wide eyes, screaming. Blue gazed at her own paws and inspected her enlarged pads. Her powerful muscles twitched. She roared so loud the entire shop shook, sending decorated liquid vessels crashing to the floor.

In her new form, she lunged at the demon with ex-tended claws and opened jaws, screeching caterwauls. She grabbed the shop owner's leg and chomped down, growling and thrashing around.

The woman tried to kick her off, squealing in pain, as she fell onto her behind.

Blue released her leg and crouched for a split second, then jumped onto her face and scratched her cheeks. She felt the warm blood trickle down her leg.

The woman defended herself, pushing and flailing, screaming at the top of her lungs, but Blue did not relent.

She fought until the woman scurried off on her knees, panting. Blue let go and ran to her human's side, lashing her tail and checking for anymore intruders. A deep rumble formed in her throat as she roared. Blue lunged forward as the woman tried to escape and grasped the demon's neck in her jaws. Her tongue thrashed and hit her feline cheeks.

Moments later, the thrashing stopped. She surrendered and gasped her last breath, her arms limp.

Blue let go. As she stared at her victim, she knew. *No one hurts my human.* She padded to her friends, and her body relaxed as her eye level returned to normal. Her fangs and enlarged muscles returned to their usual size. She became a cat again.

Blue guarded her companions and flinched at the slightest sound that met her ears. She was determined to wake her human and the others, for she knew another cat was vulnerable when they were sleeping. The proud feline scouted the room for signs of something that might help. A vessel for humans to wash their paws with water lay in the far corner, nearly out of sight. Various human objects that looked useless lay on shelves off the floor.

She noticed another curved object she had seen humans drink from with their strange mouths. With one paw before her, she investigated her surroundings further, crouched on the floor. Another paw. Her ears pricked for the slightest sounds, and she took a few more steps, continuing to see if anyone might enter the room. She looked back, swishing her tail with displeasure.

Blue reached the curved vessel and jumped onto the cool side of the washing place. She grabbed the vessel on the shelf next to the glass object, where she could see herself through it. She placed her paw on the elongated surface of the thing they used to make the water come out, and the water poured down the hole below her. Her tail swooshing, she played with the water droplets, pawing at it and drinking a few sips for herself.

She refocused on her mission and stretched her neck to see her human still lying on the floor, several tail lengths from her. She used her jaws to pick up the vessel's handle and turned her head so the open part was facing outward. It took her a while to adjust herself. She swiped the water with her tail until it finally stopped flowing. Pricking up her ears, she curiously watched the last few water drops disappear down the drain as her irises grew bigger. She moved her head back and forth, feeling the weight shift of the water in her vessel, and jumped down from the surface. A few drops spilled on the floor as she traipsed to her human.

A loud creak on the floor caused her to jump backward. She dropped the vessel from her mouth. It fell onto the floor, spilling all the water everywhere. She lifted her paws, one by one, and shook them to rid herself of the cold liquid. *I hate being cold.*

Angry with herself, she padded to her human with narrowed eyes and lowered ears, swishing her tail in annoyance. His water pouch had fallen onto the floor. Perhaps if she could open it, she could throw some onto his face and wake him. She grabbed the spout with her teeth and dragged it to his face. She bit hard, but the top stayed on. Soon, drips poured from the neck. Holes formed as she let go, then she picked it up by its middle and walked to him. She dropped it onto his head, with the neck of the pouch touching his nose.

Water trickled onto this face, but he did not wake.

She began to worry and meowed for him to awaken. She hated being without him, and seeing him so vulnerable filled her heart with sadness. Sitting on her wet hind paws, she watched his face as the last of the water disappeared from the pouch, flattening it into a mess. She jabbed at it with her paws and knocked it off his face.

Pawing at him with her forepaws, she meowed and wailed. Her voice became louder and more erratic as her tail swished. Feeling a pain inside her belly, she knew if she did not wake him up soon, she would starve. Her empty belly would surely eat itself, and she would never taste her delicious kibble again. Blue growled and realized she had used all her patience she had left in her feline body. With outstretched claws on her right paw, she swung her arm into the air above his head. She clawed his cheek, and trickles of blood dripped down his face.

That did it. Her human shot upright, flailing. "Wha-What happened?" Feeling a pain in his cheek, he touched the scratches. "Blue, did you scratch me?"

"Mayow!" She regarded him with relief in her eyes.

"Thank you, Blue. But man, that hurts! Did you have to do it so hard?"

Blue rubbed on his thighs as he slowly turned himself around to face the rest of the room.

He saw his sleeping comrades beside him. Touching his cheek again, he peered at the blood on his fingers. "I was dreaming. I thought I was back home... and I had a girlfriend. I was eating dinner with my family and... it was all a dream. It seemed so real," he told her softly. He shook his head and saw the dead creature on the floor. "The shop owner drugged us."

Blue placed a paw on his.

"Blue, we need to wake the others. You woke me up by scratching me. Is pain the only way to break this?"

She studied him with unblinking, concerned eyes.

"We should wake Araduk first. He will know how to help the others without hurting them too much."

Blue approached the snoring short creature, with his wiry beard hair all over his face. She eyed her human.

He nodded.

She noticed his upper lip hairs and pawed at them. Blue grabbed several of them on one side in her jaws, closed her mouth, and yanked her head in the opposite direction. The remaining hairs stayed on her tongue as she coughed and spat, pawing at her mouth.

"Lass! Get back here!" he hollered, shaking his head as his saliva-drenched lips sprayed the two of them with his spit. He blinked, rubbed his eyes, then touched his hairs above his lips. The short creature gazed around the room, blinking his eyes. "The bonnie, red-haired lass. She's gone. It was so real."

Blue pattered to him and sat.

"What is... What'd ye think ye're doin', moggy?"

"Araduk, we were all drugged. Blue scratched my cheek and woke me up. She yanked on your mustache. We need to wake up the others."

"Right, lad. Right. Give me a moment to collect myself." The short creature bellowed a strange, deep shrill of sound, shaking his head as his beard moved. "All right, am up. Let's do this."

One by one, they inflicted minimal but enough pain to the others to awaken them, either by a smack on the arm or a scratch on their skin. Soon, everyone rose, placing their paws on their heads, blinking and confused.

The pointy-eared creature shook his head. "I truly thought we had succeeded in our quest and I had traveled back to my father. He embraced me and... it felt so real."

Water drops ran down the strong one's cheeks as she surveyed the room. Her head hung low as her lips quivered. She placed her paws on the sides of her head. "Why did you wake me up? I was finally normal. I finally had my boyfriend back in my life, and my place wasn't covered in broken appliances and holes in the walls. Why'd you do this to me?" she turned and asked the others as they all shook their heads.

"Moira, it was all a dream. The shop owner drugged us." The pointy-eared one moved toward her, outstretching his open paw for her to take.

She pushed herself backward with her legs, her arms behind her. "No! I was happy! You took me away from that! All this time, I went along for the ride, and then I finally got to be normal, and you took me away from it?" she screamed, crying and huffing.

"I wanted to feel a sense of normality again. I don't want this strength anymore. Thought I wanted unicorns and dragons, but I don't. I wanna go home, and I wanna be normal again. Take me back."

"We all dreamed of seeing loved ones and doing the things we missed, but we're back now. We need to keep going. It was all an illusion because the tea made us hallucinate," Blue's human said, then whispered to himself, "Remind me to find that shop owner."

"Danielle, we were in bed, and I could smell the floral shampoo in your hair. I thought you were real." The shifting creature exhaled, closing her eyes as she whispered, "When will I see you again?"

Blue's human stared in disbelief. The others met his gaze—the shop owner.

The pointy-eared one stood, bracing himself on the bench, and staggered to the bloody corpse. A second tongue protruded from behind its head. He splayed a shaking paw on the counter outside the back room and used his back paw to push her. Another mouth. "She was a *futakuchi-onna* demon. They're very dangerous and cunning. I suspect she drugged us to eat us. The second mouth on the back of their head is always hungry and never satiated. They must feed or it makes their lives miserable."

"That's disgusting," the strong one said, touching her belly with a scrunched face.

The pointy-eared one stared at the deep bite marks on the demon's neck. Their teeth went all the way through her skin and out the other side. And a large bloody paw print was on the floor next to her. "Something big killed this demon. Look at the bite marks."

"Well, whatever it was, we're eternally grateful," the short one said.

Blue paid no attention to them. She took her time cleaning herself from such a horrific experience. *They should be thanking me, but did any of them stroke my beautiful fur to show their gratitude? Of course not.*

"Eat... me?" Blue's human whispered. Blue heard the stomach acid rear up through his esophagus. He turned from the group and vomited, heaving and retching.

Blue sniffed the air as a wave of vile stench filled her sensitive nostrils. She sneezed and moved farther away, keeping a watchful eye on her human.

"*Kuso,* no one ever tried to eat you?" the angry one joked as she winced, holding her head in her paws.

"Uh... no," the cat's human answered.

"Well, I've had about enough of this place," the short one said, rising.

A glowing light appeared in the middle of the group. It began as a small speck but grew and transformed into a swirling range of colors—another oval of magic. Strange sounds played from inside as the group caught glimpses of other humans and closeups of sound objects that pulsated from the whimsical touches of blues and purples.

"What is that?" Blue's human asked, his eyes glowing as he crept closer.

"I don't know. It looks far less dangerous than anything else we've seen. Maybe it'll bring us closer to Iceland?" the pointy-eared one answered.

"The music is lively. Sounds like a party. I bet there's ale. Let's go there!" The short one smiled at the portal.

"It looks fine," the angry one said.

Before anyone could say anything more, the strong one staggered to stand, wiped the snot and tears from her face, and walked right through, disappearing inside.

"Well, I guess that settles that."

Moira

Concerts and Passports

As her tears dried on her face, Moira beheld the surrounding sights and smells of the concert venue. Her skin felt itchy from all the crying for a moment as she flinched her cheeks, then the feeling vanished. She had never heard such music before, but the next thing she knew, her foot tapped on the floor and her hips moved with the beat. She bent her arms, closed her eyes, and listened. *I don't know where we are, but this music is amazing.*

The stench of sweat and beer filled the darkened, open room of the venue, called The Pageant. Colored lights illuminated the stage, while five men played upbeat, deep rock songs with alluring lyrics that rose above the singing, joyful crowd. People up front jumped and sang, with their arms waving.

Vibrations from the floor tickled their feet. The sound waves from the six-foot-tall black speakers released near deafening, melodic tunes. All around, people listened and barely spoke, fixated on the show. Behind the young drummer, a large banner that read, LUDO, waved with the back curtains. Girls danced in a group, holding their drinks in the air while swaying to the music. Other people sang loudly and clapped in ecstasy. Not an ear turned away from the inspiring sounds of requited love, epic battles, and entertaining stories.

The rest of the group looked all around with tense shoulders and zipping eyes. Such strangeness here. Moira danced in front of them, enjoying herself. They had to remain close together to hear over the loud music.

Araduk sniffed the air and let his nose lead him to the bar nearby.

"I'll have your finest ale, my good sir!" he begged, pulling himself up onto the nearby stool so he could see better.

He didn't have any money, so Tim rushed over to speak with the bartender.

The man handed Tim a bottle of water and he paid for it with his card. He gave it to the dwarf.

"Water?" Araduk yelled with narrowed eyes. He shook his head.

"Remember what happened last time you drank?" Tim asked above the music.

"That was from m' own concoction! Lad, ye never goin' to let m' have fun again, are ye?" He held the water above his head and studied the bottom. "This another one of those crispy cups of yours? It's so light." A few drops fell from the flimsy, plastic-loosened lid as he turned his wrist. He lapped them up as they dripped onto his nose and into his mouth.

Tim opened it for him and threw the cap in the nearest trashcan. He tapped his foot and swung his head back and forth, smiling. "Ya know, these guys are actually pretty cool. I might buy their album."

"What's an album?" Braern and Araduk asked him in unison.

"Oh, it's a flat, circular disk that holds music or a file to listen to on your computer or music device. I have a ton of them back home. I love music."

"And how do you know they're *cool?* You can't touch them from here," Braern asked.

"It means they're popular, good."

"Cool," Braern repeated, smiling.

Nozomi caught the eye of a green-haired girl in a black tank top connecting her thumbs together and twisting her wrist to display her fingers above her.

A third of the crowd lifted their arms, twisting their thumbs together, and rotated their palms toward their faces. Their gestures looked like butterflies.

The current song spoke of dinosaurs and time traveling.

"Did I hear them sing, 'pterodactyls?'" Tim asked. "Yup, I'm buying it."

Oh, pterodactyls. That's awesome!

Nozomi walked over and danced with the girl, their hips swaying as they greeted one another over the music. They smiled and pointed at the stage.

Braern felt the vibrations from the music as a new song played. This was even more upbeat than the previous.

Moira paused to rest, then felt herself getting into the music once again. A burning formed on her neck as if Braern's gaze was penetrating her skin. She ignored him, this time, for she wanted a few moments of peace after so much death and turmoil that had followed her everywhere the last week.

Braern listened to the music but paid little attention to the band on the stage. He watched Moira dance again, swaying her hips and jerking her body left and right to the rhythm.

She clapped and stepped side to side in place.

Braern took a deep breath and approached her.

The eccentric lead singer with glasses had introduced the song title as "Save Our City."

Braern tapped her shoulder.

She flinched. Shaking her head, she pointed to her ears.

Braern nodded and stood next to her without touching her.

At least he respects my boundaries. He's a good guy, but I ain't got time for messin' around with an elf, even one as sexy as he is.

They listened to the lyrics: *"Anything can be a weapon if you're holding it right."*

The words echoed in Moira's mind. Was this another premonition, like the ones Braern spoke about? She was determined to pay attention this time, and she knew he was too. *I'm listening.*

After the end of the song, cheers and claps filled the enormous room. A few moments of silence let the performers catch their breaths.

"Well, hello there, St. Louis!" the keyboardist greeted the crowd, and everyone erupted in woots and claps. As he spoke to the audience, Moira smiled.

Oh... St. Louis. Feels like home here. A big city with neon lights and loud music. Perfect. Moira sighed, facing forward. "I've only heard this band a few times on the radio, but I've never seen them live. This is a welcome change from being attacked by trolls, nearly eaten by a weird mouth demon, and almost drowning. I think I'll make a note to myself to go see them again if they ever come to New York. They're amazing."

"I would like to come with you next time if that is all right with you. I like them too. Much different from our music in my village, but I like them."

"You do?" she asked, eyeing him.

Braern nodded.

The new song was catchy, upbeat, and romantic.

A group of millennials wearing T-shirts with cherries and the band name on them pushed their way around the duo to get closer to the stage. One beefy, taller guy walked into her. He turned around and mouthed the word, *"Sorry,"* then disappeared into the mass of dancing bodies.

She nodded.

Moira's heart ached as she was forced closer to Braern, so their shoulders touched.

"I feel like I'm in a fairytale, listening to this one," Moira said.

"I must know, what is a *deity?*" he asked her. They turned their necks to see each other's faces half shrouded in light from the stage and darkness from the room.

"A deity? It's like a god from Eastern culture."

"And what are leprec-c-c...?"

"Leprechauns? They're short Irish people who wear green and hoard gold at the end of rainbows. There's also one on the box of that nasty cereal."

"Cereal?"

"Pfft, never mind that part."

"You are wise, milady. I'm impressed." He nodded and bowed to her.

"Yeah, if only I knew how to let myself love again." Her shoulders slumped as she returned her gaze to the front.

The lead singer was busy licking his guitar while stroking its strings with a crazy look on his face.

She laughed and stifled a smile.

"I can help with that if you will allow me to. I still have not given up on us, but I respect you, and I will give you all the space and time you need. I'm not going anywhere." Braern touched his finger to hers.

This time, she didn't turn away.

He gently intertwined their fingers while admiring the profile of her beautiful face. He slowly caressed her skin with his thumb, then brought her hand to his mouth and sweetly kissed it.

"Oh, Braern. We've been through this. I don't want to hurt you."

"I told you, you will not hurt me. I would do… *'anything for you,'*" he repeated the recurring words from the last song.

She turned her whole body to him. Her eyes glistened as he took both her hands in his without looking away. She fought the urge to run as she also fought to stay focused on his face. And those ears, they called to her.

Gently pulling his wrists, she moved their hands, still connected to his face. He kissed her fingers as she closed her eyes, smiling through a closed mouth. Taking a deep breath, she absorbed everything around her—the loud music, the feel of his hands on hers, his soft lips on her knuckles, and the smell of beer.

She ignored the drunk man shouting the lyrics to the next song behind her—something about trampolines. She giggled at the thought of how much they should be distracted right now, but they weren't… somehow. She gently released her hands from his and touched his pointed ears.

He closed his eyes, feeling her touch, and stroked her arms with the backs of his fingernails. Not wanting the moment to end, he wrapped his arms around her and pulled her close.

She let go of his soft grip, threw her arms around his neck, and hugged him tightly. Their cheeks met. Such softness. The two of them squeezed each other and felt parts of their ribs touch. Though uncomfortable for a second, they continued their embrace. She felt his bony body through his clothes as she played with his hair. Then their lips were inches away. They crept closer, feeling the music in their stomachs.

"Ye two haven't kissed yet?" Araduk asked as he bumped into Braern.

They backed away from each other.

"Perfect timing," Moira said in a sarcastic, monotone voice. She narrowed her eyes, resisting the urge to punch the dwarf square in his hair face. *Damn it, man!*

The band finished the concert and disappeared backstage. After a few moments, two of the band members appeared at the merch table to their right. The lead singer and the keyboardist smiled, posed for pictures, and autographed t-shirts and posters.

Tim walked over and told the group he'd like to wait in line.

A yearning overcame Moira as well. She felt pulled to the table, but she couldn't figure out why. Soon, it was their turn.

She watched as Braern followed her to the table. *Does he feel it too? There's some reason we're supposed to be here and talk to these guys.*

"You guys were amazing!" Moira complimented them.

"Thank you! You're the ones we felt from the stage. I'm Convy. Pmo, our drummer, wanted me to give this to you. He said, 'Find the elf and tell him he'll know what to do with it when the time is right,'" the keyboardist said, pulling a drumstick from behind his back. He shook their hands and noticed the long line of people watching, then signed it with a black permanent marker.

Braern took it and bowed. "Thank you."

Tim bought their album as Moira and Braern walked to the side to let others fawn over the band. They stared at the drumstick as the writing glowed a golden color, then returned to black.

"He a wizard or something?" Moira asked Braern.

"I'm not sure, but I believe this will help us in the future." Braern tied it to his belt next to his sword.

Moira eyed his waist and giggled. *I'm surprised no one came to kick us out, since we have a sword and a cat. But, I guess we didn't exactly come through the front entrance.* Her thoughts lingered to what was under his belt, but she shook her head and turned her gaze away from him.

Tim met up with them again, grinning at his new merch.

Blue struggled in his bag, annoyed by the loud music from the night. She rubbed her sensitive ears that throbbed from the lower bass sounds.

"Let's find Nozomi and get out of here before the exit gets too crazy," Moira said.

They returned to where they had been standing to find her making out with the green-haired girl she had been dancing with earlier. The two of them grabbed each other's waists and ignored all the moving people around them.

I'm glad someone's getting some action tonight. Sure isn't me. "Hey! We gotta go," Moira yelled.

Nozomi pried her lips away, stopping the kiss.

The girl took out her phone and handed it to Nozomi.

She typed her number into it. "Call me." Nozomi walked back to them, smiling.

"She was cute," Moira said.

"Her name is Amanda."

"Thought you had a girlfriend?"

"Do you see her here?" Nozomi asked with a frown. She scoffed and folded her arms, looking away as she rolled her eyes.

"Nope. Sorry." Moira looked away, blushing. *Didn't think she was a player, but do what you gotta do, girl.*

"There's Araduk. Let's get out of here." Tim pointed to the dwarf, whose top knot was barely visible above a small crowd of people talking.

They grabbed the dwarf and headed for the exit, politely making their way through the crowd. With people all around him, Tim held his head high with a smile.

"This is the most relaxed I've seen you in a while, dude," Moira told him. The music had put their minds at ease.

"That was my first real concert. Of course, I've attended several at church, but those were nothing like this."

"Good for you, kid. Way to live in the moment."

Moira side-hugged him as he blushed.

They stayed together and emerged into the brisk night air. The brightness of the city lights made the sidewalk sparkle. Cars passed as people spoke loudly to hear over the others. They walked down the street to a place where they could talk.

"We need to find somewhere to figure out how to get from here to Iceland," Tim said.

"We're in the middle of the Midwest. I've never been here before, so I don't know the area," Moira said. "I wish we could go to my place so—"

Another portal opened, and they fell through the sidewalk, disappearing into the weightlessness of colors once again.

*****

They arrived before a familiar door. "That's weird as hell. I wished we were at my place, and... here we are."

"Are... you all right, milady?" Braern asked after Moira froze with her hand above the doorknob. *I'm so used to meeting talking doorknobs that I'm shocked when mine doesn't say anything. So weird.*

"Huh? Yeah. Sorry." She shook her head, blinked a few times to clear her mind, and turned her key. "Home, sweet dump," she said as her door creaked open.

"Wait, we were walking on the sidewalk, outside that show... then we fell through another portal and ended up... here?" Tim asked, staring at his hands and scrunching his face. He gazed all around at her perfectly normal apartment complex.

Araduk crunched his water bottle in his hand.

Braern frowned and gazed at the tan colored buildings with dark colored doors. "You wished we would... come here and... we did?" he asked.

"Hmm... yeah, I guess I did," Moira answered.

The group stepped inside and Moira closed the door.

"Braern was able to save Tim from being swallowed by a portal. Now, you thought about your apartment and we are here," Nozomi said.

"Do we have some control over all this?" Araduk asked, peering around his friends at her messy place.

"Perhaps..." Braern said.

Chinese food and gas station trash spread throughout her apartment immediately hit Moira's senses. She frowned and held her breath. Everything else was where she had left it—junk everywhere, expired condiments in the fridge, a huge mess.

"Sorry guys. I'll take out the trash really quick. Make yourselves at home," she encouraged them and jogged to the kitchen, pulled a trash bag from the yellow and red box, and flung it in the air with a whipped sound to open the bag.

"Smells fine to me." Araduk took a deep breath. The odor did not affect him.

Tim and Nozomi made scrunched faces as they entered the living room. Nozomi surveyed the trash stuffed behind the green patterned couch, while Moira frantically gathered all the papers and magazines lying around.

Moira grabbed some junk mail from right where Nozomi was about to sit and threw it in her bag.

Braern forced himself to keep a stoic face and tried to hold his breath a few times to not smell anything. He was afraid of insulting his host.

Blue jumped from Tim's bag and sniffed the air while padding around the room. She rubbed on the sofa and rolled around on the floor, enjoying the smells.

"Well, at least someone likes this place. I've probably got another month before they throw out all my crap and officially evict me, since I've been wandering around everywhere with you guys." Moira walked to the door, looking back. She ran outside to take the trash to the dumpster. Returning to her friends, she saw the cat tearing at the bottom of the couch.

"Oh, sorry. Blue, stop that!" Tim scolded.

"Meow?"

"No, she doesn't have a scratching post. Stop it!"

He reached into his bag and placed some food on the floor to appease her.

"It's okay. I found that couch on the side of the road. I don't mind."

"She has some sharp claws, but she's usually really good about not tearing up furniture. I never believed in declawing. It's torture for them."

"I didn't know that. I'll keep that in mind if I ever get a cat." Moira closed the door as everyone sat. *That'll never happen. I can barely take care of myself, let alone a pet.*

"What's the plan? How do we get to Iceland from here?" Araduk asked, situating himself. He smiled at the cat as he sat next to Nozomi.

Blue was still rubbing on everything, and they could hear her chirping happily and smacking around junk mail on the table.

Tim smiled at his silly friend.

"All right, we need to get to Iceland to find that council. They'll know what to do to stop all this insanity," Moira said.

Tim redirected his gaze and lost his smile. He cleared his throat and straightened his back.

"Where is... Iceland? Is it truly made of ice?" Braern asked.

"Ha! No, but I hear it's pretty cold there."

"How do we get there?" Araduk asked.

"I am not flying you all the way there. I would drop dead in the ocean," Nozomi commented, annoyed.

"I imagine I couldn't fly there as well?" Braern asked.

"No, we'll have to fly in a plane."

"A plane?"

"Yup! Like I said earlier. Oh yeah, I forget you guys don't know what I'm talking about half the time. So, an airplane is a mechanical transport that flies super-fast and high in the sky. We need to make it to the airport and somehow get tickets and passports. No idea how."

"These... tickets will allow us to fly in this... air... plane?" Braern asked, trying to pronounce the words.

"Is it safe? What is this contraption made o'?" Araduk cocked his head, frowning.

"It is made of heavy metals." Nozomi scoffed at having to explain such a rudimentary topic.

"Actually, they're also made of aluminum and titanium because of their lower density that allows the plane to lift easier into the air," Tim added. He cocked his head onto his shoulder, lying back into the couch behind him.

"I didn't know that. Cool," Moira said. "Okay, so we need tickets, but they're,"—Moira opened her computer that was still plugged into the nearby wall outlet and quickly searched for nonstop flights—"a thousand dollars each, both ways. I don't know how I still have internet here. So, that's..."

"Five grand," Tim answered.

"Damn, I have, like, three dollars in my account. No-zomi, Tim, you guys got any money?" Moira asked.

"I took my mom's credit card, but it's probably maxed out now." Tim shook his head at the guilt he felt.

"I spent all my money trying to find that evil creep," Nozomi told her.

"Well, I don't know how we are going to pull this off, then. We also need passports, and those are like a hundred dollars apiece too. This is hopeless."

"What are passports?" Braern asked slowly.

Araduk was too busy scratching Blue's back and watching her roll all over his hands. He laughed. The group stared at him while he smiled, playing with the cat. He noticed everyone was quiet and looked up. "Oh, I'm sorry. What are we talking about?"

"We are trying to figure out how to get passports and tickets to fly to Iceland," Moira answered, becoming more annoyed at all the questions. "They're little identifications with our pictures on them, showing we can travel to other countries outside the U.S."

"The *U.S.* What a strange name for a land." Braern looked puzzled.

"Guys! We don't have time for this! We need to figure this out! As much fun as that concert was, we probably shouldn't have stayed there so long." Moira stood and stomped her feet, causing the floor beneath her boot to crack and split. "Crap. My landlord is gonna kill me," she scolded herself as she pulled her foot from the dent she had made on the floor.

"I have an idea. Do any of you have a passport?" Braern asked.

"I have mine with me. I came from Japan to here, so it looks different from an American one." Nozomi pulled her wallet from her back pocket and gave it to Braern.

He studied it for a moment and noticed the shimmering, hard, slick paper and her image. Various patterns reflected the light above from Moira's ceiling fan. "I think I can do a spell to duplicate this." Braern felt the smoothness of the paper that was bent in the middle. Nozomi's picture looked exactly like she does now. He waved his right hand over the passport and closed his eyes. *"Go ni naru!"* He spread his fingers one by one until they all were outstretched.

The passport duplicated itself into five; each one appeared behind the previous.

"What about photos?" Nozomi asked as Braern handed her original to her. She nodded, then looked at Moira.

Moira pointed into the air, looking nowhere in particular, and blinked furiously. "Oh! I have one of those cute, new, retro Polaroids!" She ran to her bedroom and rummaged through her closet. She grunted while moving cardboard boxes and plastic bins. She grabbed a photo box covered in sparkling gold unicorns from the top of her closet. The sight of her memory box brought her a moment of comfort.

"I got it!" She brought it back and sat in her seat. She crouched in front of Tim and quickly took his picture.

He jumped back in his seat, his eyes widening. "I wasn't ready!" he squeaked, embarrassed, as his face reddened.

"It does not have to be perfect," Nozomi said.

"Tim, it'll be fine," Moira assured him as the image slowly printed and ejected from the bottom. "Hold this." She handed it to him.

He held it by the thick white border at the bottom and ensured not to touch the picture developing from the light.

She repeated the same with Araduk, Braern, then herself. Moira pulled Braern's medium-length hair over his ears to reduce any comments from airport personnel before snapping his photo. Moira smiled with a cheesy, open-mouthed grin, while the men kept their mouths closed. After the sound of the shutter went off and the photos printed, she handed them to each of her friends.

They waited for the photos to develop.

Braern signaled with his fingers for them to hand him their photos. He wiggled his hand over their photos in the blank box on each passport, then slammed down his hand as the photo instantly merged with the passport onto the box. He did this until he'd created all the passports.

Moira told him what personal information to include on the passports and suggested their names be in English. She coaxed him until it was perfect.

He wrote with his finger hovering above as she coached him to ensure the language was readable and looked like a machine printed it. When they finished, he handed them to their appropriate person.

They nodded while admiring the craftsmanship.

"Looks real to me," Tim commented, studying his photo. "I look like crap though."

"You look fine, lad," Araduk assured him.

"Dude, you're mostly hair!"

The dwarf showed him his final product. "Of course! Look at me! I am a dwarf!" He chuckled.

"I look... almost human." Braern noticed his hair covered most of his ears.

"Well, that's a good thing. You'll fit right in," Moira said, staring at his passport. She smiled. "All right, passports. Check."

"Now, how will we pay for these flights? None of us have any money." Moira sighed as her lips blew raspberries. She relaxed against the couch, crossing her arms while staring at the ceiling.

"Let's head to the nearest airport and leave that to me," Nozomi said with a snicker.

Araduk

The Airport

Signs for the various terminals came into view as Araduk peered out the window of the metal beast they rode in. People temporarily parked on the curb by the entrances, grabbed their suitcases and bags out of trunks, and lumbered inside. A couple embraced, while the woman dressed in dark brown and cream colors kissed her husband goodbye, then dragged her wheeling bag across the cement ground to the automatic doors. Vehicles pulled up or drove by at walking speeds as pedestrians crossed the striped walkway on the road. It was a busy place for humans to gather.

The dwarf watched as people walked in all different directions. After a moment, he blinked. Every human face in his sight was replaced by a beaten, bruised, and lifeless one with broken jaws or missing eyes. *They're all my victims from the wars. They still haunt me to this day, no matter where I go.*

Araduk blinked again, and they returned to normal. He shook his head, scrunching his eyes with his hand on his temple.

The driver listened to a low hum of relaxing music. It seemed a strange tune to the dwarf's ears, but he appreciated it nonetheless. It was a welcome distraction.

Moira leaned toward the window when they arrived at the entrance that was the closest to their flight. "Terminal B, please." She signaled to the driver, pointing for him to stop.

"Braern, you need to disguise your weapon or we will be in big trouble and won't make it through security," Moira whispered to him.

"They have metal detectors. How's he gonna make it through the scanners even if he hides it?" Tim asked.

"Sh!" Moira hissed. "No idea, but we'll figure that out when we get there."

The elf nodded, closed his eyes. With a wave of his hand over his belt, the weapon vanished, but the rest of his belongings remained. "It took me many years to learn the invisibility spell without speaking," he whispered. Braern held his head high and smiled, tapping the hilt of his invisible sword.

"I have never seen a place like this," Araduk commented with a sigh. The dwarf's voice broke Braern out of his trance.

"Yes, it's very different from most anything we have in Yumerion. However, our ports are similar to this *air... port.*" Braern placed his hand on the window as his nose cooled.

He noticed Araduk's usual smile had disappeared.

"Are you overwhelmed, my friend?" Braern asked.

He could tell am distressed, Araduk thought. He felt grateful for such an observant friend.

"Aye. Everywhere I look, I see death on their faces, bloody and blackened with bruises. I feel as though I'm back at war. Funny that I was given this gift and I cannot even heal m' own mind." He hovered his shaky hand over his flask pocket.

The driver finally stopped after inching his way to find a suitable spot to drop them off. He placed a hand on the headrest of the passenger seat and twisted his torso to peer back at everyone. He turned off his music. "You've never been to an airport? Where are you from?" he asked with a grunted smoker's voice.

"I am from Lavendale, good sir," Braern answered and bowed from his seat.

"Am from Tetsu Mountain, but I've lived the last few years atop Shiro Peak at the monastery," Araduk followed suit.

"I've never heard of those places. I'll have to look them up." The driver raised an eyebrow and rotated his body forward again, tapping on his phone in its holder attached to the vent.

Moira and Tim laughed to themselves, covering their mouths.

Nozomi scoffed and pushed past everyone to exit the vehicle first. She waited by the entrance, tapping her foot and in her usual stance of crossed arms.

"Safe travels," the driver said as everyone exited the vehicle.

"Thank you." She nodded as she closed his sliding door and met up with the group.

A plane roared overhead. Braern and Araduk ducked and covered their heads with their hands. The travelers watched it climb into the powder-blue, cloudless sky.

"They're airplanes. They won't crash into us. It's okay," Moira said with a smile.

Tim rummaged through his wallet.

"What are you looking for, your passport?" Moira asked.

"No, I need my emotional support paperwork so I can travel with Blue. I don't have a carrier, but I hope my back-pack will work."

Araduk and Braern stared in awe at the automatic slid-ing doors.

"See! Humans do have magic!" Araduk said.

They walked through the inside doors, and Moira stopped to check the signs to figure out which way to go.

"Where do we go from here?" Braern asked, gawking at the people hustling and talking among themselves.

"It looks like we need to follow the arrows past this area here, then we get to the ticket counter over—"

"We do not have time for this. Follow me." Nozomi pushed past them and they watched as a family of six coor-dinated where they were headed in the busy airport.

Nozomi led the group to a restaurant with a long line of people waiting to be served. A delicious smell of cooked meats and baked breads with spices filled Araduk's nostrils.

Mmm... that's makin' me hungry!

He licked his lips.

"What are we doing here? We need to figure out a way to get tickets," Moira pointed out and panted from bustling behind Nozomi for a while.

The rest of the group had to pause and take a breath.

"I am looking for our way onto that plane." Nozomi scouted the area and watched the people go about their lives.

A few school-aged boys passed Braern. They slowed as their father continued without them, staring at his phone.

"Your ears are so cool! Where did you get them?" the boy in a blue shirt and khaki shorts asked.

"Thank you. I was born with them," Braern answered as he bent to their level to talk to them.

Moira stopped and turned around. She watched as Braern let the boys touch his ears and giggled.

Lots of *wows* and *oohs* came from the excited boys' gigantic smiles.

Braern smiled as well.

My beard is entertainin' too, lads! Ah, ye wee ones can't appreciate how long it took me to grow this thing out! Ha! the dwarf thought to himself.

Moira pushed her thighs together. She cleared her throat and looked away. "Calm down, ovaries. Not the time," she whispered as Braern waved goodbye to the boys while they hurried off to meet their dad.

Tim put his hand over his mouth and chuckled.

"What are... ova... ries?" Araduk asked.

Moira sank down and sighed. "Haven't you ever taken a health class? They're part of a woman's—" She lowered her eyebrows. "Oh, wait... never mind. I'll tell you later."

A few more kids approached Tim and tried to pet Blue.

"Hey, kids, always remember to ask someone before trying to pet their support animal, okay?"

They nodded as he took his backpack off his shoulder and carefully lowered her.

"Do you see how her tail is up?" Tim asked the kids.

"Yes," they said, matching his voice that was close to a whisper.

"That's how you know she's happy and it's okay to pet her. Now, make sure to stroke her fur in the direction of the growth, like this."

The children followed his directions and smiled.

Blue thoroughly enjoyed the extra attention and purred with half her body still in the backpack.

The kids giggled, petted her head, and scratched her chin. One of the young ones pulled her whisker.

Tim politely asked him to stop, but Blue tolerated all the touching.

"Alright, kids, say bye to Blue. We have to go," he said.

"Bye bwoo!" they all said as their parents took their hands and led them off. They looked behind them with arms outstretched in their parents' hands and smiled a goodbye to their feline friend.

Nozomi stood back and frowned, watching all this transpire. "People are staring at us. We'll never pull this off if we stay together. Meet back here in an hour."

They nodded. Nozomi walked away by herself and the others stayed together.

"We might as well find the service counter where we can get our tickets while we wait for her to come back," Moira suggested.

"After you, lass," Araduk said.

Moira led them around the airport for a few minutes.

Araduk narrowed his eyes, staring at all the humans. He furrowed his brow and slowed his pace.

The faces appeared again; this time they combined with the heads of the living humans that walked by or held conversations sitting outside restaurants. All of them were the same as before—bloodied, beaten, and bruised. Some wore metal helmets.

At first they carried vacant expressions, staring nowhere in particular. Then, as they walked, the faces turned to Araduk. A pain rose in his chest. His heart rate increased as his breathing became erratic. He shook his head and swallowed.

I'm so sorry. How can I make amends an' right this great wrong that I committed? What can I do?

They didn't answer him. He placed a hand over his heart and sighed. His right hand twitched as he felt an overwhelming yearning to stroke the side of his flask. It caused him physical discomfort in his arm and chest when he refrained from reaching for it.

In the early weeks after he was given his enchanted gift, simply touching the cool metal of his flask was enough to calm his nerves. But that didn't last. He needed to drink or the faces would never go away. He didn't have time to feel this sadness. His friends depended on him to see this quest through.

With a sigh, he reached in and fumbled in his robe pocket. He pulled out his flask, took a quick sip, and placed it back before anyone noticed.

Seconds later, the faces vanished. His shoulders relaxed as he took a deep breath. His pains vanished as his legs wobbled slightly as he walked. He was a little unsteady, but he was used to such a feeling.

That's better.

Araduk watched Moira lead them to a counter with a person standing behind a picture device with numbered keys.

It looks like the strange device in Tim's bedroom, Araduk thought.

They all approached a balding, fifty-something customer service attendant with a gray beard and a nametag that read, BILL COVINGTON.

"Hello, Bill," Moira began.

"Yes? How can I help you, sir?" He ignored her and spoke to Braern instead. The man raised an eyebrow and slid back his head when he noticed the elf's ears. He chose to remain silent and not ask.

The top of Araduk's head barely came to the counter.

"Excuse me? I was talking to you!" Moira said with a loud voice.

Oh, you better not anger the lass. She'll break your jaw!

Tim stood behind Moira and Braern, sinking his head into his shoulders, and kept quiet.

The man studied Braern for another second, then pursed his lips and forced himself to focus on Moira. "What can I do... for you... both?"

Braern opened his mouth to speak, then stepped backward.

"Yeah, I'm right here. Look, we are trying to find the ticket counter. Would you show us how to get there? Please?" She grasped the edge of the counter with one hand. She clenched her other fist. A snap sounded as she crushed a small part of the counter, sending a few fragments onto the floor. She released her hand and held her head high.

Watching her try to control her anger, Araduk gulped and took a step back. Tim followed his lead as they waited behind Braern and Moira.

Braern placed his hand on Moira's fist and caressed his fingers up her arm to her elbow.

She relaxed her shoulders and spread out her fingers with a sigh.

Good thinkin', lad.

"It's down that way and to the left after you pass the food court." He faced Braern again.

"Thank you," Moira said through gritted teeth.

As they walked away, Braern turned his head and wiggled his fingers in the air toward the man.

Bill Covington paused for a moment, then widened his eyes. He wailed and smacked his legs with a scrunched neck. The man opened his mouth wide in a shrill scream that was audible halfway across the airport. He lifted his knees and stomped his trembling feet. He made a horrible, loud ruckus all of a sudden.

The elf must've done something to him! Ha!

The customers shook their heads as a crowd surrounded the area.

Security took him away while the manager soothed the people in line and found a replacement to run the service counter.

Moira covered her mouth as the group of five headed back in the direction of where Nozomi had left them. They all laughed under their breath.

"What did you do to him?" Moira asked.

"I tricked his mind into thinking he had little flaming spiders all over his body."

"Oh my god! Serves that asshat right. I hate people like that. I'm a person too!" Moira laughed. "And thank you," she said to Braern.

"For what? The fire spiders?"

"No, for letting me defend myself. I don't need anyone to do that for me."

"I knew it was your battle, milady. Know that I am always here for you, should you need me."

Moira smiled as she wrapped her hand around Braern's arm and laid her cheek against his shoulder as they passed the food court.

"Those two are fallin' hard for each other. Mark my words," Araduk whispered to Tim as they walked behind Moira and Braern.

"I've been saying that for days," Tim said with a smirk.

"What do you think Nozomi's up to? You think she's gonna rob a bank or something?" Tim asked.

"What is a bank?" Araduk asked.

"I keep forgetting. Sorry. It's a place where people keep their money while other people borrow from it."

"And the currency here is gold coins and treasure?"

"Yeah... sorta... but here we have paper money and plastic cards the keep track of how much we spend."

Araduk nodded. "I see. Sounds complicated."

"It is. Most humans are terrible with money."

NOZOMI

AIRPORT IMPERSONATIONS

Nozomi scanned the airport and walked alone, stopping every so often to lean against a wall to locate her target. *It has been a while since I have used my observational skills like this. We need someone who appears to have money but is gullible enough to fall for my hot mess in a minute.*

While she traveled all over the human world, Nozomi was tasked with finding and capturing wanted fugitives who refused to show up for their court dates. Bail bondsmen paid her to deliver these criminals to them in exchange for a generous sum. It wasn't the most glamorous job, but it kept her fed, clothed, and she never had to stay in one place too long. She loved change. And change loved her. The two fit together like perfectly cut puzzle pieces, straight from the printer.

She blinked, catching herself gawking at a group of twenty-year-old college girls with short, plaid skirts and low-cut tank tops. They gossiped and giggled with one another, hands on their waists.

You all are going to be so cold once you get on that plane. Your legs will freeze. Such beautiful idiots.

Then, one of the girls appeared to grow red, wavy hair, and her face changed. Danielle. Whenever she stopped for a moment to think, her girlfriend filled her thoughts and overcame her senses. The familiar pain in her chest developed again. With her fist over her heart, Nozomi closed her eyes as her inner eyelids moistened. She was afraid to open them again and allow the tears to fall down her face. She had a tough girl facade to continue.

I will find you and free you, love. I promise.

She blinked again, and the girl returned to normal.

With a sniff, she shook her head, smelling an aromatic scent of hamburgers and pizza from the restaurant near the bar. She blinked several more times, and the tears vanished.

What about a businessman? She noticed a larger man with a suit, who was clearly wearing a toupeé, drinking at the airport bar. He donned a blue tie and newly polished black shoes. She removed her jacket, revealing her tight, black tank top. She ran her fingers through her hair and moistened her lips with her tongue. With palms up, she adjusted her bra and pushed her boobs together to accentuate her cleavage, then sat next to the man. Ordering a drink, she waited for him to look at her.

"Where are you headed?" he asked, staring at her chest, but she looked him straight in the eyes.

"Oh! I am heading to Iceland, actually. Such a cool place with all those glaciers and stuff," she said in a high-pitched voice, twirling her hair. Rotating her body to face him, she opened her legs and scooted her chair closer. She leaned her torso forward.

He gulped.

"Where are you heading? You look super important. Are you a bigshot CEO or something?"

"Uh..." He cleared his throat. "No, I'm the operations manager of—"

"That is so interesting. Do you travel often?"

"Yes, and I love yo—it. I love traveling!" The man blushed, adjusting his jacket. He placed his briefcase over his lap.

Nozomi finished her drink and smiled.

The man motioned for the bartender to put her drink on his card.

"Oh, thank you so much! That is so sweet of you!"

"You're... uh... welcome."

Leaning into him, she felt his chest on hers. She stifled a cough from the intense smell of his musky cologne, then whispered in his ear, "Do you want to get out of here?"

"Sure." He grabbed his briefcase with a shaky hand.

That took five seconds, Nozomi thought.

She held his wrist and led him to the nearest restroom. They quickly entered.

Two guys stared at them with wide eyes and washed their hands and left.

As the door closed, Nozomi pinned the businessman against the back of the bathroom door and leaned in, staring at him. His minty breath was a welcomed surprise. She was not usually this keen on getting this close to a man, although she had a few sexy ex-boyfriends who made her list.

The scent of cedarwood filled her lungs with a deep exhale. It was a pleasant enough smell for her to enjoy the seduction. *At least he has proper hygiene. Women are so much cleaner.*

She pressed her lips on his. For a moment, she was not kissing some random person, and she felt Danielle's softness for a second. Then it faded when he grabbed her arm. She frowned. *All right, I am done with him. I have not fed like this in so long. I need it. I cannot stop myself.*

While he rammed his tongue against her teeth, pulling her so close his belt buckle scratched her belly, her form flashed between human and fox. Hearing his beating heart in her ears, an overwhelming hunger rippled through her body. The man's spirit tingled on her lips as she inhaled his aura. The kitsune felt full of a renewed energy, more than she had in years. The man's lustful aura tasted like sweet candy as it traveled down her throat. Relaxing her body, she transformed into his likeness, clothing and all. She stepped backward as he opened his eyes.

"What the *hell?*" he screamed and left his mouth agape and eyes wide; every drop of vitality he had vanished.

Nozomi tightened her fingers together with her thumb on the outside, sucked her lips, and rammed her fist into the man's nose. He released his briefcase, and it plopped onto the floor, echoing for less than a second. Afraid someone would discover her, she dragged him to the bathroom stall and carefully set him on the toilet. She locked the stall and slid underneath the door. She adjusted her tie and grabbed his briefcase. She exited the bathroom, feeling rather strange in this new body, and pulled on her pants to readjust herself as she walked. Soon, she held her head high, puffed out her chest, and adjusted her tie. She inhaled and felt at ease in her new body.

I can do this. Think like a rich guy.

She returned to her friends' meeting spot.

Minutes later, the group regarded her in confusion with their mouths open and eyes wandering all over her new body.

"It is me. Nozomi. We need to get our tickets." She smiled, licking her lips and wanting to remember that taste for as long as possible. Exhaling slowly, she heard her off-pitch voice. *I need to learn to master the male vocal cords too.* She tried to do her best deep, manly impression, but it still did not match the body.

"How did you...?" Araduk scrutinized the body Nozomi had turned into.

"Act natural," she hissed, looking back, then quickly returned her gaze forward.

The group complied and remained silent as they followed such a strange version of their friend to the nearest customer service counter and waited in line. It was awkward attempting to make small talk. They eventually reached the front of the line.

Nozomi cleared her throat. "Hello, there. My friends and I would like five tickets, with one support animal, on your next flight to Iceland, please," she said in her new voice as best as she could, with her head in the air, and rummaged through her new bag for her wallet.

She found it, adorned with a diamond button on the front, gold trim, and black leather that anyone could smell as she removed it. She scoffed and rolled her eyes for a moment, then remembered she must stay in character. She fiddled around the many hard, plastic cards until she came across one that read, Chase Platinum Gold Saver.

"Right away, sir. One moment, please," the young man said and typed away at his computer, searching for flights.

A few moments later, the young man looked up. "That'll be $9,839.31, please. How will you be paying today?" he asked with a smile.

She handed him the card.

"Excellent. Here are your tickets. Your flight is in fifty-five minutes. You want to follow the arrows until you get to terminal B, flight five-five-seven, all the way down on your left. Thank you very much and enjoy your flight." He handed her a stack of tickets wrapped in little folders containing all the information.

She placed them in her bag and nodded, thanking the guy.

The group walked off and headed toward the security check.

"Genius!" Tim chuckled when they were out of earshot.

"Yeah! Damn, girl. You sure kept your word. Ha!" Moira thanked her.

Araduk and Braern silently chuckled behind them as they followed, still ogling the enormous building and all the sights, smells, and people everywhere.

When they reached the security check, Nozomi distributed each ticket. "Do not lose these!"

"Braern, Araduk, watch what we do and repeat it exactly, all right? This will seem strange, but this is to keep us all safe on flights," Moira educated the two men as Nozomi went first.

"Braern! Your sword!" Tim whispered, keeping his head raised as he glimpsed at the visible sword.

The elf waved his hand over the drumstick and the sword and they disappeared. "Thanks."

Nozomi approached the counter in her stolen body, placed her suitcase on the conveyor belt, and pushed it along the rolling wheels. Disguised as the businessman, she removed her shoes and belt and all the loose change in her pockets and set them on the small tray. She entered the security x-ray machine, pulling to keep her pants up, and raised her arms above her head as the lasers scanned her new body. After the beeping of the machine sounded, she shifted her stance, feeling an unfamiliar and annoying appendage between her legs.

How do men walk around with this thing?

"Next!" the security guard said.

Moira went next and followed the same routine.

Tim announced his emotional support animal was in his bag. He produced the necessary papers from his therapist to show security.

Blue remained in Tim's backpack as a little girl behind him squealed, "Look, Mommy! A kitty!"

"I see that. How cute!" the mom said.

Tim looked back and smiled, then entered the machine and raised his arms. He was exempt from needing to remove his backpack, but the security guard asked to see inside it. Tim took out Blue when he was on the other side and gave the bag to the woman guard, but kept holding one of the straps.

She checked inside with a flashlight, then returned the bag to Tim. He placed his feline friend back in the safety of her bag.

Araduk and Braern were next. As the elf walked through, the guard squinted at his ears.

"Are those ears real?" she asked, perplexed, as she rose from her seat.

Moira nervously hollered, "They're surgical implants. He's really into elves. You should see his house. Ha!"

"They are actually—"

Moira hissed at him to be quiet.

He nodded and silenced himself, walking through security.

"I'm sorry, ma'am. Could you step over this way, please?" a male voice sounded.

Moira frowned with narrowed eyes. "Ma'am?"

A female security guard instructed her to raise her arms. She patted Moira and touched her hair with gloved hands.

"Is this really necessary? I don't have anything."

"You're good." The guard stepped backward.

"Thanks." Moira scoffed and adjusted her shirt before rejoining the others. She hated that such a simple task had been difficult for her.

Braern was next. He surveyed the strange machine with the tall opening. He followed directions, stepped inside, and raised his arms.

The security guard frowned when the machine beeped.

He stepped out of the machine.

"Sir, can you step back in, please?" the security guard asked.

Braern nodded and stepped backward, raising his arms again. It beeped again. He looked down, watching his sword flicker visibly again. With a wave of his hand, the elf whispered the spell to render it invisible. He smiled with his chin up and raised his arms again.

"Sir, can you step over here, please?" the guard asked again.

He did.

"Do you have any metal pieces inside your body?"

From the corner of his eye, he saw Moira raise her eyebrows at him and nod.

"Yes," he said.

"Okay, you can go on through."

Everyone grabbed their belongings and put on their belts and shoes. Nozomi checked her ticket—they all did the same—and followed the signs to terminal B. They made it in time for everyone to board.

"Flight five-five-seven to Iceland is now boarding," a robotic female voice sounded over the intercom.

"I have so many questions, but I suppose they should wait till later... right, lass?" Araduk asked.

"Good call," Moira said.

The group was one of the first to wait in line to board. They shuffled forward as the flight attendants and service members showed them the way through the long hallway that bounced as they walked.

Araduk and Braern watched Moira, Nozomi, and Tim board the plane with Blue. The loud hum of the engine made the men uneasy. They looked between the cracks in the barrier of the plane door and the protruded hallway toward the giant mechanical contraption they were about to enter. They moved out of the way as other people started boarding in front of them.

"We are going into the belly of this... metal beast?" Araduk asked.

"I dislike this as much as you do, my friend. How can something that appears so heavy be able to fly?" Braern asked as the two looked at one another.

Moira frowned. "I thought you weren't gonna ask questions?"

"Humans are either very smart or very dumb," Araduk whispered to his elven friend so no others could hear as they passed.

The sounds of low conversations and footsteps continued behind them as they observed the giant beast they were about to enter.

Moments later, Nozomi found her window seat in first class and placed her briefcase in the overhead compartment. The rest of the group sat near her. When everyone had boarded and the rest of the group found their seats, she waited for a moment when no one was looking. She waved her hand and transformed back into her human form.

A flight attendant walked by and offered her a drink, shocked for a moment. "Wasn't there an older gentleman sitting here?" she asked, handing Nozomi the orange drink.

"No, only me. You must be seeing things."

Nozomi bit her lips and forced herself not to smile.

She watched the flight attendant as the woman swallowed hard, turned her head, walked to the back of the plane, and disappeared behind the curtain.

A giggle escaped Nozomi's lips. Her eyes crinkled as she relaxed her tense shoulders, leaning back against the chair.

"This is going to be a long flight."

Tim

Take Off

Tim's gaze flitted between Braern and Moira as he sat between them, biting his lips. "This is gonna be awkward," he whispered. Blue stayed in her backpack at his feet. The engine hummed. The sound grew louder as it combined with a high-pitched whistle. Families chatted quietly while the rest of the passengers placed their carry-ons into the overhead bins.

A shorter woman eyed Braern and smiled, struggling to place her bag in the cargo bin.

He made eye contact with her, smiled back, and helped her place her bag on the shelf above her head. His invisible sheath hit someone in the arm. "I apologize."

They rubbed the spot and raised an eyebrow at him, confused about what had hurt them.

Araduk and Nozomi sat close to one another. Araduk winked at her.

She scoffed at him and folded her arms, inching away from the crazy dwarf.

"I don't believe this heavy contraption will ever make it into the air," he said to no one as he kicked his legs back and forth under the seat. He strained his neck to watch the flight attendant demonstrate how to buckle a seatbelt and followed along.

They acted out the escape plan, how to put on the oxygen masks, and what to do if the plane reached any turbulence. The dwarf's hairs pulled at his chin as he buckled his beard under the belt. He yanked hard on his hair and hit himself in the face with his beard beads.

Nozomi chuckled.

"Oh sure, go ahead and laugh, lass," he said, giggling.

Nozomi placed a hand over her mouth.

Tim clenched the armrests till his knuckles whitened and his breath quickened. Sweat beaded on his forehead, and he closed his eyes. *I hate flying! Gotta distract myself. I can't let Blue out yet until we take off.*

The plane taxied as the whirring sound from the engine increased; they were on the move.

"Hey, Araduk! So, wanna know how a plane works?" Tim kept his gaze steadily forward, but his voice shook.

The group turned toward him from their seats. They could all see each other, sitting on opposite sides of the aisle.

"Four opposing forces happen simultaneously to make a plane fly. The first is thrust that propels the plane forward, and the next one is drag. It pushes air backward. Then the third is the weight of the plane. That is overcome by the fourth, and its opposing force, lift. Force, drag, weight, and lift." Tim smiled at how well he explained such a complicated man-made feat of physics. He loosened his grip a bit.

"Am not sure I understand, but if ye say it will work, I believe ye, lad," Araduk said, nodding. The dwarf raised his eyebrows, looking out the tiny window next to him.

Tim ground his teeth, and Moira placed her hand on his to try to soothe his fears. His heart rate lowered a little as he swallowed.

The plane shook from hitting a gap in the runway. The engine roared louder as Tim wiggled his feet and pushed his body into the back of his seat. His stomach churned as he was certain everyone around him could hear his insides twisting and turning on themselves. The beat of his erratic heart pumped in his fingers as he clenched harder. Tim closed his eyes and forced his lungs to take deep breaths.

"Would you like to stroke my fur to calm yourself, human?" Blue asked him telepathically.

Tim could feel her squirming to free herself and attend to his dire needs.

"Yes, of course I need to, but I can't bring you out of my bag until we're steady in the air," he answered back in his mind.

The two shared conversations in their thoughts, even when they were apart. It often got him in trouble in school, when he wouldn't pay attention to his studies.

The next best thing that he could do to calm himself was to caress the side of his backpack with his foot. Blue knew what he needed and rubbed herself against him. It worked. He opened his eyes.

"I don't mind this, honestly," Braern said. "Flying seems rather natural... to me, anyway. Wonder why we all weren't born with wings?"

Moira looked at him, then back at Tim. She raised an eyebrow.

"That's ri-ridiculous. Humans can't fly. We have to travel in planes like... this to fly," Tim stuttered. Talking to his friends distracted him as well.

Braern tapped his foot against his invisible sword on the floorboard as the plane accelerated. He carefully scooted it under his seat and ensured it wasn't close to anyone's feet.

"Ladies and gentlemen, please put away all electronic devices. Fasten your seatbelts and remain seated. We will be taking off momentarily," the flight attendant said by the cockpit in the front.

The plane gained speed, and Tim leaned his head and peeked out the window, his neck aching and stiff. He saw the runway going by faster and faster until the weight of the plane shifted to the rear, causing everyone to be pushed back into their seats at an angle. They were airborne.

"Look at how high up we are!" Araduk hollered as he pressed his hands and nose against his window.

"No thanks!" Tim squeaked, squinting so hard his face had reddened. He felt his body become hotter from the anxiety welling in his stomach, so much so that his esophagus had started to burn—stomach bile. *Oh no...* Tim fumbled quickly inside the seatback in front of him for the blue bag. He barfed.

Moira and Braern grimaced and leaned away from the poor kid when they smelled his stomach contents.

"I'm sorry, guys." He wretched again. "I... hate flying."

"We made it into the air. It's gonna be okay, Tim," Moira began. "Hey, what was your favorite part of our journey so far?" she asked.

He wiped his mouth, and when he closed the bag, the smell nearly vanished. He turned his head to see her smile. "Oh, uh..." He loosened his grip as his mind raced from all the interesting sights, smells, and sounds he had encountered on their journey so far. "That's easy. Meeting you guys." Tim took a deep breath and forced his gaze toward Moira's kind eyes instead of looking out the window.

Araduk was busy pressing his face against the window while fogging it with his breath.

"Is he licking it? Weirdo." *I bet they haven't cleaned those things in weeks.* The thought was nearly enough to cause him to vomit again, but he turned his attention to Nozomi. She picked at her nails, slouching with her seat belt still on. He longed to feel as comfortable as she seemed to be in such a potentially dangerous situation.

"Ew." Moira said, frowning and leaning her head away from the dwarf.

The teen shook his head and concentrated on his friends on either side of him.

"Anyway, yeah, that was pretty cool meeting you too, ya know. You're a cool kid." Moira placed her other hand on top of Tim's.

"Thanks. I don't really feel like I contribute as much as you all do, though. I mean, at least Araduk can heal, and Braern has that cool, black sword and knows magic. You've got that super strength, and Nozomi can turn into crazy-cool stuff." Tim lowered his voice to a whisper so no one else would hear. "I mean, I'm happy to be on this quest with you guys. This has been... one heck of an adventure."

"Hey, you can talk to animals. None of us can do that. That's way cool," Moira said.

"Yeah?"

"So cool."

Minutes passed and the flight attendant spoke over the intercom again. "Ladies and gentlemen, we are now thirty thousand feet in the air. You are free to move around the cabin. We will arrive in Reykjavík in fourteen hours and thirty-seven minutes. Thank you."

Several clicks sounded as a few passengers stood. One went to the bathroom, while the others scooted through the narrow walkway to talk to family. Parents helped kids find electronic devices to keep them busy. A teen with bloodshot eyes and tousled hair secured a pillow around his neck and immediately snored. One woman buried her face in an erotica novel, not paying attention to any of the passengers' shushed hustles. Flight attendants pushing wheeled carts stopped to ask if anyone wanted refreshments. Another cart squeaked by while the first-class passengers chose their snacks and drinks.

Tim smiled as he thanked the flight attendant, who handed him a tiny bottle of water and a towel. He discarded his barf bag in the trash can she opened. As he leaned forward, he outstretched his arm and turned on the little fan above him and twisted it to blow on him. The cool air soothed his burning, sweaty face. He sniffed the air and smelled a hint of cleaner. With a twist of the cap, he sipped the cold liquid, his stomach settling.

"It's so beautiful up here! Look how far away the land is!" Braern shouted with wide eyes as his nose and hands touched the tiny window. Between the clouds, he saw the green patches of land below. *These guys are hilarious with their curiosity and amazement. It's kinda fun watching them experience such mundane things for the first time.*

Moira pulled out her headphones to listen to music.

Tim hummed to himself and tapped his feet. He was finally at ease.

Nozomi looked around to ensure no one was watching her and transformed her hand into various creatures' paws—a tiger, elephant, then a monkey.

Tim laughed under his breath.

"What is this?" Braern touched a cord attached to the seat back in front of them. He inspected it, turning it every which way with a raised eyebrow.

"It's a phone, silly." Moira took it from him and secured it back on its hook.

"Actually, maybe... I should call my mama," Tim sneered and clenched his teeth, drooping half his mouth to the side. "Nozomi, you got that dude's credit card?"

"Yup." She dug around his wallet, then turned to hand it to him across the aisle.

"Thanks." Tim took a deep breath. "All right... phew. Here goes." He swiped the card on the side of the phone and dialed the number.

Seconds later, they all heard his mom's voice frantically asking who was on the line.

"Mama! *Estoy bien...* Mama, I'm okay... I'm on a plane right now... Don't cry, please. I'm okay. I promise I'll be home as soon as I can. I wanted to let you know I'm okay. I gotta go, Mom. I love you."

She was screaming so loud in Spanish that he wasn't sure if she'd heard him. He pulled the phone away and squinted as she screamed at him. He hung up the phone, sat back in his seat, and stared at the ceiling, adjusting the little airflow vent.

"She sounds pretty worried. At least she knows you're okay," Moira told him.

"Yeah, I guess. I've never been this far from home for this long."

"You and I have that in common, my friend. We are new adventurers," Braern said, smiling through a closed mouth. He nodded.

"I wish I had someone to call who was worried about me. Don't really have anyone." Moira shrugged her shoulders and sighed, looking at her feet.

"Hey, at least when you are alone, no one can stop you from doing what you want to do," Nozomi told her with narrowed eyes. "Like revenge," she murmured loud enough for the group to hear.

"You have us now. We are your family." Braern placed a hand on Moira's and regarded her with hopeful eyes.

If I wasn't sitting here, I bet they'd start making out right about now.

"Thanks, Braern. You guys are all right—especially Araduk. I mean, look at that guy's beard. It could solve world hunger by itself."

"What?" Araduk leaned over and asked with his mouth full of peanuts. A dozen wrappers lay on his lap, as a few crumbs were stuck in his beard.

The group chuckled.

The same flight attendant strolled to their seats and asked if they needed any help or if anyone would like a hot towel.

Everyone shook their head. Tim noticed Braern observed how others were using the towel and repeated that on himself. He thanked her, and she continued on her way. The rest of the group was happy with water.

Araduk twisted the bottle cap so hard the water spilled all over his lap, but he licked it all up and gulped it all down.

What would happen if we crashed? How would we get out of the plane before we explode? Tim had imprinted the locations of the emergency exits in his mind. He grabbed the pamphlet in the pocket on the back of the chair in front of him. He studied the plan by repeating it to himself. The thought of being stuck in a plane while it filled with water or fire made his heart jump. Forcing thoughts of escape, he relaxed his tense shoulders.

"Tim? You okay?" Moira interrupted his depressing scenario.

He shook his head and blinked, bringing himself down to reality. "Yeah, thinking of what would happen if we needed to get out of this plane in an emergency."

"Don't think about that. You'll freak yourself out for no reason. We would figure it out if something happened. Planes are safer than cars, remember?"

"Yeah... I guess."

NOZOMI

GRIFFIN TURBULENCE

People quieted as Nozomi fiddled with the controls to lights and the fan above her. She heard the little fan whistle and aimed it at her face. The coolness soothed her anxiety for a few moments. She fumbled through the pamphlets and other paper items in front of her in the pouch of the seat. Nothing looked interesting enough to read. *Should have brought a book with me.*

She looked out the window, her fist on her cheek. *I have been on a plane so many times that this does not phase me one bit.*

With narrowed eyes, she leaned back in her chair and enjoyed the gentle hum of the engine. The shifter listened to the conversation in front of her while she crossed her arms and sighed. The passengers in front adjusted themselves. The cloth seats stirred.

"Matt, honey, I'm gonna try to nap. Wake me up when we get to Iceland," a woman said. Nozomi heard her fiddle around in a bag of some sort and pull out an object that made a tiny tapping noise. She guessed it must've been headphones.

"Okay, Mom," the boy said.

Sounds like a ten-year-old boy and his mother.

Nozomi gazed at the vast ocean outside as light clouds passed in front of her view.

Several minutes passed, and the kid's seat moved once again. Half his face appeared in the space between the edge of his seat and the window. She watched him frown, leaning closer til his nose pressed against the glass.

"What is that?" he asked.

What is he staring at? Nozomi's interest piqued, and she leaned forward. She stared out her own window again.

About half a mile away, a swirling portal appeared. It was hardly visible through the clouds. Dark dots flew through the gateway in the sky and spilled into the human world. They grew bigger and approached the plane. Soon, she could decipher wings as the figures took on a bird-like shape. Four feet appeared under their large, feathered wings.

"What kind of bird has four legs?" the boy whispered to himself.

The boy's face fogged the glass. He quickly wiped the smear with his fist and backed away a few inches to stare in awe.

"Hey, Mom, look at this weird, bird thing flying in the air." He nudged his mom. Their seats vibrated again. The boy peered back at the strange creature flapping its wings through the cloud sky. It flew closer.

Nozomi could now see their features. Cream-colored feathers covered their bodies, and their beaks were orange and curved at the bottom. Four paws and muscular legs, resembling a lion's, protruded from below. The creatures' enormous wingspans glided and flapped. Their mouths hung open as they struggled to stay in the air.

Griffins.

"It's a griffin," Matt murmured, barely over a whisper. He touched the window again with his face.

Ah, so he does know his mythical creatures, Nozomi thought. *Wonder why they are up so high. That cannot be good for their lungs. And why are they even in the human world? Something is not right. Did the evil one do this?*

"What the...? Am I dreaming?" the boy asked himself.

She heard him slap his cheek with his hand.

You are not dreaming. I assure you, kid. Those are real griffins. She thought about telling him out loud that he was right, but decided against it. She and the others had bigger problems.

"Mom! Look!" he said a little louder. "Mom!" he said louder still. His seat moved. Likely, he was trying to wake his mother. She snorted and groaned.

"What is it, Matt? Are we in Iceland?" she asked, yawning. "I feel like I haven't been asleep that long."

"You haven't. Look at that!" He pointed out the window. The creatures vanished.

Maybe they flew in view of the other side of the plane?

"Huh?"

"What? It was right there!" he hissed and banged his fists on the window.

The other passengers peered at him while his mom tried to shush him. "Honey, maybe you've been playing too many video games lately. Nothing's there."

"No, I swear I saw a griffin flying in the air. It was coming toward us! I'm not making this up!" he hissed louder.

By now, the other passengers from across the aisle stared, with crossed arms and frowns.

"I'm sorry. My son is seeing things. He's really tired. We're very sorry."

Matt's face reappeared by his window. His face reddened. His brow furrowed. He clenched his fists and stared skyward for any sign of proof.

To her left, Araduk drooled with his mouth open, asleep. Nozomi nudged him with her elbow.

"Dwarf, wake up. This kid in front of us saw a griffin," she said quietly. She pushed him a few more times.

"Wha... Have we landed?" he asked, sucking the saliva back into his mouth and making lip smacking noises, scratching his neck through his beard. His eyes fluttered open.

Nozomi gestured with her head and nodded toward the window. The griffins appeared again from the other side. Araduk leaned in front of Nozomi. She felt his beard tickle her clavicle. He blinked.

Moira heard their conversation and reached over Tim. She patted Braern on the shoulder to wake him from his dozing trance. "Hey! That kid in front of Araduk and Nozomi says he saw a griffin."

"A griffin? Are you sure?" the elf asked, shaking his head.

"Only one? That doesn't seem so bad." Araduk leaned back in his seat again and retrieved his flask. He took a quick sip.

Tim woke up and sniffed, closing his mouth. He shook his head, hearing the ending to what they said.

"There it is again!" the boy in front of Nozomi hollered.

His mom scoffed, then peered out the window. She saw both their faces squished together. "Oh my god! You were right! What is that?"

"There's another one! It looks like they're tired, Mom!"

The boy was right. Araduk and the others witnessed the same flock of griffins he saw, mere feet from the plane, tumbling in circles with their paws on their chests, their mouths open as they panted. A tail swooshed in front of their windows and disappeared above. Araduk blinked one eye and leaned over Nozomi again. He smacked his face into the glass to see better.

"Careful dwarf. You are squishing me." Nozomi hissed.

A loud thud jostled the plane.

"This is bad," Moira said as tightened her seatbelt with quivering lips.

"Ladies and gentlemen, please make your way to your seats and buckle your seatbelts. We are experiencing some... uh... I don't even know what to call this." The captain's voice became muffled as he tried to cover part of the microphone. "We are experiencing some strange turbulence, so please remain seated. Thank you for your patience."

Soon, nearly all the passengers craned their necks to gawk at the commotion in the sky. Several screamed while others prayed and folded their fingers together with their eyes closed.

Flight attendants shoved the beverage and snack carts into their respective areas. They looked out the windows by their seats and buckled in for safety.

Nozomi watched as the entire herd of griffins was now exposed. There were dozens of them. Some opened their mouths in shock as they caught sight of the airplane. Others were curious and flew closer to inspect the enormous metal flying contraption, likely to try to catch a ride before they plummeted to the ground from exhaustion.

One ventured too close and slammed into the side of the plane, causing multiple passengers in the aisle to lose their balance. They screamed and dropped their cell phones and snacks. The other passengers helped them to stand, and they all rushed to their seats quickly.

Muffled squawks and screeches came from outside. A loud thud sounded from the roof of the plane, followed by high pitched scrapes.

Chaos and terror ensued aboard as the passengers panicked and tightened their seatbelts. Some prayed with eyes closed and hands together. Others quieted their frightened children.

Nozomi squinted her eyes, gazing at a larger bellied griffin. The creature huffed and puffed, clumsily flapping its wings at tiring speeds. It lost its balance, reaching for the outside of the plane, and slammed into the side. The nearest engine sucked the creature into it as it squawked, with all of its limbs frantically attached to the rim. The propellers in the engine were too strong. It disappeared inside as a splatter of blood drenched the windows. The slap of the red liquid on glass made Nozomi's stomach churn. She scrunched her face and shook her head.

"Lads and lassies, am afraid one of the griffins got sucked into the engine over on this side. He's gone."

"That poor thing!" Moira clasped her hands over her mouth as tears welled in her eyes, staring at the dwarf.

Then, the starboard side engine sputtered, stalled, and died.

"Tim, does this flying contraption need... uh... both... what do ye call 'em... *engines* to stay in the air?" Araduk asked.

"Yes! Yes, it does! We're gonna die. I can't believe I came on this flight. We're all gonna die!" Tim squeezed the armrests until his hands whitened.

Blue meowed to be let out of her bag and scratched at the sides.

Tim's chest rose and fell as he hyperventilated and clenched his eyes shut.

"We are not going to die," Nozomi said. She unfastened her seatbelt and stood. She stepped across the aisle to Moira, Tim, and Braern's side.

Passengers used their seat-attached phones to say tearful goodbyes to loved ones. Unpredictable turbulence shifted everyone aboard again.

"Ladies and gentlemen, we are experiencing difficulties. Please fasten your seatbelts and put on your oxygen masks immediately. We're doing everything we can to fix this error." The captain forced his voice to remain calm.

Moira watched another griffin get sucked into the port side, inches closer to the second engine. "Braern! If that engine dies, we're all dead!"

"I need to get out there and help him!" He pushed around their legs to the other side of the plane. The panicked elf hurried down the middle aisle, watching the griffin inch closer to the engine. He stopped every few feet and leaned toward the other passengers' windows.

"Can you breathe if you're up this high?" Moira asked, unbuckling her seat belt.

"Sir! Er... ma'am! You both need to get back to your seat, now!" one of the flight attendants demanded from her seat at the front of the plane.

Nozomi saw the poor griffin as it scratched and screamed to free itself on Braern's side of the plane, but it was sucked closer to the dangerous blades. Its outstretched claws held onto the metal for dear life.

"What are you doing? You cannot go out there!" Nozomi yelled after him.

Araduk left his seat and toppled over into the aisle, pushing against Nozomi. Twenty seats away, Braern leaned his head across a seat of three people to see where the griffin and engine were. He looked back at Moira who had stumbled into the aisle, bracing herself with her hands on the seats on either side of her.

Nozomi watched their silent exchange.

I hope he is not about to do what I think he is about to do.

Moira extended her arm for Braern. He maneuvered to the spot inside that was adjacent to the roaring engine and saw the griffin pulled farther toward the blades, as its feathers protruded from the engine's metal shell. The elf raised his eyebrows and swallowed. He stared at Moira with pain in his eyes.

He took a deep breath, removed his invisible belt and weapon. They dropped to the ground with a thud. Only his friends knew what that sound was.

The elf waved his hand over his body and disappeared. People screamed in shock and leaned away.

Moira tripped the few steps over and struggled to grasp Braern's belongings as she kept her gaze fixated out of the nearest window.

Nozomi pushed her way to an empty seat and watched the elf try to rescue the griffin on Moira's side of the plane.

Braern perfected his magic spell so that only his body and clothing became incorporeal. He knew not to cast the same spell on his sword or it would fall to the earth and be lost. The elf glided his invisible body through the metal shell and opened his eyes. Halfway out of the plane, he conjured a sticky substance from his hands. The goo appeared out of his palms and the bottoms of his boots.

The extreme cold turned his face white while his nose reddened. Now fully outside, he clung to the side of the plane as the wind blew his hair and clothing. He blinked constantly, struggling to see while he fought to breathe.

Nozomi felt the plane slowing as it descended, and the blue ocean had become visible through the clouds once more.

Inch by inch, Braern crawled while absorbing the goo into his hand or foot, then cast it again to appear. He clambered around the outside and onto the protruding wing. A minute later, he looked inside the engine. With one hand free, he grasped the griffin's lion-like leg and pulled it out.

The griffin slammed into him as the sticky substance disappeared. Intertwined, the griffin and elf flew backward. Braern's head hit the side of the plane, knocking him unconscious. The griffin flew away, screeching.

Back inside the plane, Nozomi watched in horror as the elf disappeared from their sight, plummeting towards the water.

"Nozomi! You're the only one who can help him!" Moira screamed, clutching his invisible sword and other belongings against her chest.

"How can I do that? I cannot do what he does! How do I get out of the plane?"

"What the hell is happening? Sit down!" the fight attendant yelled again.

"Tim! You always know what I can turn into. What
should I do?"

"Quick, lad! Or he's lost!" Araduk grasped him and
shook his shoulders.

Tim rubbed his leg against his bag with Blue inside. He
placed his hands on his head and blinked, his eyes darting
from the floor to the ceiling. "An insect? No! Something that
can withstand freezing temperatures and go through metal. A water bear! I mean, a tardigrade! They're tiny bacte-
ria-sized things with eight legs and fat bodies and a weird
head and a circle nose. They can survive in any environment.
You can go through the plane and save him!"

"I do not know what that is! I need to see a picture so
I can shift into it!" Tim whipped out his phone, turned off
airplane mode, and googled the creature. He shoved his find-
ings in front of her face. *I think I can shift into that thing.* Nozomi nodded and engrained the image of the creature in her
mind. She ripped off her leather jacket, raced to the rear of
the plane, and disappeared through the floor. She kept the
image in her mind of how Tim had described the creature.

Quickly, she shrank down to the size of an ant, watching
as the seats, people, and the inside of the plane grew enormous around her. Soon, she grew so small, fully transforming
into the bacteria. Staring at her appendages, she witnessed
her eight legs appear, swirling molecules of varied colors
bumping into each other. She flew over as fast as she could,
giving herself wings on her back to propel her forward.

Nozomi, the tardigrade, passed through multiple el-
emental layers of various metals. Then she escaped out of

the other side of the plane. As soon as she felt the cold, she transformed into a griffin, for it seemed fitting, thinking of what had transpired earlier. She saw the tiny dot of the elf out of view as he disappeared below her. Diving after him, she forced her body into a bullet shape to travel faster, her wings, arms, and legs straight against her.

The unconscious elf's clothing flapped in the wind while his back arched. Braern's arms and legs flailed above him. His eyes were closed.

"Gah!" Nozomi yelled, her tongue drying as she forced her eyes to stay open, despite them filling with tears.

She saw the ocean getting closer. Inches from the water, she reached out and grasped his body in her forepaws. He dangled in her claws. Pausing in the air, she looked up at the plane flying overhead. She flapped her wings, and the two of them launched in the same direction. Her tail tip dipped into the ocean as a wave of water sloshed behind.

Out of breath and frozen from tail to beak, Nozomi wheezed as her eyelids grew heavy. Her trembling talons held her elven friend. They made it to the shore. The shifter transformed back into a human and the two of them somersaulted onto the ground, collapsing on top of one another. With a drop of her hand onto the cold, black beach, sleep took them both.

*****

An unknown time later, the freezing, ocean waves lapped at Nozomi's fingers. She retracted them with a shiver and opened her eyes. Sand covered her cheek. Groans from Braern sounded beside her as the two of them turned to face one another.

"Nozomi? Where are we? What happened?" he asked, pushing himself up to sit with a shaking arm.

His vest and *kamishimo* top had come undone, exposing his stomach. The light from the sun shone onto a hint of muscular abs in the shadow of his shirt. Nozomi caught herself staring at his belly with wide eyes. *Damn, he is hot. How have I never noticed this before?* She blinked and turned her attention to his face.

"You saved the griffin from destroying the plane engine and, by extension, everyone aboard. I am certain they landed safely on the runway. We need to head that way," she said, pointing in the direction of the airport.

He nodded with a slight smile.

"I'm happy to hear everyone is safe," Braern uttered. He rose and held his shoulder.

"That must be where the griffin slammed you into the plane. We are both lucky we survived in the thin air up there."

"Yes, I don't care to die before I find the answers to all these burning questions. I'm grateful to you. Thank you for saving me."

Nozomi nodded, stretching her arms.

"You are welcome. On the way there, I will tell you what Tim had me shift into, in order to save you."

"Please do."

The two of them leaned on one another to stand and gaze skyward. The airport was miles away. Without a word, Braern pushed off the ground and rose into the air. Nozomi transformed into a hawk and the two flew to the airport, landing in a back area where no one could see them. They hobbled over to the entrance.

"We need to find Braern and Nozomi. I hope they're all right." Moira furrowed her brow and rubbed her wrist.

Nozomi heard Tim, Araduk, and Moira as they stepped through the automatic sliding glass doors of the exit from Reykjavík Airport. Blue was safely in Tim's backpack, snacking on some freeze-dried fish crackers.

"We're right here," Braern said in a soft voice.

They turned to see them sitting on the bench behind.

"I'm so glad you're okay!" Moira said, her lips quivering, as she ran over. She dropped Nozomi's jacket wrapped around the elf's weapons and items onto Braern's lap. She wrapped her arms around them both.

"How are you able to carry Raven? My father cast a spell on it so it becomes as heavy as a mountain should someone who intends to cause me harm try to wield it."

"Well, I don't wanna hurt you. It shocked me when you were in the hospital when we first met, but I figured out if I wrap some fabric around it, I can pick it up. It's pretty heavy though."

"And by fabric, you mean my jacket. Thank you for bringing it," Nozomi said.

Braern unwrapped his weapon and handed her the black jacket with a smile. He looked at Moira as she took a step backward.

"Ah... your strength allows you to carry my sword, but it hurts you if you touch it?"

"Yup."

The group nodded.

"Thank you for returning these to me."

"Anytime." Moira's eyesight blurred as tears formed. She hugged him again, closing her eyes. "I don't know what I'd do if something happened to you, or any of you."

Moira hugged Nozomi too. The shifter flinched for a second, placing her jacket over one arm, then wrapped her arms around Moira. As she released her grip, Nozomi watched her voluptuous lips glisten in the sun. Her hair smelled of jasmine. She squeezed her knees together as she felt a pang of discomfort between her legs. *Kuso, I need to get laid,* Nozomi thought with a sigh. *Danielle. I miss you.* She imagined her long, ginger hair blowing in the breeze.

Tim's voice broke her out of her trance. "That was some crazy stunt you guys did. I'm happy to see you too." Tim's face warmed, and he averted his eyes, sinking his head into his shoulders. "And dude! You looked like Spider-Man with your web stuff shooting out of your hands! So awesome!"

"Spider... man?" Braern asked with an eyebrow raised.

Moira sniffed back a tear and shook her head with a laugh. "It's a super hero in books and movies."

He nodded.

"Good to have ye both back with us." Araduk patted their shoulders.

Moira sat next to Nozomi and watched as the shifter placed her hands over her ears, staring at the ground.

Braern still tried to catch his breath, leaning against his rescuer. He adjusted his clothing and tightened the laces of his vest and boots. Then, the elf brushed the sand off his long sleeves.

"We can rest for a minute," Moira said.

"I've never even been out of the country, let alone Iceland. Well, except for Japan." Tim surveyed the distant city skyline.

While they spoke of what recently happened, Braern placed his belt back around his waist and adjusted the drumstick and sword. He felt such relief to have them back.

"I travel all over for work, but I have never been here before. Looks interesting. Not sure how I feel about the cold," Nozomi said in a weary voice.

"I believe my ancestors settled here long ago. I also have never traveled here," Araduk commented.

"Who are your ancestors?" Braern asked.

"I bet they're Vikings! Tell us they're Vikings!" Tim adjusted his glasses as they shifted in his excitement.

"Ye guessed it, lad. Am a descendant o' the Vikings!" Araduk patted his belly, then stroked his beard.

"So, you're human too?" Moira asked.

"Long ago, part o' m' family migrated to Yumerion an' settled thir too."

"You still look like a Viking now. Hope that's not offensive," Tim said.

"Why, thank ye, Tim. Not at all."

"And you're... Scottish too... right?"

"Aye, my family has human and dwarven ties from many generations ago."

"So, where to next?" Moira asked, surveying the land.

Before anyone could answer, they heard muffled sounds of someone talking over a radio behind them. They turned to see several police officers speaking to one another on their radios by the interior airport doors. As people walked in and out, the doors opened, and they could hear parts of the conversation.

"Someone stuffed the poor guy in a bathroom stall, then robbed him and used his credit card to fly to Reykjavík."

"I did not rob him," Nozomi whispered. "Eh, I mean, I did take his credit card... I guess I did rob him." She shrugged.

"Be on the lookout for an Asian woman, about twenty-two, with long black hair with blue highlights, average height and weight. She may be traveling with a small group."

"I am not average anything." Nozomi frowned.

The cops heard their whispers and turned their attention to the group. One pointed directly at Nozomi.

"Shi... We need to get out of here." Moira's eyes widened.

"Run!" Nozomi shouted.

They ran through the parking lot and quickly found a rideshare who spoke English and hurried in the van.

"To the city, please," Moira instructed.

They arrived and exited quickly. Nozomi used the victim's card one last time.

"Here, lemme have it for a sec," Moira said.

She handed it to her.

"Wait, what if we drop it on the ground and hope someone else uses it? Then the police would go after that person and they'll give up on us?" Moira asked.

The group stood in silence for a moment.

"I don't know how money even fits inside that little, paper-thin thing. But that sounds like a plan to me, lass," Araduk said.

Moira nodded and kept her gaze ahead and released her grasp on the card. It fell with a tiny, plastic sounding thud.

Before them, a multicolored array of buildings in bold colors was a welcoming sight. Poplar trees scattered about the city. A few natives in jackets walked around, gossiping to one another. In the distance lay massive, snow-covered mountains under the cloudy sky. The faint stench of sulfur filled their noses. They heard sirens in the distance and hid behind a restaurant.

"Ew, why does it smell like a dirty diaper here?" Moira asked, sniffing.

"I think it's the sulfur from the volcanoes," Tim said.

"You got any ideas on where to go to hide from the cops?" Nozomi asked.

Braern floated above the wall of the restaurant and placed his hands on the roof. "There's a tall tower about a mile away."

"It might be that dinosaur-sized church with the long name I saw online," Tim said.

"Let's split up for now and meet at that church in the middle of town." Braern pointed to the distant tower.

Nozomi nodded as Moira eyed Braern.

Braern stayed with the guys because he knew he could better protect them with his magic.

Blue watched through her backpack window.

Nozomi left with Moira, and a pair of black-dressed cops followed them into an alley on foot. They stopped with a wall in front of them.

Moira smirked and whispered, "They don't have guns."

Nozomi nodded.

"We want to talk to you. Please, come with us." The two officers shuffled forward with outstretched arms to appear unthreatening.

Backup arrived in a patrol car and blocked the exit.

The women stared at the cops, contemplating their next move. Nozomi threw her hair out of her face and clenched her fists. *What can I shift into? There are volcanoes and mountains here and tall buildings, so... got it!* She transformed herself into a car-sized, black mountain goat with curved horns and strong, gray hooves. "Hop on," she whispered, keeping her gaze ahead.

Moira climbed onto her friend's back, feeling the strange sensation of her bony spine on her thighs.

"What is that? *A goat?*" the cop yelled, stepping backward from its immense size.

With opened eyes and mouths, the officers backpedaled, with arms stretched in front of them.

Two more police officers arrived from the car and joined the shocked faces.

Nozomi galloped toward them.

They all jumped out of the way before hooves met foreheads.

Nozomi leaped over them and disappeared down the street, Moira holding onto her black mane to steady herself.

Moira looked ahead at the tower. "There it is! Keep going that way!"

Nozomi looked back to see the cops. She heard one radio for more backup. He paused, leaning on his car door, unable to form the words for a moment. "There's a giant... goat... running around the city. I need backup!"

They laughed, and the women headed towards the tall tower in the middle of the city.

BRAERN

THE LAND OF ICE AND FIRE

Meanwhile, the other officers chased Braern, Tim, Blue, and Araduk down the main road lined with shops. Sirens wailed as the car zoomed after them.

If I fly all over this village, the humans will feel threatened. The elf adjusted his aching shoulder as they ran. He had no choice. Braern knew they had to stay on foot or risk his friends being caught. With their belongings flinging around on their bodies, Tim zipped Blue's backpack closed so she wouldn't fall out. "Hang in there, Blue! We'll stop soon."

"Meow!"

"Stop! You're under arrest for aiding and abetting a criminal!" one officer sounded through his megaphone from the car window.

"Where are we goin' now, lad?" Araduk asked.

The four turned right down a street and around the corner of a shop selling wool sweaters and hats.

I need to lose them. But how? Braern thought.

They stopped running to catch their breath.

Tim pushed up his glasses again, then placed his hands on his knees and eased his backpack to the ground.

"I don't know how much longer I can do this, elf," Araduk heaved, then collapsed to the ground, his hand on his chest, with closed eyes.

"Me too. I'm done. My legs are Jell-O." Tim unzipped the bag for Blue to come out.

She jumped and sat on his lap, purring to lower his stress.

He ran his fingers over the top of her head and down her back. "You okay, Blue?"

She meowed and looked up at him. He placed her in the backpack again, despite her vocal protest.

"I know, but we gotta keep going. You need to go back in here for a little while again, okay?"

"No more running," Braern said. "Stay here." Pebbles crushed under his boots as he stepped from behind the side of the building.

Two patrol cars stopped in the middle of the road and blocked the width of the street.

Braern stood, legs apart, his palms facing outward at his sides. He floated in the air above them.

The police stared in awe with wide, unblinking eyes, shielding themselves with their car doors.

What was that spell Orastos taught me when we first learned to fly together? Oh, yes!

"*Kaze o tsukuru!*" he shouted. A breeze blew toward him as he seized it within his grasp. The winds blustered toward him now, his hair waving. His hands glowed, and a powder-blue light swirled around his body. *Another moment longer... there, that's it.*

The power of the wind surged through his soul, and his heart felt light and cooled. He formed a ball and stretched it to create a mini cyclone. Soon, it enlarged to the size of a building. He noticed people emerge into the street to see what was happening. The elf conjured a shield and imagined it stretching alongside the street, protecting the innocent bystanders. He doubled it and threw another one on the other side of the street, shielding those people. A second later, grimacing from the power growing unsteady, he reared back and threw the cyclone at the police cars, sending them flying backward.

He intended not to injure the police. When they were far enough away that he could hardly see them anymore, he sent a bubble underneath to lower them to the ground. They floated inside their vehicle, staring outside of their windows with shocked faces. Once on the ground again, they paused for a moment. Then they accelerated, sending screeching rubber noises echoing through the street. They turned around and zoomed away. Braern's wind magic terrified them enough to abandon their chase.

He floated to his friends and gasped for breath. "I didn't think that would work. I've... only tried it once with my father."

"That was so cool, man! You have to teach me how to do that!" Tim yelled with a giant smile, his arms waving in the air.

"Nice work, lad." Araduk patted Braern's shoulder.

"Now, let's get to that church."

*****

An hour later, the travelers were reunited.

Braern heard Moira a few feet in front of them. The women beat them there. "There it is!" she yelled as she pointed to the church.

The church towered above the rest of the red, white, and gray roofs. She looked behind and saw the police had disappeared.

"Wish I could see the looks on their faces." Nozomi chuckled.

They arrived at the long stone walkway to Hallgrímskirkja. The statue of a Viking wielding an ax sat on a curved sculpture. The church looked like two sets of musical organ pipes of varying heights that started small on the sides and made their way up to the tall tower. A white cross sat at the top, and below was a large-hand clock that read, 12:30 p.m.

"We're right behind you," Tim called. "Wait, are you a goat, Nozomi?"

The women stopped and turned to see their friends.

"'Bout time you got here," Moira joked.

Blue walked on her own. She'd had enough of being cooped up in that bag. Stretching her legs was a great relief.

"We need to get inside and go out the back way," Nozomi said as she transformed back into her human form. Moira fell off her back and landed on her feet.

"Gimme some warning next time. Damn, girl," she said with a scoff.

They hurried inside the massive church.

"Wow, it's gorgeous," Moira said, beholding the curved arches that met far above them.

Rows of orange and gray wooden pews faced the front of the church. A few people sat and prayed, and others walked around, taking photos and whispering to one another.

They moved to the side between several pews and the walls.

"It looks like a volcano in here," Tim said. His mouth stayed open as he craned his neck to look above.

"I believe that is exactly how they intended this to look," Araduk said.

"All right, we gotta do this quick." Moira retrieved a cloak that one of the Shiro Peak monks had made for her from her bag.

They followed her lead and donned their own cloaks.

Tim kneeled and fastened a tiny one they had made for Blue to her back, tying the strings under her chin as the hood sat on the back of her neck. He watched his cat friend fidget with the new fabric on her back.

"We need to keep moving," Braern said. "Not only do we have your human police that might come after us again, but we don't want any harm to come to anyone here. Death follows us wherever we go."

"Agreed," Araduk said with a nod.

They wandered past the front of the church and came to an enormous pipe organ that nearly reached the ceiling.

Tim walked behind them, slowing his pace to catch a few more glimpses of the beautiful artistry around him. "My parents would love to see this place," he whispered.

"C'mon, Tim," Moira urged.

The boy rushed to catch up to his friends and peered at Blue.

She blinked slowly at him as they walked.

"Love you too, Blue. You look so cute with your little cloak on." Tim adjusted his glasses. "But it's so cool in here. Can't we stay for another minute?"

"Sorry, lad," Araduk said.

"Here's the door. Let's move," Braern instructed and led everyone outside. "We need to get past this village. I can't explain it, but I think we need to head north."

"Not gonna lie, I was about to say that too," Moira said.

"Are we all thinkin' the same thing?" Araduk asked.

"Seems like it," Tim answered.

Blue peered at him, licking her paw and rubbing it over her ear.

"I feel something pulling us there too," Nozomi said as she stared off into the distance.

They stood, staring in the direction they were headed. The Icelandic terrain called to them.

Braern placed a hand over his heart, as if it were being pulled by an invisible thread with a hook through his aorta. The ache resonated from his chest through the rest of his body. Something wanted him to go north—for them all to go north.

They navigated out of the city and followed a grassy path leading in the opposite direction. A few arrow-shaped signs pointed north that read, HELGUFOSS.

"Still think it's pretty cool that all of us are being pulled in the same direction. Means we're a real team," Tim said to his friends.

Blue rubbed on her human's legs as they walked.

"We're already a team, kid." Moira tousled Tim's hair.

The beautiful landscape boasted green plateau hills spread over the grassy plains. Snow-covered mountains lay miles ahead, with clouds surrounding their summits. The air was colder than the elf was used to. He could see his breath as he exhaled. A shiver traveled from his nose and fingertips to the rest of his body. Volcanic sulfur filled his nostrils, yet it was only mildly unpleasant due to his other senses that fancied the area.

"It's strange not having the cover of trees," Braern said, looking around. He felt exposed in such an open terrain.

"We should hurry and find our destination—wherever that is," Nozomi said.

They all nodded in approval.

"Very well, I'll fly ahead," Braern said.

"I suppose I will be a bus again," Nozomi said and threw her arms in the air with a smirk. She transformed into a giant hawk and bent for the group to board. A scoff escaped her beak. She narrowed her eyes.

"You three should start paying me to transport you everywhere."

"Jokes on you, we don't have any money!" Moira said as she laughed.

Araduk sat in front, and Moira climbed up.

Blue crouched to the ground, her ears flat.

"It's all right, Blue. You'll be safe up there. We'll be there soon." Tim pried her claws from the earth as bits of grass and mud fell from her paws. He eased her into his backpack, zippered it, and adjusted the straps on his back. He climbed aboard and stared at the space behind Moira. The boy sideglanced at Nozomi and turned his head away, offering to sit between them.

Moira nodded, then caressed Nozomi's feathers that moved in the wind.

"That is nice, thank you," Nozomi said. "Everyone ready?" She looked back.

Braern noticed Nozomi's eyes were indistinguishable from her human form.

"This way," the elf said as he lifted off the ground.

They flew for several minutes until they reached a shallow stream with protruding rocks. It trickled to a stop at its beginning. Their shadows darkened the ground as they flew above. The creek expanded with more trickling water. Then they spotted a waterfall.

"Is this it?" Tim asked.

"It feels like it is, but nothing's here," Moira said, frowning.

Nozomi and Braern lowered themselves to the creek's grassy edge. A large boulder sat close to the middle of the rushing water that splashed into the creek below.

"I'll look over there." Braern floated to the boulder and levitated in front of it. He placed a hand on the smooth, wet rock and saw his hand disappear. Quickly, he retracted his arm and studied his fingers. His brow furrowed, seeing the ripples from the barrier.

"Do you see anything?" Moira yelled.

"I'll be right back," he said, keeping his gaze forward. Braern floated through the boulder and disappeared. He heard their voices.

"What the hell? Where'd he go?" Moira screamed.

"Oh no! Did he fall through another portal?" Tim asked.

"Braern!" Araduk yelled, panicking.

"Not again! We have to go after him!" Tim yelled, gulping the spit in his throat.

"I'm right here. It's safe. You all need to see this." The elf peeked his head through to the other side.

"I don't feel like getting wet today. Can you fly us over there?" Moira asked.

"Why not?" Nozomi answered. "Here we go." She closed her eyes, flew straight into the giant rock, and disappeared.

The barrier rippled, then stopped as they went through.

On the other side, the Icelandic terrain continued, with the waterfall behind them. They exited the other side, dry. Before them stood a broken castle, looking as if a giant had ripped off the top half with its bare hands and threw the pieces into space. Towers were incomplete, while others remained with thatched roofs and stones missing from windows. Black soot caked the entire outside of the castle walls. Shredded and broken, the entrance archway and the door lay diagonally and almost flat against the ground, as if someone had kicked it in. The massive building was as wide as a lake and as tall as an Eastern giant from Yumerion. Whimsical, colorful swirls rippled in waves in the sky. Dozens of scattered islands floated above them with craggy ground that came to points at the bottoms. The top of the islands carried various doorframes with portals inside at different angles and sizes. A few of the islands had stairs leading up to their portal gateways.

"It looks like this is the destination for other travelers like us, too," Tim said in awe. He placed his backpack on the ground and rotated it so Blue could see.

She meowed and didn't seem at all impressed.

"Wow, this is amazing. It's like a magic subway station," Moira said.

Nozomi transformed into her human form after they climbed off her. "It is beautiful."

"Such beauty. I feel a sense of peace here, but that conflicts with the sight o' this poor castle. Wonder what happened?" Araduk stepped forward.

Braern took a deep breath. "I think we should go in."

"Very well. Let's see if the council can give us the answers we need," Araduk said.

They walked to the broken door. It was ajar and off one of the hinges.

"What happened here?" Tim shook his head with a frown. "It must've been bad if they left the place like this."

"I've got a bad feeling about this." Moira rubbed her arms as they stopped.

"It's you," a shaky voice said, muffled.

They looked around to find where the voice had come from.

"You're finally... here. I can't believe it," the voice said, then cleared its throat.

"Who's there? Who are you?" Braern spun around, staring at each of his friends and looking skyward.

Moira shrugged.

"Down here."

They looked down at the slanted door hanging open on the castle.

The doorknocker wiggled its nose and moved its jaw left to right. "Phew! I haven't spoken in... over sixteen years!"

"Who are ye? And how do ye know about us?" Araduk pushed through his friends to the front so he could see. The dwarf's face was at the same level as the doorknocker.

Half its face was a lion and the other half a dragon, with intricate carved designs. Soot covered its face as it spoke. "I've waited a long time for you to return. I'm so relieved to know you're here now. You can fix this castle! It's been horrible keeping quiet for so long, but ya know how oaths go. Am I right?" The doorknocker winked at them.

Tim raised an eyebrow at it as the others stared with open mouths.

"I'm the keeper of *Verndari* Castle. You don't know who I am?"

"We have never been here. How would we know who you are?" Nozomi asked with a frown.

"Wait, you said you've been waiting for us. But this is our first time here," Moira said.

"I have. This is *Verndari Castle*. Everywhere you see is Gapureia. This is the realm between Yumerion and Earth. It's the safe place for all members of the council to meet in times of need."

"The council? Are they in there? Where are they? We need to speak with them right away!" Braern placed a hand on the doorknob and climbed over the debris, pushing the door. As it cracked and jostled, he placed one foot inside the castle. Then his world went black.

*****

Another vision. The bright imprint of the castle appeared before him, traveling the entire width of the building on both sides of him. The brightness of the lines of every door, window, and wall illuminated until the entire castle looked new. Before him, he saw rows of seats leading up as far as he could see. The seats varied in size, for he imagined all the different creatures who had come here long ago—from humans and lions to giants and dragons, each with an appropriately sized seat. Some sat. Some flew. Others came from the ground. Still others floated, nearly transparent.

A few more had their own personal pond to swim in, with water-filled bubbles around their heads.

Then the darkness swept over the council. A blurry being of green slashed and attacked the members inside. Magic flew in all directions as the sounds of wailing and screaming echoed. The green light slaughtered them all until a single bright light shone in the middle of the room. Green and yellow lights fought and swooshed past Braern. He squinted as time slowed, seeing elf ears fly past him within the yellow light.

Then time started again. The lights vanished, engulfing the entire room in a blood-red hue. Then the ground shook beneath him as a vast explosion riddled the castle to rubble before his eyes. A wave of darkness overcame him as he felt a horrific pain in his chest.

A feminine voice mumbled.

"Braern!" Moira yelled. "Braern! Are you okay?"

*****

The elf blinked and the world returned. He pushed himself up from falling against the door.

The doorknocker mumbled underneath his grasp as he removed his hand.

"I apologize. I..."

The doorknocker raised an eyebrow with its mouth open. "Last time I saw you, you had black hair. Needed a change, huh?"

"What?" Braern asked, dusting himself off, squinting.

"You're... Braern Yogensha, right? Why, I knew you when you were much smaller. You used to play outside here and worked on your spells while your parents spoke in front of the council."

"I've never been here before. What are you talking about? I don't have any... parents. I have one parent, and his name is Orastos."

"Orastos? He's still alive? Thank the gods! Why haven't you brought him with you? Where is he? I'd love to catch up with my old friend!"

"He disappeared weeks ago. I don't know where he is. Did you say, parents?"

"Yes, your mother and father."

"I don't have—" *Why did Orastos never mention parents? What did I see in my vision? This is all confusing. I don't... understand. It cannot be true.*

Braern placed his hands on the sides of his head, his arms trembling. The back of his neck pained him as he fought to try to make sense of the new information. The questions arose so quickly that it felt as if they pierced his eyes and traveled to his brain, with flaming needles stabbing every memory he thought he knew. *It was all a lie? How can this be?*

"All right, you're confusing him. Stop." Moira crawled through the broken doorway and wrapped her arms around the collapsed elf as he braced his hands on the floor.

"Braern has parents?" Tim whispered to Araduk.

"I am confused," Nozomi said. "Look, we are here to talk to the council so they can tell us where to find this guy who wants us dead."

"I'm afraid that's not possible. They're... gone." The doorknocker closed its eyes and sighed.

"What do you mean, *gone?*"

"Hey, guys, come look at this." Moira waved her arm for them to follow.

As Araduk took his last step into the castle, Braern blinked his eyes open. They focused. The appearance of the front entrance and the surrounding parts of the building moved like static and sent a ripple through the rest of the building. Not much of a roof remained as the sun beat on them from inside. In the middle of the stadium-like structure sat a large, open shell with cracked stone. Something ignited a pink color in the middle of it, and the brightness shone onto their faces. They peered inside to see a circular light.

"Wow, that's pretty."

"Hey! You, Braern and his friends! Hey!" the doorknocker called.

"What is it?" Braern asked, his hand on his head as he hobbled to the entrance.

"You need to leave now! He's coming back!"

"Who is coming back?" Nozomi's expression turned stern as she ran to the door and stared into its face, pounding the wood above with her palm. "It is him? He is the one who has been after us and who took my Danielle? Tell me where he is! I will rip his heart out of his throat! Tell me!"

"I'm afraid I don't know what you're talking about, but you must leave. Now! You cannot hope to right a wrong when you know so little. Please! I'm begging you!"

Blue stared, meowing loudly.

"Blue says we need to go, now!" Tim yelled.

"I hate to say it, but I think we should listen to both of them," Moira said as the rest of the group ran to the entrance and climbed over the debris once again.

"But you must tell me about my parents! Why don't I remember them? And where is Orastos?" Braern yelled as Moira pulled him from the doorway.

The doorknocker grew still and closed its mouth.

A distant light shone from the gateway islands in the sky.

"We need to hurry," Araduk whispered to Nozomi.

She scoffed and transformed into a hawk.

They climbed aboard, and the six of them flew out of the waterfall barrier and to Iceland. Braern floated by, his legs and arms dangling.

"Eh, that was a waste of time. We have more questions than we have answers now! Gah!" Nozomi frowned in her hawk face as she screeched and veered them toward the nearest forest.

MOIRA

THE CAMPFIRE

Moira sensed their pain and could feel it all within her mind as they stopped in silence. It was as if all their neurons connected inside her brain, sending every stressful worry into her central hub. Her head throbbed, begging for rest.

They found a moss-covered area, perfect for a fire. It was time to discuss their plan. Everyone but Nozomi gathered a few nearby branches and piled them together. Rocks jutted from the ground in a warped circle. As the sun retreated behind the trees, it left a colorful array of wispy clouds scattered about. The brisk wind cooled their aching bodies.

Blue jumped out of Tim's bag and carried a small stick in her mouth and dropped it off, as the others did. She held her tail high with her head up and pattered to Tim.

He smiled and scratched her chin. The little cat leaned into his scratches and rolled around on the ground, picking up tiny rocks and blades of grass in her fur.

Braern sighed with his head in his hand and threw a tiny fireball onto the wood, and after a few moments, a crackling warmth started.

More silence. They peered at the flames as the heat warmed their skin.

She stared at her friends. Such depressed, defeated faces. Even Araduk had lost his usual smile and perky attitude. Tim pushed his glasses further up his nose and leaned into the fire with his elbows on his knees. Blue was the only one who seemed remotely happy. For a moment, Moira wished she could be a cat and not have a worry in the world except when her next meal was.

A pain in her heart developed when she watched Braern. All her troubles vanished when she compared herself to how much he must be suffering. To know that your beloved father had lied to you for your entire life must be the most earth shattering, heartbreaking knowledge of all. She wished she could do anything to ease his turmoil, but she knew nothing would help. So much pain.

Moira bit her lip, her head shaking. *This is not where we give up. I won't allow it.* She rose and took a deep breath. "All right, we've been all over creation for weeks, thrown through portals like we're basketballs! I admit, seeing the unicorns and the dragons was exciting. I mean, the dragons were cool, until one tried to fry us... and riding one was fun... but that's beside the point. We've barely had a moment to take this all in, to question, to just breathe. We haven't had a moment to think! Traveling from one world to another and back again, again, and again, and again cannot be good for our health. I'm exhausted, you guys. *Exhausted.* I want to know why this is happening to me, to us, and how the hell we have no control over our lives anymore. Sure, my life was boring as shit before I met you all, but damn, I'm going to sit in this spot until we get some answers. I'm done. I'm not taking another damn step." She threw her arms in the air, tattered, beaten, and bruised. Her motivation left her. She collapsed onto the boulder behind her and winced at the hardness on her butt.

"Hate to say it, but I agree with the lass. Am stayin' put too. Enough o' this." Araduk plopped his rotund rear onto his large, flat stone. He stared at the fire, took a deep breath, and nearly fell asleep with heavy eyes, his knuckles on his cheeks. The fire reflected onto his irises.

The rest of the group sat on the rocks.

"I guess, even after all this time together, we still don't know each other that well. That's not gonna help us figure all this out," Tim said.

Blue sat next to him, looking up at him, requesting more chin scratches.

He obliged her.

"Figures. The cat is the only one who is happy," Nozomi said. She had her back to a tree, staring at the fire, with her hands in her jacket pockets and knees bent. "I could use a cigarette right about now," she muttered.

"I find myself unable to grasp what has happened to us all, since I have been away from my father for so long. My father... if I can even call him that... has lied to me for years. The doorknocker cannot possibly know what he's talking about. It can't be true. Can it?" Braern asked the air with a sigh and rested his elbows on his knees with his back arched. He refrained from making eye contact with anyone, like he was having a conversation with himself.

"I don't even know where all your abilities came from," Moira said.

"Yeah, we never talked about our lives before we met," Tim said.

"Well, now's the time to fix that. Who's goin' first?" Moira asked.

A thought clicked in Moira's mind as scenes rushed at her so fast she couldn't understand them. She stood upright and faced Araduk. "Wait, when did you develop your healing powers?"

"Oh... uh... over a decade ago. Why, lass?"

"Tim, what about your communication power? When did that start?" she asked.

Tim's eyes widened at the woman.

"I've had this ability since as long as I can remember... since I was a baby, I think."

"How old are you?"

"Sixteen."

Araduk shook his head and stood.

"Aye, my gift appeared around that same time for m' too, lad." He nodded.

"What are you saying?" Nozomi asked.

"Nozomi, did you realize you could shape-shift around that time too?" Tim questioned.

"I suppose. I learned to shift when I reached one hundred years old. We lived our lives as foxes until my parents taught me how." Nozomi's eyes narrowed, and she frowned at him as if he had accused her of something. She tilted her head away as she exhaled. A single tear welled in the corner of her eye that glistened in the light.

"Wow! You're a hundred?" Tim asked with wide eyes.

"Yes, 116."

"Damn girl, you look amazing for your age," Moira said with a chuckle.

Nozomi narrowed her eyes at her. "Surely, you have gathered that *kitsune,* like myself, age differently than humans."

Nozomi turned and faced away. She swallowed so loud that everyone heard her.

"Makes sense."

"When did you, Moira?" Tim asked, leaning forward.

"Um, I can't remember when it started. I think I was five or so."

Wait, that was about sixteen years ago too.

Moira's eyes widened—the muffins. "Your mom said you were talking to animals when she was pregnant with you."

"You're right! I remember I had a weird connection with our dog, Freckles. At least, that's what they told me. Guys! We all gained these special powers at the same time! Do you know what that means?"

"I'm thinking the same thing!" Moira shouted.

Silence. Wandering faces searched all around for the answer that was right in front of them.

"It can't be a weird coincidence. Is this possible?" Moira asked, gasping.

"I got into my first fight about sixteen years ago!" Moira shouted, standing. She ran her hands over the sides of her face in disbelief.

"Sixteen... wait. Wait, this is all making sense. That was the last time I took a life... during the last war I fought in with m' clan." Araduk stood as well, regarding his friends with a wide grin. He held his head high with his fists on his hips, shaking his beaded beard.

"I believe that's around the time I came to live with Orastos, but my memory is clouded. For years, I tried to remember anything from before he took me in, but I cannot." The elf moved his jaw left to right with a frown.

"Yer sayin' we were destined to meet? That everythin' happened for a reason? It cannot be a coincidence that we all developed these great powers at the same time," Araduk said.

"I... never thought of it like that," Moira said. "We were meant to find each other. All this was supposed to happen!"

"You're saying this was destiny, that fate pushed us together? For what reason? To save all these people from impending disasters?" Braern asked, shocked. "We have hardly managed to avoid many disasters on this journey, so far. It's a wonder we're all still alive."

"And if this all happened at the same time, then why now? Why us? And what happened before we changed to cause us to be this way?" Moira puzzled.

"It's more than that," Tim urged. "I think we were pushed together for something bigger, something earth-shattering, huge. And it has something to do with the portals. I can feel it."

"But what?" Nozomi asked.

"I don't know, but I think if we continue this journey together, we'll find out," Braern said. "At this point, I don't believe we have a choice but to press onward."

They nodded.

The group whispered and muttered various theories for a while.

Nozomi narrowed her eyes and stood without a sound.

The campfire still roared as the group watched her with weary eyes.

"Here we are with no more answers, only more questions. We have not learned a single scrap of knowledge about any of this, from anywhere we have been. We should've found out something important at the castle, but we *did not!* I wasted my time traveling all over with you, when all I wanted to do was find the guy who took my..." she sighed. "Tried to get away from you on that island because... I thought I saw another *kitsune*... but I am done."

"Girl, sit down. We're all exhausted, and we need time to chill out before the next bad thing happens to us. I swear, they keep on comin'!" Moira tried to assure her.

She gazed at the star-scattered night sky and took a deep breath. "I cannot do this anymore," she whispered. "I refuse! I am going after him myself." She spun around and stormed off.

Moira rose and went after her.

"Let her go. We all need to take a few moments for ourselves. If she's in such a rush, let the lass go," Araduk said.

Moira heard the annoyance in his voice, but she knew he and the others would never force anyone to continue on with them against their will. She sat down with a sigh, slapping her hands on her legs.

"But we need her." Tim watched her disappear into the trees.

"He's right. It's her right to go off on her own if she so chooses to," Braern agreed with the dwarf.

"It doesn't feel right to break up the team," Moira muttered with her head down. *If we can't stay together, I don't think any of us will make it through this alive.*

NOZOMI

MEETING THE ENEMY

Nozomi stormed off through the sparse woods. Her head vibrated as she sneered with a clenched jaw. Every inch of her body filled with rage as she transformed her hands into tiger's paws and slashed her claws through the bark of trees in her path. Wood pieces hit her in the face while she recoiled backward. Her blood boiled as she stopped in front of a rowan tree with a few crimson berries left. *I wasted two weeks playing house with these morons and I have nothing to show for it! I am no closer to finding this asshole than I was before I met them!*

"Gah!" she screamed at the top of her lungs and furiously sliced through the tree til it cracked and splintered.

"Well, hello there, beautiful. I've been looking all over for you," a familiar voice sounded behind her.

She dropped her arms as the tree crashed to the ground with a thud, causing a gust of air to fling her hair out of her face. She turned her paws back into hands. Her body stiffened as she turned around to see him. A man with umber hair faced her, wearing a black, white, and green *kamishimo* with wide shoulders and narrow front panels. A tie around his waist led to a pleated bottom that lay over his socked feet, with black sandals. His hunter-green eyes pierced her core. With a gasp, her eyes widened and her heart pumped so fast she thought it might break out of her chest. She fought to inhale enough air.

"It's you! Where is Danielle?" she yelled, exposing her teeth and standing with her knees bent and legs apart. She clenched her fists.

"Your ginger-haired slut? She's locked away. You'll never find her.

"Locked away? So, she's still alive?" Nozomi closed her mouth and spread out her fingers.

"She is... for now," the man said with a chuckle. He smiled with a closed mouth and raised his chin.

"What do you mean... for now?"

"I've been looking all over for you and your friends for weeks. Every time I opened a portal for your entertainment, you evaded my generosity. I was only trying to..."

"Generosity! You tried to kill us!" Nozomi yelled, spit flying from her lips.

"Oh, I suppose I did. Nonetheless, here you are before me and you don't have a scratch on you."

"I'll put more than a scratch on you, you..."

"Now, let's not resort to such violence. I believe you and I can come to an understanding."

She glared at him as he took several steps to the right. She stepped to the left to ensure a safe distance remained between them.

He paused. "If you deliver me your friends, I will not only tell you where your girlfriend is, but I'll free her as well."

"What? You cannot be serious."

"Oh, but I am. You see, I watched you long before you met up with them. I know you've been on the fence about going on this little adventure with them from the start. You can go back home to her and this will all be over. All you have to do is bring them to me."

Nozomi was speechless. Her eyes twitched as she imagined her and Danielle reunited and embraced in passion. But what about her friends? She had grown at least a little fond of them, even for a loner like herself. Her chest felt as if a boulder had replaced her heart and grown cold and still. She inhaled and placed a hand on her head, blinking and trembling so much her jaw ached. *What do I do? How can I betray them like that? What if this is my only chance to save her?*

"Tick Tock. Time is running out."

"Gah! All right, fine! What do you need me to do?"

"Bring them to me."

Nozomi closed her eyes as he levitated off the ground and floated to her. She refused to flinch as he caressed the back of his fingers across her cheek. She blinked, and a tear escaped her eye as she bit her upper lip.

With a deep breath, she screamed. "Help! Someone help me, please! Braern! Moira! Help!"

She heard her friends yell back.

"Nozomi!" everyone shouted in unison and ran toward the voice. She watched as their bodies came into view over a hill of grass and sparse trees. The sounds of their pounding feet grew louder.

They came into view: Tim with his backpack over his shoulders, Moira with fists ready, Braern frowning, and Araduk panting with his mouth wide open.

The man curled his hand and shot a green light around Nozomi's neck. He stared at Braern with unblinking eyes.

"Thanks, love. I'll take it from here," he said, his gaze on the elf.

Braern frowned and squinted his eyes, then turned his attention to his imprisoned friend.

Nozomi gasped, clawing at the light. The air drained from her body. She kicked and twisted.

The enemy glared at them, tilting up his head with a vacant expression. He stood his ground with his legs spread apart.

I should have known he would never keep his word. I need to break free! "Kill... him..." Nozomi choked out as she tried to kick him from behind.

The enemy squeezed his hand so the magic green ring around Nozomi's neck constricted more.

Feeling the life drain from her, she dangled, blue in the face and limp. A white light appeared in her mind, blurred by the vision of her friends before her.

Without a word, the man wiggled his fingers, and a glowing, metal prison appeared with Nozomi inside.

Her skin burned as she grasped her neck. Panting and gasping, she took deep breaths and crumpled to the ground. Hot with rage, she tried to transform into a rat to escape between the bars. She found she couldn't. "I cannot shift! He cast a spell on the bars!" Nozomi fell onto her side and grasped the cool metal with her fingers as the green light from the bars appeared over her hand. Her gaze remained on her friends.

"Let her go!" Braern unsheathed Raven with one hand and ignited a ball of orange magic energy with his other. The elf's body vibrated as he forced himself to stay fixated on the man responsible for every misstep of their journey. His face reddened with rage as he focused his energy on his fists, lighting them with magic. He side glanced at Moira, who stood with her knees bent and her fists clenched. They glared at the evil man who followed them across the worlds to end their lives. Time slowed as their turmoil had only begun.

Araduk outstretched his arms while Tim ran behind the dwarf. Blue pushed her way out of her bag and jumped to the ground. The cat trembled by his side and crouched into a ball. Her back arched and her fur bristled as she growled and hissed.

Moira clenched her fists so hard her skin broke and bled down her arms. She frowned and gritted her teeth, feeling the muscles in her face ache.

They lunged toward him, yelling primal screams, like a pack of lions leaping onto their prey. Araduk and Tim crouched close by with terrified eyes and shivering lips.

The enemy swept his arm high in the air and down to his knee.

Moira raised an arm and hollered as she ran toward him. "This is for those poor creatures you killed!" She threw a punch toward his grinning face with all her might.

He rotated to the side and avoided her. As she fell off balance, he knocked her down with a wave of magic square between her shoulder blades, knocking the air out of her.

She skidded to a halt and lay gasping on the ground, coughing and spitting.

Braern conjured a glowing ball of orange fire with one hand and chucked it at the man's chest with a grunt.

The man opened the palm of his hand, and a portal appeared with a glowing blue swirling light around it. Inside was a lake. He flung the fireball into the water, and it evaporated in a puff of steam as it hissed. He closed his palm, and the portal disappeared.

Frowning and grimacing, Braern aimed his dark blade toward him.

The enemy formed his own blood-red conjured sword that glowed brighter with every strike.

Braern reared and sliced down with his Raven.

The enemy blocked.

Braern pushed forward and plunged his weapon toward the man's belly.

The enemy skipped backward and rotated with his arms behind his back.

"You're not even trying! Fight me!" Braern screamed. The clashing of metal, sizzling of magic, and frustrated groans sounded as the two battled. The hilt of the enemy's sword rammed into Braern's nose, sending him flying.

Moira lunged forward and raised her right fist to swing at the enemy's side from behind.

A wave of light emerged from his hand as he faced his palm toward her.

The wave knocked her down, and she rolled over and slammed on the ground, groaning.

Braern looked at her and felt his entire body heat from rage within him. "Don't touch her!" He raised his sword and yelled a spell. Raven illuminated as he flew toward him. Grimacing, with both hands on his weapon, he focused on the enemy's neck, imagining decapitating him with a single swipe.

Another wave. Braern tumbled to another side and braced himself, with one hand still on Raven and his other and feet on the ground as he stared onward.

Tim and Araduk ran off and cowered behind a tree, peering out from the side.

"It's now or never, lad," Araduk said. His muscles tensed as he rose.

Terrified, the boy watched his hands tremble.

The two of them staggered toward the enemy, their eyes fixated.

He stared at them and raised his chin, gripping his fist as the cage shrank with Nozomi inside.

"Get me out!" Nozomi felt the heat of the bars burn her skin as her breathing and heart rate increased. Her prison began to shrink as she pushed her hands on the side to try to stop them.

The group glared at their enemy with heaving chests and fists clenched so tight they drew blood.

"You're the one who's been opening portals, spilling lakes into restaurants, and trying to kill us, aren't you? Why?" Moira asked, scowling.

Seconds passed before the man burst out laughing, hunched over with his hands on his knees.

Braern lessened the light around Raven and lowered his sword.

Moira unclenched her fists, raised an eyebrow, and tilted her torso back.

"Wha...?" Tim said, frowning behind Araduk.

"Wait, wait, wait. You all are too much. I'm sorry," the enemy said between laughs, wiping a tear from the corner of his eye.

The group eyed each other with shaking heads and hunched shoulders.

Braern narrowed his eyes and gritted his teeth, staring at the man in front of them.

"Name's Schism. Pleased to make your acquaintance." He outstretched an open hand, bowing with the upper half of his body, twisting one leg over the other. "Well, I mean, that's the name I gave myself. We humans have such an interesting language. Who knew such a word would perfectly describe all that is me? What do you think?"

They stepped backward to prepare for another attack.

"To answer your question, yes, that was me. Pretty cool, huh?" Schism straightened his posture. "And I gotta say, I've been looking all over for this one. She's mighty tricksy." He glanced at Nozomi as she struggled to free herself.

"You know her?" Moira asked.

He nodded, sucking on the corner of his lower lip, smiling.

"I don't understand. Ye merged creatures together, nearly drowned innocent people, and ye keep comin' after us," Araduk sneered.

"Yes, yes, and... let me think... yes. But that's all water under the bridge, so to speak. Ha! Water... too soon?"

"Gah! Why are you doing this?" Nozomi screamed. The bars stopped shrinking before her spine snapped, her knees nearly crushed against her chest.

"Why? Because I'm destroying everything they worked so hard to build. Serves them right. They should've let me—"

"Who's *they?*" Braern asked through gritted teeth.

"You mean the council?" Moira said. "What did you do to them?"

"Nothing they didn't deserve. Now, I don't suppose you'd all surrender and let me have my way, would you?" Schism asked with an upbeat pitch.

"Never!" Moira yelled.

Braern spit and curled his upper lip. He channeled light energy to envelop his sword once again. "What do you know about the council? I was told my... real parents used to be..."

"Your parents? Wait, you can't be? I knew you looked familiar." The man shook his head and pointed a finger at Braern. "You must be that elf kid who almost got the best of me... but your hair's different. It must be you. You... haha... I can't..."

The man laughed and exhaled. His friendly demeanor vanished as his nostrils flared.

"You're the reason I couldn't fulfill my vow to myself for sixteen years. I searched *everywhere* for you! Where were you hiding?!"

"I've never seen you before in my life! I don't know you!"

"You're lying! You gave me this scar. I nearly died by your hand and you were just a kid!" the man roared and grabbed a handful of fabric in his hand to reveal a long, white scar across his chest.

"I didn't hurt you! I told you I don't recall meeting you! What do you want from me... from us?"

"What do I want? Ha!" he laughed. "I want every last connection to the *verndari* to lie down and die by my hand. That's what I want!"

"You can try, asshole. We won't go down without a fight," Moira said through her clenched jaw.

"What a shame. Very well, then. I love a challenge." Schism removed all emotion from his face. He watched as their fists and jaws clenched tighter. "But before you go too crazy, you might be interested in this fluff ball here." He pulled an orb containing a small creature from thin air. Light glowed around it, illuminating the victim.

"Master Kabu!" they screamed in unison.

"Don't... listen to him," he begged, banging on the glass orb. All the electric shocks around them drowned out his tiny fist sounds.

"Saw this little guy helping you, and I had to teach him a lesson. You understand, right? Can't have him interfere with my plan," Schism said, his head up. He twisted his wrist and moved his fingers, one by one, back to his palm to form a fist.

The orb shrank at lightning speed, the sounds of every bone in Master Kabu's body snapping all at once. Blood spurted everywhere as the rabbit inside was crushed into a puréed mess of organs and bones. The orb fell to the ground and shattered into a million pieces, spraying their legs with red.

"How could you...?" Tim asked from behind his tree, clenching his belly.

Blue covered her eyes with her tail as she flattened herself more.

"We didn't even have time to save him," Moira whispered. Her cheeks reddened as a tear streaked her face.

Blinding light surrounded Schism as his short, tousled hair flew upward. A neon-green beam shot skyward as he filled his hands with portals of swirling light. They grew larger above his palms. He threw two at Braern and Moira, and they sank into the portals below them and disappeared. He tossed two more under Tim, Blue, and Araduk—gone. He flung the last one under Nozomi.

No one remained.

*****

Each of them arrived in different places between Earth and Yumerion.

Moira shivered as the piercing cold and snow surrounded her, alone in a blizzard.

Braern treaded water in the middle of an ocean while the stars reflected on the water and sheathed his sword, splashing water on his face.

Tim appeared at the top of a tree in the great rainforest in Brazil. Blue clung to the branches, swaying in the night sky, meowing for help. He pulled her close to him, crying.

Hearing only the sounds of her breath, Nozomi, buried in the earth, clawed through the surrounding dirt in every direction.

Araduk's stomach rose to his chest, and his heart pounded as he fell through clouds, seeing nothing but sky below him.

Schism wiped his hands with a nod. He stood, alone again, and smiled.

BRAERN

BATTLE OF THE PORTALS

Seconds later, in unison from their varied locations, the five of them screamed as their hands lit with brightness. Portals appeared, and they climbed through them, returning to crash to the ground before their enemy. After righting themselves, they glanced at each other, then at him. Nozomi brushed dirt off her chest. Araduk straightened his beard. Braern flung his arms in the air as water drops pattered on the ground. Tim cradled Blue and froze like a statue. Moira rubbed her arms and exhaled.

Schism raised his eyebrows in shock. "Welcome back. I didn't think any of you could harness the power of the portals. This will be fun."

Araduk and Tim froze, peering at Schism in sheer terror. They ran behind the trees and peeked over as Blue followed.

"There's nothing we can do. This is their fight now," Araduk assured him, his hands on Tim's shoulders.

Tim looked down to ensure Blue was safe. He sighed with relief and watched the battle transpire.

Braern, Nozomi, and Moira charged as their own lights appeared in various colors around them.

Schism braced himself with palms in front.

Braern swung his sword, but he deflected.

Moira punched; he moved out of the way.

Nozomi transformed into an Eastern dragon and exhaled her lungs. She spat a wave of fire toward him.

He flattened his hand, raised it up to his forehead, and vanished. Then he reappeared at Braern's side.

The elf sensed his presence and pivoted to his left. Schism conjured his own sword, as Raven was inches from his nose. They clashed and swung, grunting and moving away from the others.

Braern swung high.

Schism blocked and plunged his magical weapon into Braern's abdomen. He fell to the ground, holding his side in a fetal position, yelling in agony.

Araduk ran to him, with wide eyes on Schism. Tim followed.

"I got ye, lad," the dwarf said with a wavering voice, flashing his gaze between Schism and his battered friend. He hovered his hands over him and healed him quickly.

Several feet away, Nozomi flew toward him, and Moira ran to attack. The women charged side-by-side.

Schism raised his arm as a wave barrier sent them flying.

They skidded to a halt.

Braern relaxed his tense facial muscles as he peered at the wounds that vanished with his pain.

"Thank you!" he yelled as he rose and flew off toward their enemy.

"Any... time," Araduk answered. They ran off and hid behind a nearby boulder.

"Perhaps this will change your minds." Schism lifted his arms in the air as a gust of wind nearly blew them over.

They crossed their arms to shield their faces from the dirt flying.

He can harness the power of wind too? Why is his technique similar to mine? Braern thought.

"What is he doing?" Moira yelled through the howling of the wind.

Two portals formed and grew larger from Schism's fists. He lowered them to ground level. One revealed a farm in the United States with sleeping sheep in a grassy field, while the other showed a centaur playing with his three small children while his wife smiled close by. With a turn of his arms, the portals faced one another.

Shocks of electric energy whizzed and popped between them like two lightning storms against each other. Soon, the portals looked like two ends of a pair of black holes, pulling their gravities inside one another. The sheep and the centaur were involuntarily drawn together. Baaing and roaring echoed through the air as the two creatures fought to run in the opposite direction. A burst of light nearly blinded everyone. They closed their eyes.

They opened them to witness the portals' energies had waned, and the pictures inside them both were black. The light between them faded to reveal a creature unlike any they had ever seen—an amalgamation of a centaur and a sheep. Its fluffy wool covered its body as its mighty hooves pounded the ground, causing cracks in the dirt. Its snout protruded, dripping with black ooze from its mouth. Muscles gleamed as it shook the wool from its eyes.

"That doesn't seem so threatening," Moira whispered.

Braern and Nozomi kept their eyes on the enemy and the creature.

"Kill them," Schism said, curling his hand and throwing a jolt of green energy at the creature. It recoiled forward, then straightened its back as its eyes glowed green. The creature yelled, reared on its hind legs, and ran forward, hands outstretched.

"Never mind!" Moira shouted.

They jumped out of its way, and it galloped toward them, arms open, its neck clicking and shifting as it lost control over its own instincts.

Braern glared at Schism, feeling a surge of energy inside him, then the centaur slammed into him. The full force of its muscular body crushed his chest. He fell backward and skidded to a halt several yards away, one hand clenching his ribs, coughing.

Nozomi snarled as smoke rose from her dragon mouth. She panned between the centaur and Schism, grinding her pointed teeth and growling. Her whiskers twitched as her head shook with rage. "I'll handle him! You take care of that beast!" she yelled to her friends.

Her enemy frowned as he stepped backward from her, hands out in front of him. He looked surprised that she was coming after him.

"Tell me where Danielle is!" she roared as she zipped through the air, pushing up grass and dirt around her at top speed. She flashed by Schism as he sidestepped to avoid her. Nozomi crumpled her body against the bark of a tree, then pushed herself off and flew toward him again, snaking through the air with mouth open and saliva spraying.

She slashed her foreclaws at her right, then her left, alternating her arms.

He placed his hands behind his back and skipped backward across the earth, evading her every move with ease.

She growled with rage. Belligerent, with tears streaming from her eyes, she lunged forward again, but he moved several yards away.

He lifted his hands, and a portal rapidly appeared.

"I haven't had this much fun in years!" Schism laughed, barely breaking a sweat.

She tried to stop her scaly body but fell through into a dark ruin of rocks atop a sea below, with stars blinking above her. The atmosphere was frigid against her scales. Watching the portal shrink, she knew she had to act fast. She zoomed through at the last second, returned, and stopped herself in midair. She flipped around, then crashed into him as he fell to the ground with a thud. The portal closed and disappeared. She had him.

"Now we finish this," she snarled and clawed at his chest, slicing his clothing as blood splattered.

Schism raised his injured arms and touched the bottoms of his palms together to form a glowing, green energy from his hands. It grew to the size of a dragon. He threw his arms forward, and the magic blasted into Nozomi, forcing her backward. She flailed in the air as she fought to right herself.

Disoriented, the world spun around her.

*****

Down on the ground, Moira clenched her fists, her thumbs across her fingers.

The centaur reared and galloped toward her.

She lunged her arms forward to grasp its skin in her hands. She heaved and lifted it above her, struggling to steady herself, and threw it against a nearby protruding rock.

Bones cracked and splintered as the force of the throw shattered its back legs and muscles. Shifting again, the creature rose and faltered toward them, with bones sticking out from his hind legs.

Braern and Moira raised their brows and eyed one another as it charged at them. They felt the guilt overwhelm them, but readied their fists and sword for another round.

This time, it ran to Braern and threw its open human hands at the elf with a vacant expression.

He reared his sword above his shoulder and swung at an angle as it reached him. He slashed off its human arms, sending wool fragments through the air.

It fell on its side, writhing in pain as it fought to rise again with only two working limbs.

Moira watched with a heavy heart. "It's not going to stand again."

Braern glanced at Moira as they stood over the poor creature. He lifted his sword in the air and plunged it into its chest, spraying blood across their clothes as the creature struggled and kicked.

It coughed up bodily fluids that oozed from his mouth and eyes. The kicking and flailing slowed, twitching, then it stopped. The creature lay motionless on the ground. Dead.

Braern slowly retracted his sword and felt a wave of pain overwhelm him.

Moira held her head low. "It didn't deserve to die like that."

They both looked up to see Nozomi and Schism sparring several yards away, with magical energies flying around them in circles, crashing into the air.

"He's the monster."

"We need to go help her, now," Braern said, tightening his grip on his weapon. A rush of power surged through him while watching his friend struggle.

Schism and Nozomi flew toward the pair. They thrashed and fought and knocked Moira across the ground, dirt and rocks scraping her bloodied cheeks, rendering her unconscious.

Something inside Braern snapped as he stared at her unmoving body. It was as if a hammer slammed into his ribcage, all the way through to the back of his spine, his heart shattered and crushed.

Lights appeared several yards away and flooded the surrounding area, traveling toward Braern, sword in hand. The energy consumed him as he screamed.

"Braern," Moira squeaked, awakening and turning her body to face him. Blood dripped from her mouth.

Something's not right. I... can't control this. I can't...

"I don't know what's happening. Stand back!" Braern backed away from her out of fear that he might hurt her. A glowing, white light appeared from the drumstick tied to his belt. He peered down but couldn't will his limbs to move. His body shook as his mouth quivered. His eyes opened wide as he stared at Moira.

Without a word, she scooted backward, away from him, with her palms facing him. Her chest rose and fell as she fought to catch a breath.

Nozomi and Schism ceased fighting and watched the elf, surrounded by light. In seconds, Schism conjured a portal with both his thumbs clutched together, palms facing Braern.

"No!" Nozomi swung her claws at his arms.

The portal increased to the size of the elf, and he bent his elbows then forced the portal to fly towards Braern, just as Nozomi sliced into his arm with her claws, sending blood spurting. As the portal traveled closer to the elf, it grew staticky. The surrounding light flickered, dimmed, then disappeared.

Schism watched in horror.

"How did you do that?" he yelled, his face twisted in anger and disbelief.

The elf rose in the air, sword in hand, as he thought of all the questions that had gone unanswered on their journey. He had parents. Orastos was gone. He watched innocent creatures die, and his friends suffered and had nearly lost their lives all because of Schism. He longed to watch his body grow cold and still as new energy flooded into him from around them.

He felt lights glow from his arms, legs, and head. Five portals appeared and grew larger. Closing his fists, he commanded them to shrink in his mind, but they didn't. Instead, they increased in size.

"How am I doing this?" he yelled. "Moira, run!"

She lay motionless and terrified, gasping for breath. She stared at him, then turned, staggered to stand, and ran in the opposite direction.

A clash of energy grew from his torso and spread outward.

Schism stood with wide eyes and an open mouth as the wave engulfed them all.

Layers of portals facing all different directions surrounded all seven of them. Araduk and Tim appeared farther off, watching and holding one another. Schism and Nozomi stared as she transformed into her human form, unable to concentrate on keeping her dragon body.

"Nozomi, everyone, get out of here!" Braern yelled, focusing on the enemy.

Nozomi ran to Moira, and the two women held each other as the light blinded them. They shielded their eyes with their hands.

Tim, Araduk, and Blue joined them, and the group gazed onward.

"He's gonna sacrifice himself for us," Araduk said, his arms in front of him, shaking.

"No!" Moira screamed, reaching out her hand for him, blood dripping into her mouth from her head wounds.

A wave of wind traveled toward them, causing them to huddle closer together and shield their eyes as their hair blew backward.

Tim grabbed Blue and held her next to his chest, afraid she'd be blown away.

Braern flew toward Schism through a layer of ocean, splashing and spitting a salty taste from his mouth. He saw a blurry version of the enemy through the water. He opened his mouth, and bubbles blew from his nose. He emerged, dripping wet, and ran as the surrounding energy cracked and sparked.

Schism fled as they flew through layers of magical energy ovals, through water, air, ground, and a thunderstorm.

They flew through a variety of portals and vastly differing environments that lasted less than a second in each.

Braern felt his body overheating. His muscles ached as he fought to focus his energy on the evading enemy. He zipped through the portals after him.

Schism groaned in frustration and returned toward the others, watching Braern's friends struggle to shield themselves from the elements.

Enraged, the elf's hands glowed as two energy balls grew and enveloped the entire area.

The elf yelled louder than he ever had in his life, feeling his jaw nearly unhinge with how wide his mouth opened.

Nozomi, Araduk, Tim, Blue, Moira, and Schism stopped and stared at him as greater waves of energy enveloped them all. A blinding light appeared above them. Everyone ceased fighting and covered their eyes with their hands.

Ripples formed in the air and hurled toward them all. Their bodies froze, even Blue's. Not a leaf moved. Even the bacteria in the air stilled. A single large portal appeared next to the light. Time stopped. It sucked the six frozen friends into it in a split second, then disappeared, leaving Schism behind.

Darkness.

Braern, Moira, Araduk, Tim, Blue, and Nozomi found themselves in a floating destination of pure blackness. There were no lights, no sounds, no vibrations. They illuminated individually from within their cores and could see one another. Even the cat's color was visible as she pushed herself through the air and floated, without gravity, above Tim.

"What is this place?" Tim asked, searching in every direction for some semblance of something familiar.

"I've no idea, but it sure beats dying at the hands of that psycho," Moira commented.

"Ye got that right, lass." Araduk smirked.

"I had him," Nozomi whispered, staring at her trembling hands.

"Braern, are you okay?" Moira asked, trying to swim toward him but without luck.

The elf floated, his body limp, as he fought to catch his breath, the burning of his muscles subsiding. Static sparks of energy jolted through his body from the residual power he conjured. His vision blurred, then steadily appeared clearer as he refocused on his friends.

"Something stopped me... I almost had him," Braern said, gasping to breathe.

"Ye almost took us down with ye, lad," Araduk said softly.

Braern wept, his chest aching.

With the elf's arms at his sides, a white light appeared. A familiar hunched shape formed before them as he could decipher wings, a robe, and a long tail with a white tuft on the end. He turned his back to Braern until the elf floated closer. The form flew in the air with his legs crossed, his tail swishing underneath him.

Braern heard deep, humming tones. The sounds filled their ears as he closed his eyes and listened. He no longer had control over his legs, but they guided him forward. As he was a few yards away, a head with a long white beard and pointed ears and curved horns turned around to face him. The face he had longed to see again was in his sight. *Are my eyes deceiving me? Is he real?* Braern thought. He landed on a dark platform that appeared under them. The elf's arms flopped to his sides while his legs could no longer support his weight. Braern fell to his knees as a new wave of tears trickled down over the last tears that pulled at his cheeks. His lips quivered as he opened his mouth to speak.

Before he could utter a word, a raspy, aged voice filled his ears. The dragon turned around with arms outstretched. With a weary smile on his face, he finally spoke the words Braern had longed to hear for weeks. "Took you long enough, my boy. We have much to talk about."

*****

What did you think about this book?

I would very much appreciate an honest review on Amazon when you're finished. If you have time, I'd also appreciate an honest review on Goodreads. Thanks so much for supporting a self-published author. I wouldn't be here without my amazing readers!

COMING IN 2022

SCHISM

AMALGAM ORIGINS

ELLIE HOLLAND

COMING IN 2022

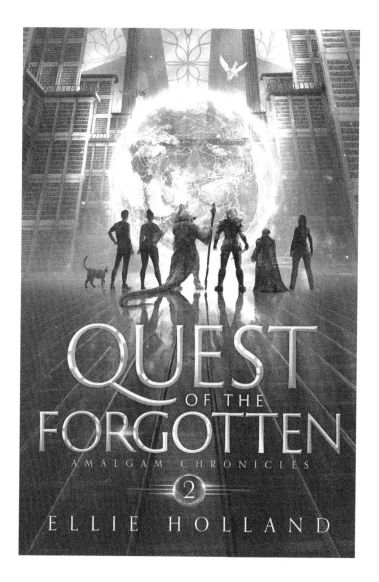

GLOSSARY

Alicorn- pegasus with a horn like a unicorn

Ao River- "Blue River" by the Fire Wyrm Swamp

American Airlines Center- hockey stadium in Houston, Texas

Araduk Lightbringer (formerly Araduk Ironspine/ pronounced AR UH DOOK)- healer dwarf from the Tetsu Mountains who became a monk after swearing a vow to never hurt anyone again.

Arigatou- "thanks" in Japanese

Arigatou gozaimasu- "thank you very much" in Japanese

Artemis- powerful alicorn who resides at Shiro Peak Monastery

Aye- "yes" in Scottish

Bairn- "baby or child" in Scottish

Baka- "stupid" in Japanese

Basilisk- a mythological reptile

Blue- the cat who claimed Tim as her human

Bonnie- pretty or attractive in Scottish

Braern Yogensha- (pronounced BRAY URN) elven mage raised by a wise, old dragon

Centaur- four legged mythological creature with the torso, head and arms of a human and the bottom of a horse

Chipotle- place of delicious burritos in the USA

Chijimu- "to shrink" in Japanese

Churro- fried dough treat

Chimera- three-headed mythological creature who is the elder of the verndari

Chimon- Orastos's and Braern's doorknocker at Lavendale Library who guards their workshop. He was once a creature until he did something unspeakably wrong and now spends an eternity as their doorknocker.

Crescent Stones- stones shaped like moons that are close to the Fire Wyrm Swamp

Danielle- Nozomi's girlfriend who was kidnapped by Schism

Demo- "but..." in Japanese

Devdan "Schism" Elberos- (pronounced DEV DAHN ELL BEAR OHS) the villain who wants to destroy everything the verndari council built because they wouldn't allow him to be a full-fledged member of their council as a portal guardian

Ent- living tree that can pull up its roots and walk

Ent Village- village where the ents live

Ever-Changing Lands- Large area of lands that are sentient and can change into any environment they choose

Faerie- magical creature with a humanoid body and wings in Yumerion

Faun- creature of mythology that is half-goat and half-human, similar to a satyr

Fire Wyrm- enormous white, wyrm who breathes fire and lives in its own swamp

Fire Wyrm Swamp- place where fire wyrms live to the north of Lavendale

Futakuchi Onna demon- demon from Japanese folklore that has the body of a woman with an extra, insatiable mouth hidden inside the hair on the back of her head.

Gapureia- (pronounced GAH POO ER EE AH) magical subway station for verndari to travel to and discuss protecting the portals and the realms of Earth and Yumerion

Geta- Japanese sandals

Gin Whiskey- (pronounced GEEN whiskey) strongest alcohol known between Earth and Yumerion. 100% proof. Araduk possesses a never-ending flask of it that he acquired from a witch by working for her for five years.

Gomen- "sorry" in Japanese

Gomen nasai- "I am so sorry," in Japanese. This is more formal and sincere than "gomen."

Go ni naru- "become five" in Japanese

Griffin- mythological creature with the body of a lion and the head and wings of an eagle

Hai- "yes" in Japanese

Hainu- strong, fast, ferocious winged dogs from Japanese folklore

Hallgrimskirkja Church- tall church in Reykjavík, Iceland that was designed to be similar to a volcano, which is common in the country

Helgufoss Waterfall- waterfall outside Reykjavík, Iceland with a portal to Gapureia

Hidogaru- "to expand" in Japanese

Houston, Texas- where Tim's family lives

Inoshishi- Japanese boar and favorite meat in Lavendale

Irasshaimase- "welcome" in Japanese

Isabella Rodriguez- Tim's mom

Izanagi/Izanami suns- gods/suns in Yumerion who created the world

John F. Kennedy International Airport- airport in New York

Kakusu grass- "concealed grass" in Japanese. The grass can rip itself from the ground and walk with a curious personality. It is native to the Ever-Changing Lands.

Kamishimo- Japanese traditional dress of samurai warriors on Earth and kappurai warriors from Yumerion

Kappurai- warrior caste of Yumerion

Katana- Japanese sword that has a curved, single-edged blade and long grip to accommodate two hands. This is the weapon of choice for Devdan "Schism" Elberos.

Kasa Obake- an umbrella demon from Japanese folklore

Kaze o tsukuru- "make the wind" in Japanese

Keryth- The soul in The After who sends a message of a prophecy to Orastos in Yumerion.

Kimono- T-shaped Japanese wrapped garment that is worn left side wrapped over right, unless the wearer is deceased

Kin- "family" in Scottish

King Carrot- king of the rabbits in Rainbow Rabbit Burrow

Kirei ni naru- "become clean" in Japanese

Kitsuka- land dolphin creature that can be found outside Rainbow Rabbit Burrow in Yumerion

Kitsune- (pronounced KEET SU NAY) Japanese mythical shape shifter who prefers the form of a beautiful woman or a fox. Nozomi is a kitsune. The most powerful kitsune have nine tails.

Kuso- "shit" in Japanese

Lavendale Forest- forest where Braern and Orastos live in the village of Lavendale

Lavendale Library- library where any creature can come to gain knowledge from any world or realm

Lenleonette- sentient queen tree of the Ever-Changing Lands and friend to Araduk

Ludo- St. Louis based band that formed in 2003 with 5 members (Pmo is the drummer and Convy is the keyboardist)

Manhattan Memorial Hospital- hospital in New York where Moira takes Braern when she first meets the injured elf

Maria Rodriguez- Tim's sister

Master Kabu- "master turnip" in Japanese. He's a rabbit mage and healer of Rainbow Rabbit Burrow

Meganai Cave- "Cave of the eyeless" in Japanese. The troll lived here.

Midtown Park- park in Houston, Texas

Miguel Rodriguez- Tim's dad

Mijo- "son" in Spanish

Moya Island- "Misty Island" in Japanese

Moggy- nickname for a cat in Scottish

Moira Washington- (pronounced MOH EE RA) woman with super strength that she has trouble controlling

Moira's apartment- where Moira lives/lived

Mon- (pronounced like MOAN) medieval Japanese currency from the samurai era

Museum of Natural History- museum in New York City where Moira works/worked

Niji Woods- "rainbow woods" in Japanese. Rainbow Rabbit Burrow is located in the Niji Woods.

Nozomi Hayakawa- (pronounced NOH ZO ME HA YA KAH WA) Japanese shapeshifter kitsune who has a fox form with two tails.

Orastos- (pronounced OH RAS TOHS) powerful 1,000-year-old dragon mage who raised Braern since he was an elfling

Owaru- "stop" in Japanese

Platypies- (pronounced PLA TEH PEES) blend of harpies and platypuses that Tim names

Portal- gateway of power for creatures to travel from one place to another. Portals can also be summoned by experience portal guardians.

Princess Plum- lives in Rainbow Rabbit Burrow and is princess of the rabbits

Rainbow Rabbit Burrow- place where the rainbow rabbits live

Reykjavík, Iceland- place on Earth where the main characters travel to in order to find the Verndari Castle. It has the portal to Gapureia.

Rokado- (pronounced DOH KAH DOH) Braern's raccoon-dog friend

Ryu Valley- "Dragon Valley" in Japanese. This is Telzraug's home and valley of the dragons.

Queen's Library- library in New York

Satyr- mythological creature with the body of a human with a goat's tail, ears, legs, and horn

Sandshoe Crabs- giant, harmless creatures that live in Yumerion that resemble horseshoe crabs from Earth

Sanshouo Lake- "Salamander Lake" in Japanese (pronounced SAHN SHO OO OH) Lake in Yumerion, where Nozomi travels to and wades in the water as a fox

Shiro Mountains- (pronounced SHI DO) snow-capped mountains to the north of Lavendale where Shiro Peak Monastery was built

Shiro Peak Monastery- a monastery the portal guardians travel to where Artemis, the alicorn, and the other monks live

Shoji- Japanese style paper and wooden doors that slide

Swamp salamanders- salamanders found in Fire Wyrm swamp

Tabi- Japanese socks with a slit between two toes

Tea Garden- Japanese inspired garden with bridges, streams, and places to drink tea

Tetsu Mountain- Araduk's previous home, where he lived with the dwarves and commanded their army

Telzraug- dragon who is thrown through a portal and tries to burn down a hockey stadium on Earth

The After- the afterlife where souls travel to after they die

The Pageant- the location of the concert that the main characters travel to and listen to music from the band, Ludo. The venue is located in St. Louis.

Thir- "there" in Scottish

Timothy Rodriguez- sixteen-year-old nerdy kid who travels with his beloved cat, Blue

Timoteo- Tim's nickname and "Timothy" in Spanish

Torii- Japanese gateway marking the entrance to a sacred area like a shrine or monastery. There is a *torii* gate at the bottom of the mountain steps of Shiro Peak Monastery.

Unicorn- mythical creature with the body of a horse with a magical horn

Verndari- portal guardians and protectors of the realms of Yumerion and Earth

Verndari Castle- castle where the verndari council of portal guardians meet and discuss matters from Yumerion and Earth

Wakaranai- "I don't understand" in Japanese

WOW- World of Warcraft

Yakusha- device that can translate words with magic that Master Kabu gave the portal guardians

Yatta- "I did it" in Japanese

Yer- "your" in Scottish

Yume Fountain- (pronounced YU MEH) fountain outside Lavendale forest

Yumerion- fantasy world of The Portal Guardians

Yutakana tabi- "Prosperous Journey" in Japanese

Ludo

In chapter 30, the portal guardians meet the band Ludo! I received permission from the band to include them in my book. Thanks Tim Convy, Tim Ferrell, Andrew Volpe, and Matt Palermo (Pmo), and special guest Adam Brooks!

The two songs with the lyrics mentioned in the chapter are "Anything for You" and "Broken Bride." They're an amazing pop-punk, humorous, romantic, and vividly imaginative band. If you want to check them out, this is their site www.ludorock.com and their Facebook is www.facebook.com/LUDO Give them a listen! You won't be disappointed! I recommend starting with "Love Me Dead" if you're new to the band.

Made in the USA
Monee, IL
09 April 2022

93712401R00254